The Legend of Dalton Manor Series

The Legend of Dalton Manor Series

The Complete 4 Book Collection Third Edition

By T.L. Stevens

Copyright © 2017 Cloud Fire Books

All rights reserved under International and American Copyright Conventions. By payment of the required fees or by downloading this e-book, you have been granted the nonexclusive, nontransferable right to access and read the text of this e-book on-screen. No part of this text may be reproduced, transmitted, downloaded, decompiled, reverse engineered, or stored in or introduced into any information storage and retrieval system, in any form or by any means, whether electronic or mechanical, now known or hereinafter invented, without the express written permission of Cloud Fire Books.

This novel is a work of fiction in which names, characters, places and incidents are products of the author's imagination or are used fictitiously. Any resemblance to real persons, places or events is completely coincidental.

ISBN: 979-8-9917568-8-4 (Paperback)
ISBN: 979-8-9917568-7-7 (eBook)
ISBN: 979-8-9917568-9-1 (Audiobook)

Library of Congress Control Number: 2025921110

Printed in the United States of America

**Dedication**

I dedicate this series to K.M. who inspired me to get back to writing. As well as my loving and supportive husband and family. I want to thank all of you for your encouragement, nudging and feedback. You reminded me to keep trying and to never give up hope.

I also want to encourage you to leave a rating and review, especially if you enjoyed this series. Much thanks to all of you who take the time to this and share my books with others. I truly appreciate you doing so.

If you want to see what happens next look for the sequel

Emerging Branches (Book 5)

SERIES TABLE OF CONTENTS

Book 1

Heading off to college was something Ally never thought she'd do. When the school hosts a Halloween party at a supposedly haunted manor she's hesitant to attend, but she goes. Ally never believed in haunted houses or legends, until...

1

The Gift

TABLE OF CONTENTS

<u>Chapter One</u>

It had been a spur of the moment decision. Simply put an excuse to leave the house, but it was one of those things Ally could look back on and see it had made a huge difference in her life. Like a chance encounter or turning left instead of right. Something you don't think is going to have any impact on your life. Yet, here she was two years later doing something she had never really given any thought to.

Making the final turn onto Main Street towards the highway surprisingly calmed her heart. The all too familiar shops, restaurants and empty buildings flooded Ally with forgotten memories. Recalling her first kiss outside the ice cream parlor made her smile. Memories of watching countless parades with her parents and having pizza with friends at Tony's Place would always be cherished times. Happiness was abruptly replaced with sorrow when the charred remains of the dry cleaners came into view. It had been numerous years without a single thing being done to the fire ravaged building. Ally couldn't help but remember the young life that had been lost there.

Engrossed in her thoughts Ally didn't notice she was now on the open road. Glancing in her rearview mirror she could scarcely see her small town fading away.

Glenbrook had been the only home she'd ever known. Leaving for short visits even with her family used to frighten her. Ally had grown up feeling safe in her small town, where everyone looked out for each other. No, Glenbrook wasn't perfect it had its issues and sorrows, but as a whole it had been a safe haven to grow up in. Now she relished the idea of attending college in a city far from home. No sooner had she finished packing everything she could squeeze into her little hatchback did she find herself bubbling with anticipation. The further away she got from her hometown the more courage and excitement built within her. Ally was one of the very few that did more than talk about leaving Glenbrook she was on her way out.

Leaving was a hard sell to her parents until the partial scholarship arrived tipping the scales in her favor. Without it Ally believed she'd have lived her entire life in one place like her parents and grandparents. If she were completely honest with herself there was a time not so long ago when that would have sufficed.

School was scheduled to start in a week giving her enough time to settle in before classes started. As the single lane roadway became a multilane highway thoughts of the unexpected note from her soon to be roommate came to mind.

Dear Ally,

Hello, my name is Rose and we'll be rooming together. I'm so thrilled my family agreed to let me live on campus, even though our home isn't too far away. I look forward to seeing you soon.

Have a safe trip,
Rose

Ally was thankful to be rooming with a local although she didn't understand why Rose's family would pay the added expense. Ally mailed a similar note to Rose adding her cell number and arrival date. She hoped to receive a call or at least another note from Rose with her cell number before she headed for school. However, neither of those happened.

Nervous excitement fluttered in Ally's stomach when the freeway sign announced her exit in three miles. She had never slept in the same room with a stranger and that realization made Ally's stomach flip flop. When a stranger appeared in town it only took a short amount of time before it was discovered which family they were related to and the reason for their visit. Before long the person was no longer a stranger, but they didn't sleep in Ally's home let alone her room. A list of what ifs began swirling in her mind: "What if Rose snored or worse, what if Ally did?" "What if their personalities clashed?" "What if she drank or did drugs?" "Now you're getting ridiculous Ally," she whispered aloud to herself.

Exhausted from the nearly seven-hour trip Ally silently thanked her father for teaching her to read a map. In no time, she found the freshman dorm she had been assigned to. Finding a place to park proved far more difficult than she expected. Making several laps through various parking lots left her frustrated. Pure desperation had compelled others to be creative in their parking forcing Ally to fight the urge to park next to a fire hydrant.

"Sure Ally have your car towed the first day," she told herself. Tears began to well in her large brown eyes when out of nowhere an empty spot appeared right in front of her. Without hesitation Ally sped into the spot afraid it would disappear as quickly as it appeared. Resting her head on the steering wheel she jumped when her cell rang. Flipping the phone open she saw "unknown caller" flashing on the screen.

"Hello?"

"Hello Ally it's Rose. I'll be right down to help you unload."

"Oh my gosh thank you," was all she got out before Rose quickly said you're welcome and hung up.

Ally was puzzled and wondered how Rose knew she had arrived. Then she realized she hadn't told her where she was parked. She couldn't call her back; she didn't have Rose's number. Staring at the screen trying to figure out her next move she was again startled. This time by a gentle knock on the passenger side window. Hazel eyes framed by flowing red hair peered through the passenger window. A bright smile featuring the whitest and most flawlessly perfect teeth she'd ever seen flashed at Ally.

"Rose?"

"Yes, it's me" she answered motioning Ally to roll down the window so they could speak in a normal tone.

Giggling Ally apologized then reached over the bags on the seat and began to roll down the window. Straining to get the window down Ally didn't notice Rose going around the backside of the car. Rose tapped on the driver's side window drawing Ally's attention to her. Opening the door Ally looked up at the statuesque girl in front of her. Her flawless complexion, tailored clothes and manicured nails were something out of a glamour magazine. Ally felt herself staring and suddenly wished she was wearing something other than torn jeans, a faded T-shirt and flip flops. Several ash blonde curls had broken free from her loose ponytail. Tickling her face and neck adding to Ally's desire to hide her appearance.

"You must be exhausted," stated Rose who then instructed Ally to grab her purse and follow her upstairs. Grabbing her purse, she tried to lift one of the bags from the passenger seat when another unfamiliar voice this time male rang in her ears.

"Please allow us, Miss Ally. We are more than happy to take care of that for you."

Ally spun around in the seat so quickly she bumped her elbow on the steering wheel. Noticing several men standing around her car made her forget about the pain radiating in her arm. The fear she felt must have been apparent on her face. Rose stepped in front of the man and leaned down towards her.

"It's all right Ally. These are the movers my family hired to move us. They moved me in yesterday. My family figured it would be easier if they stayed another day and moved you in too"

Skeptical and unnerved by this excessively generous offer Ally stayed seated. Unable to accept their help. Questions raced through her mind, "Who was this girl?" "What in the world did her family do?" "Why would they offer to pay movers to move someone they don't even know?"

"My apologies Ally. We've frightened you."

Searching for the right answer caused more questions to race through her mind. If Ally confirmed she was scared she would sound like a baby. If she said she wasn't then how would she explain why she was sitting there clutching her purse with a death grip?

Before confirming or denying anything Rose gave her a way out, "We can help the movers if that makes you more comfortable. Let me go change and we'll get started." This sounded like a reasonable compromise. Everyone except Rose grabbed something and headed towards the dorm. It was clear that with all the help it wasn't going to take long to get Ally moved in.

The lobby of the dorm was bustling with students lugging their belongings in every imaginable way onto the elevators or down various hallways. Noticing the crowd of unhappy students waiting for the elevator made Ally sigh remembering they were on the fourth floor. Following the movers as they turned away from the crowd she braced herself for the stairs. Beginning to reconsider the idea of allowing the movers to handle this. A small plastic sign pointed down one of the hallways toward the stairwell. However, Rose made an unexpected turn and happily announced, "Here we are this is much better."

In front of them were two elevators with only a handful of students waiting. Within moments Ally was upstairs in her room flopping on her bed. It was then that her body overrode her mind. Lazily she handed the keys over to the movers. Relinquishing all power of her belongings and car to them.

As the noise of the movers faded into the background a wonderfully sweet scented breeze flowed through the open window next to Ally's bed. With her eyes still closed she turned her face into the breeze taking a deep long breath trying to capture the fragrance riding on the wind. A vivid mental picture of an abundant flower garden in full bloom filled her head; with jasmine covered trellises, rows upon rows of gardenias, lilacs, honeysuckles and countless other aromatic perfumed flowers. The image was so clear she could almost see bees buzzing from one flower to another happily at work.

"That's the last of it Miss Ally," announced the mover she'd given the key's too. He handed them back to her letting her know he locked her car. Quickly sitting up Ally took the keys thanking him profusely for all the help. A simple nod was his only response before leaving. Rose spoke up before Ally could thank her and casually stated she'd be back shortly.

"That's weird," thought Ally watching Rose leave, but figured it would be a good time to call home. Ally told her mother about Rose while she unpacked and all the wonderful and unexpected happenings. Attributing them to the wealth she believed Rose to have. Through the course of the conversation Ally agreed with her mom that neither beauty or wealth could have created an open parking spot or extra elevators. By the time she hung up the phone she was convinced Rose simply had a charmed life. Secretly Ally hoped it would rub off on her.

Ally unpacked enough clothes to fill her tiny closet leaving the rest for later. Her meager perfume and makeup collection only took up one drawer in the bathroom. Another welcome surprise came when she realized there wasn't a second door leading to another room on the opposite end of the bathroom. Having one bathroom for the two of them was going to be so much nicer than sharing it with four girls. Ally chuckled at the thought of how many other wonderful surprises may lay ahead not knowing another was just minutes away.

Chapter Two

"I'm back," alerted Rose carrying elegant paper bags by their handles. A savory aroma filled the room causing Ally's stomach to growl loud enough for Rose to hear. "Good you're hungry," she teased.

Ally blushed in agreement wondering what shade of red she had become for the second time since her arrival. She already felt self-conscious about how she looked. Ally had always believed herself to have above average looks up until now. When she was faced with her stunningly beautiful roommate. There was nothing exceptional about Ally's freckled face, naturally curly hair or athletic build, but she had always been one of the prettiest girls in Glenbrook. Feeling very much the small-town girl she struggled to find something to say. To her relief Rose asked her to bring her desk chair over so they could squeeze together at Rose's large desk to eat.

It was interesting how each side of the room had its advantages. Although Rose's desk, dresser and closet were bigger Ally had far more privacy, a window and full length mirror. The desks formed a natural barrier between the beds reaching a couple feet shy of the ceiling. Ally sat down and noticed several class books already stacked on the upper shelf of Rose's desk.

"If you would like we can go pick up your books tomorrow."

"That would be great," answered Ally looking down at the meal in front of her, "This looks delicious. Thank you," hesitating for a second before piercing a bite size chunk of beef she added, "Its almost too pretty to eat but I'll force myself."

Rose smiled then gracefully lifted a small morsel to her mouth. Every move she made was fluid and exquisite. It was like watching a skilled ballerina perform. If appearances meant anything the two of them would have nothing in common which began to worry Ally. This would make for a long year if that were indeed the case.

Ally bit into the most tender flavor-filled piece of meat she had ever tasted and inadvertently released an audible sigh. The blush it brought to Ally's face made Rose smile with delight. So far, all Ally was contributing to their new friendship or at least she hoped it would become a friendship was a form of amusement.

Before she knew it the two were engrossed in conversation discussing class schedules, favorite movies and such. To Ally's amazement they had several things in common from their love of ice skating to both of them being an only child. Which was the only information Rose shared about her family. Ally felt a strange connection with Rose as the conversation flowed easily. It was as if they had known each other all along.

Finishing the last bite of the chocolate soufflé Ally thanked Rose for the most delicious meal she'd ever had.

"I'm glad you enjoyed it. I'm going to get comfortable then we can talk some more," said Rose pulling fashionable pajamas from a dresser drawer.

An unexpected knock on the door caused Ally's heart to skip a beat making her wish Rose hadn't gone into the bathroom. It was almost 11:00 PM and as far as she knew they weren't expecting anyone. Another knock, this time much more demanding.

From the bathroom Rose shouted, "Is someone here?"

"Yes. Are you expecting someone?"

"I'm not. Are you?"

"No."

"Did you look through the peep hole?" questioned Rose stepping from the bathroom.

"Not yet."

Pushing past Ally, Rose peered through the peep hole then swung the door open. A short blonde holding two plastic cups by their rims in one hand stood there prepared to knock again.

"You're not Jessica!" she slurred.

"No. I am not."

"Where's Jessica? Why are you in our room?"

"I'm not in your room," declared Rose blocking the doorway as the girl attempted to step inside.

"Hey, what's your problem?"

"At the moment you are."

Anger blazed in the blonde's eyes as she stepped forward straining her neck to look Rose in the eyes. This was far more than her impaired balance could take. A split second later she was stumbling backwards landing hard on the hallway floor.

Flashing back to another place and time Ally recalled her mom standing guard at her bedroom door. Her father was yelling orders about cleaning up after herself. Covering her ears with her pillow she turned her eyes to the soft glow coming in her bedroom window. How she hoped her mom could get him calm and in bed before she had to get ready for school. Ally remembered her fun and happy dad from years earlier. Now he spent most of the day looking for work and the remainder of it at local bars hiding from his problems.

He resented the fact that his wife had to get a job even though without it they wouldn't survive. Combining her tiny paychecks with his unemployment checks barely covered household expenses. When the factory lost its major contract a large portion of employees were laid off causing an unpleasant ripple throughout Glenbrook.

Families were forced to move, others like Ally's family barely got by and still others dug themselves into a deeper hole by their actions. Ally knew her father's drinking would soon dig them into a hole they couldn't get out of.

The once bustling little town was no more. Businesses closed and homes were left abandoned. Life as Ally knew it drastically changed in a matter of months. Guilt about leaving her mom alone to deal with her dad washed over Ally. Although she found a smile when she thought about a very special conversation with her mom. Repeatedly Ally's mother told her there was a better life out there for her. There was a quiet strength in her mom that she never really knew existed until the last few years.

The slam of the dorm room door brought Ally back to the present. Smirking with delight Rose said, "I don't believe she'll give us any more trouble." Ally had missed whatever happened between Rose and the little blonde. Just like at home she had learned to disconnect from confrontations. Disappearing into her own head making it easier to bury the horrible memories deep in her mind. It was ironic that having experienced all the past drunken face offs between her parents and learning to disconnect from a situation would now shield her from a present one.

"Are you all right?"

A quick shake of her head cleared away the memory and Ally forced a smile, "Yeah, I'm fine." She gathered up the mess from dinner shoving it back into the paper bags. "I'm getting tired I think I'm going to get ready for bed."

"Of course, you had an awfully long day."

Ally climbed into the strange bed feeling both happy and sad. She was on an adventure she never thought would become a reality. In the back of her mind she knew her mom would have a tough night dealing with her dad. Ally was sure he had used her leaving as an excuse to hit the bar since he wasn't there when she called home. He would use anything as a reason to justify going to a bar. Even poor weather had become a regular and valid excuse.

With deliberate effort Ally pushed aside all the snide comments her father had made in the months leading up to her leaving. She focused her attention solely on her mom's encouraging words overflowing with so much love and pride it brought tears to her eyes. Ally could not only hear it in her mom's voice she could feel it deep within her chest pumping new life into the brokenness her dad had caused.

"Good night Ally," whispered Rose.

"Good night."

Chapter Three

A skilled cyclist whizzed by Ally as he navigated his way through the crowd of pedestrians rushing to their classes. Confused and lost students scrambled about adding to the nerves she was feeling about her very first college class. The sudden stops and about turns of some of those in the crowd caused numerous collisions or near misses. The past week had sped by with all that needed to be done making Ally wish she had arrived sooner. She didn't feel quite ready for this.

With Rose's help, she had accomplished all the things on her to do list except finding a part-time job. Between the scholarship and a more than generous gift from her grandparents Ally was set until spring. She was thankful she was able to find and purchase used books for all of her classes. It was a huge help in keeping her from depleting too much of her limited funds. Now it was up to Ally to earn enough for next semesters books and any other necessities that came up. She knew she couldn't hold out for her dad to get his act together enough to find work. She had stopped believing in him long ago. No matter how convincing his plea's and apologies sounded or how many good days he had. She accepted the sad truth that it was only a matter of time before he slipped up letting her down again.

How she longed for the father of her past. The strong, confident man who lovingly swooped her up in his arms when he got home from work tickling her face with his mustache as he covered her with kisses. Resentment continued to build over the last few years as she watched him repeatedly hurt those who loved him most. It was that resentment that made her more determined than ever to succeed at school. Between not wanting to return home to watch the continued destruction of her family or face the embarrassment of what she viewed as failing. If she admitted defeat and left college. Ally was resolved to do everything within her power to remain in school.

She was unsure if it was the sound night's sleep she'd recently been getting or the excitement of what was to come but something inside her was changing. A trait she rarely exhibited was becoming a driving force. Ambition now ruled her mind. For the first time in her life she was putting herself first. She had come to the realization that she couldn't stop her dad from choosing to drink his sorrows away. He had made his decision and now Ally felt it was time to do the same. Her needs and wants now came before trying to fix others. Choosing to reach her goals by focusing on what she needed to do gave her confidence. However, her mom's influence reminded Ally that she didn't have to become self-centered to have success. She could remain true to herself and still work hard at fulfilling her dreams.

Taking a seat in the large classroom Ally scanned the room for a familiar face. Perhaps someone from her dorm that she often rode the elevator with or walked past in the lobby. Most of her time had been spent with Rose preparing for classes to begin leaving little time to mingle with others. Something she now regretted.

"Boy it's packed in here," commented a high-pitched voice. "Hi I'm Susan. You are?" she asked, extending her hand.

"Ally," she said shaking Susan's hand.

"It's nice to meet you," smiled the pretty brunette dumping her bag on the desk. While she arranged her belongings, hung her sweater on the chair and silenced her cell phone she continued to talk. In the few minutes before the professor introduced himself Ally learned where Susan was from, which dorm she was in, how many siblings she had and that she wasn't a morning person. Making this her least favorite class already.

If Susan noticed the smirk on Ally's face she showed no sign of it. Nor did she need to breathe as words continued to flow out of her mouth. Genuine excitement bubbled from every inch of her captivating Ally with the most mundane topics. This girl could read a dictionary out loud and keep you riveted. Making you want to listen.

"Oh, the professors ready. We better stop talking," whispered Susan leaning towards Ally.

Hiding an amused grin behind her hand Ally nodded in agreement stifling her laughter. "Yes, 'WE' need to stop talking," she thought to herself. If nothing else this class would be quite entertaining. Which would get two days of the week off to a good start.

Halfway through class it became evident that the professor found Susan's enthusiasm less than desirable. Apparent to everyone except Susan, who continued to raise her hand until class was dismissed. The professor stopped calling on her and eventually focused his attention on every other section of the class. Making sure he kept from making eye contact with her. An added benefit to this behavior was that Ally was swallowed up in the black hole surrounding Susan and wasn't called on once.

"It was very nice meeting you Ally. I'll see you in a couple days. I've got to get to the other end of campus for my next class."

"Nice meeting you too," Ally replied. Wary that saying anything more would launch Susan into another over sharing session causing her to be late for her next class.

There was just enough time for Ally to grab breakfast before she had to be to her next class. To her dismay the cafeteria was packed. Overflowing with hurried and impatient students she was forced to limit her choices to the pastry and cereal bar. "No hot meal this morning," she told herself as the enticing smell of pancakes and bacon engulfed her senses. Resulting in her making a mental note to eat breakfast before her first-class next time. She could only hope there'd be less people willing to get up that early to eat.

Worn out from a busy day of classes Ally lounged in the shade of a large tree. Thankfully the heat of the mid-day sun was held at bay by the maze of branches above her. Ally shut her eyes and listened to the leaves dancing in the cool breeze mimicking the sound of a gentle rain. Soaking up the beauty of the moment all cares and responsibilities disappeared for the time being.

"Hello Ally. Whatcha doin?"

There was that familiar high pitched voice again. Without opening her eyes Ally knew it was Susan. With such a distinct voice, it was easily remembered. Especially since she had heard so much of it earlier.

Ally responded through squinting eyes, "Relaxing for a moment."

"Wish I had time to relax with you, but I've volunteered to help with the big Halloween party next month. There's still so much to do. Flyers should go out this week if you're interested. What am I saying? Of course, you're interested. It's gonna be a great event. I'll bring you a flyer personally. Gotta run," and with that she was gone.

Heading back to the dorm Ally meandered along less used pathways enjoying the quiet. Adjusting to such large crowds was taking some getting used to. Not knowing or at least recognizing everyone around her was a strange and foreign feeling. Glenbrook had only one high school so eventually everyone ended up in the same place.

She was slowly learning that there were some benefits to a small town and to her surprise she was beginning to miss them. Always having at least, a couple friends in each class with whom a common history was shared. Strong bonds had been formed over the years filled with sleep overs, broken hearts and shared secrets.

The problem with sharing secrets meant that sometimes they proved all too harshly who your true friends really were. When Ally's dad crashed into a tree in their front yard arriving home drunk it soon became the towns latest scandal. Intense emotions of betrayal still lingered after nearly three years. She wasn't sure the hurt from some lifelong friends would ever go away. This brought her full circle to appreciating the ability to disappear on the large campus and jammed classrooms.

She was hardly even noticed by people on her dorm room floor let alone a hot topic for the masses.

Heavy footsteps behind her broke the trip down memory lane. As they quickened and drew closer Ally's body tensed. Her mind raced with options of what to do. Before she could decide a bulky male overtook her carrying large oversized duffle bags in each hand. He rounded the next corner still at a full run and relief washed over Ally. Not only because he was gone but that Rose came around the same corner. She couldn't understand how the two of them hadn't collided. Either way Ally was thankful Rose wasn't run over. It would have been like being hit by a train ending badly for Rose.

"How were your classes?" questioned Rose as they stopped together on the path.

"They were good. I met an interesting girl in my first class."

"Interesting?"

"Funny interesting," Ally clarified. "She's quite the talker," now chuckling as she replayed some of Susan's funnier points in her head. "How was your class?"

"Rather boring I must say. The professor speaks in a completely monotone voice making everything she says dull and lifeless."

Picturing Susan jabbering away in that class popped into Ally's mind. "Too bad Susan isn't in that class. She'd liven it up in no time."

"Perhaps she would but I'm going to see if I can transfer to another class."

"Oh, that bad?"

"Yes, that bad. As a matter-of-fact I'm heading to the admission office to see about switching before it's too late. I don't imagine I'm the only student in the class with the same idea."

That simple conversation carried Ally back two years. Parting ways she continued her walk to the dorm reliving that fateful morning.

Chapter Four

Through swollen eyes Ally applied the final coat of mascara in hopes it would help camouflage the evidence of a tear-filled night. Letting her sun kissed curls hang loose around her face provided another layer of protection she could hide behind.

The high school campus was bustling with final preparations for career day. Ally was neither interested in attending or helping out. She was merely using the event as an excuse to arrive early at school. She wanted to get out of the house before her dad woke after passing out on the couch around dawn that morning.

"Good morning Ally. I didn't know you were helping set up."

Raising her face ever so slightly to Mr. Griffin her favorite teacher she replied, "Oh, I'm not."

His warm smile and friendly eyes switched to puzzlement. Adjusting his thick framed glasses, he questioned her about her early arrival. Not wanting to share the horrible night with anyone Ally soon found herself hanging posters and setting up tables and chairs.

Before long various business professionals and college recruiters began arriving. This was the first career day the school had scheduled in years and based on the few in attendance. It didn't look like it would be much of a success. Ally thought there would probably be more booths than students in attendance, but hoped other students would use the event as a reason to get out of something like she had. She didn't want Mr. Griffin to feel bad about organizing the event.

To avoid going to class and appease Mr. Griffin, Ally agreed to stay. Assisting in any way needed until the end of the event. Ally inattentively flipped through the college brochure one of the recruiters had handed her on his way in. She was so focused on thoughts of her horrible night she failed to notice he had returned.

"Do you plan on going to college?" questioned the stout man.

Unaware of his presence Ally was startled and jumped bringing a crooked smile to his face. "No," she sputtered closing the brochure.

For a moment Ally thought she misspoke and said yes because he launched into a full-length spiel about the college he represented. Half listening, Ally watched his double chin fight against the tight collar of his shirt held secure by an out-of-style blue tie. She felt bad that he was trying so hard to sell her on attending college. Tiny beads of sweat appeared at his receding hair line as the morning sun rose higher in the sky.

When he was finally finished Ally thanked him. To her dismay he stood there in front of her until she politely agreed to think about it. Even though she knew she'd forget him and all he said as soon as he walked away. No one in her family had ever gone to college and she didn't plan on being the first.

"You know you have the grades to get into college," it was more of a statement than a question. Mr. Griffin continued, "There are scholarships and grants available. You just need to apply. I'd be happy to help you with them and make sure you take the right classes over the next couple of years."

Something deep inside Ally made her hesitate before speaking. The words "No, thank you," wouldn't leave her mouth no matter how hard she tried to say them. An internal battle raged inside her while Mr. Griffin pulled several packets from a file box.

Random thoughts frantically darted through Ally's mind each struggling to be fully heard. Rubbing her forehead in an attempt to subdue the chaos only made flashbacks from the night before more clear. Beginning to spiral into the pain her father left in her heart was abruptly replaced with the sensation of pure tranquility. It commanded her attention. Eased her heartbeat back into a normal rhythm and slowed her breathing.

Free of doubt Ally calmly smiled at Mr. Griffin and confidently announced, "I'd like that," pausing for dramatic effect she stated, "I'm going to go to college."

Hearing those words in her own voice come out of her mouth made her feel the way Mr. Griffin looked. Full of bewildered amazement. Cheerfully he began to ruffle through the selected packets and stacked them in order of importance.

The confusion she felt over her spontaneous decision paled in comparison to the overwhelming and nonsensical peace filling her. There was no logic, no reason to feel anything but regret or fear over her decision. Yet even when she tried to convince herself she had made a huge mistake and take it all back it was swiftly eliminated. Ally was swept up in an incredible feeling of repose and confidence. Ally felt convinced she was on the right track to something amazing.

It was unclear even to Ally how she had arrived at this point. Retracing her steps back to the moment she awoke that morning Ally remembered being afraid she'd disturb her dad while getting ready for school. Waking him before last night's beers had been completely slept off meant more heartbreak was on its way. She was even more terrified that if she waited too long he would definitely be up before she left. There was no doubt there was trouble just waiting to explode. Ally wanted to be anywhere but at home when it surfaced with its typical vengeance.

Thankfully Ally remembered career day was taking place. Giving her the perfect ruse to leave much earlier than normal. In the blink of an eye she decided to take it. She slipped from her bed in one fluid motion, tip toed to her parent's room and whispered the little white lie to her mom about having to help with career day. Lots of practice at silently getting dressed and moving around the small house had become an art form. Ally was ready and on her way in no time. Creeping to the front door she kept a watchful eye on her snoring father. Silently she closed the door accomplishing her goal of leaving without being detected.

Little did she know that the little white lie about helping at career day would become the truth and lead to a major life decision. If she had known what was to come. Would she have decided to tell that lie and escape to the safety of school?

Firmly closing the door to her dorm room, she told herself "Yes." There wasn't a doubt in Ally's mind that she had made the right decision. The unexplained calm that had flooded Ally's being when she agreed to attend college had remained with her. The only valid reason she could come up with was the support and guidance of an awesome teacher. A teacher who helped her believe in herself and chase dreams she didn't even realize she had.

She knew first hand that the right teacher could make a significant difference in the lives of their students. Ally understood Rose's desire to change classes and hoped she'd be able to find a better fit. Without Mr. Griffin's direction Ally believed she wouldn't be where she was. Days before leaving she personally gave him a heartfelt letter letting him know exactly that.

Just as Ally hung up the phone after telling her mom about her first day Rose returned. Pleased by the success she had at switching classes. This came as no surprise to Ally adding this to the lengthy list of success's Rose continued to have. It was more evidence to back up Ally's belief of the charmed life Rose led.

"Would you like to have dinner before we get started with our studies?" asked Rose.

"Sure. I can't really focus on an empty stomach. Besides we'll beat the dinner rush if we go now."

Over dinner Ally shared the story of Mr. Griffin and how she ended up at school. Carefully leaving out everything about her dad. No one here knew those ugly private details and she truly liked it that way. It was the complete opposite of how it had been back at home. She also appreciated the fact that Rose never asked any prying questions, but took everything at face value.

"So did you always plan on going to college?" asked Ally curious about Rose's story. To this day Rose remained tight lipped about her family. She never brought them up or went home to visit. Although it sounded like they were close by.

"Yes. I always knew I'd attend college," she replied appearing uncomfortable. "It's getting crowded in here we should probably head back."

Stepping into the evening breeze Ally got a whiff of those amazing flowers from the day she moved in. "Oh my gosh. Where is that smell coming from?" she asked looking all around.

Shrugging her shoulders Rose picked up her pace. Making it difficult for Ally to keep up. The height difference between the two of them always made walking together interesting, but now Rose was almost sprinting.

"Are we in a hurry?"

"I forgot that I need to take care of something."

"What?"

"It doesn't matter. You go on back to the dorm. I'll see you later."

The captivating scent wafted through the air again this time much stronger.

"Don't you smell that Rose?"

Rose inhaled deeply, "The flowers?" she asked, seemingly unimpressed.

"Yes!" Ally answered waving her arms to add exuberance to her reply. "Isn't that the sweetest most marvelous scented flowers you've ever smelled?"

"It is very nice."

"Nice?" That's one word Ally would have never thought to use. With Rose's vocabulary, Ally couldn't understand why Rose would select such a small insignificant word to describe the amazing fragrance in the evening air.

"I really have to take care of something. Please forgive me."

Ally yelled to Rose as she watched her nearly run from her. "Where's it coming from?" but Rose was already too far away to hear her question.

After several failed attempts to find someone who might know where she could find the origin of the flowery bouquet Ally reluctantly went back to her room. Taped to the door was a folded piece of paper with Ally's name written on it. There wasn't anyone in the hallway nor were there notes on any other doors.

Concerned about what the note might contain Ally quickly unfolded it only to discover it was a flyer for the Halloween party Susan had mentioned. Written at the top was a message from Susan complete with a smiley face.

Ally,

This is only a rough draft of the flyer, but it has all the important stuff on it.

Susan :)

35

Chapter Five

By the time Ally's alarm went off Rose had already left for her morning run. Ally stumbled out of bed and glanced at the Halloween party flyer left on her desk. Rose must have returned well after Ally was sound asleep. Even though she had tried to stay awake for her.

How she wished she had been able to discuss the Halloween party with Rose before leaving for class. Halloween had never been a favorite holiday for Ally. She only enjoyed the fun light side of Halloween. Things like smiling jack o' lanterns, bobbing for apples, trick or treating with family and friends. The dark scary side was not something she appreciated. No haunted houses or horror movies for her. The party sounded like fun with the Victorian era theme and the fact that it was being held off campus at a nearby manor. That was in no way enough to entice her. Ally wanted more information before seriously considering it.

She hoped that Rose being a local might have more details about the party than the flyer listed. If not, she would have to wait to talk to Susan about it. Which she knew wouldn't be a problem considering how much Susan carried on about everything and even more so if it was a favorite topic.

Returning from her longest day of classes Ally was thrilled to find Rose waiting for her with pizza and soda. Rose greeted her happily as she sat cross legged on her bed dressed in the most casual outfit Ally had seen her in. Other than her running gear. Her long red hair was pulled back into a high ponytail causing her hazel eyes and bright smile to stand out even more.

"Boy that pizza smells good I'm starving," said Ally throwing her backpack on the floor. "Thank you so much."

"It's my pleasure. I figured you'd be tired and hungry by the time you finished your classes and would like to stay in for dinner. Plus, we didn't get to finish talking yesterday."

"No we didn't. Where'd you have to go anyway?"

"That's not important but I will say mission accomplished," beamed Rose.

Ally was too hungry and fatigued to investigate this any further and decided to let it go. She had learned over the past couple weeks that if Rose didn't want to discuss something she wouldn't no matter what you tried. Rose always managed to masterfully change the subject or make the issue in question suddenly seem too unimportant to keep discussing.

After inhaling two slices of pizza Ally leaned back against the wall feeling quite content. A breeze blew the

Halloween flyer off her desk landing at her feet. "Oh that reminds me. Do you know anything about the Halloween party the school has every year?"

"I have heard it mentioned, but I don't know all too much about it."

"Here's a rough draft of the flyer. Susan, the interesting girl I met taped it to our door sometime yesterday. It looks like fun, but I just want to know more about it before making a decision."

Rose took the flyer, looked it over and agreed that it looked like fun. "We would get to go shopping for costumes," she exclaimed with pleasure.

"That's true."

"Why wouldn't you want to go?"

"If they're going to have zombies chasing me or popping out from behind something. I'd rather stay home."

Rose contemplated Ally's answer then began to explain how she didn't believe it was that type of party. Telling her it sounded much more like a costume party with dancing than a gore fest. Ally remained unconvinced. She decided to put her decision off until she talked to Susan. She figured with Susan on the party's committee she would be a better source of information. Rose reminded her that if they were going to attend the party they would have to acquire dresses before what few were available were taken.

Nodding Ally said, "Point taken. I better get some of my homework done before I get even more tired. Thanks again for the dinner. What do I owe you?"

"You're welcome. Nothing it's on me." This was Rose's normal response when Ally asked about helping pay for things. A small part of Ally was beginning to expect this answer and cheered when she heard it. However, a much bigger part of Ally reminded her that it wasn't right to take Rose's generosity for granted.

Focusing on her assignment proved to be a difficult task. Ally's mind kept wandering back to the party. She didn't want to miss out on what could be an exciting fun filled night. However, she couldn't even afford to rent a dress. This concern reminded her that she still needed to find a part-time job. Exhaustion prevailed and near midnight she climbed into bed.

A dream filled night caused Ally to stir nonstop until her alarm rescued her from the tangled mess of nightmarish images. She couldn't remember much about the dreams. What little she could recall was blurred and vague, but there was an air of secrecy in them. She chalked it up to her fears, wariness and indecision about the Halloween party. That was surely the cause of her unconscious playing games with her throughout the night.

Between classes Ally made a point to stop by the main billboard on campus. It was full of colorful adds stapled, tacked and taped on top of each other. The adds ranged from available tutors to used cars for sale. There were only a few for part-time work. None of which Ally was qualified for.

"Whatcha looking for?" It was Susan's upbeat voice from behind her.

"Hello Susan. I'm looking for a part-time job."

"Find anything good?" Susan questioned as she began placing the Halloween party flyers on the billboard. This did little to distract her. "So did you get the flyer I left on your door the other night? I figured since I wrote your name on it no one would touch it. Well at least I hoped not. Aren't you excited? It's going to be so much fun. Not to mention we get to dress up. I mean how great is that? Think of the fun we'll have finding a dress. Gosh who'd ever think I'd need to shop for a Victorian dress?" questioned Susan. This time actually pausing for Ally to answer.

"It does sound like fun, but I was wondering if it's going to be..." Ally hesitated. How could she express her fears without sounding like a big baby? At last it hit her, "a blood fest with gore all over the place. I don't really like bloodshed it makes me queasy." There, that sounded a little better. Blame it on a weak stomach instead of fear.

"No, it's going to be a real class act. Everyone is supposed to dress and act like ladies and gentlemen from the Victorian era. The only thing we've compromised on is dancing to today's music instead of the boring stuff they had back then. If we stuck to that no one would come." Susan laughed at her own comment with such enthusiasm Ally found herself joining in.

Agreeing that it sounded like fun Ally let Susan know there was a good chance she'd be attending. The fear of being frightened had nearly been eliminated. All she needed to do now was figure out how in the world she'd budget for a dress before the costume stores ran out.

"What kind of job are you looking for? Maybe I can help you find one."

"I don't have much experience other than bagging groceries at our local market," confessed Ally becoming more convinced that she wouldn't be able to find a job.

"Well, that's something. Give me a couple days. I'll talk to a few people and see if there's anything I can come up with. By then I hope you'll decide you're for sure coming to the party. Then we can plan a shopping date for our dresses."

"Thank you Susan. I really appreciate that."

"That's what friends do. Hate to cut this short, but I have to hang the rest of these flyers. We want the biggest turn out in years."

"Friends?" thought Ally. It wasn't that she didn't like Susan or wasn't thoroughly entertained by her, but they hardly knew each other. She was just becoming comfortable with thinking of Rose as more than a roommate. Even though she wanted them to be friends. The pain of being terribly hurt in the past by lifelong friends had taught Ally a lesson. To be a bit more cautious about who she considered a friend and how close she'd let them get. She never wanted to be hurt like that again. Ally viewed this college experience as a new beginning. Where things would be different, herself included.

She was off to a good start keeping the mess of her family life to herself and limiting her calls home to when Rose wasn't in the room. For the most part Glenbrook was a faint memory that she could easily push away when it crept into her head. Remembering how conversations would end abruptly when she entered a room didn't happen here. No whispering or sideway looks from people she'd grown up with when out and about. No one had a clue about the pain filled secrets buried deep within her and if things went as planned no one would ever know.

The single fear Ally couldn't seem to bury was that of not being able to stay in school. There were times she found herself crying in the privacy of the shower at the mere thought of leaving her new life full of possibilities. This was another reason Ally thought she had a bad night's sleep for the first time since her arrival. "Don't worry Ally you'll find something," she tried to convince herself.

A moment of jealousy swept over her as she envied the charmed life of Rose. Who appeared to have more than enough. Ashamed of herself Ally shook it off remembering how much Rose had already done for her. There had never been a time when Rose was stingy or boastful of the privileges her family afforded her.

There hadn't been even one time when Rose asked for something in return or looked annoyed at always footing the bill. Rose gave generously and it always seemed to make her happiest when she surprised Ally with something new. Ally figured it was like parents watching their children experience Christmas for the first time. Allowing them the privilege of seeing it through young innocent eyes again. Reminding them of the magic Christmas morning once held for them.

<u>Chapter Six</u>

"How did today's interview go?" Rose asked timidly since all the previous times she asked had made Ally feel like a failure.

Susan had made good on her offer to help Ally find a job. This had been her fifth interview this week causing Ally to lose hope. "They said the same thing as the rest. That they have a few more interviews before they make their decision."

"I hope you don't mind me asking but why the sudden urgency to find employment?" Rose's voice was sincere and laced with obvious concern.

How could Ally explain financial worries to someone she believed never experienced them. Especially about something as trivial as renting a dress for the upcoming Halloween party? Afraid that it would seem completely absurd to Rose who had been discussing in great detail the styles she favored. Ally struggled for an answer.

Just the day before Ally and Susan had run into Rose during lunch in the cafeteria. It had been quite the entertaining contradiction. Watching Rose speak in her elegant way while Susan chatted away vigorously covering multiple topics at the same time. Ally had been exceedingly amused while listening to their exchanges. It was as if they were from different worlds. Nonetheless, Rose maintained her poise and never once appeared annoyed with Susan's endless rambling.

Ally had hoped the two would meet although she was concerned that their obvious differences may cause a problem. At least for Rose. Susan seemed to have this "ignorance is bliss" thing going on. Particularly when it came to her noticing that some people, even professors, wanted her to simply close her mouth for a while. A long while.

During their shared lunch, it had been decided that all three of them would attend the party. Susan's normal excitement level reached new heights. Her words building in speed and pitch as she gave them the inside scoop regarding party surprises. This helped Ally feel more comfortable and at ease about attending the party. Now her only worry was obtaining a dress. Which had lessened a bit when Susan gave her so many job leads. Unfortunately, none of them had panned out, but Ally remained optimistic.

Ally was learning how different life away from home was. Unlike her experience at the local market in Glenbrook Ally hadn't been hired on the spot at her first job interview. She kept reminding herself that growing up in front of the market owner's eyes was a major selling point when she applied for a job. There was also the fact that the owner had gone to school with her grandfather and they were friends. Ally was now convinced that put her at the top of the applicant list.

Here, she was just like every other college student scrambling for a job that would accommodate her class schedule. There wasn't anything setting Ally apart from the mass of applicants.

"Ally? Did you hear my question?" inquired Rose.

Snapping back to the moment Ally took a deep breath realizing she had missed a question. They were all supposed to go dress shopping this weekend and without any real job prospects Ally would need to back out. She decided to tell another little white lie based on what she believed Rose's question to be, "I've got far too much homework to catch up on. I don't think I'll be able to go shopping for a dress."

"That's not what I asked. However, I believe you've alluded to the problem weighing on your mind."

Ally was quick in denying the discovered truth. Stammering for the right words to argue her case failing miserably. Skeptical of Ally's attempts to persuade her into believing the homework story Rose smiled victoriously. "The three of us are going shopping as planned. I don't want to hear another word about it."

At the mere sight of Ally's mouth beginning to open in protest Rose lifted her hand silencing her before any audible noise could escape. With a rather smug look on her face Rose grabbed her backpack and headed off to her final class of the day. Leaving Ally feeling like a scolded child.

Unclear by what Rose intended to do Ally began imagining all sorts of things. "Was Rose planning on buying her a dress?" "Did she have a job up her sleeve?" Either way Ally felt a sense of relief sweep over her. Partly about the dress concern, but primarily about the possibility of finding a truly good friend.

By the time Saturday rolled around Ally was still clueless about Rose's plans. Any time she tried to find out what the plan was the topic of conversation was changed. Ally figured if all else failed she would simply say she didn't find anything she liked. Putting an end to this entire thing.

"Oh my gosh, these things are itchy," complained Susan fussing with the high collar on the first dress she tried on. "Yeah. I'm not going to be able to handle this all night." She quickly retreated to her dressing room unzipping the dress as she went.

Searching the racks Ally now began to run her fingers over the fabric trying to detect which dresses might also be itchy. She didn't want to spend the entire night scratching and being uncomfortable. Selecting a possible contender Ally lifted a pink dress from the rack surprised by the weight. "Wow, this is heavy. Those poor women they must have been grouchy and miserable all the time."

Rose smiled and shrugged as she continued her search. By this time Susan had reemerged in another dress. Appearing quite happy with her selection. After several trips to the dressing rooms both Rose and Ally gave up and decided they would need to look somewhere else.

On their way to another costume store Rose noticed a small vintage shop. Pulling into the open parking stall right in front of it she said. "Perhaps they'll have something in here."

The store was quaint with multiple scented candles that were losing the battle against the musty smell of old used items. Faded books lined oversized dusty book cases, men and women's hats hung from the numerous hooks scattered haphazardly on the wall-papered walls and sure enough there were a few dresses hanging on small circular racks. There was far too many nooks and cranny's in the store to notice everything, but it was clear it held quite the eclectic collection of antiques.

Studying an old perfume bottle Ally lost sight of the other girls. The pale green glass dwarfed by the metal cap with its black atomizer made her wonder if it still worked. Ally gently squeezed the black bulb releasing a fine mist into the air. Surprisingly the scent was pleasant enough. Turning to see if she'd been caught she found herself standing alone in a far corner of the store. It was then that she noticed the store clerk had also vanished. Growing worried she heard Rose's voice from the other end of the store. "Ally would you come here?"

Making her way through the maze of intolerable looking chairs Ally couldn't imagine being comfortable in them. Their high straight backs and thinly cushioned seats were less than welcoming. Ally soon spotted Rose walking towards her with a gorgeous blue Victorian dress. "Oh my gosh that's beautiful," gushed Ally reaching for the dress.

"The dressing room is just through there," pointed the clerk from behind Rose who was followed closely by Susan.

Ally hadn't really known what she was looking for in a dress unaware of what was worn back then but this dress answered that question. Grabbing the dress carefully she sauntered towards the dressing room making sure not to drag it. The dress was also void of any musty smell. It actually had a light floral scent to it. Ally figured Rose or the clerk had lightly sprayed perfume on it before handing it to her.

In no time Ally emerged smiling brighter than she had in a long time. The clerk had assisted her and even supplied a pair of shoes to complete the outfit. Standing on the small platform surrounded by three full length mirrors Ally admired herself. Soon catching sight of the smiling faces of Rose and Susan behind her. Everything was falling into place then reality reared its ugly face. The price tag scratched Ally's arm reminding her she couldn't afford to rent a dress let alone buy one.

Her downcast face crushed the happy moment for them all. It was Rose to the rescue again. "I know what you're thinking and you don't have to worry about it. Everything is already taken care of."

"You can't buy me this dress," Ally grabbed the price tag and nearly fell off the platform. Assisted by the clerk she regained her balance, "Rose I'm serious I won't let you spend that much money on a one-time party dress."

"I'm not buying the dress Ally. Mrs. Anderson has agreed to let you borrow the dress for the evening with my promise that it will be returned safely."

The clerk interjected quickly noticing Ally's look of disbelief, "If Miss Rose say's you're a friend of hers and can be trusted then that's all I need."

Susan stood in the background speechless for the first time since they'd meet. Her tearful eyes and shaky smile was more than Ally could take. She found herself overcome with emotion. Afraid to cry on the dress she quickly wiped away escaping tears with the back of her hands. "How do I thank you for this?"

"Your obvious excitement and happiness is all I need. Now go change before you cry all over the beautiful gown," teased Rose with an undercurrent of seriousness.

Watching the clerk bag the dress made Ally want to pinch herself. This was all too wonderful to believe. Thinking she couldn't be any more surprised she watched the clerk tuck the shoes she'd worn with the dress into the bottom of the garment bag.

A continuous flow of "thank you, thank you, thank you" were said by Ally as they left the store and headed to their next stop. It was rather humorous to see Susan interrupt her parade of appreciative comments to Rose by changing the subject. In no time Susan was back to her old self jabbering up a storm from the rear seat of Rose's spotless car.

By the end of the day all three were successful in finding a dress of their choice. Now all they had to do was wait for the party itself which now felt like a life time away. No longer having any worries about the party and feeling completely at ease about going Ally couldn't wait to tell her mom all about it. Then on second thought she decided to wait until after the party.

She didn't want to be talked out of it by either one of her parents. Ally could already hear her dad saying that a college party was nothing more than an excuse to drink or do something else careless. Wouldn't that be ironic? Ally refused to let anyone ruin this for her. She would simply avoid calling home until well after the party; knowing this wouldn't cause great concern since her calls had become less frequent over her short time there.

The last time she had spoken to her mom things were still bad at home. Her mom was now working another part-time job leaving her more exhausted then before. Her mom never said so but Ally believed that the second job was also a way to spend more time away from home as well as supplying another much-needed paycheck.

It had become a sad but true fact of life. Ally preferred not to know what was going on at home. Feeling guilty about leaving her mom alone to deal with her dad and worrying about what he would do next had proved to disrupt every aspect of her life. The easiest way to avoid that was to not call home. She wasn't going to risk destroying her excitement about the party with a simple call and that was that.

<u>Chapter Seven</u>

The last few weeks had gone by painfully slow for Ally. She had even started running a day or two with Rose to help speed things up. Swamped with homework and continuing to look for a job still managed to leave far too many free hours.

Attending a high school party in Glenbrook didn't vary much from any other day in town. It would be the same group of kids hanging out whether it was called a party or not. The college's upcoming Halloween party was going to be a real party. There would be countless people she didn't know in an unfamiliar location with costumes and tons of surprises she had been privy to thanks to Susan. The party was the buzz around campus. No matter where she was Ally would hear groups of students discussing with great anticipation their plans on attending. Ally hoped the manor chosen for the location would be large enough to hold the number of people she believed were going.

The night had finally arrived. Leaving the campus grounds almost empty as everyone prepared for the party. Ally admired her reflection and the perfect fit of the deep blue Victorian dress. She couldn't help but wonder how she'd do moving in the dress. The gown had multiple layers of fabric making it heavy not to mention the dress's train. Although it wasn't a particularly long train it would still be trailing behind her all night. She hadn't walked in the dress much while at the vintage store leaving her oblivious to just how difficult the simple act of walking was going to be. How Ally wished she had done some practicing before the big night but it was too late now. She'd just have to find a way to manage.

"Beautiful" announced Rose through a hoarse voice.

Ally turned to see her roommate standing in the bathroom doorway with her red nose, glassy eyes and uncommon pasty complexion. Rose had been sick for nearly a week now and wasn't showing any sign of improvement. It made Ally terribly sad that she wasn't going to be able to attend the party with her and Susan. "Thank you, but you should be in bed Rose."

"I may have to miss the party," commented Rose before sneezing several times. Then added, "I'm not going to miss you getting ready."

"It's the most beautiful dress I've ever worn," Ally said turning back to the full-length mirror, "I'm just glad this isn't the daily style of dress anymore it's a bit much for every day."

"It's missing something," replied Rose lifting a tiny black box towards her.

Ally took the box and after rubbing her fingers across the black velvet she slowly opened it. "It's beautiful." Examining the locket Ally noticed tiny clusters of flowers nestled among swirls that complimented the heart shape perfectly. Engraved on the smooth back side were the initials "E & H"

"Oh my gosh. Thank you," mumbled Ally reaching to hug Rose who stopped her from doing so with a series of dry coughs. Waiting for the cough attack to stop Ally felt bad for leaving her friend in her time of need. "I should stay home with you."

Rose shook her head and her hazel eyes flashed with more life than she'd exhibited in a week. Her look said all she wanted to say and Ally conceded defeat.

Even though Ally had waited with bated breath for this night to arrive a wave of nerves momentarily gripped her. She had held onto hope that Rose would have recovered by now and the three of them could have gone as planned. Remembering she still held the open jewelry box in her hand Ally looked at the gift and smiled. Her nerves about attending the Halloween party without Rose slowly eased. Her excitement once again taking center stage.

"Let me help you put it on." The silver chain twinkled happily in the light as the locket was lifted from the box. Rose fussed with the clasp while Ally took hold of the locket. Glancing at the engraving again she wondered who "E & H" had been while carefully trying to open the locket.

"It won't open" said Rose still struggling with the clasp, "that's why I got such a good deal at the antique store."

Not wanting to risk breaking the beautiful gift Ally gave up and shrugged her shoulders. Finally, the clasp gave way and they both smiled with a sigh of relief. Ally turned around lifting her curls from her neck and laughed when she stumbled on the train of her dress.

"I knew it would complete the outfit," boasted Rose. It was one of the rare moments where she showed pride in herself.

Rose was correct. The locket complimented the look adding the perfect finishing touch to the dress. Ally should have expected this from Rose with her natural sense of style. Other than her current sickly state she always looked picture perfect.

Losing herself in the fantasy come to life Ally stood there soaking in the image before her hardly recognizing her own reflection. The anticipation of the night ahead caused a sly smile to form on her face causing Rose to smile through her misery. The sound of girls giggling down the hallway reminded her that she needed to get going. Ally didn't want to miss a moment of the evening ahead of her.

Dalton Manor sat on acres upon acres of land a few miles outside the next town. The road leading to the manor was a bit more deserted than Ally expected. She thought she may be lost until she noticed two masterfully crafted lamp posts along the road drawing her attention. The elegant party sign instructed the party goes to the turn off the highway and proceed down the unpaved road. Whoever had created the flyers had masterfully duplicated the lamp post scene along the highway. Making it easy to point the party goers in the right direction.

Pulling down the tree lined driveway Ally half expected to see the headless horseman riding alongside the dirt road with her. When the enormous house came into view Ally understood why the location had been selected. The moon peeked through storm clouds casting distorted shadows on the weather-beaten house. Mesmerized by its eerie beauty Ally didn't notice Susan approach the car until she knocked on the window startling her.

"Isn't it great Ally? This is going to be so much fun," rambled Susan before Ally had the car door fully opened. "I've been looking for your car. How's Rose feeling? I'm so bummed she's missing this. It's a shame she got sick."

Ally could hear the hum of Susan's voice continue as she struggled from the car. Nodding automatically as she slowly rose to her feet. Before venturing toward the house Ally ran her hands down the bodice of the dress then fluffed the skirt to make sure it hung correctly.

Although the clouds were threatening rain it had yet to materialize. This eased Ally's concern over ruining the bottom of the dress by dragging it through mud. She couldn't forget for a moment that the dress was borrowed and had to be returned to Mrs. Anderson in the same condition it was in when it left the store.

Reaching the steps Ally grabbed the front of her dress lifting the ruffles clearing the way for her feet to move. Before taking the first step she closed her eyes and silently hoped she wouldn't fall. With the first step Ally felt a firm yet gentle grip on her arm, "Allow me," announced a husky voice.

Ally locked eyes with the most captivating sapphire eyes she'd ever seen, "Th, th...thank you," she stammered. Unable to take her focus off the alluring blue eyes that were as intent on her as she was on them. The numerous steps to the porch which had moments earlier been something to dread had now become too few steps. Upon feeling the strangers hand release her arm a wave of concern rushed through Ally. Would he disappear as quickly as he appeared?

With a nod this kind gentlemen ushered her into the grand entrance. Engrossed in her surroundings Ally didn't notice the handsome stranger vanish into the crowd. A massive curved stairway lead upstairs where a few people stood talking. Incapable of venturing past the red ropes with an "Employee Only" sign. Clearly the second floor was off limits to the party goers. No longer was there concern about the manor being large enough to hold the number of guests in attendance. The grandeur of the manor was awe inspiring. Adding to the dreamlike feeling Ally had been having since she dressed for the evening. Never in her wildest dreams had she even considered that something like this would be happening to her.

She had left Glenbrook knowing there was a great big world outside of the town limits, but all this was indescribable and unbelievable. No matter how hard she tried to capture this evening she feared she would never be able to fully relay how wonderful everything was. Rose wouldn't be able to completely appreciate just how thrilling it was to be there. "Poor Rose," she thought to herself. At that precise moment Ally realized her concern over her helpful escort disappearing had come to fruition.

Susan's boisterous laughter burst through her disappointment bringing her back to reality. It was only then that Ally noticed all the students whizzing by her going from one room to the next. Susan was on the dance floor without any sign of a clear dance partner. Completely lost in her dancing but Ally wanted no part of that. The mere act of walking in her dress was difficult enough.

Ally searched the crowd for those unforgettable eyes making her way down the painting lined hallway. The subdued candle light made it hard to make out much of the paintings. Despite the dim light she was drawn to one particular piece of artwork. In the muted flickers of the candle flames she struggled to make out the features of a man standing in the shadows of the manors front porch. Moving closer to the painting merely obstructed what little light the candles offered. Forcing Ally to take a step back.

"That's Mr. Dalton the owner of the manor," whispered Susan in Ally's ear giving her a fright. "Legend has it that Mr. Dalton is a powerful warlock cursed with immortality."

Ally interrupted, "A warlock?"

Without skipping a beat Susan continued, "Day's before his one year wedding anniversary his wife suddenly got sick and died. Mr. Dalton refused to lose her so he cast a spell trapping her soul inside his anniversary gift until he could release her soul into the body of another. When that body grows old and eventually dies he re-traps her soul only to repeat the process. Locals say he repeats the process even to this day," Susan stated without any tone of teasing.

For a moment Susan had Ally enthralled by the story she told. Then a smirk crossed Ally's face, "Oh that's a good one Susan a surprise you forgot to tell me about?"

"No, it's true. I told you about all the surprises we planned well almost all the surprises, but really Ally this is true." The hurtful look on Susan's face tugged at Ally's heart so she encouraged her to continue with the legend.

"As I was saying, legend has it that Mr. Dalton has continued to release and trap his wife's soul throughout the decades. It's rather romantic to have someone move heaven and earth to live with you forever. At least I think so," and with that Susan turned and headed down the hall back towards the music.

Refocusing her attention on the painting in front of her Ally stared intently at the figure in the shadows. Still unable to make anything out. She felt a strong need to see the face of the dark figure. Unsure what was motivating her, but unable to pull free from the desire. The longer she studied the murky silhouette the more determined she became until her eyes began playing tricks on her. Leading her to believe the figure had begun moving in the darkness slowly making its way towards the sunlit steps.

Chapter Eight

Edmund stepped from the shadows into the brilliant morning sun ready for that afternoons gathering. There were final preparations to be completed before his guests began arriving. He was determined to make sure every detail lived up to his expectations.

His servants had been up before dawn in hopes Edmund would be pleased with their efforts. The head chef had prepared his favorite breakfast and served it at a table set for a king. The picturesque porch that framed the entire front of the manor provided Edmund the perfect vantage point. Hidden in the obscure morning shadows he enjoyed his meal while maintaining a watchful eye over his staff.

Without so much as uttering a sound he commanded everyone's attention with his imposing presence at the edge of the porch steps. The entire staff paused from their work to acknowledge his majestic appearance. Scanning the expansive grounds brought a heart melting smile to his captivating features easing the staff's tension causing a wave of excitement to run through the lot of them. They reviled in a sense of accomplishment. Feeling relief for the briefest of moments before quickly returning to the job at hand.

Satisfied with the progress outside Edmund proceeded indoors to verify the kitchen staff were also on schedule.

This was to be the very first festivity held at the manor in decades. Not a single person knew what to expect. Their minds were filled with curious thoughts of who Mr. Dalton was and what the old abandoned manor would look like. This year's harsh winter had taken its time before reluctantly melting away. Edmund's eloquent and opulent invitation to the late spring event helped distract the local socialites from the bitter cold. Their days were filled with preparations for the reception from selecting one's attire to rehearsing a pretentious greeting filled with false humility. Everyone who was anyone would be in attendance. High society was more than ready to celebrate their riches and status in full view of each other. Each vying for what they viewed as being the winner of the day. The crème de la crème of the elite.

Edmund had waited far too long for this day to arrive. He had almost lost count of how many bleak and miserable winters he'd gone through. At last, he felt the time had come to reintroduce Dalton Manor to the world and reclaim his family's place in it. What better way to avenge his parents then from behind enemy lines? He'd kept his existence a secret for more than half a century covertly watching and learning about his intended prey.

Discovering each individual's desires, faults, strengths and weaknesses in order to calculate their demise. Simply wiping out the village didn't allow for a lifetime of suffering. That is what Edmund wanted them to struggle through. He wanted; no, he needed them to feel the intense pain their ancestors had inflicted on him. Strategizing and planning his revenge over the decades was the only happiness he found in his everlasting existence.

The murder of his parents had left Edmund alone. The carefree teenage boy he once was may not have been physically killed that summer night but emotionally he was dead. The only surviving emotion was pure unadulterated rage. An insatiable anger that was continuously fueled by the hatred he felt for the angry mob that took his parents and the rubble of a life they left him with.

Over the years he had mastered his craft. Driven by the emptiness in his heart Edmund grew into a supremely powerful warlock. Unlike anything the villagers could imagine. His parents combined force didn't come close to the expertise or caliber of power he had reached. His mother's gentleness that once lived within him had been replaced with a maddening need to have someone pay for his misery. Even his father's appreciation for the differences between the humans and themselves now only served as an added source of exasperation.

As the years passed the legend of Dalton Manor with the family of witchcraft practicing demons had been all but forgotten. The memory of their fiery deaths or their very existence had long since faded into the background. No longer did guards stand by the road blocking the driveway entrance to the burnt remains of the manor. The reason for keeping people away for their own safety had become folklore. Gone were the men who deliberately set the manor ablaze making sure it burnt to the ground with his family trapped inside. Edmund could still hear their cursing and cheering at the destruction while his parents shielded him between them. It was then that his parents merged all their remaining power and granted Edmund immortality.

"Mr. Dalton sir," said the head butler interrupting Edmunds repulsive memories as he stood motionless in the foyer.

Without saying a word Edmund turned towards Arthur. His deep blue eyes raging at the thoughts still lingering in his mind. Arthur remained motionless carefully balancing a silver tray on each hand waiting for Edmund to speak. Considering both options before him Edmund pointed to the table setting of choice. Arthur gave a slow nod then turned and walked away leaving Edmund struggling to contain himself.

Glancing at his pocket watch he was surprised to see how much time he'd spent reliving that horrid night and continued on to the kitchen. The smell of roast duck, sweet potatoes, freshly baked bread and countless other dishes brought a grin to his face wiping away his scowl. Watching the bustling activity in the kitchen did more than amuse him it lifted his spirits. All the hardworking cooks scrambling about to make sure everything was just right reminded him how mundane a human's life was. With a simple wave of his hand the entire party would be ready, but he understood how important it was to keep his true identity a secret. He couldn't risk his plan being detected or worse failing.

Having a full staff of helpless humans was a necessary evil. An instrumental part of his plan. Wanting to fit in with the upper-class Edmund understood he had to appear to be one of them. No matter how ridiculous he believed it all to be or how much he preferred to limit being in the company of humans. Over the years he had surprisingly become fond of a select few on his staff. Edmund had grown to enjoy their company while listening to their simple stories. Since they had all been selected from great distances away he planned on excluding them from his revenge. Not only were their families uninvolved with his past many of them had proven to be useful in one way or another. Similar to farmers keeping cats around to catch rodents or cows for their milk. The humans at the manor served a purpose.

Edmund retired to his room for a moment closing the door behind him. Sitting on his dresser was the remnants of the only family portrait that had survived the deadly fire. The treasured and irreplaceable picture with its burnt edges protected by the glass of the much too large frame was the only thing left of his parents. Other than himself. The descendants of that murderous mob may have forgotten what their families did, but Edmund had not. Each and every day since the death of his family he not only remembered the tragedy, he trained, focused on and prepared to make someone pay for their evil. Tracing his fingertips along his mother's face he recalled her contagious laugh and briefly smiled. Turning his focus to his father he felt the confidence and vigor that exuded from every part of him. An all too familiar tinge of pain radiated in his cold heart.

"Today it begins," he stated to the faded canvas that held what was left of his parents. Their smiling faces full of love and plans for their family's future coexisting among the humans was his father's dream. Edmund had stood in front of their warm embrace for the portrait, but all that remained of him was from his forehead up. Every other part of Edmund had been consumed by the fire. He was beyond thankful that his mother and father's faces were spared. How differently he viewed the humans from how his father did. Living among them sickened him. If not for his intense desire to make them pay for his parent's death, he would never have contact with them. A knock on the door was followed by Arthur's gravelly voice announcing the guests were arriving.

Checking his reflection in the mirror Edmund straightened his bow tie, smoothed his vest with his large hands and put on his friendliest smile. His natural charisma and charm would aid in his efforts to win over the guests. His hope was to become a trusted friend allowing him to enjoy the fruits of his labor first hand. He wanted them to come to him for guidance or consolation during their troubles. The very same troubles he deliberately caused in their lives. Peeking out the bedroom window he could see the carriages delivering their high society cargo to the manor. Filled with a sudden charge of anticipation Edmund quickly headed outside to greet his guests.

No one knew anything about him yet each invitation had been accepted and responded to quickly. The mere fact that they were elegantly worded, created on the finest linen and stamped with his signet ring was enough to impress the influential members of society.

With their self-appointed nobility and financial status, they all felt superior to not only those less fortunate but amongst each other. It was a never-ending battle to become the epitome of wealth and prestige. Although a family may be included or accepted into this exclusive circle Edmund had seen them turn on one another in the blink of an eye. Loyalty was almost unheard of. The superficial relationships most of them had were far too easily severed.

"Stupid humans" whispered Edmund under his breath watching a newly arrived guest be greeted by another. All the hustle and bustle of climbing out of carriages and introductions ceased when Edmund was announced by Arthur.

As expected, his obvious good looks drew quite a reaction from the available ladies. Knowing they were there for no other reason than to inspect a new possible suitor he intentionally ignored them. Standing behind their parents they each lifted their fans covering their faces deliberately leaving their longing eyes visible. Edmund stifled his laughter as he could see their reaction to him in his peripheral vision. He made his way onto the lawn with long strides then proceeded to shake hands with the gentlemen. His towering stature was level with a few of their top hats, but for the most part even their tops hats couldn't reach his shoulders.

"It's a pleasure to meet you," repeated Edmund making the rounds through the now large crowd. The cook rang the dinner bell calling everyone to the feast being served. Taking his seat at the end of the head table Edmund welcomed his guests with a well-rehearsed speech delighting his audience with his eloquence.

Casual conversations intertwined with pompous comments were carried out during the meal. Edmund was determined to capture has much as he could. He simultaneously listened to all of them deciphering what could be of use to him. A particular conversation however, drew his attention away from his scheming. A young woman's sweet voice danced above all others like a song and her relaxed yet willful way of talking intrigued Edmund. Excusing himself from the table he headed in the direction of this musical voice.

Heads turned anxiously waiting for him to walk in their direction causing his intended target to stop mid-sentence leaving him lost for a split second. His highly tuned senses had already zeroed in on her breathing while she spoke earlier. He quickly identified the young woman sitting at the farthest table. She was facing away from him as he approached but her father had spotted Edmund and rose to greet him.

"This is a splendid way to spend the afternoon Mr. Dalton. My family and I would like to pass along our gratitude for such a wonderful meal." The man's handshake was strong and assured.

"It's my pleasure, Mr.?" questioned Edmund. This was one of the few families he hadn't researched before the luncheon.

"Mr. Beck."

"It's an honor to meet you Mr. Beck. You and your family are welcome any time."

Before Edmund could be introduced to Mr. Beck's family another man interrupted the conversation. Obviously concerned and insulted that his family had been passed over. Edmund turned towards the aggressively rude intruder visibly dissatisfied with the behavior. This unfortunately allowed Mr. Beck to excuse himself taking his family with him. Mr. Beck turned back giving a disapproving glance at the impolite behavior of his fellow guest. A smug sneer of triumph was returned by the invader adding to Edmunds irritation.

The entire time Edmund dealt with the unwanted intrusion forced upon him he remained focused on Mr. Beck's daughter. He could hear her enchanting voice commenting on the splendor of the manor and its vast grounds. Edmund had enhanced the manor along with the grounds to a level unseen before. A sudden breeze tossed her waist length hair about making it come to life as it reflected the sunlight on its golden strands. How he wished he could send the man in front of him to the moon but his common sense took hold forcing a stop to those thoughts.

Puzzled by the overwhelming desire to meet this woman Edmund felt stumped. Why should he be the slightest bit interested in her? Just when he thought the sound of her lovely voice couldn't be matched her laughter rang through all the commotion lifting his mood to forgotten heights. Abruptly Edmund ended his conversation with his rude guest then turned to follow the Beck family.

Watching her laugh with her entire body brought an uncontrollable smile to his face. Quickening his gait Edmund closed the gap between them. His eyes locked on the movement of the young woman's layered cream and blue dress as she appeared to glide over the lawn. The train of her dress obediently trailing behind her graceful steps.

"Mr. Beck," said Edmund upon reaching them.

Simultaneously the family turned towards him. At last he could see the woman who had captured his interest. Her exquisite face took his breath away causing a strange unfamiliar sensation within him. Edmund suddenly became aware of his own heartbeat which began picking up pace while he soaked in the beauty in front of him.

"Mr. Dalton, allow me to introduce my lovely wife Cora and our only daughter Helene."

Chapter Nine

Both women curtsied in silence almost in unison with one another. Helene's petite size mirrored her mothers, as did her long flaxen hair. Her eyes were like those of her father a warm rich chestnut full of intelligence and strength. Edmund found himself lost in the depth of their mystery. Similar to looking into a wishing well filled with the hopes and dreams people had cast into it.

"It's my pleasure to make your acquaintance," replied Edmund. Eagerly awaiting the sound of Helene's angelic voice, but as expected she remained silent allowing her father and mother to carry the conversation. Edmund tried to capture every delicate move Helene made while Mr. Beck discussed his recent business travels.

"Would you care to see the stables?" Edmund asked Mr. Beck after noticing the intricate brooch Helene wore on her lace bodice. The gold framed onyx stone contrasted brilliantly with the ivory carving of Pegasus. The proud creature rearing tall with wings held high appearing like he was ready to fly from the black gemstone that held him. Helene's face lit up with excitement and she stared at her father until he acknowledged her enthusiasm. Her impatience brewed just below the surface waiting for her father's approval. How desperately she wanted to remain with the men on this excursion.

"Thank you Mr. Dalton for the invitation, however I believe Helene and I would prefer to have a cup of tea with the other women. You men go ahead and enjoy the horses," responded Mrs. Beck.

The reddish flecks in Helene's eyes came to life, they sparked and glinted with fury at the idea of not seeing the stables and the number of quality horses she imagined they housed. This resulted in a clearly visible change in her stance. Holding her breath behind a clenched jaw Helene forced her frustration down into her feet. Well-hidden underneath the multiple layers of her dress. From a distance her foot tapping would have gone unnoticed but the gentle sound of her shoes knocking against the ground delighted Edmund.

Mrs. Beck gave Helene a disapproving look. One that Edmund believed had been used numerous times before. This did little to subdue Helene who turned her focus to her father. The two of them had quite the silent debate resulting in her father's next words. "Cora I would like Helene to accompany us. After all, we are in the market for a new horse. This is an excellent opportunity to make sure we buy a horse Helene will appreciate.

Especially because she will be the primary rider of the mount."

A sly smile of gratitude beamed from Helene's face. Respectfully she kissed her mother's cheek before telling her to enjoy visiting with the other women. Still very much displeased Cora accepted defeat and excused herself from the group. The further away Cora got from them the more alive Helene became. Her lively spirit which seemed to be embraced by her father appeared to be a source of concern for her mother. Edmund had to agree with Mr. Beck and found Helene's self-assuredness a welcome change of pace. Within minutes of reaching the stables Helene began venturing off by herself. She seemed to be searching for something in particular while her father made sure to keep her within view.

"Oh father he's gorgeous," squealed Helene from the far end of the stables. Her boldness took over. She opened the gate and stepped into the stall with a very large gray horse. Edmund and her father rushed to the stall after losing sight of her. Preparing to subdue the horse with a spell Edmund was astonished to see Helene stroking the horses neck while carrying on a full conversation with him.

Realizing she wasn't alone Helene turned towards Edmund speaking directly to him for the first time, "What's his name?"

"Storm," replied Edmund trying to hide the fact that she had taken his breath away for the second time.

"Storm," she repeated looking the horse square in the eyes. Her friendly interaction with the powerful animal engrossed both men. Edmund watched in admiration as Helene connected with Storm in a way he had never seen before. The horse was magnificent in both beauty and brawn remaining aloof around almost everyone else at the manor. Edmund rode him regularly while all others chose to keep their distance. His size alone was daunting. When combined with his sometimes-headstrong behavior Storm was usually admired from afar.

The time spent in the stables was far too short for Edmunds liking. Before he knew it, he was escorting Mr. Beck and Helene back to the party. The gentleman side of Edmund understood that it would be improper to spend any more time away from his other guests. He couldn't risk offending them or fail to see his plan for revenge materialize. Helene had briefly made Edmund forget the reason for hosting the gathering in the first place. As they drew nearer to the crowd he was quickly reminded of why he was surrounded by the humans he despised. The sound of their boasting voices and laughter cleared his mind of everything except vengeance.

Edmund attended to his other guests who were eagerly awaiting his return. Playing the part of the gallant, well-mannered host so convincingly his absence was soon forgotten. Edmund carried on meaningless conversations with the other guests while covertly listening to Helene describe Storm to her mother with remarkable detail. He picked up on the concern in Cora's voice when she responded. The older women sitting with them didn't know how to react to Helene's excitement and viewed her enthusiasm as a problem to be handled.

Edmund remained fixated on the women's conversation. He appreciated Cora's comments as she kissed her daughter's forehead before lovingly saying, "My sweet Helene, you are so much braver than I. The world is yours for the taking. I have no doubt you will blaze a path for those behind you to follow."

Cora had the authority to speak freely being one of the long-standing women in charge of arranging social affairs and keeping order. These women held the power to accept or ostracized individuals at their discretion. A power most of the socialites lived for. Their days were filled with gossip and meddling in an absurd effort to maintain their own status in town. Cora's brave comment to her daughter persuaded Edmund to consider that she was doing something very similar to what he intended to do. Become one of them to secure one's safety. The whole "keep your friends close but your enemies closer" way of thinking. Even though Helene's gusto for life may be frightening to her mother it was clearly something Cora wouldn't allow anyone to disapprove of.

Guests began departing when the afternoon sun started its descent into the early evening sky. Mr. Beck approached Edmund thanking him again for his hospitality leaving Cora and Helene safely inside their carriage. Although Edmund was disappointed at not being able to say good-bye to Helene he was thankful for the opportunity to invite Mr. Beck back to the manor. He wanted to discuss a possible business venture. Edmund had decided he wanted to get to know Helene better which meant he had to go through Mr. Beck.

With the final guests on their way the staff began clearing the mess left behind. Their day was far from over, but the thrill of such a successful luncheon had reenergized them. They all missed the interaction with people from town. The staff were expected to remain at the manor day and night. Except for a select few who were sent on occasional errands. Almost all of the food served had been grown on the property. Even the ducks were hunted there. It had only been within the last year that some were allowed to venture into town for supplies. It was a clever way to start laying the ground work for Edmunds plan. In an effort to pique the interest of the towns people his staff began appearing in town on a regular basis. Strangers were quickly noticed in the tight knit community. Edmund's well-mannered servants with seemingly unlimited funds doing his bidding were sure to catch everyone's attention.

Edmund had cast a spell on his entire staff wiping out all memories of life before working for him. Their lives at Dalton Manor were all they could recall not even realizing they couldn't remember their families or childhoods. They were the lucky ones. Their poor families knew they were gone and missed them. Many had searched in vain for their lost family members. The spell also veiled his staff from anyone who may recognize them. The powerful incantation made them look like complete strangers even to their own parents. As time went by generations passed away and the missing family members were forgotten.

Edmund took a seat on the porch swing meditating on the Beck's carriage. Keenly aware of its location and the happenings inside. The banter between the three of them tickled him so much he found himself chuckling. Their behavior was unlike any humans he had watched over the years. He soon found himself filled with enjoyment as he eased dropped on the Beck family. It occurred to Edmund that this must have been what his father had enjoyed and spoke of when he discussed living side by side with the humans. His father had never feared the humans nor had he ever imagined the hatred they would have for him and his family once it was discovered what they were. His father's good natured heart and willingness to accept everyone for who they were had ultimately cost him and his wife their lives.

Anger erupted in Edmund when the memory of losing his parents rushed back in. He was even more upset with himself. How could he have made such an amateur mistake? How dare he let Helene distract him to the point of almost forgetting his mission for the day. Instead of remaining completely on task he had allowed a mere human to lead him off course. This was unacceptable. He had waited so very long to wreak havoc in the lives of the villagers. Feeling like he had let his parents down with his insane infatuation for this young woman he refocused his attention.

Edmund knew he had to regain control if he was to be successful in his plan. He decided he would meet with Mr. Beck as planned. Then never see or speak to any of them again. He thought of sending them away to make sure he wasn't tempted to check up on Helene whenever the memory of her beauty floated into his mind. There was no room in his life for distractions. Particularly from a woman who would never accept the real him.

"Can I get you anything?" asked Arthur noticing the unhappy look on Edmunds face believing he was disappointed in the afternoons event.

"A cup of tea."

"Of course sir."

Upon his return, Arthur had gathered the courage to question Edmund about his obvious dissatisfaction with something. "Is there something troubling you sir?"

Edmund noticed the concern on Arthur's face. Knowing that the kind elderly man took great pride in his work he concluded that Arthur believed he had failed in some way. Edmund put his mind at rest by saying, "No Arthur. The gathering went extremely well today. As always you handled every detail with tremendous care."

This brought a smile of satisfaction to Arthur's face. He thanked Edmund for his kind words. Arthur had become a trusted confidant over the years something Edmund didn't expect but was greatly appreciative of. He was the first staff member selected soon after his parent's death. There was a long history between the two of them and Edmund knew he could always turn to Arthur. With everything except what he was and what he intended to do.

That simple fact confirmed why Edmund had to wipe Helene from his existence. If he couldn't expose himself to Arthur after so many decades together. How could he possibly get involved with Helene?

Chapter Ten

Over the next couple weeks Edmund made countless trips into town always making sure the Beck family wasn't there. He remained focused on the family line that was responsible for leading the murderous mob that killed his parents. Edmund wanted nothing more than to bring retribution down on the lot of them. The Bennett family now the main land owners in town were thrilled at the prospect of Edmund wanting to expand the acreage around the manor. Edmund trusted that the greed of these humans would blind them to his vengeful plot. Their unappeased hunger for more and more money made them salivate with anticipation. They were already spending the money they planned on earning from their potential business dealings with Mr. Dalton.

Edmund struggled but managed to eliminate thoughts of Helene by letting his hostility rule his heart during the day. Leaving her to haunt his dreams when he finally gave into sleep. Awaking throughout the night with memories of her in the stables or laughing whole heartedly with her parents. As much as he wanted to forget her very existence she lingered in the deepest recesses of his mind.

The night before his business appointment with Mr. Beck Edmund found himself anxious about their meeting. Wishing he hadn't scheduled the meeting in the first place. He could have easily wiped it from Mr. Beck's mind, but something he couldn't explain had prevented him from doing so. Visualizing the home of Mr. & Mrs. Beck quickly transported Edmund there. Helene sat at the piano playing a happy little melody while her parents listened lovingly. Watching her fingers dance across the keyboard mesmerized Edmund as much as the song itself.

"Helene come join us," beckoned her father while the last note hung in the air.

"Yes, Father," she answered taking a seat on the sofa next to her mother.

"Tomorrow I meet with Mr. Dalton to discuss a possible business venture and I want to discuss something with you before then."

Helene's expression showed he had piqued her interest. She glanced at her mother as if to ask if she knew what he was going to say. Her mother smiled a coy smile turning to her husband. Secretly Helene hoped it had something to do with the amazing gray stallion from the stables. She had been trying to figure out a way to ride the superb animal since she first laid eyes on him. How she hoped this would be the perfect time to bring it up if her father didn't. With great anticipation, she eagerly waited for her father to continue.

Mr. Beck cut to the chase, "It was blatantly obvious that afternoon at Mr. Dalton's home that he has taken a liking to you Helene. He had a difficult time taking his eyes off you."

This was not at all what Helene was hoping to hear, "I hadn't really noticed."

"Oh I beg to differ my daughter. I believe you noticed. You are far too observant and intelligent to not have noticed."

A shrug of her shoulders was Helene's only response before trying to change the subject, "I was hoping you wanted to discuss Storm. Perhaps to schedule a day that I could ride him or even better set up a time to discuss buying him from Mr. Dalton."

"I may be able to persuade Mr. Dalton into letting you ride Storm, but the horse is not for sale. There is no reason to discuss that topic of conversation."

Cora glared at her daughter's sigh of disappointment and with raised eyebrows sent a clear message to her daughter to tread carefully. Mr. Beck's silence spoke volumes as he patiently waited for Helene to give him her undivided attention.

"As you were saying Father."

"Not only do I believe Mr. Dalton wants to discuss business. I expect him to discuss his desire to court you."

Edmund watched in disbelief as Helene's face showed utter dissatisfaction with this idea. He couldn't remember having any woman be less than thrilled with the prospect of spending time in his company. Let alone the possibility of being courted by him.

"Oh Father," was all she could get out before having to take a few deep breaths to balance her shaky voice. "We know nothing about the man. Except he is obviously good looking and has an abundance of money. Did you not see all the other available young women swooning over him?"

"Yes I did. They did very little to hide their yearning. However, I'm confident you also noticed his eyes were constantly on you?"

"That's only because he viewed me as a challenge. Something I'm sure he's quite unaccustomed to. He doesn't appear to be a man who has ever had to work for anything in his life especially the company of a woman. He's clearly wealthy and blatantly handsome. Which means he's another arrogant, selfish, spoiled man who knows nothing of hard work, loss or humility. I'm sure the only thing he loves more than his wealth is himself."

At this point Mr. Beck rose from his chair and in a stern voice reprimanded his opinionated daughter, "You listen here young lady. The only part of your little rant which was correct is that we don't know anything about

Mr. Dalton. Other than he's affluent and good looking. You are making rather large speculations about all the rest. Something I know you yourself disapprove of."

Helene knew better than to respond to her father's outraged words. Lowering her eyes to the floor she waited for him to continue. Unfair judgements in her family were quickly dealt with and Helene knew she'd crossed the line. Her mother placed her hand over Helene's giving it a gentle squeeze reassuring her of their love as her father continued to scold her behavior.

Cora's subtle display of affection was enough to calm her husband's voice. "Helene, look at me," he requested. When she made eye contact with him he went on. "Have you experienced unfair judgment because of your wealth and beauty?"

"Yes."

"Then you know how unjustified and hurtful that is. Aren't you guilty of the same assumptions with Mr. Dalton?" After Helene answered his question he knelt in front of his wounded daughter looking her dead in the eyes.

"Judging someone based on nothing more than the money or looks they have or don't have is wrong. You know this Helene. You are clumping Mr. Dalton in with all those who've caused you pain in the past. That behavior is just as unseemly. Your mother and I have raised you better than that. Let your opinion of the man come from your experiences with him. Give him a chance to show you who he truly is before unfairly deciding who you think he is."

Helene nodded in agreement feeling ashamed of her behavior. She was usually on the other end of this type of conversation and was baffled as to why she had such strong negative feelings about a man she had just met. Somehow he had put her at odds with her own beliefs.

As the Beck's retired for the night Edmund returned his focus to the manor. It was late in the evening and most of the staff had gone to their quarters. Enjoying the view from his bedroom window Edmund admired the star filled sky. He replayed Helene's words over and over in his head. She had been terribly wrong about him. He knew all too well about loss. The emptiness that prevailed within him had not lessened over the decades. There wasn't a day that went by when he didn't think of his parents or wish he had the power he now possessed. He believed things would have played out differently if he had.

For some unknown reason, he needed Helene to know she was wrong about him. Her opinion of him mattered far too much. Confusing Edmund even more. There was nothing logical about the way she made him feel. His racing heart at the mere thought of her, the inability to breath normally in her presence or this growing urgency to prove to her that he wasn't anything like she imagined. Appreciating the loveliness of a woman wasn't new to him, but this was so much more. There was an all-consuming need to know everything about her. To make her happy, to push everything else aside and focus entirely on her and her dreams.

The thought of bringing a smile to Helene's face eased his pain for a moment filling him with peace. No matter how short lived that might be it was making a difference. An unexplainable sense of tranquility like he hadn't felt since losing his parents was overtaking him on a regular basis. What a welcome sabbatical from the anguish he had been living with. Believing nothing in the world except revenge could bring him happiness had proven to be a truly sad existence. Helene had given him a new hope, a hope that made simply existing a thing of the past. Was it possible to live and enjoy an immortal life?

At last the thought of living for eternity didn't seem unbearable. Somehow Helene had shined a light into his dark world bringing about a change in him. A change he didn't see coming. One that he had stopped aspiring for or even allow himself to envision decades ago. Dreaming of a life filled with joy, laughter and love merely intensified his loneliness.

As expected Edmund dreamt of Helene throughout the night. What he didn't realize was that Helene was laying in her bed wide awake unable to sleep. Her insomnia brought on by continuous thoughts of him.

Chapter Eleven

Tossing and turning unable to get comfortable Helene sat straight up in bed huffing loudly. Her mind wouldn't shut off regardless of what she tried. Counting sheep, humming a lullaby all ended up at the same place. Dalton Manor. The memory of Edmund was clear and detailed from his hypnotic blue eyes to his deeply smooth voice. It was only then that she realized she had taken in all his appealing qualities despite her best efforts.

Frustrated that she couldn't erase him from her thoughts she pulled the covers over her face letting her head crash back into her pillow. Forcing her eyes shut she pictured herself as a little girl playing on the tree swing in her front yard. Taking slow deep breathes she remembered the gentle swaying making her tense body relax and sink deeper into her mattress.

The next thing she knew she was staring at the sheet still on top her face completely unaware of when her eyes opened. Hours later she drifted off to sleep. Pure exhaustion finally conquered her over-active imagination. As Helene sank deeper into her slumber her unconscious mind picked up where her consciousness had left off. There was no escaping Edmund Dalton. Whether awake or asleep he permeated her thoughts.

By this time the eastern part of the night sky began to glow with a hint of color. Soft yellowish-orange hues were the first pale signs that morning was on its way. Silence laid across the valley like a warm safe quilt as early dawn went primarily unnoticed. Waking from another dream Edmund rubbed his tired eyes wondering how long he'd been asleep this time. Stumbling to the window he caught sight of the amazing sunrise. He watched the illumination of light in the distance become a striking blend of deep orange and red as the sun rose from behind the rolling green hills. In all its glory, it still paled in comparison to his latest dream of Helene.

Unable to control his curiosity he envisioned the Beck's home finding himself watching Helene in her restless sleep. Helene's eyes fluttered rapidly beneath her eyelids intensifying his curiosity. It was obvious that she was dreaming and he had to know what her dreams contained. Placing his fingertips against his temples he closed his eyes joining Helene in her dream. To his enjoyment she was at Dalton Manor wandering around the grounds in the same dress she wore to the luncheon. She was even more enticing than he remembered.

Hovering over her from a distance he waited nervously to see what secrets her dream would reveal. Edmund realized that there was no one other than Helene in the dream. Soon she started running towards the stables. Upon reaching the empty stables she collapsed into tears causing Edmunds heart to ache for her.

"Helene," whispered Edmund from the far end of the stables making himself visible to her.

Slowly she raised her face to him and in a shaky voice uttered one word, "Away."

Edmund was crushed at her harsh word. The sight of her tear stained face made him wish he hadn't revealed himself. He didn't know what he'd done to make her disdain him so, but it was painfully obvious that she loathed the very sight of him. He couldn't change her feelings even if he wanted to. Human feelings were theirs and theirs alone. They were far beyond any power witchcraft held. If there were a spell to prevent humans from hating witches and warlocks it would have been cast centuries ago.

"Everyone's gone away," added Helene extending her hand to Edmund who rushed to her side. With his heart racing he helped her to her feet.

The panic was evident in her delicately soft hand as it quivered within his. Being a true gentleman he released her hand once she was standing and stepped back to an acceptable distance. It was completely improper for an unmarried woman to be unescorted in the presence of an eligible bachelor. Dream or no dream Edmund would behave properly in hopes to gain her trust.

Before he could reassure her Helene woke from her dream expelling him from her presence so suddenly he was confused at being back in his bedroom. A lingering fog hung over him while he stared blankly at the sunrise now filling the skyline with color. The sensation of Helene's hand in his seemed so real. He had to remind himself that it had only been a dream.

With very little sleep Helene wasn't happy about the full day ahead of her. Her mother had scheduled social affairs and errands in town while her father handled business deals. Including the one with Mr. Dalton. This thought brought her back to her dream where she stood alone with Edmund in his stables.

"Helene dear are you awake?" asked her mom through the slightly opened door.

"Yes, Mother."

"Very good. I want to get started with our day so be quick my dear."

Helene nodded in agreement as her irritation grew from having spent all night thinking and dreaming about Edmund. He on the other hand was ecstatic from the knowledge of Helene dreaming about the manor and being able to spend time with her. Even if it wasn't real. At least not yet.

Edmund kept himself busy all morning until Mr. Beck's arrival. Although they discussed everything they needed to cover he purposely left things undecided. Making it necessary to schedule another appointment. Due to Mr. Beck's existing travel plans they wouldn't be able to meet again for a few weeks fitting perfectly into an ingenious idea Edmund came up with. He relished the thought of having more time to organize his plan of action. Edmund believed he would not only pull his plan together but end up with the result he hoped for.

As evening fell Edmund lounged in an oversized chair in the study restlessly waiting for Helene to climb into bed and sleep. Listening in on Helene with her family he smirked at the sound of her repeatedly yawning. Assuring him it wouldn't be long.

"Good night Mother. Good night Father," was music to his ears. In no time, he could sense a change in her breathing signaling she had drifted off to sleep. To his delight her dream picked up almost where it left off the night before. Edmund watched her standing in the shade of a large tree located near the stables. Wasting no time Edmund made his move.

"Beautiful day," he remarked from behind her.

"Yes, it is," she answered turning to face him. Her hair pulled into a graceful bun highlighting her slender neck triggered something deep inside Edmund. Controlling himself he noticed the same brooch as before on the sweetheart neckline of her short sleeved lavender dress.

"I can't help but notice your stunning brooch."

"It was a gift from my father's travels to Greece. He knows how much I love horses and Pegasus is the ideal horse. How I wish he were real." Blushing Helene turned away, but continued, "I used to dream of riding him as a young girl soaring high above the trees and landing way up on a mountaintop simply to soak in the view."

Edmunds smile beamed with adoration while he listened to her carry on about Pegasus and the many adventures they shared over the years. The sweetness in her had returned. No longer did she seem irritated by the mere sight of him.

"Do you believe in magic?" he questioned knowing he probably wouldn't like her response.

"No, not real magic. It's just the silliness of a young girl, but wouldn't life be delightfully wonderful if magic did exist?"

Edmunds heart leaped for joy as he heard genuine sincerity in her answer. "Helene would you accompany me to the stables? There's something I would like you to see."

Together they walked side by side making sure to leave an acceptable distance between them. They were completely in step with each other while enjoying a simple conversation. Random people came in and out of view reminding Edmund that he was in Helene's dream. There was only so much control he had over her dream not to mention a limited amount of time. Helene headed straight for Storms stall finding it empty. Edmund then took her out to the adjacent arena.

Helene's eyes came to life at the sight of the majestic Pegasus rushing to greet them. Edmund stepped into the arena taking the bridle in his hand and lead the mighty creature towards Helene saying, "Helene, say hello to your old friend."

A large lump in her throat prevented her from speaking. Wiping tears from her cheeks she locked eyes with Edmund. The gratitude that filled her shined through the tears gathering in her warm eyes making him wish he could freeze that moment and hold onto it forever.

"Would you like to go for a ride?" he asked mounting Pegasus. Still unable to speak she took hold of his hand as Pegasus bowed to help her be lifted on. "You may want to hold on tight."

Before Helene fully processed what Edmund had said Pegasus bolted through the stables. Forcing her to wrap her arms firmly around Edmund to prevent her from falling off backwards. Clearing the stables within a few strides they were soon gaining altitude causing her to burst into joyous laughter. Edmund soaked in the pure sound of her heavenly laugh. He could also feel her laughter as her body shook rhythmically against his. Having her so close to him full of life and happiness made Edmund feel more alive than ever before. Pegasus swooped low over a crop field then headed high into the cloudless sky.

"This is better than I remember," said Helene in a hushed voice gently laying her head against Edmund's shoulder blade. This unexpected moment was agonizingly broken by the sound of someone knocking. Reality came bursting in dissolving their flight into nothingness.

"Helene are you all right?" asked her mother.

Rubbing her eyes Helene mumbled, "Yes."

"You were making noises in your sleep. I thought you were having a nightmare."

The dream flooded back filling Helene's heart with sadness that it ended when it did. She knew she wouldn't be able to recapture the fantastic flight. No matter how desperately she wanted to.

Chapter Twelve

Throughout the following days Helene found herself wandering back to her dream reliving the splendor of it all. There were numerous times her mother had to repeat herself due to Helene's constant daydreaming.

"You seem distracted Helene. Would you like to discuss what's on your mind?" asked her mother realizing this too was missed. "Helene," she stated in her best mom voice.

"Excuse me Mother. Did you say something?"

With a chuckle, she answered, "Yes, I did. I said you seem distracted and asked if you'd like to discuss what's causing you to be so preoccupied."

Helene had always been close to her mother. Even though she was much bolder and outgoing than her mom it was an attribute Cora admired in her daughter. Helene understood her mother's only concern was how society may view her unconventional behavior and what affects it would have on her life. There wasn't anything the two of them didn't feel comfortable discussing so why should this be any different? Helene asked herself.

"Do you recall my dreams of riding Pegasus when I was a little girl?"

"Of course, my dear. You have always had quite the imaginative mind."

"I dreamt about Pegasus the other night."

"Interesting," replied her mom curious as to where this was going.

"It was." Helene paused trying to shrewdly organize her many thoughts. Unhappy that Dalton Manor and Mr. Dalton had played such a significant role in the dream made her cautious. How should she continue? Finally, she went on, "It was different from any of my previous dreams."

"In what way was it different?" asked Cora not wanting to lead Helene in any way. She wanted to hear the honest truth from her daughter in her own words.

"It was more real, more fantastic than ever before........it was like I could feel the wind on my face and smell the musky scent of his cologne surrounding me."

"Cologne?" Cora stopped mid-stitch on the quilt she was working on and looked up at her daughter. "Pegasus was wearing cologne?" Unsure she'd heard Helene correctly she anxiously awaited an answer.

Blushing Helene realized she hadn't put her thoughts into the order she had wished. Using her fan in an attempt to try to cool the heat radiating from her face she scrambled for the best way to answer. How was she to let her mom know she had dreamt about the very man she had condemned so harshly days earlier. To her relief her father was away on business. There wasn't a chance of him interrupting their intimate conversation. That fact helped her decide to share all the confusing yet mystical details of her dream.

"No, Pegasus wasn't wearing cologne. It was Mr. Dalton's cologne."

"Do tell my dear." Cora now on the edge of her seat placed her sewing needle into the pin cushion.

"I was standing near the stables at Dalton Manor and Mr. Dalton offered to show me something at the stables. Mother, it was Pegasus!" she exclaimed. The excitement now evident in her speech and mannerism. "He and I went for a ride. We flew over crop fields then up into the bright blue sky. It was remarkable and so much more vivid than I remember."

Cora sat across from her daughter with an endearing smile intently listening to Helene describe in great detail everything from the suit Mr. Dalton wore to the interrupted flight they shared. At which point Cora understood the heart-breaking expression on her daughters face when she had woken her.

"You have feelings for Mr. Dalton." It wasn't a question; it was a matter-of-fact statement based on her mother's keen observation. Cora had noticed that long lost sparkle in her daughter's eyes return on their first visit to the manor. "It was clear the moment you two laid eyes on each other that something was there. Your rant regarding him the other night confirmed my suspicions."

"I don't want to feel anything for him," confessed Helene.

"What frightens you so?"

"He's too perfect. He's handsome, physically fit, intelligent, wealthy, well-mannered, loves horses and is more than I could hope for. Why is he still unmarried?" Helene then answered her own question, "There's something terribly wrong with him something behind those captivating eyes or he's..."

Before Helene could finish her sentence and begin a new rant her mother broke in. "Let's use your logic my dear. Why aren't you married? You're beautiful, educated, talented, humorous, have a large dowry and are well behaved most of the time," teased her mom, but the light-hearted jab backfired. She watched the all too familiar torment flare in Helene's eyes as hurtful memories swiftly filled her head.

Helene gave a weak smile in response to her mom's effort to lighten the mood, but was still feeling things she didn't want to feel. She was so attracted to Edmund it scared her beyond reason. There had only been one other man in her life that she ever imagined marrying and he had destroyed her years earlier. Cora knew this was playing a huge role in Helene's resistance towards her feelings about Edmund.

"Helene my dear, you can't make Mr. Dalton pay for what happened in your past."

It was time to face her fears and release the thoughts that had been bouncing around her head since that fateful day at Dalton Manor. "I'm so afraid mother. I feel more for Mr. Dalton than I've felt for anyone before. Although I don't even know him...." A lump in Helene's throat choked out the words trying to escape her lips.

"Love is terrifying Helene. Even if you've never been hurt by it. It's natural for you to feel the way you feel. However, if you don't chose to move forward and take a chance on love you will be forever stuck in the pain and misery of the past." Taking her daughters hands in hers she squeezed them gently wishing she could remove the sorrow from Helene's heart. "It's time to let go of the hurt and forgive him. Only then will you be open to a new love. The love you hope for and deserve. It's the only way to keep from missing out on true love."

A single tear escaped Helene's welling eyes knowing her mother was right. The wall she'd built around herself had protected her from being hurt by love. Nonetheless it had created a new misery stemming from her loneliness. Which she attempted to suppress by staying busy. Now that Edmund had stepped into her life the loneliness she tried so hard to ignore screamed out in despair. Begging to be replaced with more than exciting and daring adventures. Pushing the limits of society would no longer fill that void.

Realizing her daughter had kept so many emotions buried deep within her shattered heart Cora joined Helene on the sofa. Wrapping her arms tightly around her daughter Cora could feel her body tremble. This simple act of empathy opened the flood gates. Helene sobbed all the tears she had kept locked away for years until there wasn't any left. Wiping her puffy eyes dry she felt a sense of relief wash over her.

Helene cleared her throat and whispered, "Thank you Mother. You're completely right. It is time for me to stop allowing the past to rob me of my future."

"That's my girl," beamed Cora. At last, she saw the same strength and confidence her daughter exhibited in every other area of her life return to the hope of finding love.

Feeling lighter on her feet than she had in a longtime Helene almost danced over to the piano where she played happily until bedtime. It was unknown what lay ahead, but this new openness to love made her antsy with anticipation. She would put the lessons learned to good use and find the man of her dreams. The man she'd been longing for. The one she had begun to believe didn't exist. Whether or not Mr. Dalton would be that man had yet to be determined.

Edmund watched Helene sleep sound for the next couple weeks never once intruding on another dream. He no longer had to investigate her dreams trying to understand why she felt the way she did about him. He now knew the reason and it only made him want her more. He was no stranger to the sting of a broken heart. Although they each handled their distress differently it was a common ground they shared. Perhaps the two of them united would mend their shattered hearts.

"Was it possible to dream that big?" Edmund wondered. "Could a true and complete love make each of them whole again?"

Recalling happy memories of his parents Edmund smiled with a new-found optimism of experiencing what they had. A genuine and selfless love that stood strong to the very end. The passionate tender looks they shared, the way his mother giggled with his father, their ability to always make Edmund feel safe and loved even in the midst of a deadly raging fire. A strange blend of sorrow and hope for a happy future pulsed through his veins. Becoming keenly aware of what his parents had always wanted for him...........a family of his own.

It was decided in that moment. He would ask permission to court Helene once Mr. Beck returned from business. To help pass the time he would continue to sabotage the enemies of his family with everything from bad business ventures to missing heirlooms. Edmund watched with pleasure as the humans argued and blamed each other for one thing or another finding it amusing if nothing else. Although it was a far cry from the destruction he had planned for them it would do for now.

The urgency to avenge the murder of his parents was replaced with an urgency to begin his life with the most beautiful and intriguing woman he'd ever met. Edmund was so captivated by Helene that he pushed aside the fact that she was human. Losing sight of all the complications it would present.

Finding himself missing Helene to the point of physical discomfort he chose to see if she was dreaming during the midnight hour. The full moon subtly illuminated her room magnifying her beauty. Motionless she slumbered peacefully without a care in the world. Her mind thoroughly relaxed and dream free leaving him no way in. Edmund would have to settle for the scenic view of her sleeping. Something he found to be more than enough.

"Sleep well my sweet Helene," he whispered before bringing his vision home. With a bewitching mental picture of Helene snuggled in her bed he quickly drifted off to sleep with the soothing sound of an early morning rain storm.

The storm hid the dawn enabling most of the villagers to remain in their beds on this dreary morning. Before long the gentle rain transformed into a heavy downpour. The morning sky grew darker as bellowing clouds shut out any sign of light until lightning erupted across the sky. Each bolt twisting and turning as it shot towards the earth. Soon the first explosive boom of thunder rumbled in the sky growing in intensity until it rattled people from their sleep.

Nature continued to unleash its fury on the valley. Wind pulled trees from the ground when their roots were unable to take hold of the sopping wet ground. Even Dalton Manor felt the effects of the storm causing the electricity to suddenly go out leaving Ally standing by candlelight in the hallway. Girls shrieked in the darkness while the boys whistled and hollered with excitement bringing Ally out of the trance that had kept her eyes locked on the painting.

"Ally," shouted Susan feeling her way down the hallway.

"I'm here," Ally answered moving closer to the sound of Susan's footsteps.

"Now what are we going to do?" grumbled Susan.

"Oh, this isn't part of the entertainment?"

"I'm good Ally, but a thunderstorm is a little more than I can plan. Some of the guys are going to check the fuse box and I thought you should come back to the party until the lights are fixed."

Very happy with this idea Ally agreed and rejoined the party goers. Soon haunted stories were being shared. Halfway through the first story Ally made her way back to the grand entrance doing her best to drown out the remainder of the far too creepy story.

"You don't like scary story's?" questioned a young man.

"Not really," admitted Ally.

"Then why attend a Halloween party?" He could see he'd embarrassed her and quickly changed the subject, "I'm Artie, maybe I can tell you a different type of story."

Chapter Thirteen

Ally was thankful that her and Artie's conversation helped to stifle the voices from the other room. Intrigued by Artie's offer she thought for a second and brushed a loose curl from her eyes. Torn between wanting to avoid the scary stories being told in the adjacent room or being alone in the dark with a complete stranger Ally remained glued to the floor.

Sensing her discomfort Artie gathered the few remaining candles from the hallway and sat them on the floor near the stairway. "We can sit here and still be visible to your friends."

Confirming his theory Ally took a seat on the stairs feeling much better after noticing Susan was keeping a watchful eye on her. A fire had been lit in the main room adding a sinister glow to the house. Nervous laughs echoed about as the spookiness of the night grew. The storm showed no sign of relenting its grip on what was supposed to be an enchanting night making Ally wish she had stayed home to take care of Rose.

"Would you like to hear a different kind of story? It'll take your mind off everything else."

Leery of what his story might entail Ally hesitantly asked, "What kind of story?"

"A love story."

With a tilt of her head she gave him a skeptical look. Ally wondered what kind of love story a male college student would tell. This had to be a ploy to get something he wanted and she wanted no part of it. As she began to get up he held his hands up and politely asked her to wait.

"I just thought you'd like to hear more about the legend of Mr. Dalton. I saw you admiring the paintings earlier," he blurted out quickly trying to keep Ally from leaving.

"That's not a love story it's just another scary story." Now she was getting mad and would have left the party if the storm wasn't increasing in force.

"That's where you're wrong.......I'm sorry I don't know your name." During that short sentence his voice went from sounding almost urgent to calm and collected.

"Ally," her answer was more of an automatic response than a desire to continue talking with him.

"Hello Ally, it's a pleasure to meet you," he said extending his right hand hoping to make her comfortable.

Ally shook his hand not wanting to be rude and asked, "So the story of a cursed warlock trapping his dead wife's soul in an anniversary gift isn't scary?"

"That's not the entire story Ally it's simply a small piece of the story being used to keep the legend alive."

"Oh yes, you're right. Mr. Dalton takes the lives of other women to bring his wife back. There's a love story if I ever heard one." Ally's words dripped of sarcasm not a common occurrence for her, but her growing fear at the continuing darkness and stormy night had her very much on edge. At this point she just wanted to be back at the dorm.

"Instead of debating what type of story it is how about I share it with you. Then you can decide?"

Feeling pretty much out of options Ally agreed to listen. This seemed to be the lessor of the other two evils she was faced with. Leaving was far too dangerous. Not to mention it would be an impossible feat not to ruin the borrowed dress. Besides the sounds coming from the other room proved the haunted stories were getting more terrifying.

Artie took a seat a couple steps above Ally. He leaned back against the wall and stared off into the distance before beginning. "Mr. Dalton first met his future wife at a gathering right here at the manor. Their attraction for each other obvious to everyone in attendance. They each tried unsuccessfully to deny their feelings and once they both worked through their doubts and fears there was no separating the two."

Baffled by Artie's recollection of Mr. and Mrs. Dalton's meeting over a century ago she interrupted him, "How could you possibly know how their meeting went or what they were feeling?"

"I work here at the manor. It's part of my job to know the entire legend. When the manor isn't being used for parties or weddings I give tours and part of the tour is sharing the romance of Mr. Dalton and his wife."

Relief washed over Ally realizing she wasn't in danger. She was simply being given a run of the mill account of imaginary people used to sell tickets, but she was fortunate enough to get a private tour with special effects and all. Laughing at herself she inquired about one thing, "People get married here?"

"Yes, there have been countless weddings held at Dalton Manor. It's an impressively beautiful place when it's not decorated for a Halloween party. Now as far as weddings go there has never been a more splendid wedding here than the first wedding. The wedding of Mr. and Mrs. Dalton."

Smiling at Artie's skillful segue back into the story Ally gave him her undivided attention. Prepared to enjoy the free entertainment.

"After a brief courtship Mr. Dalton proposed to Helene on a cool autumn morning. With tears of joy streaming down her face Helene trembled when Edmund carefully placed the one-of-a-kind engagement ring on her finger. The square diamond sat above a halo of sapphire stones that matched Edmunds eyes. She imagined the life they would share making Helene believe her heart might burst with happiness."

Unexpectedly the lights came back on causing Artie and Ally to squint from the brightness. Cheers roared through the manor but then it was dark again. "Guess they're having more trouble than they thought they would," commented Artie.

"Shouldn't you be helping?" wondered Ally.

"There's enough staff helping with the lights. I'm to remain here until the lights are repaired and make sure nothing goes wrong." Then added, "There's always staff at the manor."

"Why?"

"To protect it."

"To protect it from what?"

"Vandalism and theft. Helene's engagement ring is in a display case upstairs with dozens of other priceless artifacts."

Ally's mind buzzed with curious questions. "Was this legend based on real people? Could this all be true? Well, everything except the warlock part. Settling on the belief that Artie's story was a cleverly mastered rendering to drum up business she found herself wondering what the engagement ring looked like." She had to see the ring for herself.

The lights flickered a few times then stayed on. Once again the music quickly filled the house and the manor appeared as it had when she arrived. Susan artfully skipped her way over to the stairs beaming with excitement. Ally marveled at her ability to skip in her gown.

"That was close. I thought we were going to have to call it a night. Who's your new friend Ally?"

"This is Artie."

"Hello again Susan. We met at one of the party committee meetings." Artie could tell she didn't remember him. "It was quite some time ago and I wasn't there long. I had work to do."

"Oh yeah, I do remember seeing you. I'm sorry it's all kinda a blur after so much planning and organizing." Turning her focus back to Ally she asked her if she was ready to dance.

"Not yet," quipped Ally. "If it's okay with Artie I'd like to finish hearing the legend of this manor," then almost in a whisper added, "Perhaps I could take a look at the engagement ring he's been describing."

Artie smiled in agreement to Ally's hesitant request then confirmed with them both that no one else would be allowed upstairs.

"Yeah, that's fine. We hadn't planned on permitting guests upstairs any way. Ally you're gonna love it. It's a wonderfully bittersweet story and wait till you see the ring. It's the most gorgeous piece of jewelry I've ever seen. You two have fun. I have a few things down here I have to help get done. A couple more surprises for our guests. The whole lights going out fiasco put us a little behind so I gotta get to it."

"I believe that's the shortest amount of talking I've ever heard from Susan," joked Artie.

"Yes, it's never boring when Susan's around. You've got to love that about her."

Artie glossed over Ally's comment taking her hand to help her up the massive stairway. He opened the velvet ropes to allow them through making sure to secure them once Ally was safely on the second floor. He led her into a large room that over looked the back part of the manor. Flipping on a couple light switches the contents of several glass cases were revealed. There was so much to take in, clothing from the Victorian era, silver display trays lined with colorful perfume bottles etched with brilliant artwork. A complete table setting with labels for the various glasses and silverware made Ally chuckle out loud.

"I'm not even sure which side of the plate the fork goes on let alone four forks."

"Meals were an event to be enjoyed and relished back then unlike today's food from a paper sack."

"That's true," agreed Ally having never thought of that before. "Where's the engagement ring?"

Artie pointed to a smaller case that stood alone at the far end of the room. Inside the case was a woman's fan, a discolored journal, several jewelry pieces and Helene's ring sitting high above them all on some sort of pedestal draped in black velvet. The square diamond sat at an angle on the band giving the illusion that the square was diamond shaped. A uniquely beautiful way to display the large diamond perched high on its setting. This allowed the angular halo of rich sapphires nestled below the gemstone to frame the radiant stone perfectly. Artie's description didn't do the ring justice.

"Oh my gosh, that's beautiful!" squealed Ally having never seen a ring so breathtaking.

"Mr. Dalton designed the ring himself personally selecting each stone. Then he instructed the jeweler to destroy the mold when complete and promise to never recreate the ring."

Ally could only imagine how Helene must have felt being given such a stunningly impressive ring from the man she loved. Regardless of how the story ended Ally now thought it possible that Artie was right about it being a love story. She wanted to know how it all went so terribly wrong. Looking up at Artie she asked him to finish the story.

Chapter Fourteen

Artie walked over to a window peering into the empty darkness. Breaks in the clouds appeared allowing the full moon to shed light into the gloominess of the night. The moonlight exposed the destruction left behind from the storm which had slowed to a gentle sprinkle. Just about the time Ally was going to ask Artie if he was okay he cleared his throat and began. His voice steady at first, then gradually becoming raspy when he got to the wedding day. The entire time keeping his eyes focused on the view from the window.

It was as if Artie could see the wedding taking place. Ally was thoroughly impressed with his masterful storytelling. It became apparent how incredibly skilled Artie was at his job. Drawing Ally into the story to the point of her joining him at the window. She needed to see what he was looking at.

"The sun was just beginning to set when Helene took her first step down the aisle towards Edmund. A violin quartet played softly as Mr. Beck walked his only child down the rose pedal path. Swans glided across the lake near the shoreline as if they were invited guests. It was more than Helene imagined her wedding day to be. Her fairy tale had come to life, but like most fairy tales there was heartbreak on the horizon."

Ally swore she heard Artie's voice crack while he took a moment before continuing. "Mr. and Mrs. Dalton spent their first blissful year of marriage traveling the world. There was so much they wanted to see and do before starting the large family they both hoped for. Having a lifetime ahead of them there was more than ample time to fill the manor with children."

Clapping from downstairs broke the moment, "What's going on down there?" asked Ally turning away from the window.

"It's the actors preparing to entertain the guests with a few shows," answered Artie. "I'll have you back downstairs before the main attraction."

"What's the main attraction?"

"If I tell you that it'll spoil it for you. Don't worry Ally the first few plays aren't something you would enjoy. They're more of your classic horror filled Halloween tales."

"Oh. Then I'm even happier to be up here."

"Now, where was I?"

"You were saying the Daltons wanted to have lots of children someday."

"Yes, that's right. Children were years off and they knew once they had them they would do less traveling. Mr. & Mrs. Dalton wanted nothing more than to raise their family right here. Dalton Manor was more than their home. It was the place where their most cherished memories had taken place. No matter where their travels took them there was no place they loved more than Dalton Manor. It was where the two of them met, where Edmund proposed and where their magical wedding took place. When their first wedding anniversary approached Mr. and Mrs. Dalton returned home from their travels.”

A mixture of screams and laughter repeatedly found its way upstairs while Artie continued to share the deep love Edmund and Helene shared. He spoke as if he had known them personally creating such vivid characters Ally could picture the happy couple enjoying life to the fullest. She imagined Helene putting on one of the gorgeous displayed gowns and envisioned her spraying perfume on her neck drawing Edmund close to breathe her in. It truly was a love story. The type of love story that only happened in the movies Ally told herself. Now believing this all too perfect legend was nothing more than an amazingly crafted theatrical show she waited for the climactic end. Never expecting it to affect her. Especially since she thought she already knew the ending.

“Can you see the stables in the distance?” asked Artie pointing out the window.

Ally cupped her hands over her eyes blocking the light from the room and searched the large yard for stables. Far off she noticed an outline of a long building confirming it was the stables she asked, "How many horses does that hold?"

"Dozens, but there was one horse that Helene favored to everyone's amazement including Edmunds. It was a large gray stallion by the name of Storm. Most people were taken back by his size alone, add his wild nature to the mix and he was usually left alone. Until Helene arrived Edmund was the only one capable of controlling the head strong animal. There was a unique connection between Helene and Storm. It was as if they understood each other in a way no one else did."

"It sounds like they shared a common spirit an untamed nature not wanting to be stifled," Ally chimed in surprising herself more than Artie with her input.

"Perhaps that was it," agreed Artie smiling at the fact that Ally was enthralled by the story. "Days before their anniversary Helene went for her morning ride. Unknown to Edmund she had made plans to pick up his anniversary gift figuring it would be the best time to sneak away without him knowing what she was up to."

Ally's mind raced ahead to Helene catching a cold and dying like Susan had explained earlier that evening. Her eyes glazed over and her mind played the story out which didn't go unnoticed by Artie.

"Ally are you still with me?"

Ally blinked in embarrassment and quickly returned her attention to Artie. Apologizing she said, "I'm sorry Artie, I don't mean to spoil the story but Susan already told me she got sick and died."

"That's one version circulating. Would you like to hear the truth of how it really happened?"

Intrigued by this turn of events Ally nodded in agreement paying close attention to Artie's words she waited to hear new information. A strange look washed over his face making it appear that he was aging right there in front of Ally. A seriousness penetrated his eyes forcing her to lower her gaze with uneasiness. Attentively she listened to him continue the story.

"Enjoying the ride back to the manor Helene kept Storm at a gradual pace allowing her to take her eyes off the road. She unwrapped Edmund's gift one more time before arriving home. Smiling in approval at her selection Helene was soon lost in her thoughts. Imagining Edmunds reaction when he opened her heartfelt gift made her giddy with anticipation. Feeling completely overwhelmed by the love they shared she failed to notice Storm's ears perk up and the change in his gait.

Oblivious to the fear Storm was feeling she was nearly tossed from the saddle when the steed suddenly reared up neighing loudly. Her entire body was jolted when Storms front legs landed hard on the ground and before she could tighten her grip he bucked again this time striking his front legs aggressively. No sooner was he on all fours did he begin kicking his back legs wildly in the air flinging Helene to the ground. Seemingly possessed Storm repeatedly reared and kicked shaking the ground with every thunderous stomp. Intense pain radiated throughout Helene's body. Struggling to open her eyes she caught sight of Edmunds gift. The silver goblet now laid among the wildflowers lining the road reflecting the brilliant sunlight. In between painful gasps Helene whispered Edmunds name then fought hard for her next shallow breath.

Edmund's heart skipped a beat putting every cell in his being on high alert. Filled with electrified zest he shouted "Helene!" towards the East where her broken body lay. He had been admiring the anniversary gift he bought for his wife, but now the locket was gripped so tightly in his hand that it dug into his palm. He shut his eyes tensing every muscle searching frantically for any sign of her. As his vision raced across the countryside he caught a glimpse of Storm galloping full speed back to the manor. Following the road his heart shattered at the horrifying site of Helene face down on the hard-dusty road.

With a flash of his hand he was at her side. Ever so gently he lifted her into his massive arms causing a whimper of pain to escape her lips. The soft familiar curves of her body were gone. Storm's heavy hooves were far too much for Helene's tiny frame leaving a mangled mess of bones barely contained within her skin. Her stunning face left untouched except for the dirt on her left cheek. Edmund raised an unsteady hand and lovingly wiped away the dust revealing a developing bruise. Even with all the power he contained there was nothing he could do to save her. Helene's shattered body was beyond repair. Even for such a consummate warlock. The wife he adored and loved more than life itself had been brought to deaths doorstep. Feeling utterly helpless for the second time in his life he roared unrecognizable words at the universe.

A devastating ache devoured him as he watched Helene's breathing become even more shallow. The realization that he would live an eternity without her seemed to slow time. Separating his thoughts into manageable pieces. Latching on to one thought in particular Edmund pried the locket open between his fingers. Concentrating solely on a formidable spell he made sure to recite it flawlessly word for word.

Having never reopened her eyes to see Edmunds distressed gaze Helene took her last breath. Her body went limp in his arms filling him with immeasurable pain. It became excruciating clear that she was gone. Using the ball of his hand to clear his eyes he stared at the photo inside the locket. Consumed with panic he waited. Relief and solace washed over him when he noticed Helene's eyes begin to blink in the photo. "I have you my love. You are safe." Carefully he closed the locket sealing it with a kiss and whispered, "I will see you soon." Edmund took a deep chest lifting breath while clutching the locket tightly within his hands.

Ally remained in stunned silence surprised by the pool of tears in her eyes. She waited for Artie to continue until the hush between them became awkward. It was only then that she noticed the entire house was dead quiet. Even the rain had stopped. Giving the unexpected silence an ominous feel.

"I better get you downstairs before the big event."

"That's the end?" questioned Ally wanting answers to the multitude of questions she now had.

"Not exactly, it's more like the beginning," was Artie's only response before heading for the door. "Come Ally I don't want you to miss this."

Unsatisfied with where Artie left the story she stood her ground, "I'd rather hear what happened next and miss the big event."

"My apologies Ally, but I have a part to play in the final show. I have no choice but to go down stairs."

125

Ally stood motionless and in utter disbelief that he had left her alone in the room. Standing there she replayed Helene's appalling death over and over in her head raising more questions. Several minutes passed before Ally began looking around the room at Helene's belongings now feeling a mystifying connection to the items. Taking a long final look at the engagement ring Ally wondered why it had been taken from Helene. "That's it!" she shouted determined to find Artie and have him finish the story. She headed downstairs stomping her feet angrily with every step.

Securely taking hold of the railing with one hand Ally began down the stairs struggling to hold her dress up with the other hand. The rain had made the old house humid and hot drawing attention to how burdensome her dress was with its multiple layers of fabric. A warm sensation overtook Ally making her feel like she'd faint. Fearful she would tumble down the steps she looked around the manor only to find she was alone. Pausing for a moment she noticed there were no voices or sounds other than her own breathing.

"Hello!" Ally cried out but there was no answer. A chilled breeze blew in from the open front door. The fresh air cleared her head momentarily then the same warm dizziness returned knocking her off balance.

"Are you ill?" said the same husky voice from earlier that evening. Supporting Ally in his strong arms this handsome man assisted her safely outside and gently sat her on the porch swing.

The cool air felt great and Ally breathed it in deeply. For a quick second she felt better and then everything began to spin forcing her to lean forward catching her head in her hands. Through half closed eyes she noticed the opened locket swinging from her neck. Scooping the locket into the palm of her hand Ally struggled to see the photo inside. Her blurred vision causing her to blink repeatedly until she recognized the eyes of the stranger in the black and white photo.

Terror swept over Ally making her sick to her stomach as she watched the woman in the locket's photo morph into herself. With all her might Ally tried to yank the locket from her neck, but the chain and clasp held tight.

"Helene, my love," exclaimed Edmund taking her hands into his before gently moving the locket into his own. Pausing for a moment he grinned at the frightened face of Ally now in the black and white photo. Edmund snapped the locket shut bringing a radiant smile to Helene's face.

"Will there be anything else Mr. Dalton" questioned Rose from behind him.

"No, that will be all Rose you may return to the garden," he answered wrapping his arms tighter around Helene who was struggling to get to her feet.

With a curtsey Rose turned and walked across the sloshy green grass through the garden gate. Deadly silently she stood in front of the center rose bush. Before long she felt herself fading away. In an instant, she was standing behind Ally who was weeping uncontrollably.

The wonderfully familiar scent of the mystery flowers from school captured Ally's attention. Turning away from the blackness of the closed locket she couldn't believe her eyes. There in front of her stood Rose.

Book 2

Was Ally truly trapped within the legends curse? Had magic, something she thought to only be fantasy stolen everything from her? There is only one thing Ally wants and that is to escape her captivity.

129

Closed Heart
TABLE OF CONTENTS

<u>Chapter One</u>

Darkness enveloped Ally causing Rose's voice to be lost in its impenetrable vastness. As the minutes passed Rose became more concerned for Ally who laid motionless on the ground. By now, Rose was shouting Ally's name in hopes of reviving her. It didn't work, so Rose began shaking Ally by her shoulders trying desperately to bring her back around.

Gradually the murkiness began to give way until Ally heard her name far off in the distance. Subtly her fingers flinched and under closed eyelids her eyes roamed wildly searching for light. Ally scrunched her face and fought against the empty blackness that held her. Eventually her eyes opened ever so slightly.

"Ally, Ally can you hear me?" pleaded Rose.

"Rose?" whispered Ally barely audible.

"Ally, it's Rose. I'm right here with you," Rose assured.

With quivering eyelids Ally mumbled incomplete sentences about being scared from a nightmare. When her eyes finally opened fully her thoughts and words became clearer.

"Oh, Rose," she exclaimed looking up at her friends troubled face. "What a terrible nightmare. I was trapped in the beautiful locket you gave me." Ally sat up with help from Rose and continued. "It was so real my heart is still racing and....."

Rose lowered her eyes, slowly shaking her head side to side making Ally look at her surroundings. They were outdoors in a large field of tall green grass surrounded on all sides by a dense forest of huge old trees. The sun hung brightly in the vivid blue sky and fluffy white clouds resembling cotton balls changed shape as they lazily blew by. In the distance the soothing sound of a stream filled her ears. Watching a flock of small birds fly overhead made Ally feel like she had landed in a fairy tale. The astounding world around her reminded Ally of travel brochures with their perfectly awe inspiring images. So often those pictures encouraged people to travel to exotic destinations. Much to the delight of the travel agent.

The last memory she could recall raced in and she quickly spun around to see a shimmering black spot shrinking before her. Horrified, Ally turned back to Rose who was seated beside her with sorrow filled eyes. Her bleak expression confirmed what Ally was almost too frightened to ask.

"I'm in the locket?" asked Ally before answering her own question. She stated in a cold emotionless statement. "It wasn't a dream."

"No Ally, it wasn't a dream," replied Rose just above a whisper.

"How?" "Where?" "I, I........," stammered Ally trying to make sense of what had happened. It started to become too much when every human emotion flooded her senses. Questions filled her head and tears rushed from her eyes encouraging Rose to take her hand in an effort to calm Ally down, but this only infuriated her.

"You!" shouted Ally pulling her hand away. "You did this to me." Fighting with the weighty dress she managed to get to her feet, "I thought you were my friend," Ally yelled stomping away. After about a dozen steps Ally realized she didn't know where she was going or if she was in further danger. There was no way for her to anticipate what could happen next. This situation was beyond comprehension. Ally's logical mind repeatedly screamed at her, "This couldn't possibly be happening!" Being sucked into a locket was something from a fantasy movie not real life.

Dreadful thoughts persuaded Ally to stop walking away from Rose. She was the one person who could possibly help her or at least know what to do next. Reluctantly, Ally turned back to face Rose and it was at that moment that it dawned on Ally. Rose was also inside the locket. Feeling like her head might explode Ally dropped to her knees in the tall grass noticing that she was no longer wearing the borrowed blue Victorian dress, but a pale lavender dress.

Unable to take anymore Ally began sobbing incapable of catching her breath. Rose rushed over to Ally and wrapped her arms around her. Rose sat quietly hugging Ally allowing her to cry until her tears ran dry. Peering up at Rose through swollen eyes Ally begged for answers without uttering a single word.

"You're exhausted Ally. Let's get you somewhere comfortable so you can rest," coaxed Rose rising to her feet.

This made no more sense to Ally than the fact that she was trapped inside a piece of jewelry. Her puzzled expression revealed her thoughts. "Comfortable?" she thought. Of all the questions banging around her head how to get comfortable wasn't one of them.

"I'll take care of it Ally, all I need you to do is remember a favorite place where you felt happy and safe. Leave the rest to me."

Rose made it sound so simple, like they were back in the dorm room having a casual conversation over dinner. How in the world could Ally focus on a happy memory? Her life had ended, or had it? Was she dead? Terrified at the possible answer her mind protected Ally and jumped from those unspeakable thoughts to a long-lost memory. A summer spent with her family along the coast when she was little.

Floral scents filled the air around them, but the scent was quickly replaced with a salty ocean breeze blowing swiftly through the trees. The gentle sound of the stream was drowned out by crashing waves. Seagulls squawked overhead beckoning them to follow. Curiosity brought Ally to her feet who then made her way toward the ocean sound. Upon reaching the trees she could see the stream she'd heard earlier ambling its way through the forest. With Rose by her side she continued on until the forest opened up to reveal a seaside cliff high above the ocean. On the sand, not far from the shore sat a vaguely familiar beach house. Ally was sure she'd seen it before with its large wrap around porch lined with mix matched lounge chairs. The collection of wind chimes hanging from the eaves played a happy symphony inviting the girls to visit. The musical sound strengthened Ally's hazy memory as she gazed at the house.

Rose pointed out a steep narrow stairway leading down to the beach. The treacherous looking steps made from large flat stones failed miserably at welcoming Ally. The stairs began near the streams descent off the cliff then steeply meandered towards the sand far below. Without a word she hesitantly headed for the steps, stopping abruptly realizing it would be an even more dangerous trek in the dress she wore. How she wished she were in her own clothes then suddenly she was.

"You're doing great Ally keep it up," encouraged Rose who was following close behind.

Remarkably, the memories or thoughts that crossed Ally's mind were coming to life seconds after she thought them. She somehow understood that Rose was the key. This was both exciting and frightening.

"That I cannot do," bemoaned Rose.

Ally had thought of reversing time. How she longed to go back before the party to when she received the locket. No matter how hard or how much she focused on this thought nothing happened.

"There are limits to my ability. I can't change what's happened. All I've been given authority to do is make your time here as pleasant for you as possible."

"Where is here?"

"There's plenty of time to discuss where, how and why. For now, let's get you to the beach house. You don't realize it but it's the middle of the night and you need to rest."

Looking up at the afternoon sky Ally disagreed. Rose quickly commented on Ally's thoughts before they left her mouth helping to avoid the argument Ally was preparing for. "That's creeping me out Rose. Get out of my head!"

"All in good time, but for now I have to monitor all your thoughts so I can set everything up to our liking."

"What I'd like is to be back home," stated Ally through a cracking voice.

"Ally please, let's get back to your happy memory of the beach. It's for your own good."

A barking dog splashed in the waves chasing the seagulls from the sand. "Cap?" thought Ally. "Captain!" she yelled at the top of her lungs. The dog responded with a wagging tail and happy barks. The two hurriedly made their way to each other with Ally stumbling more than once on her race down the dreaded steps. Throwing her arms around the neck of the large yellow Labrador momentarily made Ally forget where she was. Rubbing her hands over his wet fur made her laugh like the little girl who had picked him out so many years ago.

Captain had died just when Ally began to need him more than ever. He always slept at the foot of her bed, but when Ally's father began drinking and losing his temper, Captain had strategically moved to the floor in front of her door. This prevented her father from entering the room.   Captain's massive size proved to be a wonderful door stop and if her father persisted a warning growl quickly made him storm off.

Ally couldn't believe her trusted friend, confidant and guardian had come to be with her. Showering him with praise and constant petting Captain wagged his tail across the sand with happy excitement. "Good boy, you're such a good boy," repeated Ally staring into his large brown eyes.

"Shall we get inside?" questioned Rose.

Ally glanced over at the beach house which by now was becoming a clearer memory. The smell of food wafted through the air making Ally painfully aware of the hunger she had been ignoring. Brushing the sand from her legs Ally and Cap followed Rose towards the house. Climbing the few steps onto the porch caused more memories to rush in. When the familiar sound of the squeaky second step made it to Ally's ears a smile crossed her face. She realized it wasn't one summer she had spent there with her family but several. How could she have forgotten all of them but one?

Opening the front door Rose motioned for Ally to enter, "Dinner awaits," she added closing the door behind them.

The sights, sounds and smells of the house stopped Ally in her tracks. "Oh I loved it here," exclaimed Ally. Each corner of the room and nearly every piece of furniture held a memory. The phrase, "If these walls could talk" came to life in that moment. It was like the walls were talking or shouting at Ally. Lost memories of happy weeks spent in this place became crystal clear causing tears of joy to break free from Ally's still swollen eyes.

"Dinner is served," beckoned Rose from the kitchen.

"It smells wonderful."

"Come on Captain I wouldn't forget you," called Rose to the large dog placing his bowl on the floor.

Feeling safe Ally enjoyed her meal recalling even more childhood memories which she willingly shared with Rose over dinner. The two sat and talked for hours like they had back at the dorm. It wasn't until Ally decided to go to bed that she remembered where she truly was. The harsh reality hit like a ton of bricks. Literally knocking the wind out of her.

"Ally there's no use getting yourself all worked up again. You head off to bed while I clean up and we can talk tomorrow morning. I promise I'll answer your questions."

Emotionally drained Ally didn't have the strength to argue with Rose. Fatigued in every possible way she headed upstairs to the room she'd spent so many wonderful nights in. Passing the large master bedroom, she stopped briefly and curiously wondered if her parents would be there. As expected the room was empty, but how she had hoped it wouldn't be. Cautiously she opened her bedroom door and noticed the closet was full of all her favorite clothes. Investigating further, she discovered the dresser held her most comfy pajama's and on top of the bed lay the quilt her grandmother had made for her.

Random pieces of her life that had never been at the beach house now filled it. Rose was surrounding Ally with so many things that brought her comfort and happiness. She hadn't even thought of them and yet here they were. To her surprise having Cap with her at the beach house along with some memory filled keepsakes were making it more and more difficult for Ally to complain about her current situation. Even Cap's favorite tug toy was quickly discovered launching the two of them into a play session. Before too long Ally finally collapsed on the bed. She slept deeper than she ever had in her life. Captain took his rightful place at the foot of her bed remaining her devoted protector.

Throughout the night Ally's dreams were happy and filled with love. Anytime the slightest hint of darkness or terror crept in it quickly vanished only to be replaced by another heartfelt memory. Ally's childhood may have been void of too many material things, but she was never short on love while growing up. At least not until her father became someone she no longer recognized.

It was Cap's friendly nudge that woke Ally from her slumber. Stretching and yawning she slowly came to.

Sweetly she petted Cap's head as he rested it on the edge of the mattress. He happily wagged his tail and the brushing sound on the hardwood floor made Ally giggle. How she had missed their morning wake up routine, nudge, pet, wag and up we go. Cap made audible noises only a dog could make encouraging Ally to her feet. The cool floor sent her feet back up into the warmth of the bed. A disapproving bark echoed in the bedroom. Cap now stood at the door almost demanding that Ally get up.

"Boy you haven't changed," grumbled Ally locating her fluffy white slippers under the bed. Still half asleep, it wasn't until she opened the bedroom door and saw the long forgotten hallway of the beach house did everything come crashing back. Cap ran down the hall to top of the stairs and began spinning in circles encouraging Ally to follow. The exhilaration she felt from her wonderful night filled with happy dreams and Cap's playful way of waking her from her slumber disappeared without a trace. Dreaming about being back at the beach house was one thing, but actually being there because a warlock trapped you in a piece of jewelry was an entirely different story. How could Rose do this to her?

Chapter Two

The smell of breakfast raced up the stairwell refocusing Ally's attention on her growling stomach. "How long did I sleep?" she wondered. The last thing she remembered was eating a rather large meal before bed and here she was famished again. Reaching the bottom of the stairs she spotted the morning sun through the open windows rising over the calm ocean. The picturesque sight transformed Ally's frown into an appreciative smile.

Rose peeked out of the kitchen, "Good morning Ally. I suspect you slept well."

"I did," replied Ally letting Cap out the front door.

"I'll answer your questions just like I said I would last night. Now come and sit down for breakfast. You can get started with your questions during breakfast if that's what you would like."

Without another word Ally followed Rose into the kitchen unsure of where to even begin. Rose patiently waited for Ally to finish the mouthful of blueberry crepes she was enjoying. Drinking the last sip of her milk Ally leaned back in her chair, crossed her arms and stared off into the distance. Moments later she refocused her attention on Rose who had begun clearing the dishes.

"This is crazy," exclaimed Ally afraid if she said anything more she would burst into tears. Her emotions were just under the surface and she was doing everything she could to keep from spiraling into the depths of despair.

"I understand Ally."

"Do you?" shouted Ally her emotions now boiling over. "I'm supposed to believe I'm in a locket cursed by a warlock? That I'm not dreaming all of this and magic is real?" Ally's voice now brimming with fear, "Am I dead?"

"No Ally, you're not dead. Mr. Dalton doesn't want you dead he just needs to use your body for a while, so he's put your soul inside the locket for safe keeping."

"Safe keeping!" At this Ally rose to her feet, slammed her hands down on the kitchen table and shouted, "Well I was using my body!"

"Please Ally, let me start from the beginning and take your mind off where you are for a while."

"Yeah, like that's possible." Pacing the floor Ally let question after question pour out of her mouth then she stopped and glared at Rose, "You're here too. Why are you here? Why would you help him?" Tears overflowed Ally's eyes and wiping them from her face she mumbled, "I thought you were my friend."

"Let me tell you a story of friendship Ally and perhaps you'll see that I am your friend. The type of friend who will do anything for the friend they deeply love and cherish."

A glimmer of hope pulsed through Ally's veins. "Could Rose help her?" wondered Ally. "Had Rose joined Ally in the locket to help her escape?" Moving into the living room they made themselves comfortable and Ally anxiously waited to see if there was something Rose could do.

Clearing her throat Rose began, "Have you ever had a friend that you could always count on Ally? One that you knew would do anything for you without expecting anything in return? One that you could tell your deepest secrets to in complete confidence and know they'll never tell another person as long as they live?"

"I thought I had, but I was terribly wrong."

"Then you should understand. When and if you truly do find that one in a million friend you would do anything in the world for them no matter the cost."

Ally was equally intrigued and puzzled, "Go on."

"Helene and I met when we were very young. Years before we thought about boys or of anything serious for that matter. Our days were filled with playing, laughing and sharing our silly little girl dreams."

"Helene?" skepticism covered Ally's face. "Helene from the warlock story?" Ally didn't want to even hear the names Helene or Edmund. The only thing she wanted from Rose was her help to get out of the locket.

Rose could see the anger building in Ally, but she remained calm and said, "Yes, Ally. Helene was, is my very best friend."

Ally couldn't find the words to express herself so she resorted to rolling her eyes and scoffing loudly. The frustration and anger building within her was subdued by an unknown force leaving her speechless and calm. Resuming her position on the couch she returned her attention to Rose all the while inhaling deeply. A soft breeze blew in through the open windows bringing with it the wonderfully sweet scent of blossoms. Once the room was filled with the tranquil reassuring aroma Ally thoroughly relaxed.

"Neither Helene or I had siblings so we became like sisters. There wasn't anyone or anything that came between us. Even when high society frowned on Helene's boldness and outgoing personality she remained a class act. Being appreciated for one's beauty wasn't enough for her, she wanted to be loved for her intelligence, strength and daring side. Her parents loved this about her even if it was a major concern for her mother Cora."

Rose took a deep breath and for the first time appeared to be hesitant and shy. This was a side of her Ally didn't believe existed. The self-confident red head that always took control had been replaced by a timid wounded young woman fighting to regain control.

After a few moments of silence Rose continued, "I on the other hand would lose my temper without the slightest warning. A behavior completely unacceptable for a lady. Especially a lady of my family's social standing. No amount of beauty, money or status allowed for this. Temper tantrums were frowned upon for children let alone a grown woman. Even I couldn't predict when a sudden and inappropriate outburst of anger would hit. Needless to say, when Helene and I came of age the men asking permission to begin courting me were less like gentlemen and more like tyrants. Maxwell was a master at hiding who he truly was. Not only from my parents but from me. He and I were married in a grand ceremony. Maxwell spared no expense in creating the wedding of all weddings. It had everything a young woman could dream of. All too soon I would discover the wedding and most importantly the marriage was missing the most important element. The love of a good man. I was just another beautiful item to be checked off Maxwell's list. Unfortunately, he took much better care of his inanimate objects than he did me. I learned early on in our marriage that displeasing him in anyway would cause me pain. Sometimes more than I thought I could bare."

Ally grew more confused as Rose continued to speak about a marriage that took place decades ago. Believing in the story about a warlock and his lost love was difficult enough. Now Ally had to believe that her college roommate had actually known them. How was any of this possible? The more Ally heard the less she understood.

"Magic Ally," was all Rose said before she dived back into the story. "I'll never forget the first-time Helene and Edmund saw each other," gushed Rose with a renewed spark in her eyes. "He was so handsome and regal, there wasn't an eligible young lady at his luncheon that wasn't dying to be noticed by him. No one was surprised when Helene's exquisite beauty captured Edmunds attention, but many hearts were broken that afternoon. Their mutual attraction was evident from the beginning so I was flabbergasted when Helene avoided discussing him."

Ally studied Rose's face watching carefully for any sign that she was being untruthful. After all, Ally's trust in her had been destroyed by her betrayal, but the honesty and genuine emotion behind her words captivated Ally. With a twinkle in her eye Rose repeated a conversation from the past.

"Did you enjoy yesterday's luncheon?" asked Rose.

"Yes, it was very nice," answered Helene.

"Nice?"

The two stared at each other for minutes before Rose cracked a sly smile, "You're going to make me pry?"

"There's nothing to say."

"Don't play coy with me Helene. Have you've forgotten who you're speaking with?"

Helene didn't say a word, but lifted her cup of tea to her smiling lips. Placing the cup back onto the saucer Rose could see Helene's mischievous mind hard at work. At last she said, "Mr. Dalton has a stable full of beautiful horses. There was one particular steed I'm hoping to persuade my father into purchasing for me."

"Horses? You want to discuss Mr. Dalton's horse stables? Helene you're deliberately being evasive about Mr. Dalton."

"What about Mr. Dalton?"

"Have it your way Helene, let me explain what we all witnessed yesterday. Neither of you could take your eyes off each other. When you and your father walked off with Mr. Dalton I thought Margret Bennett was going to come after you with her parasol and hit you over the head with it. She was so angry she probably would have if her father hadn't taken her arm."

"Margret Bennett can have Mr. Dalton for all I care."

"Excuse me?"

"He's too perfect Rose. If something is too good to be true it usually is. How could a man with so much wealth, intelligence and good looks still be single? There must be some horrifically ugly secret about him. I can't tell you what it is, but I'm sure it's lurking just below that handsome exterior."

"So you agree he's handsome?"

"Of course I do, I have excellent eye sight. As if his chiseled features weren't enough all he needs to do is look at you with his hypnotic blue eyes and you're captivated. I was lost in them immediately and that was just the beginning. When he greeted my father his deep voice resonated throughout my body triggering my heart to melt. I could have listened to his velvety smooth voice all day, especially while he discussed his prize horses. I searched for a flaw in him harder than I've ever tried before and I couldn't find one. Whatever is wrong with him must be terrifying and I for one don't want to find out what it is. I hope I never have to see him again as long as I live." Helene stared off in the distance trying hard to persuade herself into believing her last comment.

Rose managed to keep quiet and watched Helene's face become flush at the mere thought of Edmund. It was apparent that Helene had very strong feelings for him and she was doing her best to destroy them. Rose knew all too well why and spoke up, "Helene I know your heart was broken, but you can't hold every man accountable for that. There is still hope for you. You could find the love you dream of, but only if you open yourself up to the possibility." Rose took her friend's hand and looked her square in the eyes before saying, "Be thankful my friend. You still have a chance to find real love."

Hearing the hurt in her friend's voice and watching a solitary tear roll down Rose's bruised cheek made Helene smile a sad smile. She lost count of how many night's she'd spent hoping Maxwell would finally come across someone bigger and meaner than he during his travels. Especially when he was in a drunken rage. They both believed the only way out for Rose was if she ended up a widow. Then she could marry a good man and be taken care of, but thus far Maxwell had always come out the winner. Returning home feeling more powerful and entitled then when he left.

"I know Rose, I'm so afraid of having my heart broken again or ...?

"Or ending up like me," muttered Rose completing Helene's sentence. "I'm not telling you to marry Mr. Dalton in the morning, all I'm saying is pursue it a for a while. Get to know each other and see what happens. Who knows, maybe you'll tire of his good looks and charm." This made them both burst into much needed laughter.

In the day's that followed Rose and Helene enjoyed rides in the country, long talks and just being lifelong friends. Maxwell was away on business and was not expected back for another few weeks. Helene's family hadn't heard from Mr. Dalton and it was beginning to bother her more than she cared to admit. Keeping this to herself she watched Rose become more like the girl she grew up with. A result of Maxwell having been gone for such a long time. His time away allowed Rose to do some healing both physically and mentally. It broke Helene's heart to know her friend was hurting and there was nothing she could do to help.

The entire town lived in fear of Maxwell and his temper. Not only did his substantial physical size dominate the men in town his financial status did as well. Those facts alone inflated his ego to dangerous proportions. With the towns people paralyzed in fear he boldly seized the unofficial position of town leader. Using it to do as he pleased knowing no one would dare disagree with him. If he couldn't buy what he wanted he resorted to threats. Always making good on them and showing the towns people he was capable of anything.

Ally sat stunned at the details of Rose's horrendous marriage and the town's acceptance of her husband's behavior. She began to feel like she was in a dream inside of a dream being pulled deeper and deeper into another world. The reality she once knew as her life seemed like a foggy and distant memory. Rose had accomplished what she sat out to do. She had helped Ally forget where she was for a little while.

"If you're willing Ally I could stop telling you the story and show it to you," commented Rose in a calm yet sorrowful whisper.

"Show me?" Ally questioned doubtfully.

"Yes, I can take you back there to witness it all first hand." Rose saw terror flash in Ally's eyes persuading her to explain further. "If you allow me I can show it to you like a feature film. You would be a spectator not a participant and would be completely safe. You would not actually be there. Think of it as watching home movies."

Terrified and exhilarated at the same time Ally considered the chance to witness life way back when, and to bring history and Rose's story to life. What else could possibly happen to her? She no longer had a physical body to worry about. Immediately Ally's mind shot down a rabbit trail. She wondered how she could sit on a couch or feel an itch if she didn't have a body, but Rose cleared her throat bringing Ally back. There was so much she didn't understand and yet she couldn't think of a good enough reason not to take Rose up on her offer. Coming out almost like a dare, she said "Sure Rose, show me."

Ally's acceptance of Rose's offer made her flash her beautiful smile.

Chapter Three

An ocean breeze rushed through the French doors carrying with it the sweet smell of the college's mystery garden. Ally turned her face into the wind and breathed deeply to confirm the scent was really there. There was absolutely no doubt in Ally's mind. She recognized the aromatic scent only this time it was more powerful than she'd remembered. The perplexed expression she gave Rose who was now seated on the couch next to her helped to begin the conversation.

"It's Mr. Dalton connecting with me Ally," stated Rose without hesitation. "Whether he has something to say to me or wishes to grant me extra power to accomplish a specific task. He sends it through the magical garden at the manor. Riding on the wind the aroma filled air current transports his message or magical gift right to me. No matter which decade each of us may be in there's always air surrounding us. It's rather ingenious if you ask me," boasted Rose with a twinkle in her eye and yet Ally couldn't help but notice there was also a tinge of sorrow in her eyes.

"I don't understand. Why don't you hate him Rose? I know why I'm here. He's using my body for his dead wife, which when I say it out loud still doesn't make any sense, but you don't seem to be bothered by it. As a matter-of-fact, you helped him get to me." Ally's voice became agitated as she refocused on what had happened to her.

Rose took hold of Ally's hand. Her eyes pleading for her to calm down. "That's why I'd like to show you more of the story Ally. I believe once you've heard the full account of what transpired you will have a better understanding."

"I'll never understand Rose. My life was taken from me!"

In an instant, the sun filled room became dark. Storm clouds overtook the clear blue sky within seconds. Cap burst into the house barking loudly. A cold powerful wind rammed the house slamming the wooden shutters repeatedly against the siding. Thunder roared in the distance and crackles of lightning hit seconds later. Ally could physically feel an intense fury surrounding her even though nothing but Rose's hand was touching her. That strange fact made her blood run cold.

"Ally, it's of upmost importance that you remain focused on me. I need to show you everything for both our sakes."

Preoccupied with the storm raging outside and the icy sensation on her skin Ally didn't even hear Rose shouting at her. It became abundantly clear that they were not alone and this scared Ally into submission.

"Rose, please, please make it stop," cried Ally pulling her legs to her chest trying to sink into the oversized couch. With every muscle clenched in fear Ally tightly shut her eyes to avoid what she may see. She quickly covered her nose and mouth trying unsuccessfully to block out the familiar floral scent that now overpowered the house. This brought Ally to her breaking point. Tears found their way out of her firmly closed eyes. Suddenly becoming aware that Rose was speaking in an unknown language was bad enough, but when a rumbling voice replied back, Ally screamed, "I'll be good!" over the deafening rumble.

With one last thunderous boom that shook a few art pieces off the walls the house was once again engulfed in sunlight and warmth. Seagulls now perched on the porch's railing preened themselves. The ocean waves sluggishly embraced the shore and calm filled the room once the smell of flowers vanished. Ally peeked through narrow slits in her eyes making sure the coast was clear. Cap laid on the floor in front of her wagging his tail and nuzzling her legs.

"Ally, I need you to trust me and let me share Helene and Edmund's love story with you."

"Love story?" thought Ally. "How could something so evil possibly know anything about love?" argued Ally.

"Ally I'm begging you. Please don't talk about Mr. Dalton like he's a person incapable of love. You don't want to see him angry."

"Isn't that what I just saw?"

"No."

That one word reply made Ally feel more fear then she had just experienced. Allowing Rose to show her what she wanted now seemed like the safest thing to do. It was then that she noticed her senses and emotions were intensified and exaggerated beyond anything she'd ever known. Like a scene from an old black and white movie that had been transformed into technicolor. This world with its boldly vibrant colors and heightened sounds appeared beautiful to the eyes and ears, but Ally knew she wasn't safely at home and perhaps never would be again. The unsettling gift of a picture-perfect world was in a strange way a comfort for Ally. It allowed her to get lost in its mind-blowing beauty and forget where she was if only for the briefest of moments.

"Okay Rose, give me some time to pull myself together and we'll begin...begin this.....what do I even call it?"

"An adventure into love."

Ally listened for a hint of sarcasm or cynicism in Rose's voice but it wasn't there. "I think I'm ready," announced Ally several minutes later.

Smiling, Rose took Ally's quivering hand and asked her to relax. Following Rose's instructions Ally took several deep breaths, closed her eyes and gently laid her head back on the inviting couch cushion. Silence filled the room and Ally felt herself slip into the space between being awake and asleep. The faint sensation of Rose holding her hand was the last thought she had before her mind began spinning faster and faster. Memories, photographs, ideas, dreams and even fantasies sped through Ally's mind. Anything Ally had ever seen or thought was right there in front of her. It was a kaleidoscope of visual pictures. Some flashed by briefly while others seemed to float and dance in midair for quite some time before moving on.

Ally's expressions would change from happiness to remembrance. Any flicker of sadness or pain on Ally's face made Rose quickly push on to the next visual. "We're almost there, Ally," mumbled Rose filled with relief. Rose settled on one of Ally's fondest memories with her Grammy. Picking apples from several of the trees in her grandma's cluttered backyard. Dodging the numerous potted plants and random sitting areas Ally ran back and forth with her arms full of apples. She kept this up until the basket she was dropping them into overflowed. Ally had to carry the ones that didn't fit into the house. Before long Ally could smell her Grammy's delectable apple pies baking in the oven. She remembered how she would impatiently sit at the table waiting for one to be ready to eat. Ally especially loved devouring a piece of pie while it was still warm and gooey.

A smile quickly turned into giggles as Ally's heart overflowed with happiness and love. She didn't even mind the floral scent entirely refilling the room. While Ally happily sat there relishing in this beautiful memory flowering vines began to wind themselves up the cottage walls until the ceiling was covered. Gardenias, jasmines and several other fragrant blooms burst from the floor and furniture. There wasn't anything but Ally, Rose and the couch that wasn't completely swallowed up by the delightfully spontaneous garden. Even Cap found himself tangled in the patch of jasmine he now lay upon. Serenity engulfed the room helping Ally to finally sink deeper into the spacious couch.

"Helene, wait up!" hollered Rose kicking her horse and encouraging him to catch up to Storm. Helene's musical laugh echoed through the trees. Reaching the river Helene skillfully brought Storm to an abrupt halt. Dismounting, she led him to the water's edge, caressed his damp neck and said, "You're such a good boy."

By the time Rose arrived Helene was already ankle deep in the river splashing water on her flush face. "There you are Rose. Won't you join me? The water is so refreshing."

"Do we have to do this every time?"

Playing coy Helene asked, "What are you referring to Rose?"

With an annoyed smirk Rose splashed Helene making her burst into laughter. Rose cinched up her dress trying not to get it too wet and joined Helene in the rushing water. "You know what I'm referring to," Rose said before candidly shouting, "Mr. Dalton!"

"Is he the only topic of conversation you know Rose?" scoffed Helene turning away.

"No, but he is the only topic of conversation you won't discuss with me." Rose's long silky red hair blew in the wind creating the illusion she was on fire and figuratively she was. Her growing frustration over Helene continuously avoiding any discussion about Mr. Dalton was making her temper flare.

Helene conveniently ignored Rose and walked over to focus her attention on Storm. The magnificent stallion standing guard over the two of them.

Calming her temper Rose walked over to her best friend and placed a loving hand on her shoulder saying, "Helene do you remember the first time we came to this spot?"

Helene smiled and nodded, "Yes, we still needed a riding escort when we rode our pony's out here. Good old Theodore he was such a gentle giant....well at least around us."

Reminiscing about Helene's long deceased family footman reminded her of how much she missed him. Theodore was so much more than the First Footman, he was a wonderful storyteller, a great listener and defender of the family. Most of all, he helped teach Helene and Rose to ride exceptionally well. Each of them soon discovered their unwavering love of horses during those daily rides. It didn't seem possible that he'd passed over five years ago.

Sitting on the river bank in the shade of a large Black Willow tree the two girls continued their stroll down memory lane. "Helene this is the place where we pledged to be honest with each other and share our deepest secrets. We may have been naive young girls back then; however, I took our promise to be like sisters to heart. I'm sorry to discover you didn't."

Bowing her head and placing a hand over her stabbed heart Helene whispered softly, "I remember Rose and I'm incredibly sorry for my behavior." Raising her face revealed trepidation in her chestnut eyes. "What am I going to do Rose? Mr. Dalton haunts my dreams and during the day I can't stop thinking about him. I visualize him with me all day. He's there sitting next to me at the piano watching me play, riding with me into town, laughing, talking and falling..........."

"Falling in love?" interjected Rose when Helene didn't finish her sentence.

Helene admitted just above a whisper, "Yes."

"That's wonderful Helene. I can see that he feels the same way about you. We all can."

"I know Rose." Pausing to regain control of her voice she finally confessed, "I'm so very afraid. I picture our life together and it's more than I could have ever dreamt of. I just can't risk it."

Perplexed Rose questioned Helene, "What exactly are you afraid of risking?"

"It's too much happiness for one person to have. He's too perfect. I know it sounds crazy, but there's something holding me back. An unknown force screaming at me to beware."

"Helene we've discussed this before. Let him court you. You don't have to marry him anytime soon. Actually, you don't have to marry him at all if things don't go well. Helene, you have choices unlike I did," Rose's voice cracked and her eyes filled with regret. She took a deep breath then beseeched, "Please explore them. If you don't you may never forgive yourself. All I'm asking is for you to get to know him and give him a chance to ease your fears. Helene if there's anyone who can stand up for herself and not be forced into something it's you. What if your fears are nothing more than ghosts from the past trying to destroy any hope for happiness?"

"My mother expressed that same thought to me as well," Helene confessed.

"She's right Helene. Building walls around your heart and never letting anyone else in means Luther wins. He wanted to destroy you when he called off the wedding. If you keep holding on to the pain he inflicted on you, you're helping him accomplish his goal. Don't let him get away with that. He's moved on and no matter what he claims we all know it wasn't because he fell in love with Nellie. He fell in love with the grand status that marrying the Governor's daughter would secure for him."

After about fifteen minutes of contemplating both Rose's and her mother's words Helene stood up. With a renewed feeling of confidence, she announced with fire in her eyes, "You and my mother are right. I've spent enough time licking my wounds and living in fear. It's time I dust myself off and act like the young woman my parents raised me to be."

"Oh, it's so great to have you back Helene. I've missed you so much. No more taboo topics. The possibility of love and marriage are now up for conversation," cheered a thrilled Rose.

As the two casually rode back to Dalton Manor Rose hoped with all her heart that Helene had truly decided to give love another chance. When they reached the stables Mr. Dalton and Helene's father came out to greet them.

"What wonderful timing Helene. Mr. Dalton and I have completed today's business."

Edmund took hold of Storm's reins keeping him still while Helene dismounted. "Thank you Miss. Beck for riding him today. I've been terribly preoccupied with work and he has been a little neglected."

"You are welcome Mr. Dalton. It's my pleasure," blushed Helene breaking her eye contact with him when she felt the heat in her cheeks.

Her blush did not go unnoticed by anyone. Rose and Mr. Beck smiled happily at each other while Edmund was beside himself with jubilation at Helene's newfound ease around him. There was a softness in her voice that was only evident when he watched her at home with her family. Even the subtle changes in her movements made it clear that her guard was down. What exactly that meant had yet to be discovered and Edmund's heart pulsated with hopefulness.

Mr. Beck helped the girls into the carriage and shook Edmunds hand more vigorously than usual adding a wink of his eye. Once inside the carriage he squeezed his daughter's hand firmly and kissed her forehead ever so gently. Helene's heart swelled with happiness at the mere sight of her father's beaming smile. Everyone had noticed her obvious change of heart and they couldn't be happier. However, the joy they felt over having the Helene they knew and loved return paled in comparison to the exuberance she was holding at bay within her heart.

No words had to be spoken on the ride home. At long last a large part of Helene had come out of what could only be described as a coma and she was complete again. Nothing was off limits, the world and all it had to offer laid out in front of her. All that she needed to do now was choose what it was she truly wanted. The excitement Helene felt over what was too come was equal if not outmatched by the thrill of anticipation Edmund was feeling.

Chapter Four

Helene headed upstairs to her bedroom after an unsuccessful search. She couldn't help but pause on the same step where weeks earlier she had secretly sat listening to Edmund ask her father's permission to court her. A memory she believed she would cherish for a lifetime.

"Mr. Beck it's been an honor working with you over the last few months. I hope you have found me to be an educated, respected and established gentleman."

"I have Mr. Dalton. Especially for such a young man."

"I have come to your home today to discuss something of even greater importance. Frankly sir, it's of upmost importance to both you and I."

Helene held her breath, trying to eliminate every other sound except Edmunds rich deep voice. She grasped one of the bulky balusters with her hand becoming aware of the dampness on her palm. She then leaned in closer pressing her warm cheek against her clinched hand. Ablaze with exhilaration and hopefulness her body shook involuntarily.

What seemed like an eternity of silence went by before Edmund cleared his throat and said, "Mr. Beck, if it pleases you sir I would like to humbly ask your permission to court your daughter Helene. She is an amazingly beautiful and fascinating young woman. Her intelligence and lively spirit intrigues me. A trait uncommon in most and one I truly believe would pair well with mine. Without a doubt, I can promise there would never come a time when I would try and stifle her adventurous side. It's one of the qualities I admire most about your daughter," Edmund took a breath which felt like an eternity for Helene.

When he began to speak, his voice faltered making him clear his throat before continuing, "With your permission Mr. Beck, I would like very much to get to know her better. I understand you may need some time to consider this and discuss my request with your wife. Please take as much time as you need to contact me. I appreciate you meeting with me and vow to respect whichever answer you give me. Thank you, sir."

Edmund's shadow moved across the floor causing Helene to rise to her feet in panic. Stumbling she made it to the top of the stairs, but not without being heard. The men rushed out of the main salon to find Cora standing at the top of the stairs.

"I'm sorry my love I dropped my sewing kit on the floor and some of it tumbled down the stairs."

"That's a relief my beloved I thought you had fallen," exclaimed Mr. Beck with a sigh. "As long as you're well I'm well." Thankfully the men hadn't caught her strewing items from her sewing kit down the stairs.

The two men headed for the front door giving Cora the chance to glance back at her quivering daughter doing her best to say motionless against the wall. Smiling at her mother she retreated to her room feeling as if she was about to jump out of her own skin. The excitement of knowing she may soon be courted by Edmund and the terror of almost being caught snooping had left her jittery.

Lounging on her bed trying to calm her nerves Helene was startled by a knock on her door. "I have tea for you miss," announced one of the servants.

"Come in."

"Your mother said you may want some chamomile tea. Are you feeling ill?"

"No, I'm just a little tired."

Without another word Helene was left alone to enjoy her favorite hot beverage. Cora's timing was as usual perfect. She knocked on Helene's bedroom door just as she finished the last drop of tea. There were times when Helene appreciated her mother's skill of being at the right place at the right time and tonight was one of them. What a disgraceful and embarrassing situation Helene would have caused if she had been caught snooping.

"Helene may I come in?"

"Of course Mother."

Without so much as a word about the stairway incident Cora informed Helene that her father wished to speak with her. Helene tried her best to calm her growing excitement while following her mother back downstairs. By the time they reached her father's office Helene found herself less excited and more apprehensive.

Mr. Beck sat behind his large mahogany desk lazily rearranging piles of paperwork. The seriousness on his face prevented Helene from noticing Cora standing at his side stifling a smile.

"Close the door behind you Helene."

Feeling uneasy about what was happening Helene now searched her mother's face for any sign of reassurance. Cora's eyes gave her away. They were glimmering with happiness in stark contrast to her stoic expression easing Helene's mind.

"Samuel my love that is quite enough. You have created a dramatic mood and set the stage. Please get on with it," pushed Cora with a loving nudge against his shoulder.

Before Helene could react or even notice he had moved from his leather chair she was wrapped securely in her father's arms. Holding her like he would never let go he whispered, "I love you more than you will ever know my dear sweet daughter."

"I love you too Father."

Guided by her father Helene took a seat in one of the ornate chairs positioned near the large bow window. Samuel knelt in front of his daughter. A very uncommon position for him. She believed the last time he knelt in front of her was to clean badly scraped hands after a fall off her pony. Feeling very much like that wounded little girl Helene's curiosity built. What was it he was having such a hard time saying to her?

"Your mother and I have always encouraged you to be yourself. To explore your ambitions, to be brave and smart while never forgetting you are a lady. We are so proud of the woman you've become. Our hearts broke when Luther called off your wedding and we've longed to have our Helene back. We have missed our daughter so full of life and hope. It wasn't until recently that you've come back to us." Turning his gaze to his adoring wife he took her hand saying, "We couldn't be happier."

Lifting Cora's hand to his lips Samuel tenderly kissed the love of his life then turning back to Helene he continued. "We have always hoped that you would find a love that surpasses the love we share. Today we believe our hope for that type of love may come true."

"Father?"

"Mr. Dalton has asked my permission to court you." A sly smile crossed her father's face, "After discussing this with your mother we have both decided to give him a resounding yes. We will send a note tomorrow morning informing Mr. Dalton of our approval."

Unexpected tears flowed from Helene's eyes and she wrapped her arms around her father's neck in gratitude. The flood gates were then opened. All her fears and pain that had been locked away came crashing through those tears. The very tears she had refused to shed for far too long. Her broken heart was mending and an acute awareness of the possibilities in front of her soon changed her crying into laughter.

"It's time to celebrate. Let's get dressed and enjoy a night out. How does a lovely dinner at The Copper Tavern and a moonlight walk through the park sound?"

"That sounds splendid my love. Let us go freshen up and change. We'll be down shortly," replied Cora.

Cora and Helene headed up the stairs and Samuel teased, "Shortly?"

Helene's mind returned to the present and smiled at the cherished memory of that night. That glorious night when she learned that she was to be courted by Mr. Dalton. She still believed it would change her life for the better. Here she was weeks later anxiously awaiting

Edmund to return from business out of town. He would call on her for the very first time the following afternoon.

"Helene what took you so long? Were you able to find what you were looking for downstairs?" questioned Rose riffling through Helene's jewelry box.

"Oh I'm sorry. No, I couldn't find the sheet music then I was distracted."

"Distracted? Oh, let me guess Mr. Dalton?"

"Perhaps," giggled Helene.

The two of them spent the rest of the day discussing the events of tomorrow. Helene tried on dress after dress. She also sprayed so many types of perfumes in her room trying to select the perfect one that the smell soon found its way downstairs.

A knock on the door interrupted their fun. "Mrs. Griggs your husband is here," announced the housekeeper from outside the closed door.

Rose stopped breathing and her back stiffened before answering. She hadn't expected Maxwell to return for another week. "I'll be right down," she stammered through a clenched jaw.

"Of course my lady."

Helene smiled a sorrowful smile at her friend knowing there was nothing she could say that would help. Together they slowly walked down the stairs and found Maxwell drunk as usual boasting about his latest business conquest. Samuel sat unamused by his story or behavior. Upon seeing Rose enter the room Maxwell lifted her off her feet holding her so firmly a wheezing breath slipped from her mouth. His narcissism prevented him from even considering he was the cause of her gasping for air. In all honesty Helene was shocked by his next words. He had actually noticed Rose's change in breathing.

"Oh my, are you sick?" questioned Maxwell as he quickly pulled his arms away from her. His sudden and unexpected release made Rose drop to the floor hard. Everyone noticed one of Rose's ankles roll underneath her when she landed. Everyone that is except for Maxwell. Ultimately his question and reaction to Rose's wheeze helped Helene understand why he had noticed her wheezing. It wasn't over concern for his wife's health, but his own. Maxwell had not only abruptly dropped Rose to the floor he had stepped away from her. He didn't care if she were ill, he only cared about her making him sick. Just when Helene believed Maxwell couldn't be any more of an atrocious human being he proved her wrong.

"No dear, I'm fine. It is good to see you. You're home early," replied Rose. If her husband noticed the nervousness in her voice he thought nothing of it.

Maxwell didn't hear anything after no dear and went on to drill Rose on why she wheezed. Samuel had listened to enough and broke in saying, "Mr. Griggs I'm sure you're exhausted from the long trip home and are looking forward to a good-night's sleep in your own bed."

"I am, thank you," he slurred and with that Maxwell excused himself, but not before taking an all too firm hold of Rose's wrist. He then pulled his wife through the front door and down the porch steps. He was nearly dragging her behind him on their way to the carriage.

Helene's face expressed terror. She had an idea of what Rose was in for as she helplessly watched her best friend timidly climb into the carriage. They didn't even get to say goodbye to each other. All the joy had left Rose the moment she realized her husband had returned. Guilt boiled inside Helene for doing nothing more than standing there watching Rose leave with him.

Cora broke the awkward hush between them, "Helene why don't I help you with tomorrow's preparations? As long as we stay away from the perfume bottles. The entire house smells of nothing else."

"How can I even think about tomorrow? You saw him, he's drunk again. Please tell me you see it," begged Helene. "Rose isn't herself around him. She's terrified."

Neither her mother or father could answer her. No matter how much they despised Maxwell and his pompous behavior their hands were tied. He was far too powerful of a man to be taken down easily. The entire town had grown to understand that Maxwell would not tolerate any sort of interference in his life. The past examples he made of those who angered him by interfering was proof enough. He wasn't to be questioned or challenged. No one knew how Maxwell finagled an agreement with the local beat cops, but they appeared to turn a blind eye to his misbehavior. Whether it was through blackmail or menacing threats towards the officers or their families Maxwell appeared untouchable. Helene honestly believed he would even be allowed to get away with murder. Causing her to be even more fearful for Rose's safety.

Later that evening Edmund watched in anguish as Helene paced the floor of her bedroom. He was unclear as to why she was up for most of the night and deep within he worried it was because of him. Was she having second thoughts about beginning their courting? At long last she reluctantly climbed into bed falling asleep much easier than she thought she would. Impatiently, Edmund waited to make his move.

Helene's dreams were a jumbled mess. He hadn't seen this before, the entire town at some point made an appearance. Everyone that is except for Edmund. Her dream bounced from one place to another and from one person to another so quickly Helene thrashed in bed.

All of sudden Helene was standing on the covered porch of the town's largest church hesitant to enter.

Edmund drifted by her and entered the church as a single note rang from the bell tower. A battered and bruised Rose lay in an elaborate coffin while townsfolk paid their respects. Helene now stood at the rear of the church unable to take another step. Edmund couldn't take any more and stood next to her in her nightmare. Feeling his presence, she spun around and melted into his strong arms bursting into tears. Holding her close and feeling her intense pain stirred something inside him. He already knew he had extremely strong feelings for her, but up until that moment he hadn't truly known the depth they reached.

Holding her close even in her dream elated his being. His body tingled with electricity making him feel more alive than ever. There was no more darkness surrounding him there was only light. An overpowering and blindingly bright light coming from the woman he so desperately loved. Edmund promised himself that he would marry her someday very soon and would find a way to live with her forever. He had no idea how he would make it happen, but he didn't have a choice. There was no life without her.

Screams echoed through the Beck's house waking Helene from her nightmare. In a cold sweat she sat shivering on her bed and within minutes both her parents rushed into the room.

"Helene! What is it?" yelled her father scanning the room for an intruder.

"He killed her," Helene shrieked. The mental picture of Rose in a coffin was burnt in her mind. Her pristinely beautiful face swollen and discolored turned her stomach. Helene gagged and coughed at the memory of her dearest friend lying dead in an extravagant coffin causing more tears to stream from her eyes.

Cora brushed Helene's hair from her face and lifted her chin. "Helene you've had a horrible nightmare everything is fine my dear."

"We don't know that Mother. What if he really did kill her?"

"Who are you talking about?" questioned Samuel.

"Maxwell," was all she could get out before weeping uncontrollably.

"I'm sure Rose will arrive tomorrow as planned and will help you prepare for your outing with Mr. Dalton. You'll see she is just fine," comforted her father.

Samuel and Cora's attempts to ease her mind didn't help, it only angered her more. Before Helene could open her mouth in protest a calm reassurance came over her. Wiping her face dry she recomposed herself and surprisingly agreed with her parents.

Before long the entire household found themselves enjoying a restful night's sleep. Edmund went as far as to confirm that Rose remained alive by putting Maxwell into a deep sleep. Although to his dismay his arrival was a little too late. Maxwell's handiwork had already been left behind. New bruises were gradually beginning to darkened on Rose's beautiful face as sleep evaded her.

Ally pulled her hands free from Rose breaking the spell. Dissolving into nothingness the indoor garden vanished leaving no evidence it ever existed. With piercing eyes Ally studied Rose who sat motionless. Deep sorrow had changed her stunning face. Making her look haggard and years older. Her model worthy beauty shrouded behind a mantle of pain.

Rose knew all too well the questions Ally wanted to ask. She gave her the answers before Ally said a word. "My beauty and wealth were no match for my fiery temper Ally. There wasn't a true gentleman who would marry a woman like me. A woman who was completely unpredictable with my exaggerated and volatile emotions. I was my own worst enemy. Regardless of which emotion I was feeling it would unfortunately lead to an over-the-top temper tantrum. It's my fault I ended up with Maxwell. He was the only man willing to deal with my unbridled outbursts and capricious behavior."

Ally shook her head, "No Rose, no woman deserves to be treated that way. I don't care how bad your mood swings were or what decade you live in. It's just plain wrong."

Rose smiled a sad yet extraordinary smile at her, "Thank you Ally that's wonderful of you to say."

For the rest of the night the two cried, laughed and spoke honestly about their lives. It was as if they were back in their dorm room. Just two friends sharing secrets throughout the night, but this time secrets that were inconceivable. There was so much pain between the two of them and for the night Ally lost sight of her own heartache and focused on her friend Rose. People say "Time heals all wounds," but as far as Ally could tell Rose was still suffering greatly from her past. Ally shuddered to think how much worse Rose's marriage had gotten.

When the sun began to rise, Ally slumped on the couch and drifted off to sleep. Rose placed a quilt on her and quietly left the room. Standing on the porch Rose watched the sun rise above the ocean surface painting the sky with an ever-changing color palette.

Chapter Five

The midday sun shone through the living room window straight into Ally's eyes waking her from her slumber. Dazed from the long emotional night she lazily looked around the house and found herself alone. Had she been dreaming? Unsure of where she was Ally rushed to the front door. The sight of Rose sitting on the beach with Cap brought it all back into focus.

So much had happened in a very short amount of time or had more time passed than Ally realized? What day was it? How long had she been there? Did time even exist where she was or were the days and nights an illusion? Trying to summarize all that happened caused her thoughts to quickly spiral out of control. Dizzy from the trail of thoughts Ally leaned forward and put a shaky hand against the wall. Reopening her eyes, she noticed a gold necklace swinging from her neck. The delicate piece of jewelry with several daisies woven together along a swirled chain was uniquely beautiful. Each daisy held a tiny pink stone and the largest flower creating the grand centerpiece held the biggest stone of all. Grasping the unfamiliar necklace Ally tried to examine it closer, but the short chain made it difficult. Ally didn't remember noticing it before, surely she would have noticed it in the shower. Ally ran her fingers along the necklace and realized there wasn't a clasp. Fighting against the chain she did all she could to remove it. The chain wouldn't give. A strong earthquake knocked Ally to the floor. She couldn't help but wonder if it were a consequence or warning for her efforts to separate herself from the necklace.

"Ally!" shouted Rose rushing in the door. "Stop! You will die."

Already unnerved by the violent earthquake Ally held her breath and verified the necklace still hung from her neck. Releasing that breath, she glared up at Rose, "I'll die? Isn't that something you should have mentioned?"

"Yes Ally I should have, but you were doing so well and had yet to discover your jewelry. I thought I had more time before I needed to tell you," she answered helping Ally to her feet.

"I'm going to lose my mind! Please just let me go home. Let this all be a bad dream. I can't take this anymore," bawled Ally running up the stairs. Cap barely made it in the room before Ally slammed the door behind her. Hours passed slowly as she methodically went through all that had happened coming to the conclusion that she was helpless. A prisoner in some unbelievable fantasy, one you only read about, but for her it was all too real. Even the aroma of a marvelous dinner from downstairs had no effect. Watching the sun sink behind the cliffs she wearily climbed into bed wallowing in her agony.

Rose quietly paced outside Ally's door arousing Cap who whimpered. Ever so gently Rose opened the bedroom door and let Cap out. Ally laid sound asleep in the morning light. She was buried under the covers with one foot sticking out slightly from beneath her Grammy's quilt. Silently Rose closed the door. She knew better than to rush Ally. Rose had seen this before and understood what needed to be done. There was however one major and rare difference, Rose viewed Ally as a true friend. Something that had never happened in all this time.

Walking along the beach and watching Cap chase the waves Rose summoned Edmund pleading for an audience. Closing her eyes, she allowed the fragrant breeze to envelope her. Building into a gusty wind it spun faster and faster around her until she felt herself becoming weightless. Then in a flash she could no longer feel her body.

Edmund waited inside the manor until the time was right. In the blink of an eye he was transported to the flower garden. He then walked through all the thriving plants to the red rose bush which sat dead center in the garden. A single long stem rose sprouted and began blooming from bud to a full blossom in seconds. "Come forth Rose," commanded Edmund.

Rose lowered her gaze as Edmund came into view. His presence always impressively powerful, "Thank you, sir."

"Why have you taken me away from my love?" he questioned, "If she wasn't still weak and napping I would not have granted this meeting."

"My sincerest apologies Mr. Dalton, but as you know Ally is having a difficult time."

"That is her fault. She could create the world of her dreams if she'd simply let go of her desire to get back to her old life. My concern is not with her it is with Helene. It is our time to be together to love and enjoy life again." His tone was stern and his expression even more so.

"I agree Mr. Dalton. This is your time. You know I'm more than happy to assist Helene and you in bringing your happily ever after to fulfillment. I have never wavered on the promise I made to you both and I never will, but Ally is different..."

"Different?" interrupted Edmund. His annoyance over leaving Helene's side was blatantly evident in his speech and countenance.

"Yes," mumbled Rose before briefly pausing. "Throughout all this she and I have become genuine friends," her comment made no visible change to

Edmunds mood. He didn't appear to be more or less displeased so she took a chance and continued, "Ally is special I'm sure you can see that. I would like to help her with this transition as much as I possibly can. Perhaps if I could spend more time with her than I have with the others. In doing so it may reveal what is so different or dare I say special about her."

"Whether you two are friends or not is of little consequence to me; however, I do agree that she possesses something uncommon. It would be a shame to waste a potential talent," admitted Edmund who appeared to be seriously considering Rose's request. He had always been extremely diligent in selecting his staff and although he had never considered what Rose was proposing, he couldn't help but wonder if she had made a valid point. Could Ally be of more use to him than just a body double for Helene?

Rose smiled when Edmund's demeanor eased. She understood his irritation. Bothering him after he was reunited with Helene was almost unheard of over the decades, but Rose felt the interruption was necessary. Rose watched Edmund ponder and waited for the right moment to ask him for a favor. When his eyes glowed with excitement over the thought of adding another skilled warrior to his arsenal she knew it was time to speak up.

"Mr. Dalton, I do have one more request. Ally has never experienced real love, it's all fairy tales or romantic movies to her. After her first love finally got what he wanted from her he then left her brokenhearted. She unfortunately joined the ranks of so many young girls who were fooled by a smooth-talking and falsely devoted boyfriend. The emotional scars he left her with still cause her severe heartache. Ally is even too afraid to dream about having love someday. If she could see and hear from you directly and feel the eternal love you have for Helene it would be of great help......to all of us."

Flashing his unforgettable smile, he nodded in agreement. His anger at her intrusion had dissipated leaving behind the charismatic man who won Helene's heart and persuaded Rose to help him when he lost her.

Not knowing when Edmund would fulfill her request she rushed back to the rose bush returning to Ally who slumbered into mid-afternoon. Filled with confidence that Edmund would prove to Ally that real love is about giving and not taking from the one you love, helped Rose wait patiently for Ally to awake.

"I'm hungry," announced Ally tugging on the oversized T-shirt she slept in.

Fearful that anything she said would upset Ally, Rose smiled and without saying a word heated up leftovers from the night before. The silence between them was deafening then Rose had an idea. Retreating to an adjacent room she began to quietly play a soothing tune on the baby grand piano. It wasn't until she was well into the third song that Ally entered the room.

"I didn't know you played? I'd ask where the piano came from, but what's the point?" snorted Ally.

Rose ignored Ally's snide remark and continued to play. The next song she played was one she knew Ally would recognize and Rose hoped for the best. When Ally began humming along to the familiar song Rose craftily stretched the song out giving Ally more time to calm down. After a final climactic round of chorus's Rose stilled her fingers above the keys. Having let the tension in the room fade away she turned to Ally saying, "I would like to help you Ally in any way I can, but as I've explained there are limitations to what I'm allowed to do."

"Basically, we're trapped inside an old Victorian locket with no way out and if I remove this new necklace I'll die?" Ally's words dripped with resentment. "Did I miss anything?" she added sarcastically.

Shaking her head and whispering "no" in response to Ally's last question Rose then took a seat near her. Not wanting to hold anything else back Rose shared another secret. She carefully pulled a gold chain from under her blouse revealing an ornate white rose hanging below a few gold leaves. Ally remembered seeing a similar bracelet on Rose when they met.

"I'm not exactly trapped inside the locket like you are." Before Ally could say a word, Rose hushed her and continued, "It's better if I show you."

Reaching across the small table between them Ally said, "Then show me," as she angrily grabbed Rose's hand. Surprisingly within moments Ally was relaxed enough to be shown what she needed to see.

Edmund stood next to his dresser mesmerized by the old faded picture of him with his parents. He no longer felt the intense pain he had lived with for so many years. Missing his parents would never go away nor would the hatred towards the humans who wouldn't tolerate his kind. Nevertheless he had shockingly found a human that not only tolerated him but loved him more than he thought was possible. Edmund believed there was only one love in existence that surpassed Helene's love for him. It was the love he had for his sweet wife Helene. He adored, treasured and loved her more than life itself.

His reflection in the dresser's mirror couldn't hold the devoted love overflowing from his heart. Triggering the mirror to ripple with every buoyant thump of his heartbeat. Picking up Helene's anniversary gift he imagined the stunning locket around her delicate neck. The room filled with a soft warm glow as he mediated on this mental picture. She had touched every part of him. Even his extraordinary power was magnified with a newfound energy. Helene's love had transformed Edmund into the man he was sure his parents had wanted him to be.

This perfect moment of anticipation in giving Helene her gift was shattered when he heard her faint breathy call of his name, "Edmund."

Ally swayed in her chair while she accompanied Edmund over the countryside on his frantic search for his wife. The gruesome sight of Helene's damaged body on the dirt road made Ally turn her head. Her attempt to look away was to no avail. Something or someone snapped her head back so all she could see was Helene. Artie's skillfully recited story at Dalton Manor was being played out in front of her eyes. Watching it unfold made his gift of storytelling pale in comparison. Ally's heart broke at the sound of Helene's gurgled breathing. It had moved from a folktale to a movie in which she somehow was part of. Ally wasn't sitting comfortably in a theater seat she was a participant standing right next to Edmund watching Helene take her last shallow breath. Tears raced down Ally's face when Helene's body went limp and the color in her face drained away. It was a sight never before seen by Ally leaving her with a memory she could do without. No longer were Helene and Edmund merely fictional characters in a well-rehearsed skit. They were actual people even if one of them was an immortal warlock. In a trance like state Ally watched these two come to life characters in the most tragic moment of their lives.

Ally witnessed the locket all shiny and new capture Helene while Edmund spoke in the same strange and hypnotic language Rose used at the beach house. Once a photo of Helene formed inside the locket and came to life blinking at Edmund he released a deep cleansing breath. The words "I will see you soon," spoken by Edmund were now completely understood by Ally. She believed he knew exactly what he was doing even if he hadn't figured out all the details.

Edmunds gut-wrenching emotion overtook the country side. Fierce winds pulled fully grown trees root and all from the earth. Hail bounced against the hard ground and thunder and lightning filled the sky. Inside an invisible bubble the couple and Ally were protected from the storm around them. Edmund swooped Helene up in his arms and the next moment he carefully laid her lifeless body on their bed.

Edmund immediately returned to the dreadful scene of the accident feverishly searching for an answer.

Storm had already made it back to the manor leaving nothing more than faint hoof prints. The unusual pattern didn't go unnoticed by Edmund, but the rain quickly erased what was left of them. He wondered if Storm had proven to be too much for Helene. Throwing his arms and head back Edmund roared and raged at the sky sounding more like an untamed beast on the hunt than anything close to human. Bellowing until his voice cracked he fell to his face in absolute misery. Sobs of despair echoed throughout the valley. Lightning lit up the darkness causing a flicker of light to catch his attention. Curious he staggered over and picked up the silver goblet Helene had bought for him.

Wiping both his eyes and the goblet dry he struggled to read the engraving.

"To my darling Edmund.
Happy first anniversary my beloved.
Yours forever, Helene."

Without hesitation and in a blink of an eye Edmund was by Helene's side thanking her with sweet kisses for his anniversary gift. "You are correct my sweet we will be together forever," he stated clutching the locket.

When the hail became sheeting rain, Edmund moved to the foot of the bed planning his next move. The massive storm blocked out any light giving the illusion of night. Time stood still for Edmund as he plotted what to do next. It wasn't until Edmund heard loud panic-stricken pounding on the front door of the manor that he noticed the clock on the wall. Three o'clock? It had almost been twelve hours since Edmund lost the love of his life. His heartache distorted time making it felt like mere seconds had passed while simultaneously making it feel like an eternity had gone by. The mental picture of Helene taking her final painful breath once again shattered Edmund's weary heart.

The only thing that stopped Edmund from spiraling into despair were Arthur's sudden knocks at the bedroom door. They were quick and filled with an uncommon urgency persuading Edmund to respond. Carefully he cracked the door open revealing Arthur's distraught expression. The strange look in his eyes convinced Edmund to listen to the trail of words Arthur had been spouting.

"Arthur slow down. What has happened?"

"It's Mrs. Griggs sir, she's been carried in by her butler."

"Helene is resting. Please inform them that I'll be down shortly," instructed Edmund after reining in control over his emotions.

Edmund came into the main parlor to find Rose dripping water and blood onto his tile floor. Her face swollen to the point of making her almost unrecognizable. Bruises of every color covered her face and hands. When a female servant searched for the origin of the blood she soon discovered numerous slash marks lining Rose's forearms.

"I didn't know where else to take her Mr. Dalton sir. The town doctor refused to come to the house and care for her."

"Where is Mr. Griggs?" questioned Edmund.

"Mr. Griggs rushed out to tend to issues this storm has caused at his office. If I may be so bold sir, this storm saved her life."

Edmund issued explicit orders to the staff to make ready a room upstairs before asking Rose's butler for more details.

"Mr. Griggs was in a villainous mood when he arrived home from the office. A business deal had gone wrong and he went on a rampage the moment madam greeted him at the door. If the storm hadn't suddenly hit causing him to hurry off, I do believe we would have lost her," stated her butler. He was clearly distraught over seeing Rose in such a battered state and Edmund knew he had taken a terrible risk by bringing her to Dalton Manor.

"Does he know that you've brought her here?"

"I don't believe so. I waited until I thought he would be too far off to notice the carriage leaving the mansion."

Edmunds mind and heart sped with excitement. Taking a deep breath, he managed to hide his inappropriate enthusiasm. The butler was then given detailed instructions to return to the Griggs home and release Mrs. Griggs horse into the forest. Edmund had him repeat the explanation of how Rose slipped out without anyone catching her until it sounded unrehearsed. Once satisfied he sent the courageous butler on his way.

The manor buzzed with preparations for moving Rose upstairs leaving Edmund alone for a moment with her. This gave him the opportunity to stop the flow of blood racing from her arms and puddling on the floor. Over the next few hours she regained consciousness. Once Edmund felt she was strong enough the staff carried Rose upstairs to the bedroom across the hall from where Helene's body laid. He continued to slowly and deliberately heal Rose as to not raise suspicion by the manors staff.

By late afternoon Rose could answer questions with a nod of her head. Edmund ordered the staff to tend to her every need and to inform Rose that unfortunately he and Helene would be out that evening celebrating their anniversary, but she was safe at the manor.

Early the next morning Edmund accompanied by a nurse entered Rose's room. With the nurse standing at the far side of the bed Edmund suspended her in time allowing him to speak openly to Rose knowing what he was about to say would keep her focused solely on him.

Chapter Six

Rose struggled through blackened eyes to make the blurred figure in front of her come into view. Edmunds conspicuous good looks still found their way through her diminished vision. A fractured jaw kept her from speaking, but her tearful and anguished eyes spoke volumes. With a questioning expression, she looked towards the door and Edmund knew she was wondering why Helene was not by her side.

Pulling a chair next to the bed Edmund took a seat. The entire time reassuring Rose that she was safe for the time being. As of yet Maxwell did not know her whereabouts. This helped calm Rose even though her thoughts were dominated as to where her lifelong best friend was. Rose couldn't think of any plausible reason Helene shouldn't be there consoling her. Wedding anniversary or not Rose needed her. The anger she felt was nothing compared to the feelings of betrayal that gripped her. This only intensified the pain in Rose's already throbbing head.

Edmund held a silver hand mirror in his hand. The beauty of its delicate scrolls, small flowers and roses were indistinguishable to Rose's swollen eyes. Squinting to make Edmund come in clearer only caused the sensation of piercing needles to shoot through her eyes.

Surrendering to the pain she felt not only throughout her body but in her heart made her turn her face away. Giving up the fight to open her eyes she let them relax and close.

"Rose I need to speak with you," stated Edmund feeling lost and helpless with Helene's lifeless body in the adjacent room. His urgency made no impression on Rose. The tears trickling down her cheeks reminded him of his sweet compassionate Helene. She had spent several nights crying while discussing her fears for Rose with Edmund. She was petrified of what could someday happen to her dearest friend. Edmund recalled many a night when Helene tossed and turned in bed over those fears. Those memories of his wife and her love not only for him but for others softened his heart.

Edmund's sudden movement to pull a handkerchief from his pocket made Rose jump nervously. Her reaction was more evidence of the life she lived behind the gilded walls of her home. "Let me help you," coaxed Edmund gently.

Rose remained quiet and unmoving causing Edmund's grief to bubble to the surface. It brought him to the brink of taking what he wanted. His anguish building as the memory of the morning sun dancing lively across Helene's motionless body replayed in his mind. Edmund struggled to remain the man Helene so desperately loved. An eternal battle seethed inside him.

He wanted his wife back this very moment; however, he knew causing more pain to Rose would break Helene's heart. That was something he never wanted to do.

"Rose, you cannot go back to your husband. From what I've been told you could have lost your life in this attack. If the sudden storm had not hit you probably would not be here," said Edmund softly. His rugged deep voice scarcely above a whisper.

Unstoppable tears flowed from Rose and even though she knew Edmund spoke the truth she had no choice but to return home. Maxwell would soon find her and drag her home. Whimpers of hopelessness filled the room. The pain and sorrow on her face reminded Edmund of the day he realized his parents were gone. A very small part of her almost wished she had died and even though Edmund would never admit it to anyone he too had struggled with the very same thought. Primarily when he first escaped the rock cocoon his parents used to save his life.

Holding the mirror in front of her Edmund impatiently pushed on, "When you are ready Rose."

Never before had Edmund called her by her first name sparking more questions she wanted answers to. Helene was suspiciously missing. Instead of her best friend it was Edmund sitting with her and speaking to her like never before. Fearful chills ran up Rose's back and she felt intense panic for Helene wash over her. Had Helene confronted Maxwell? No, that couldn't be it. Edmund would never allow Helene to be harmed, but that would explain her absence. A morbid curiosity overtook her and she snatched the mirror from Edmund. Holding it on her lap she gathered the courage she needed before slowly lifting the mirror to her face. With a minuscule wave of his fingers Edmund cleared her eyes making it possible for Rose to see the full effect of Maxwell's cruel and heavy hands.

Rose shuddered in disbelief before dropping the mirror to the floor shattering the glass into thousands of shards. Her body violently reacted to her own reflection. She began hyperventilating over the grisly sight. Rose's beautiful face unrecognizable even to herself.

"I can help you Rose," offered Edmund. It was enough to bring her out of her spiraling downfall.

Unable to speak Rose moaned once as if to ask, "How?"

Rose watched Edmund pace the room before saying, "Where do I begin?" Moments passed slowly before Edmund turned abruptly. Without so much as a quiver from his lips he spoke, "Rose I need you to listen very carefully to what I'm about to say."

Refusing to give into the intense pain Rose forced her eyes to open as much as the swelling would allow. A web of puzzlement, disbelief and complete terror gripped her. Astonished, she watched Edmund remain eerily motionless the entire time speaking to her.

"How? What's happening?" Rose yelled inside her head. Her panicked expression conveying her thoughts.

"Remain calm Rose there's much I need to say." Edmunds voice resonated throughout the room like thunder.

Not sure whether to believe her own eyes she watched Edmund become exceedingly more impressive than normal. His magical being no longer hidden from view. It couldn't be explained. There was no real physical change or improvement to his already flawless features and yet there was something impressively different about him. There was a defined regal air surrounding him and power exuded every part of his being captivating Rose.

In disbelief Rose fixed her eyes on Edmund's every move. He bounced about the room in nervous excitement before stopping at the foot of Rose's bed. He allowed her time to soak in the now obvious visual change for a few minutes. He resembled the rising sun shining just above the horizon and yet her eyes weren't blinded by the radiant light flowing from him. She continued to study his appearance until she noticed something. Rose realized the nurse had been standing in the exact same place all this time completely motionless.

199

"She's frozen," exclaimed Edmund.

"Frozen?" thought Rose pulling the sheet up to her neck causing pain to radiate in her arms.

"I froze her so we could speak in private," he stated. Fearful even the slightest move he made would add to Rose's fear Edmund remained absolutely still. Impatiently he waited for Rose to turn her eyes back to him.

There was no way to ease into this. As soon as Rose refocused her attention on him Edmund simply stated, "I'm a warlock Rose. A very powerful warlock."

Their strange one way conversation came to a halt while Rose tried to process what she had just heard. Part of her believed she was dreaming, but the aches throughout her body convinced her that this was all too real.

Without waiting for Rose to come back to reality Edmund continued, "You're unfamiliar with the legend of Dalton Manor it's been far too many years. Allow me to summarize for you. This is the home I grew up in with my wonderful parents both who were like me. My father had a fondness for you humans. It's this fondness that made him unafraid and if I do say so myself foolish around your kind. He never deliberately performed magic in front of anyone, but he also never worked terribly hard at hiding it. As I grew so did the stories and eventually hatred towards my family." Edmund paused to funnel his feelings into something other than himself. This time resulting in dozens of small tornados spreading over the countryside.

Rose searched her memory remembering nothing about a legend. Her already aching head now pounded with a wave of new thoughts. One word questions bounced to the forefront of her mind, "Legend?" "Warlock?" "Years?" "Frozen?" "Helene?"

"On the worst night of my life an angry mob of humans led by someone very much like Maxwell burnt this house to the ground. My father's pleas for mercy and understanding fell on deaf ears. The frenzied mob couldn't see past the hatred in their eyes. There was no convincing them that we weren't a family of dark magic demons and my father not wanting to risk my future refused to use magic to fight back. As a last resort, he and my mother used their combined power to save my life by giving me immortality. It took every ounce of their power and strength to protect me from the blazing fire. Leaving them without the ability to save themselves. Their drained bodies created a rock-solid cave around me shielding me from the savage flames and murderous mob. I awoke from the spell a decade later to find my home in ruins, my parents gone and all alone for the first time in my life."

Rose sat intently listening to every word. Not understanding how any of this was possible or convinced she even believed the things Edmund was telling her. Either way Rose remained keenly focused on him. With a simple nod of her head Rose encouraged him to continue.

Carefully he only told Rose what she needed to know. Edmund continued his story leaving out his plan of destruction for the mob's descendants. He not only needed Rose on his side he wanted her to be a willing participant for his beloved Helene's sake. Edmund's steadfast commitment to put Helene first held strong. If there was the slightest risk of causing her harm Edmund would rethink his agenda. Even bringing her back to him had to be something Helene wouldn't frown upon.

"I've had a long lonely life Rose. One filled with far too many years of heart wrenching pain, loneliness and anger, that is until Helene came into my life. She is the love of my life. The one who brought me back from a mere existence to experiencing love and happiness far beyond my wildest dreams. You've witnessed our love first hand and you know what a difference Helene makes having her in your life. She's been your safe haven and true confidant while your life has turned from bad to worse. Rose, you know there's nothing Helene wouldn't do for you. If it were within her power she'd wipe away all your pain and give you the life she wishes you had."

Rose nodded in agreement as Edmunds words still hung in the air. It was true. Helene would move mountains if possible to spare Rose the misery she lived everyday with Maxwell. This reminded Rose, "Why isn't she here? Where is Helene?"

The desperation and sorrow on her face grew when she glanced at the door shaking Edmund's resolve. This realization helped him to truly realize what she and Helene shared. It was a love shared only by true sisters. It didn't matter that different blood pulsed through their veins. What mattered was they had become sisters by every definition. Their bond exceeded anything Edmund had witnessed over his lifetime convincing him that his plan was the best available option.

"I promise I will take you to see her very soon Rose." With that Edmund hushed Rose to sleep not only for her sake but because he needed to check on Helene. He understood that he'd thrown an awful lot of inconceivable information at Rose. He wanted to give her time to absorb at least a portion of it. He also wanted her body to do some natural healing before moving forward with his scheme.

Helene's body was frozen in time, similar to what Edmund had done to the nurse, but he imagined this would hold for only so long. He believed he needed to achieve his covert objective within the next couple days or risk losing Helene forever. Edmund wasn't entirely sure how long the powerful spell he used to trap Helene's soul would last.

Sitting in his large velvet chair by the window Edmund opened the locket to check on Helene. Her saddened and fearful face cut him to his core. Through a cracking voice he spoke, "My sweet Helene, I know you're frightened. Please rest assured that you will be back in my arms very soon. An opportunity has presented itself and it's better than I could have imagined. I love you my dearest."

Edmund closed the locket tight not wanting to weaken the spell that contained Helene. Having little choice, he knew it was necessary to help Rose heal faster. He was not only pressed for time with saving Helene, but he knew Maxwell would soon leave his flooded office to find Rose missing and come looking for her. An insight he never gave any thought to echoed in his head. All the suffering Rose had endured at the hands of her husband gave Edmund a new disturbing perspective on humans. He had witnessed their greed, unwillingness to accept differences in people and their ability to blindly rally behind the angry words of one outspoken individual. Having witnessed the various evil humans hold within did nothing to help him understand the pure brutality Maxwell showed Rose. Edmund would fight hell's fury himself to protect Helene from any harm. There wasn't any part of him that could reconcile the savage wickedness Maxwell showed his wife with the willingness Edmund had to lay down his life to save Helene's. If there had been a spell to trade places with Helene on that dirt road he wouldn't have hesitated, but there wasn't any magic that could break his parent's spell. The immortality his parents had gifted him was permanent.

Arthur knocked on the bedroom door announcing lunch was ready reminding Edmund that he hadn't eaten since breakfast the day before and he knew it was causing suspicion to fester in the manor. Helene had not been seen returning from yesterday's ride, yet Storm was back in his stall. Edmund was aware that the rumors about her whereabouts were gaining momentum. Weighing his options Edmund froze the entire manor even stopping a mouse mid-jump off a wooden crate in the cellar.

At long last the time he had dreaded over the years had arrived. He had gone over this conversation countless times in his mind; however, it gave him very little consolation. Walking to the door Edmund released Arthur from the frozen spell showing him in after concealing Helene's presence.

A concerned Arthur entered the room. He fully expected exuberant happiness to be alive and well in the manor not this dense dark cloud that had covered them all. Timidly he placed the platter on the small table next to Edmunds favorite chair. Turning to leave he was surprised to feel Edmunds hand on his shoulder.

"Arthur would you please stay?"

"Of course sir. Is there anything else you need?"

"Yes, I need you to remember how close we've become over all these years," answered Edmund doing his best to keep his voice from cracking.

As if quoting a playwright's script Edmund explained in great detail who and what he was from the building of Dalton Manor to the present. Hoping to strengthen their bond Edmund recapped favorite memories from the first time they met all the way up to the magnificent wedding Arthur helped plan. Nervously he let Arthur know he had been with him for over a century.

Unwavering from all he had heard Arthur bowed graciously and said, "Mr. Dalton it has been my honor to serve you over the years. Which you've explained is far longer than I realized. I have enjoyed my life here with you watching you change from a bitter angry young man into the loving man I always knew was buried deep within. Helene has brought such peace and complete happiness to us all. I wish for no other life than the one you've given me."

Edmund could hardly believe his ears. He knew Arthur had a heart of gold, but this was downright unexpected. No matter how much Edmund wanted to believe Arthur could handle the truth his heart was filled with doubt. What a relief for Edmund to share his deepest secret with the man he'd grown up with. The man he thought he could trust with anything had proved to be such a man.

In an unheard-of expression of gratitude Edmund hugged Arthur and sincerely thanked him. A tremendous weight had been lifted from Edmund leaving him feeling refreshed and filled with confidence. He was no longer alone in his endeavor. He now had a proven confidant to help him with his plan. For the second time in one day he had an unexpected revelation about humans. Arthur helped him to understand Helene and Rose's friendship better than ever.

Chapter Seven

Exceptionally rare nerves coursed through Edmund making him hesitate. He carefully watched Arthur's face for any hint of deception, but Arthur's eyes revealed only one thing, his loyalty to the Dalton family. Edmund held his breath before dissolving away the veil that hid Helene's broken body upon the bed. Arthur couldn't believe his eyes and dropped to his knees in sorrow. Absolute shock at the sight of her mangled body made Arthur unable to move. His lungs tightened and refused to release its last breath.

"I was unable to save her Arthur. Storm's hooves crushed her beyond my power. If only I had gotten to her sooner, then maybe?"

No longer able to contain his emotions Arthur stood on wobbly legs. He shuffled towards Helene with an uncharacteristic slouch. "My sweet Lady," he muttered taking her tiny hand in his. Her shattered body contorted, bloody and bruised made him turn his face away.

"We can have her back," reassured Edmund.

"How?" whispered a grief-stricken Arthur.

"I've placed her soul safely inside my anniversary gift until I can release her into another body," answered Edmund pulling the locket from his lapel.

Without needing any further information or explanation as to how this could be accomplished Arthur questioned, "How can I be of service?"

Knowing there was little Arthur could do at the moment Edmund gave him the task of watching over Helene so he could return to Rose. Having the support of Arthur meant he would be able to move things along more quickly. Edmund's heart thumped with eagerness knowing he would soon embrace his beloved Helene.

Leaving everyone except the three of them frozen Edmund hurried back to Rose's room feeling invigorated. He could only hope that this conversation would go as well as the one he had with Arthur.

Feeling extremely groggy from the sleep Edmund had placed her in Rose found herself unsure of what was real. It all came crashing back when she attempted to sit up in bed. The truth about why she was at Dalton Manor became agonizingly real when she noticed the bloody bandages on her arms. Flashbacks of protecting her face from Maxwell's riding crop resonated through her. She could hear his angry voice interrupted by the cracking sounds of the whip and the intensely sharp sting of each lash was burned into her memory. No matter how hard she tried she couldn't remember why or when the beating stopped. Her last memory was of herself cowering on the floor of their massive bedroom accepting that Maxwell would take her life that very night.

Edmund filled in the blanks, "You were brought here by your butler." He went on to explain that Mr. Griggs had left in a hurry when a sudden storm hit because it had caused an issue at his office. Edmund went as far as to mention all the butler had shared and how they worked out a plan to delay Rose's husband from finding her.

Nodding Rose agreed that sounded like Maxwell. She had always been thankful that he cared about his work far more than anything else. His determination and drive for more power and money often kept him away from home leaving her to live without fear while he was gone. Rose bounced between thoughts of thankfulness for the sudden storm that saved her life and distress that she survived another attack, each one worse than the one before. The horrible thoughts of what waited for her at home couldn't be shaken and her entire body shook involuntarily in anticipation of what would be.

Edmund pondered how ironic it was that Helene's death had ultimately saved Rose from hers. That was it. Edmund would present Helene's tragic and sudden death as a way of her unknowingly sacrificing herself to keep Rose alive. That would surely persuade her to help.

"Life is full of unforeseen twists and turns Rose. Sometimes those very abrupt shifts can cause a person to make unimaginable choices," said Edmund trying to ease his plan into action. Glaring deep into her eyes Edmund continued, "Rose you do realize you cannot under any circumstances return home." It wasn't a question it was virtually a command.

No matter how much she agreed with Edmund she saw no way out and her thoughts ran wild. Maxwell had the vast majority of the town in his pocket and without his consent they didn't make a move. No one ever questioned her injuries or his treatment of her. The sad truth was most of the townspeople felt secure in their safety. Mainly because Rose bore the brunt of his atrociously savage behavior. Edmund watched Rose's expression shift from immense sorrow to complete devastation.

Aware that Rose was far too weak to deal with what she viewed as a hopeless situation Edmund stilled her mind. This helped her drift off to a natural sleep. He needed her physical body to heal in order to insure the greatest success. While Rose slept, Edmund erased the majority of the damage Maxwell had done. There weren't any internal injuries of which Edmund was extremely grateful. As night fell he stood back to relish the work he had completed. Rose now looking like herself slumbered peacefully.

211

Edmund also needed rest if all was to go well. Returning to his room he relieved Arthur of his duty. "Sleep well my friend we have an eventful morning."

With a nod Arthur retired to his quarters. Reclining on the chaise lounge Edmund recalled all the times he found Helene reading there for hours on end. Making him briefly smile. Her tiny frame snuggled up against the headboard and sloped back of the Recamier sofa always brought a grin to his face. Although a perfect fit for his petite Helene it proved to be quite the opposite for him. It took very little time before he enlarged the sofa to hold his strapping body comfortably. Repositioning himself prompted a remnant of Helene's perfume to escape the velvet fabric. Edmund inhaled the floral scent only to bring a woeful smile to his face. Kissing the locket sweetly he whispered, "Good night my love."

Haunting images flowed through Edmunds unconscious causing him to fall off the lounge several times throughout the night. When the first rays of the morning sun found their way into the room Edmund's eyes burst open. He believed today was the day it needed to be done and he had made up his mind that nothing or no one was going to stop him.

In no time, he was dressed and waiting impatiently for Rose to wake on her own. Edmund sensed her heart race when she became aware of where she was. Quickly conjuring up an appetizing breakfast he strutted into her room. To her surprise she was famished and able to sit up in bed without any pain. Dominated by her hunger she ate until she felt like she would explode. After a final sip, she placed the coffee cup back on the table and noticed her arms were free of bandages.

Without thinking she spoke for the first time, "How long have I been asleep?" The sound of her own voice startling her. It was clear and vibrant sounding like her old self. She wondered if everything she could remember from the other night had been a dream.

"It's been one night since we spoke last," answered Edmund staring off into space. The lack of movement from his lips put to rest any notion Rose had about Maxwell's attack being a nightmare or that the legend of Dalton Manor hadn't been discussed.

Physically her body felt renewed, but her mind and emotions struggled now more than ever to hang on to sanity. Fear of Maxwell's impending arrival nearly caused her breakfast to come up.

Rushing to her side Edmund gently spoke to her out loud fearing his continued use of magic would push her over the edge. "I understand your concern Rose and you have every right to be fearful."

As if on cue Arthur entered the room and cleared away the dishes. He spoke to Rose in such a polite matter-of-fact manner that it remarkably eased her fear. Arthur's calm demeanor and casual conversation perfectly set the stage and prepared Rose for Edmund's next words.

"I have to say Rose until yesterday I had no idea the depths of your friendship with Helene. Arthur helped me to further understand how deep human relationships can be. He proved to be the same kind of friend to me that Helene is to you."

"Helene!" Rose's face turned as red as her hair. "Don't speak to me about our friendship. She hasn't been in here once to see me. There's nothing she or you could say that would ever help me forgive her. She abandoned me in my darkest hour," shouted Rose. She was even too mad to cry and wanted nothing more than to leave Helene's home that minute. "Edmund would you leave me alone so I can dress and be on my way?"

"Will you be returning home?"

All-encompassing fear gripped her subduing the anger she was feeling. Convulsive gasps escaped her mouth as she wrestled with the fear of her husband and the betrayal of Helene.

This was not at all how the morning was expected to go. Edmund knew it wasn't going to be easy, but the multitude of emotions Rose was feeling complicated his already formidable task. Upsetting her more could put his entire plan in jeopardy.

"I don't know where I will go, but I will not stay here one more minute. Please excuse me Mr. Dalton I have to get ready and be on my way."

"Rose you don't mean that. You are understandably upset. You almost died a couple nights ago. Please let me help you."

"Thank you Mr. Dalton I appreciate your assistance and I'm thankful that you helped me. I can only surmise that my recovery is your doing; although, I'm not sure how that's possible. Frankly it's still unbelievable. Whatever you did and however you helped me means I'm indebted to you, but as for your wife. I'd prefer to never ever see her again."

"Rose let me explain. There's so much more you don't know."

"I don't want to hear it!" her voice strong and determined.

Arthur returned to the room and stood guard by the door. His stance sending a clear message that Rose would not be going anywhere.

"Are you keeping me captive?" screeched Rose now painfully aware that she was hollering at a warlock. She'd seen only a small tidbit of what he was capable of and the all too familiar fear of a powerful man came crashing in over her.

"No Rose you are my guest and Helene's dearest friend. She would never forgive me if I let any harm come to you."

"Stop, just stop," pleaded Rose. "I never thought there was anything that could break our bond, but she found away. Please Mr. Dalton, Edmund, let me leave before I have to face her. I don't have the strength for that. I've already told you there's nothing either of you could possibly say that could take away the hurt she's caused me."

Squatting near the side of the bed and peering deep into Rose's weepy eyes he uttered the most painful words he'd ever spoken, "My beloved Helene is dead."

A new level of terror throbbed through her veins. Unable to comprehend what had just been said she begged Edmund to repeat himself. She must have heard him wrong. She would not and could not accept what she thought she heard.

A morbid curiosity drove Rose to ask a horde of questions. She wanted to know what happened, when it happened and mostly she wanted to see Helene. Confused by what day it was and when she'd last seen Helene alive Rose hoped it would be possible to see her friend one last time. Edmund smiled at the sound of Rose referring to Helene as her friend. It was a small step in putting his plan back on track. He desperately wanted

Rose to be in complete agreement with his proposition knowing it would bring great pleasure to his dearest Helene.

"Are you sure you would like to see her?"

A subdued nod was her answer. Speaking with the lump in her throat would have been an unbearable if not impossible task. At last a muffled "Yes," found its way out of her mouth causing her to swoon back into the bed drowning in her grief.

Feeling helpless Edmund recalled how he wished he could have magically changed Helene's initial feelings about him. Human free will and emotions were untouchable, but he had to try. His efforts to ease Rose's distress failed miserably. There clearly was no way to hold power over her emotional breakdown. Unlike Edmund's ability to force his painful feelings out of his body into something else, dreadfully painful human emotions remained trapped within the body of those being tormented. Edmund could not expel the pain Rose felt. The devastating news of Helene's passing brought Rose to the brink of unconsciousness. Watching her suffer through the acceptance of the news triggered mental pictures of Helene's death to replay in his mind. The anguish building inside of him was forced out creating yet another rampaging storm.

Arthur held his post struggling to keep from being caught up in the hurt permeating the room. Grieving for dear sweet Helene was to be done on his own time. For now, he had to have a clear mind and assist Edmund in bringing Helene back safely.

Chapter Eight

Short of breath Rose dried her eyes having exhausted all the tears she had left. Edmund sat at the far corner of the room blankly staring out the window patiently waiting for Rose to finish mourning her situation. Arthur had left the room momentarily to collect one of Helene's bathrobes for Rose to borrow. He found Edmund and Rose so deep within their own thoughts when he returned he wasn't sure they even noticed he had briefly stepped out.

Taking charge of the situation Arthur laid the garment across the foot of the bed saying, "When you're up to it Mrs. Griggs."

Nothing more needed to be said. Rose understood she would be taken to see Helene. Even though her mind raced with questions there was nothing to say. Her trance like gaze confirmed to Arthur that she understood. Clearing his throat before leaving the room brought Edmund to his feet.

"Please call for us when you are ready miss and we will help you get across the hall."

Deep in thought Edmund lost track of time making it feel like mere seconds had passed since they left the room before hearing Rose call for them. Through her strained and cracking voice, she begged Edmund for help in finding a way to do what she needed to do. Say good-bye to her lifelong friend. Pulling a handkerchief from his pocket Edmund handed it to Rose before carefully lifting her to her feet. When she finished wiping her face Edmund and Arthur steadied Rose and assisted her across the hall.

Before taking hold of the doorknob and opening the bedroom door Edmund did what he could to prepare Rose. "Helene had a horrible riding accident. I'm not sure what transpired, but it appears that she was.......crushed by Storm," explained Edmund choosing to rephrase his words from stomped to death to crushed by Storm. He was hopelessly trying to brace Rose for the hideous sight of her dearest friend. He knew it would be a difficult and shocking sight for Rose for it continued to remain agonizing for him. Looking at his sweet broken Helene was an insufferable task.

With curtains drawn the room was dark making it hard for Arthur and Rose to see anything. Edmund's eyes however saw everything bright and clear. Adjusting to the darkness Rose noticed a silhouette on the bed freezing her in her tracks.

"That's close enough," she stated. With each deliberate blink her eyes adjusted until she recognized Helene.

Edmund steadily pulled the curtains open inch by inch until the subdued sunlight hit Helene's beautiful face. He purposely prevented the light from being too bright. This kept it from fully capturing the heart wrenching evidence of her accident.

Pulling away from Arthur, Rose staggered to Helene's bedside and dropped hard to her knees. Overcome with emotion she didn't even notice how hard she hit the floor. Gently she took hold of Helene's hand and lifted it to her cheek, "No Helene not you!" Helene's ice cold hand lifeless in hers confirmed that her friend was truly gone.

With bated breath Edmund studied Rose's reaction waiting for the opportune time to make his move. It didn't take too much longer before it presented itself.

"If you're a warlock why didn't you save her?" Rose's voice now angry.

"There wasn't enough time to heal her injuries. The damage was far too severe. Perhaps if I had gotten there sooner."

"You call yourself a warlock!" growled Rose. If she heard the agony in Edmunds voice she overlooked it or simply didn't care.

"Mrs. Griggs," scolded Arthur. "No one is more destroyed by her death than Mr. Dalton. He lost his beloved wife, the love of his life, his entire reason for living."

In a humbler tone and with a steady stream of tears rushing down her face Rose asked, "You healed me why not her?"

"She left me moments after I found her. It all happened so quickly there wasn't anything I could do in the little time I had," replied a guilt stricken Edmund.

The sound of Edmund's faltering voice further suppressed Rose's temper. Turning her focus back to Helene she scrutinized the obvious injuries as best she could in the dim light. Feeling queasy, Rose placed her forehead on the bed next to Helene. Silently she absorbed all that had happened over the last few days. She had lost her best friend and almost her own life.

"When did this happen?"

"The day your life almost ended," Edmund answered.

Rose shook her head and groaned, "It should have been me."

Here it was. The opening he was hoping for. "Helene's death is what prevented your death," announced Edmund as if announcing dinner were ready.

"How?" questioned Rose still holding Helene's hand securely in hers.

"In my overwhelming grief my emotions took control. I sent them out into the world before they consumed me. Which became that powerful storm that sent Mr. Griggs to his office. Holding my beloved's body after she departed was far too much to bare. I had to expel my pain and anger. I was being devoured by my emotions and I knew if I didn't find a way to control them Helene would have been lost forever. Be thankful that I did. Without that unbridled storm your life would have ended as well."

"That sounds like Helene. She found a way to protect me until her last breath." There it was. Rose had freely chosen to view Helene's death as a sacrifice that rescued her from death's door.

"Yes, it most certainly does," agreed Edmund before setting his plan in motion. "But in all fairness, you would undoubtedly do the same for her. If it were within your control of course," Edmund said with assurance hoping for confirmation from Rose.

"Of course," agreed Rose without hesitation. "There isn't anything I wouldn't do for Helene." Fighting back the lingering tears Rose silently wished she could trade places with Helene. It was Helene that had a life full of love and endless possibilities while Rose had the exact opposite. She wished more than ever that Maxwell had killed her. Consumed by her thoughts and fearing that

Maxwell would show up at any moment Rose vocalized her feelings, "Why couldn't it have been me? Oh, Helene it should have been me."

At last Rose was ripe for the picking and after smiling at Arthur he made his move. Jerking the curtains fully opened he revealed the ghastly sight of Helene's injuries in their entirety. Making it perfectly clear that she could not come back from them. Sickened by the sight in front of her Rose jumped from the bed and crashed into a lamp.

"If you really mean that Rose there is a way," pressed Edmund.

"A way? A way for what exactly?"

"With my help you can trade places with Helene."

His comment boggled her mind. Rose shook her head becoming fearful of what Edmund was capable of. She moaned the words, "You would kill me?"

With a tilt of his head Edmund answered, "Not exactly."

This did nothing to ease Rose's mind. Wanting to find an escape she glanced at the door only to find Arthur standing guard again. There was no way out and she wished even harder that Maxwell had ended her life the other night.

"Please Rose let me explain. You said yourself that you would do anything for Helene."

Rose screamed, "Killing me won't bring her back!"

"No it wouldn't that's why I have no desire to kill you Rose. Please let me explain," Edmunds voice remained steady and on point.

Pulling the locket from his lapel he motioned for Rose to join him at the window. Tentatively she approached him driven more by curiosity then by fear. Admiring the locket Rose asked if it belonged to Helene.

"It is the anniversary gift I'm going to give her."

Rose noticed Edmunds odd choice of words. He spoke as if Helene was merely asleep and would wake to his gift. The more she heard the less she understood. It was exactly the way Ally was feeling as Rose showed her a first-hand account of the legend of Dalton Manor.

"It's true I was unable to save Helene's body," Edmund paused in an effort to retain control. "However, I was able to retrieve her soul," explained Edmund with a tinge of happiness.

Covering her face with her hands Rose wobbled on unsteady legs. Edmund stopped her from falling and lowered her onto Helene's lounge. Rose opened her eyes to find the room spinning about making her queasy.

"Lay back Rose," comforted Edmund.

In a dream like state Rose looked around the room trying desperately to focus on something. Pain radiated through her head making it impossible to zero in on a single thought. At last her eyes began to focus on the locket which Edmund now held close to her face. Dainty flowers, intricate swirls and the initials E & H gradually came into view. The locket was beautifully made and complimented by a delicate silver chain which sparkled merrily in the morning sun now bursting through the clouds.

"I don't understand," Rose murmured.

"Inside this locket is Helene's soul. She's been there since the day she died."

The puzzled expression on Rose's face encouraged Edmund to continue, "Before she took her last breath I was able to summon her soul from her dying body and enclose Helene safely within my anniversary gift."

"Helene is in the locket?"

"Correct," whispered Edmund before ever so carefully opening the locket to reveal Helene's face.

Pulling Edmunds hand even closer to her face Rose studied the picture inside. Noticing Helene blink and smile at her refilled her eyes with tears. "Helene?" With a nod of her head Helene reassured Rose that it was truly her.

Suddenly closing the locket Edmund said, "That's enough. The spell is weakened if the locket is open to long."

"Where is she? Is she all right? Can you get her out?" questioned Rose.

"She's safe and yes I can get her out." Edmund stood from his kneeling position next to the lounge. With long hurried strides Edmund paced the floor. Abruptly turning back toward Rose, he announced, "I can bring her out Rose, but only with your assistance."

"You need me to help you?"

"Yes Rose, Helene and I desperately need your help."

Befuddled and hopeful by Edmund's words Rose asked, "What could I possibly do?"

"With your permission I would place Helene's soul into your body," stated Edmund his eyes shining with excitement.

Rose felt herself losing control and used a pillow to hide behind. The events of the last few days were more than enough to handle. Now this? Being faced with having Helene's soul in her body was preposterous. Unsure of how much more she could take she remained stationary on the lounge. Soon growing numb to it all. Self-preservation took over and she persuaded herself that she was dreaming.

"Mrs. Griggs?" Arthur's voice broke through her denial. Rose gave no response so Arthur repeated himself more forcefully this time, "Mrs. Griggs!"

Throwing the pillow across the room she turned towards the sound of Arthur's voice the entire time telling herself she was back at home. Refocusing on Edmund and Arthur standing there in front of her she faced the truth. She was in a real-life nightmare.

"Mrs. Griggs please help bring Helene back to us all," pleaded Arthur.

"How?" she cried.

"Allow Mr. Dalton to release Helene's soul into your body."

"Then what happens to me?" asked Rose terrified of the answer, "If Helene's soul is in my body then where...."

"I can grant you the life you've always wanted Rose," interrupted Edmund. "A life full of love and happiness, a life that would always contain Helene. A life that is never-ending."

"How exactly would you accomplish that?"

Suddenly a loud and forceful pounding came from the manor's front door. Within minutes Rose could hear Maxwell's venomous voice echoing throughout the house. His fury undeniable as he shouted, "Where is my wife? I know she is here!"

A panic-stricken Rose began to tremble and cry. She turned to Edmund with a heavy heart and pleaded for help, "Please, don't let him take me home."

"I can keep you from him for eternity Rose. My plan is the perfect solution. All I need you to do is to agree to bring Helene back to us all."

Arthur returned to his place at the door as Maxwell's voice became louder. His heavy stomping up the grand stairway announced Maxwell's impending arrival. The entire time cursing all those at Dalton Manor. Edmund remained motionless. He silently stood next to Helene carefully watching and waiting for Rose to agree.

"I agree Edmund. Please hurry and do whatever needs to be done," begged a terrified Rose as the sound of Maxwell's verbal threats drew closer.

One corner of Edmund's mouth curved into a smile before freezing Maxwell in his steps causing an immediate hush over the manor. For added effect Arthur opened the door exposing how very close Maxwell was to them. Rose looked at her husband's distorted face burning with hatred, his fists clenched and the veins on his neck bulging. That particular moment in time would remain a ghastly mental picture for Rose. She would carry it with her for the rest of her existence.

Rose pressed her hand against her chest trying to calm her racing heart. Underneath her hand she felt a cold object forcing her to take her eyes off Maxwell. Edmunds beautiful anniversary gift now hung from her regal neck. The locket snapped open shooting light rays into the room making everyone expect Edmund shield their eyes from the blinding light.

"Thank you Rose," gushed Helene.

Rose opened her eyes for the briefest of moments to see Helene smiling in front of her. With a warm hug and kiss on the check Helene disappeared into the dazzling glare.

As quickly as it began the light was gone and Rose was left standing in the distance watching Edmund wrap Helene in his arms. After a passionate kiss, he lifted her off her feet and swung her in circles. The sound of their laughter echoed through the dissolving circle of shimmering black.

Rose eased her hands away from Ally. Nervously she waited for Ally's reaction to what Rose had shown to her. To her pleasure Ally's eyes no longer showed anger or betrayal. Her lovely brown eyes displayed the warm kindness of a friend.

Chapter Nine

Ally sat motionless astonished by what she had just seen. She couldn't pull her eyes off Rose no matter how hard she tried. The mental picture of her appallingly battered face kept Ally's eyes locked on her. She couldn't even imagine what her husband had done to cause such damage to her stunning face. Remembering the obvious terror in her eyes when Maxwell stood frozen before her would forever be branded in Ally's mind. One thing became clear. The entire legend or curse of Dalton Manor was in fact a love story. Although for Ally it wasn't a romantic love between a warlock and his deceased wife, but a love story between friends. Friends that would literally die for one another.

"Rose I'm so sorry for everything," said Ally. Her tears and somber tone expressed her sadness for all she had learned.

"Thank you Ally."

It was painfully obvious to Ally that Rose was shaken to the point of pure agony by having to relive such horrible memories. The anger she'd felt towards Rose had all but vanished leaving behind feelings of deep sympathy. She didn't know where to go from here or how to unify her lost life with this fantasy world. The only thing that did seem clear to Ally was that Rose was as much a victim as she was.

The afternoon sun lit up their dark mood blanketing the room with it's warm inviting brilliance, "Let's go outside and enjoy the cool breeze," urged Ally.

Smiling her radiant smile Rose nodded in agreement. Following Ally out onto the sand they made their way down to the water's edge. Before long the two were engaged in easy conversation splashing and kicking the gentle waves. Rose was correct in saying she and Ally had become friends in college although this was something Rose always tried to keep from happening. Viewing a potential host for Helene as a friend was dangerous. Time would prove it was even much more dangerous than Rose could have imagined.

With the mood beginning to lighten Ally dared to ask, "Is there anyone else here?"

"Here?"

"In the locket," Ally looked around at the sea side cliffs, the powder blue sky and the endless ocean adding, "We are still in the locket, right?"

"Yes, we are Ally," Rose answered ignoring the first question.

Trying again Ally said, "So it's just you and me in this big world?"

"For now," replied Rose before running into the waves.

Unsure if she had upset her Ally decided to let it go, for now. This was the first-time Ally remembered being the one looking out for Rose. It was something she never thought she would have to do. Rose was confident, strong, determined, intelligent and beautiful. There wasn't anything she couldn't handle or so Ally had thought. Now Ally knew that deep within her perfection were century old wounds, inconceivable torment and loneliness. Ally wondered if Rose looked back on her decision to help Edmund as a curse or a blessing.

"That's a wonderful idea," agreed Rose coming back to the shore.

Turning towards the house Ally saw a raging fire, two whitewashed Adirondack chairs and a small table with all the fixings for s'mores. Unnerved by the fact that Rose was still listening in on her thoughts Ally made herself push it aside letting those emotions fade away as they raced back to house.

Skipping dinner and filling up on s'mores left the girls feeling content. With over filled belly's they quietly watched the sun sink into the ocean. The luminous colors of the sunset took Ally's breath away. It was tremendously more beautiful than any she had ever seen. There wasn't a painting or picture that could compare.

Adding another log to the dwindling fire helped Ally feel like she was more than an observer in this strange land. Until that moment Rose had done everything from bringing her thoughts to life in the blink of an eye to all the cooking and cleaning. Understanding that Rose had been in the locket for decades caused Ally to surrender to a similar fate. At least for the time being.

The star filled sky and soothing sound of the gentle waves pushed away Rose's trip down memory lane. Ally slouched in the chair with her eyes half closed. When her head bobbed forward startling her awake Rose laughed and Cap barked as if to say, "Go to bed."

"It's been quite a day Ally. You should head up to bed."

Too tired to argue Ally lazily rose to her feet and turned towards the house before abruptly turning back, "Do you sleep?"

With a smirk Rose answered, "Yes, but I don't need much."

With a shrug Ally headed inside and was asleep before her head hit the pillow. Rose sat patiently waiting for the fire to burn itself out before covering it with sand and water. It was no surprise when Rose felt herself begin to dissolve into the sweet floral scent that encircled her. The familiar sensation of evaporating from one reality to another was old habit.

Trying to bring her surroundings into focus Rose recognized Dalton Manor's silhouette in the distance. Waiting for her eyes to clear made her other senses more acute. The strong odor of a horse drew closer while listening to Edmunds voice inside her head saying, "Helene is asking for you."

The exhaustion felt from the day she had with Ally dissipated. Then she discovered she was now seated on her horse. With a swift kick, she pushed her horse into a full gallop and headed straight for the manor. A stable boy was waiting for her near the front steps. After nearly jumping from the saddle she quickly raced to the door holding her ruffled dress out of the way.

Before she could knock Edmund opened the front door looking as debonair as ever. Only now his face beamed with love. His eyes overflowed with exuberance. A sight for sore eyes and Rose couldn't help but smile. No matter how much time passed between hosts or how distressed Edmund became when Helene was away. He came back to life when she returned.

"She's in the parlor," boasted Edmund pleased with her quick recovery.

"That is wonderful," exclaimed Rose.

Entering the parlor Rose all but jumped for joy when Helene greeted her with her priceless smile. She summoned Rose to her with the simple gesture of extending her hand. With a gentle whisper Helene welcomed her friend, "You're safe."

"Of course I am Helene please don't fuss over me," encouraged Rose pulling a chair next to the couch asking, "How are you feeling? I've been so worried."

"I'm a little weak, but I'm feeling much better. Dear Edmund looks after me every minute. He won't leave my side."

"That sounds like him."

"My fever caused me to have nightmares. One especially frightening dream kept reoccurring," Helene's eyes became sad and tearful.

"They were just bad dreams Helene nothing more," interrupted Rose.

"I know, but they seemed so real," Helene's voice faded in and out causing her to repeatedly clear her throat. "Where is Maxwell?" she struggled to get out.

"He's away on business," assured Rose.

Helene released a calming breath then closed her eyes and let her head fall against the couch. Edmund thinking Helene has passed out rushed to her side. Hovering over his beloved he glared at Rose with questioning eyes.

Helene lovingly kissed Edmunds cheek making him turn his focus solely on her. Desperate to help he asked, "What can I do my love?"

"Perhaps I need to rest for a while."

That simple statement sent Edmund into action. In one fluid motion, he scooped up Helene blanket and all into his mighty arms and carried her up the stairs to their room. Helene waved goodbye to Rose and nestled her head into the crook of Edmunds neck feeling completely protected and loved.

After the two of them disappeared from view Rose headed out to the garden. To her surprise she did not return to the beach so she wandered around the well-kept garden. Her long stem rose bush front and center was now surrounded by dozens of varying flowers. Each and every one of them held a story all its own. The large oak that offered the garden partial shade during the heat of day was the oldest vegetation near the garden. With its massive trunk and expansive crown of branches the mighty oak commanded attention. Standing proud and protective over the ever-growing magical garden.

"Lady Rose," Arthur's voice rang with excitement.

Rose turned to greet Arthur, "Oh it's so good to see you."

"Yes, it's been much too long my lady."

Nodding in agreement Rose questioned, "How's Helene doing with this transition?"

"She's doing as well as can be expected. It always takes longer than Mr. Dalton would like it to take, but he knows the routine."

"I was a little surprised to be here so soon. I was afraid something had gone wrong."

"I must admit she did give us all a bit of a scare. Physically her host body is incredibly strong, but Helene's repeated nightmares are causing unusual bouts of fear. Edmund was concerned the lack of rest would make the new body expire before it's time."

"Is that why I'm here?" asked Rose.

"Yes, Helene's main concern was for your safety. Nothing short of seeing you face to face was going to ease her mind...."

"Now she can get the rest she needs," broke in Edmund.

"I'm happy I could help," Rose curtsied.

"We all are. Arthur, would you excuse Rose and I?" Everything about Edmund displayed a seriousness.

Arthur retreated into the house leaving the two of them standing there in utter silence. The hush between them lasted much longer than Rose was comfortable with. Edmunds expression gave no clue to his thoughts. He began wandering through the garden enjoying its beauty and ever so carefully tending to any need. Although the garden had a full-time gardener it wasn't uncommon to catch Edmund looking after the flowers himself.

"Rose I want to apologize to you," Edmunds voice was sincere.

Taken back by his words Rose stood frozen in place. Unable to say a single word. In all this time, Mr. Dalton had never apologized to her for anything.

"Please forgive me for not thanking you nearly enough. You have been nothing but helpful in bringing my Helene back to me time and time again. Without your willingness to assist me I may have lost her forever."

"Of course Mr. Dalton. You don't have to apologize. I made you a promise and I intend on keeping it. Seeing Helene alive and well is thanks enough. The love you two share is one of a kind. I shudder to think of the pain she would suffer if that was ever taken from her."

"Thank you Rose. I feel the same about the love she has for you. You are truly her sister and she would be devastated if something were to ever happen to you. Her concern for you had us worried to the point of thinking this switch may fail."

"What do you suppose caused such strong fears?" asked Rose wondering if there was anything she could do to help.

"I'm not entirely sure. I thought I had them under control until today. Throughout the day her nightmares only got worse and the fear of losing her very best friend overpowered her. Nothing I said would console her. That's why I decided to bring you to her."

"Very unusual."

"Extremely," agreed Edmund. "Was there anything unusual that happened with Ally today?"

"Not that I can think of. I shared the day I helped Helene come back to you. Something I've done before although not often. As I mentioned in our conversation the other day Ally is having a particularly difficult time. Not only is her body extremely strong as Arthur mentioned, but so is her will. I decided to share my part in helping you bring Helene back because I thought it would help her accept what's happened. Besides, I still believe she could be an asset to you," added Rose.

Mulling over Rose's answer Edmund lazily twiddled a fallen leaf between his fingers. Rose never ceased to be amazed at his magical power. She began to feel herself dematerializing as he remained deep in thought. Rose soon found herself back on the beach. Edmund had returned her sensing she needed to return even though he was mediating hard on whatever was on his mind.

"You weren't kidding when you said you don't need much sleep," teased Ally joining her on the sand.

"How would you like to go to breakfast?" asked Rose now knowing what Edmund had been thinking.

"Go to breakfast?" repeated Ally.

"Yes, I think it would be all right. In all honesty, I think it would be a good thing for us both."

"Where could we go?" Ally asked with a rejuvenated energy in her voice.

"This time it'll be my choice, but very soon I'll let you chose."

Unable to hide her excitement Ally hugged Rose saying, "Let me go get changed then we'll go," halfway up the porch steps Ally turned and asked, "What should I wear?"

"I think you'll find an appropriate dress hanging on the back of your bedroom door," answered Rose beaming at the sight of Ally's eagerness.

Chapter Ten

Edmund sat peacefully watching Helene slumber well into the night. Whenever he noticed her begin to wince he joined her in her dream. Helene stood in the Griggs home shouting for Rose. The house was empty, dark and silent. Helene's voice echoed throughout the rooms creating a spooky feel. All the elaborate and ornate decor gave the mansion a museum feel much to Rose's dismay. It wasn't anything like the warm inviting home Helene had created at Dalton Manor.

Helene's spine chilling calls for her friend became too much for Edmund. Cautiously he eased himself close to her making sure not to startle her. Their uniquely devoted bond kicked in and Helene instinctively turned into her husband's protective embrace. Her body shuddered in his arms before melting into him.

"There you go my love," reassured Edmund.

No words needed to be spoken. Helene was home in his arms. Her fears ceased bringing her back to a restful sleep and she could still feel Edmund holding her secure when she began to wake. Helene soon realized she wasn't dreaming. Her husband was truly lying next to her with his arms wrapped snuggly around her. With a sigh Helene released all remaining tension soothing her nerves entirely.

Bestowing a tender kiss on her hand Edmund asked, "How are you feeling my love?"

"Better now that I'm here with you," she murmured.

"You will always be here with me," declared Edmund with such authority Helene almost forgot about the nightmare she was having.

"I have no doubt," agreed Helene, "It is not losing you that troubles me........it's losing Rose."

"I would never let that happen my dearest you must trust me on that."

"My mind knows that but in my heart, I feel like she's slipping away. The nightmares may vary, but one thing holds true she's gone. No matter where I search she's nowhere to be found."

"My dear sweet Helene, Maxwell is gone on business I can't even remember the last time he was in town. Rose is perfectly safe."

"That's just it Edmund. These nightmares are different. Maxwell is suspiciously absent from them. It's as if there's a new threat. Something I can't see, but I can feel," Helene expressed and showed Edmund the goosebumps that were forming on her arms.

Over the next hour Edmund calmed her fears lulling her back to sleep. Uneasy that a similar nightmare would haunt her until morning he remained in her dreams lovingly watching over her throughout the night. He kept her happily busy until sunrise. They went horseback riding, enjoyed a picnic by the lake then Helene joyfully played the piano while Edmund sang along. Sacrificing one or several nights sleep for his beloved to keep her safe was something he did willingly.

Within the week Helene was stronger. She had even made a few trips to the stables to visit with Storm. His extraordinarily gentle nature around her only made Edmund wonder all that much more. What really happened on the day of her death? The special attachment they shared had been strengthened after Helene's passing. After her first visit to the stables Storm's emotions were uncontainable when away from Helene. If allowed he would have stood guard by her bed, but he settled for standing below their bedroom window where she could answer his neighs or peek down at him.

The unknown cause of that tragic day made Edmund continuously worry. Helene had no knowledge of Edmund keeping watch over the two of them whenever they headed out for a ride. Edmund would forever make sure the events of that dire afternoon were not repeated. Not once had there been the tiniest reason for concern. This only added to the frustration he felt about not knowing what truly happened.

Resembling a ray of sunshine Helene descended the stairway humming a favorite song. The high collared yellow dress cinched at the waist with a bright red band complimented Helene's tiny waist. Rows of small red diamond shapes flowed from below the band to the bottom red ruffle of the dress. The vividly bright dress paled in comparison to Helene's cheerful expression.

Arthur greeted her, "Good morning Mrs. Dalton," stopping her in her tracks.

"Arthur, we've gone over this. Please call me Helene," she scolded with a heart melting smile.

"Of course my lady."

Giggling at his sideway nod she knew he would never do as she wished. It was improper for him to address her so casually, but this was part of their morning routine.

Helene joined Edmund on the porch where breakfast was being served. Sharing a passionate kiss Helene and Edmund made the servant blush before returning to the kitchen. Sitting down Helene noticed a small pink envelope tucked under her plate. Smiling gleefully at her husband she asked, "What have you done now?"

"I know our anniversary is only days away my beloved, but I can honestly say that is not from me."

Baffled and intrigued Helene broke the wax seal and peered inside. She quickly recognized the insignia from the shop where she had bought Edmund's anniversary gift. Folding the envelope closed she tucked it back under her plate and began fiddling with her napkin.

Teasingly Edmund questioned her about its content until Helene's face was flush. She was soon stammering incomplete sentences trying to avoid the topic of their anniversary. Finding her irresistible he swooped her off her chair sending the basket of sweet breads into the air and placed her gently on his lap.

"You're laughing at me," she retorted doing her best to appear angered.

"I don't know what I did do deserve you my love," said Edmund giving her a thorough squeeze.

Peacefully they held each other and watched the morning sun climb high in the sky. Swans filled the lake appearing to chase the sunlight glimmering on the tranquil waves. Everything was right with the world. Helene glowed with happy thoughts of celebrating their first year of marriage bringing her back to the envelope's contents.

"I suppose we should finish our breakfast," suggested Helene freeing herself from Edmunds arms.

With his plate empty, Edmund rose to his feet saying he had work to complete. Before leaving he earnestly kissed Helene's mouth like he had on their wedding day. Leaving her breathless and feeling overjoyed with her reaction Edmund headed for his study. He knew Helene wasn't enjoying her meal. She was completely preoccupied with the unknown contents of the envelope below her plate. Helene listened carefully until she heard Edmund announce his wishes to be undisturbed for the next few hours. Now she felt secure in opening the letter and reading its full contents.

Dear Mrs. Dalton,

The silver goblet you ordered has been completed. I will be away for the next few days. I've given orders to my errand boy to bring the goblet to the manor. He was given strict instructions to go to the servant entrance and to give the box to your housemaid.

Sincerely,

Mr. Brewer

Helene's heart raced as she ran inside to find her housemaid. Elizabeth had not mentioned a box being delivered when she helped Helene dress that morning causing concern for the goblets whereabouts. The look of panic on Helene's face was quickly erased when her housemaid presented her with the box after she burst into the bedroom.

Locking the bedroom door Helene snatched the box from Elizabeth's hands saying, "Thank you so much," then she sat nervously on the edge of the bed. With fumbling fingers Helene pried the box open, removed the velvet bag and carefully pulled the goblet from within.

"Oh my lady that is gorgeous."

Helene pleased with Mr. Brewer's work and Elizabeth's honest reaction became giddy with excitement. She wasn't sure she could wait the couple days until their wedding anniversary. How she longed to give it to him this instant. Anticipating the elation on Edmunds face when he read the inscription brought happy tears to her eyes.

Edmund sat in his study feeling content and pleased with himself knowing Helene was safe in their bedroom admiring the goblet he had sent to the house. Preventing her from traveling into town for the gift was his first order of business upon her returning to him. Every day ahead was filled with the unknown, but he knew all too well what happened long ago on this very day and he never wanted to risk history repeating itself. Assured that his beloved was safe at home gave him the relief he needed to relax and the following days passed slowly but uneventfully.

Tip toeing back into the bedroom Edmund admired his handy work. Fragrant floral bouquets of every color, shape and size filled the room. They lined the dressers, sat on window sills and covered the floor leaving only a narrow path from the bed to the door. Helene's nose began to twitch upon discovering the aromatic fragrance. Rolling onto her back she enjoyed a lengthy stretch concluding with a good rub of her sleepy eyes. Edmund chuckled at the sight making Helene open her eyes to look at him. With her puffy eyes and mussed hair, he fell deeper in love with her. This untidy half asleep woman was his very reason for living.

"Happy anniversary my beloved Helene," beamed Edmund holding a tray filled with all her favorites. Fresh fruit, ham, eggs and a variety of still warm muffins was sat in front of her.

"Happy anniversary my darling," Helene said squeezing his hand.

"Would you like coffee or tea this morning?"

"Tea please," answered Helene trying unsuccessfully to smooth her mane of hair.

"You look beautiful my love," declared Edmund with a loving smile.

Reminiscing over breakfast about their wedding day brought laughter and joy to them both. It didn't seem possible to either of them that an entire year had passed. They had seen so much in their travels and grown to appreciate their life together more each day. Helene reveled in her absolute happiness.

Taking Edmunds face into her hands she looked deep into his eyes and whispered, "I will love you forever darling. Even death won't keep us apart. You will always have my heart. There's nothing in the world that could change that."

Her words carried far more truth in them than she understood. Edmund kissed her lips firmly hiding his misty eyes. Pushing the tray clear from her lap she pulled Edmund close urging him back into bed.

Morning became afternoon before Helene readied herself for the day. Elizabeth buttoned every last button before tying a perfect bow on the bustle of Helene's dress. Admiring the finished look the two of them grinned at Helene's reflection.

"Elizabeth would you fetch Edmund's gift?"

"With pleasure my lady."

In no time Elizabeth returned with the skillfully wrapped gift with its oversized gold ribbon dwarfing the box. After a careful inspection of the present Helene was ready, "I've never been so excited to give someone a gift."

"Your face says it all," snickered Elizabeth who had lost her love after decades of marriage. Seeing Helene so very happy reminded her of what she once had. Now an old widow she felt honored to be around young love and to be reminded daily of how grand it was. Elizabeth would be forever thankful that she too had experienced true love. A love which is pure and true was something Elizabeth knew was all too rare. She counted herself extremely fortunate to not only have experienced that type of love herself, but to witness the same type of love between Edmund and Helene.

It was no surprise when Helene found Edmund sitting on the bench placed at the sight where they exchanged wedding vows and it triggered heavenly wedding flashbacks. Her regal Edmund standing motionless at the end of the aisle entranced by her approaching beauty. His adoring eyes fixated on hers pulling her towards him erased everyone around them. In that moment, nothing existed for Helene except Edmund. The entire world disappeared leaving the two of them in a place all their own.

Edmund's compliment brought her back to the present, "You grow more breathtaking with each passing day my love."

On cue Helene blushed and lowered her gaze only to bring her warm chestnut eyes back to his and say, "Thank you as always darling."

"What do you have there?"

"It is your anniversary gift," announced Helene pridefully.

"What a happy coincidence I have your gift as well."

"Oh please Edmund open your gift first."

"Your wish is my command," replied Edmund with a bow. Methodically Edmund opened his gift deliberately driving Helene crazy. He roared with laughter when she lost control and offered him assistance ripping the paper away from the box with both hands.

Helene's excitement kept her from breathing while Edmund read the inscription out loud,

"To my darling Edmund,
Happy Anniversary my beloved.
Yours forever, Helene."

Although he had the engraving memorized he always made sure to read it like it was the first time he had seen it. His thankful reaction always fresh and new to Helene leaving her brimming with ecstatic love.

"Now it is your turn, my sweet Helene," said Edmund pulling a small black velvet box from his pocket and handing it to his love, but not before adoringly kissing her hand.

Taking the box Helene's eyes began tearing up with eager anticipation. It didn't matter to her what was inside the box. What mattered was Edmund her beloved husband had given it to her. Helene's heart swelled with a single thought, "This was to be the first of a lifetime of anniversary's they would share."

Chapter Eleven

With deliberate and slow breathes Edmund took in every move of Helene's dainty fingers watching them leisurely trace the velvet box. The expression on her face filled him with such love his vision blurred from the tears building in his eyes. His Helene had returned because of Rose's help. Once again they were celebrating their first wedding anniversary. Something that had been taken from them both; although Helene had no idea that was the case. Drying his eyes so he could focus on Helene brought an exuberant smile to her face. Losing themselves in each other's stare reminded them both of how truly deep their love was.

Blowing a kiss to Edmund before carefully opening the jewelry box was a tradition. One Helene started when he had given her his first gift. They could remember it like it was yesterday. Walking several feet in front of their chaperones Edmund guided Helene over to a park bench. Sitting an appropriate distance from her he bashfully handed her a small wrapped box.

"What is this?" blushed Helene.

With his award-winning smile and a wink of his eye he said, "You will have to open it to find out."

A mixture of emotions tossed Helene's stomach about. She knew it was too soon in the courtship to be an engagement ring, but a large part of her hoped beyond hope that it would be. An internal argument between her logical mind and emotional heart ensued.

Growing concerned that he had moved too fast in presenting her with a gift. Edmund began to squirm uneasily on the bench hoping the chaperones had not seen the exchange. Was he mistaken on how he believed Helene to feel about him?

With as much control as she could muster Helene smiled. Her mouth quivered despite her effort to appear at ease. She saw something in Edmunds eyes that she'd only seen in her dreams. A heart wrenching sadness had clouded his eyes, filling her heart with misery and breaking it into pieces. Slyly she watched the chaperones and carefully picked the perfect moment to blow Edmund a kiss as not to be caught. With that small and sincere gesture his happiness reached new heights and he eagerly waited for her to open his gift.

Inside the meticulously wrapped box was a skillfully made courtship brooch. The white porcelain oval trimmed with gilded edging pictured a young couple strolling in a park. The artist's talent clearly evident in the fine details of the couple's facial expressions and elaborate clothing. It was the most beautiful brooch Helene had ever seen. Far above the expert craftsmanship, what Helene appreciated most was what it represented for the two of them. It was becoming clear that Mr. Dalton planned on making Helene his Mrs. Dalton.

With a gleeful giggle Helene exclaimed, "Oh Mr. Dalton it's beautiful. Thank you so very much. I love it," then boastfully she added, "I will wear it proudly."

Overjoyed Edmund jumped to his feet and with a zealous smile summoned the chaperones over to them. Cora hurried over and sat next to Helene admiring the gift she held in her hand. In no time Cora pinned the brooch onto her daughter's high lace collar. She then took a few steps back and admired the meaningful gift.

Now here they were husband and wife celebrating their first wedding anniversary, exchanging gifts and being so much more in love than that day on the park bench. Leaving her trip down memory lane Helene lifted the top of the box exposing the gorgeous silver locket Edmund had made especially for her.

"It's exquisite my darling," squealed Helene her voice high with excitement.

"I'm so glad it pleases you," answered Edmund his voice cracking with emotion.

Throwing her arms around his sturdy neck Helene hugged Edmund with all her might. With closed eyes, she felt his breathing match hers and swore their heartbeats did the same. Neither wanting to end the embrace they chose to savor it for as long as they could.

"My apologies Mr. Dalton and my lady," interjected Arthur bowing his head respectfully.

Unhappy about the sudden interruption Edmund scowled, "This better be of upmost importance."

"It's Miss. Elizabeth sir..." Arthurs voice matched his distressed expression.

"Elizabeth?" confirmed Helene.

"Yes, my lady. We found her unconscious at the top of the stairs."

Together Edmund and Helene dashed toward the house with Arthur close behind. Elizabeth had been moved to her room where she now laid resting. Her face void of almost all color she forced a smile for Helene when she burst into the room.

"Elizabeth," cooed Helene cupping her hand in hers. Elizabeth's cold clammy skin sent fear throughout Helene.

Elizabeth repeatedly tried to clear her throat causing a terrible coughing spell. At last she caught her breath and spoke softly, "Helene, cherish every moment." Her voice fading with every word and her eyes bouncing between Helene and Edmund making it clear as to what she was referring to.

Beginning to cry Helene studied Elizabeth's final moments. There wasn't any fear or pain exhibited on her face. With a calm peaceful expression and eyes fixated on something or someone in front of her she gasped, "Martin," with her final breath.

Helene knew all too well who Martin was. Elizabeth spoke of her late husband on a daily basis. Turning in the direction of Elizabeth's stare she expected to see Martin standing there greeting his wife with waiting arms.

Rushing into Edmunds caress Helene felt secure. Sobbing a mixture of sorrowful and happy tears Helene leaned into Edmunds solid chest. Second only to Cora, Elizabeth was another source of age-old female common sense. Helene had grown to rely on her almost weekly pearls of wisdom. There wouldn't be a day where she wouldn't miss Elizabeth's smile, thoughtfulness or little gems of insight. She would be forever missed, but Helene found great joy in the thought of Elizabeth and Martin being together at long last. Picturing them in a warm hug after all these years gave Helene some peace over losing her trusted and beloved housemaid.

Edmund envied Elizabeth being reunited with her husband. Immortality had lost all its appeal when Helene lost her life. He always knew it was only a matter of time before death separated them, but he assumed they would have a long life together before he faced losing her. Helene's fatal accident proved his assumption to be terribly wrong. Now he spent nearly every moment worrying about her safety and constantly planning for a replacement body. Leaving very little time for him to completely relax and simply enjoy having Helene with him.

Rose had continued to do her job exceptionally well over the years which helped to ease Edmund's mind. Helene was rarely trapped in the locket for more than a few weeks or so after a body gave out. Suddenly Rose's comment about Ally having a talent he could use completely distracted him.

Noticing his distant gaze Helene whispered, "Edmund are you all right?"

"Yes, my love. How are you feeling?"

"I can't believe she's gone. She was her usual happy self this morning," Helene glanced back at Elizabeth whose eyes had been closed by Arthur. "It doesn't seem real."

Speaking from more experience than Helene understood Edmund agreed, "We never know when our time is up my love. Elizabeth was correct in saying we should cherish every moment."

"We will Edmund," promised Helene before placing an emotion filled kiss on his lips.

Edmund took the jewelry box from Helene's grip and reopened it. Without saying a word Helene turned, lifted her thick long hair allowing Edmund to place the locket around her neck. She pressed the locket into her bosom causing her sad tears to be replaced by happy ones.

Knowing there was nothing more she could do Helene said a woeful goodbye to Elizabeth. After leaving the room the staff quickly began death rituals from stopping the clocks to hanging black ribbon on the knob of the front door. Not one detail was overlooked.

The manor had gone from a day of celebration to a day of mourning within hours. This was not the anniversary anyone had planned. Hearts broke for Helene and Edmund as their special day was overshadowed by death. Stunning photographs of the two of them were turned face down and the mirrors were covered in dark fabric. All the rituals stole what little bliss they had left from this morning.

Edmund was dumbfounded by the unexpected turn of events. In all the years of bringing Helene back to him Elizabeth never had so much as a cold. Unsure how this could have happened or what to do next Edmund found himself in unfamiliar territory. Clearing his head made him notice Helene was nowhere to be found. Rushing from room to room throughout the manor he began shouting for her, "Helene!"

Arthur stopped him in his tracks and calmly stated, "Miss Helene is on the porch swing".

Patting Arthur on the shoulder Edmund ran outside to find his wife curled up in one corner of the swing with her dress pulled up around her legs and feet. Her eyes now beginning to swell from crying Edmund sat on the opposite end of the swing warming her tiny feet in his hands. Remaining silent he gave her the time she needed to absorb the day's events.

He was surprised by her words when she finally spoke. In all seriousness Helene calmly said, "I'm glad Elizabeth is where she should be. At long last she is with Martin the love of her life."

"You're not bothered by her passing?"

"I'm going to miss her so very much and I'm heartbroken that she's gone, but..." Helene stopped turned her face from Edmund and struggled to go on. "I believe it would literally kill me if I ever lost you."

Tenderly he held a kiss on Helene's forehead for longer than normal helping him to hide his gloomy expression from her. Internally Edmund wrestled with the memory of losing his wife and he knew she would see that he was hiding something. He disliked the turn the conversation had taken, but agreed with Helene knowing full well that if he wasn't immortal her death would have killed him.

"I would want it to kill me," remarked Helene in a monotonic tone.

Dazed by her comment Edmund shuttered at the thought of her wishing for death, "My darling, don't speak like that."

"I'm serious Edmund life wouldn't be worth living without you. I would die of a broken heart."

Her words cut him like a knife. That was the reality of his very existence. Living an eternal life with a broken heart knowing his wife was actually dead. Finding a way to bring her back over and over wasn't ideal, but not doing so was out of the question. On exceptionally rare occasions, Edmund would be the only one who could see through the mask that everyone else saw. The strange face and body being used would momentarily peak through the magic tormenting him with the fact that it wasn't truly Helene. At least not physically, but it was Helene's soul held safely inside the otherwise shell of a body. That fact alone caused the body double to move, speak and laugh as if it were actually Helene which helped hide the truth. Edmund was sure he would have lost his mind without the exceedingly powerful spell he used. The incredibly robust magic was strong enough to keep the truth hidden from view for the vast majority of the time. More importantly it never allowed anyone else to see Helene was not really there.

"I understand my love if I ever lost you I couldn't go on," whispered Edmund in her ear.

A sad smile crossed her face, "Let's hope that day is far, far off in the future. After we've had a family and watched our grandchildren grow up and get married.

"Agreed," was all Edmund could muster. Quickly taking the focus off of them he questioned, "Did you notice anything unusual about Elizabeth this morning?" his curiosity about what caused her sudden passing was growing in intensity.

"No, she was her usual self. I know our anniversary was bittersweet for Elizabeth. She bubbled with joy at our happiness, but it also brought back the pain of losing her true love. She missed Martin beyond words. Rarely if ever did she speak of the day she lost him. It was far too painful for her. The memories she did share were of their happy times. I hope I never forget her contagious smile when she spoke of Martin."

"Elizabeth was a remarkable woman."

"Yes she was and now she's with her remarkable husband where she longed to be and for that reason I'm happy for her."

Helene's selflessness was one of the many reasons Edmund loved her. There was no hiding the pain she felt about losing Elizabeth, but true to form Helene chose to remove her feelings from the situation and focus on someone she loved.

With a beaming smile Helene shared the mental picture she was focused on with Edmund, "I can see them together hand in hand walking into the sunset."

Caressing Helene's hand Edmund smirked at her adorably cliché comment. "Speaking of sunsets we're expected at the Copper Tavern for our anniversary dinner. Would you like me to send notice that we're canceling?"

Helene hesitated when Elizabeth's words "Cherish every moment" came to mind. Although going about the rest of the day as planned felt wrong Helene couldn't keep Elizabeth's words from looping around in her head. Conflicted with wanting to celebrate her anniversary and honoring Elizabeth she sat motionless unable to answer. Her heart debated with itself until she heard Elizabeth's voice from behind her, "Helene cherish every moment." With a jolt, she turned towards the voice and caught the smell of Elizabeth's favorite perfume.

Helene unafraid answered back trusting that Elizabeth was listening. "Yes, ma'am," she agreed. Truly feeling that Elizabeth would be upset if she didn't celebrate her first wedding anniversary.

Edmund unfazed by Helene speaking to the empty space behind her appeared to be listening to her conversation with Elizabeth and patiently waited for her answer.   Sensing Elizabeth's presence Helene smiled saying, "No Edmund we should go. Elizabeth wants us to."

"I agree my love, she does."

Chapter Twelve

Ally ran upstairs to her bedroom gushing with excitement. Where could Rose be taking her? Would there be others when they arrived at their destination? Was there a way out?

The modest sun dress highlighted Ally's defined arms and calves. It was a bit longer than Ally typically wore making her feel somewhat uncomfortable in the dress. Focusing on the delicate pattern and sweetheart neckline made her notice the newfound necklace shining against her tan skin. Ally had to admit it was an outfit she would buy for herself even with the longer length.

Slipping on a casual pair of sandals she found tucked in the closet Ally hurried down stairs. Rose had changed into a long cotton skirt and black blouse. On anyone else the simple outfit would be overlooked, however Rose made it look like a runway hit. Her subtle makeup, simple half up hair style combined with her model figure and face would have destroyed Ally's confidence in her appearance if she hadn't grown accustomed to this scenario. Ally was the "girl next door" pretty type who was fortunate enough to room with the gorgeous girl who never took herself too seriously.

"Very pretty," complimented Rose.

"Thank you, it's not too long?" asked Ally sheepishly.

"Not for where we're going?"

A small part of Ally was terrified as to where they were going, but a much bigger part of her was filled with an insurmountable feeling of anticipation, "Where are we going?"

"Come with me and you'll see," answered Rose heading down to the shoreline.

Fog began to roll in as they got further and further from the house until it was no longer visible through the haze. The waves soothed Ally's growing nerves with their rhythmic sound. Soon the fog became so thick she could hardly see Rose walking beside her.

"How can you see where we're going?" Ally asked peering into the white murkiness that surrounded them still unable to make anything out.

"As long as we stay at the water's edge and continue walking we're on course."

"Are we almost there? I'm too hungry to hike much further for breakfast," joked Ally attempting to hide her mounting fear.

"Yes, just a little longer," reassured Rose.

It wasn't another five or six steps before the sun burst through the fog. Ally quickly spotted an old steamship tied to a large dock. Black smoke bellowed from the smoke stack alluding to the fact that there were people on board. Ally pulled her sandals off quickened her step and giggled when she heard men yelling orders from the deck of the ship.

Nearly running when they reached the dock Ally stopped dead in her tracks when she saw a man waving at them from the bow. All the excitement she felt about seeing another person instantly shifted to fear of the unknown. Who was on that ship? Was she putting herself in more danger?

"Is something wrong Ally?" Rose questioned.

Before Ally could answer a member of the crew was cheerfully on his way to join them. His uniform pressed and tidy kept him from running towards them. His attire shouted dignity and structure not exuberant behavior. Standing tall with perfect posture he looked very much the proper sailor except that is for the large grin on his face. With his back towards the ship he playfully winked at Rose.

"Ally I'd like you to meet Seaman Kidd. He will escort us aboard the ship," stated Rose as if there was nothing out of the ordinary about the morning.

"It's a pleasure to make your acquaintance," greeted Seaman Kidd before moving between the women and offering his arms to them.

In autopilot mode Ally lifted her hand almost shoulder height into the crook of his arm. She felt like a child next to him and even Rose seemed shorter. Although he looked close to their age there was something in his eyes that reminded her of her grandfather's eyes. It was only then that she realized Rose's beautiful hazel eyes had the same bygone appearance. An elderly wisdom and strength from lessons learned over the years. Busy considering what this meant Ally hadn't noticed the casual light hearted conversation Seaman Kidd and Rose were involved in. By the time she broke free from her thoughts they were halfway up the boarding plank.

Once aboard Ally repeatedly apologized for not greeting Seaman Kidd and completely forgetting her manners. No matter how hard she tried there was no way to understand how she was a prisoner inside of a locket. Now she was faced with the fact that it wasn't only she and Rose but an entire world or so it seemed.

Seaman Kidd interrupted Ally's string of apologies, "You are as sweet as I've heard Ally. There is no need to apologize to me we all understand what you're going through," and with that being said men and women exited doorways, came down the steps of the upper deck and emerged from below deck.

"Welcome Miss Ally," cheered the crowd simultaneously.

Rose took Ally's arm to steady her as the shock became overwhelming, "How about that breakfast? This is too much to handle on an empty stomach," said Rose.

In a whirlwind of activity Ally was ushered through beautifully carved walnut doors into a large and elegant dining room. The room glowed with a romantic feel from the oil lamps scattered about. Ally looked at everything surrounding her but saw nothing. It was all too much to take in. Her legs weakened and her knees buckled then with a thud Ally landed in the seat pulled out for her by a waiter.

Rose teased, "Are you seasick already?"

"Seasick?" snapped Ally. Her anger clearing her thoughts, "What's going on?"

"We're going to have breakfast like I said."

"Really? That's all you can say?" but before Rose could answer Ally continued on her rant. Her emotional rollercoaster gaining speed, "Who are all these people and where exactly are we?" Ally's voice now booming in panicked anger.

That explosive question left everyone frozen in place creating an eerie silence. Like puppets on a string all controlled by one puppeteer every one of them slowly turned their expressionless faces towards Ally. Episodes of old black and white horror shows came to mind immobilizing Ally in her fear. Incapable of moving or breathing normal she came close to fainting. The usual floral scent filled the ship soothing Ally's nerves like the day she moved into the dorm. Closing her eyes and breathing in the sweet fragrance Ally went back to that day full of hopes and dreams.

"Ally you don't have to stop dreaming you can have the life you've always wanted. All you have to do is accept that you're here and make your dreams come true," said a strong deep male voice from inside her head. Ally knew she had heard that voice before but couldn't remember where? Strangely it suddenly didn't matter nothing mattered other than she was hungry.

"So what's good for breakfast?" asked Ally with a smile.

"Oh everything is good Ally. You haven't eaten until you've had one of Chef Davis's meals," exclaimed Rose filled with jubilation.

"Wonderful. I'm famished."

With that the rest of the morning went off without a hitch. A full course breakfast like none Ally had ever experienced passed before her. Laughter and conversation between bites made the meal even better.

Sitting back feeling fuller than she liked Ally noticed an interesting tie clip on the gentleman across the table from her. The gold clover sparkled against his black tie, "What an unusual but stunning tie clip," commented Ally.

"Thank you Miss Ally," was all he said before excusing himself.

Ally watched him walk away and noticed how well dressed he and everyone else was. The men were all in suits and ties the women wore dresses as long or longer than hers. Curious Ally asked, "Does this ship have a dress code?"

Rose was quick to answer, "Not necessarily a dress code it's merely the style of clothing people are used to."

"What people?"

"All those aboard The Vision."

"The Vision?"

Casually Rose replied, "The ships name Ally. We're on Mr. Daltons ship The Vision."

"So everyone here is dead?" murmured Ally afraid of the answer.

"Do dead people eat breakfast?"

Rose's answer did little to calm Ally. "Well I'm not alive anymore Rose and I ate so what exactly am I?"

Disregarding Ally's question Rose posed a question of her own, "Do you see any other unique pieces of jewelry Ally?"

Now knowing what to look for Ally soon noticed everyone had at least one piece of jewelry on. The women were easy. Their earrings or bracelets all glistened as if directly under a spotlight. The men proved to be more difficult prompting Rose to explain that she needed to look for stickpins, watch chains and cuff links, a "man's type" of jewelry as Rose put it. All the kinds of jewelry men rarely wore in Ally's time.

"What do you see in common with all the different jewelry pieces?" Rose's tone was serious and direct.

It didn't take long to discover the similarities in the jewelry. "They all have flowers or leaves of some sort."

"What is on your necklace Ally?"

"Pink daisy's."

"What do you smell when Mr. Dalton is near or when he summons me?"

"Flowers. The most sweetly scented flowers I've ever smelled."

Rose sat quiet watching and waiting for Ally to try and put things together. In her waiting Rose recalled how lonely the locket had been when she first arrived and how she loved that it was now filled with life. People who understood and knew firsthand what she had gone through. What a wonderful gift to not spend eternity alone.

With frightened eyes Ally asked, "He's taken the lives of all these people? How many times has he brought Helene back and why the men?"

"Unlike you and I Ally most of those here were not used to bring Helene back."

"He's a narcissistic monster!" shouted Ally running out to the deck noticing they were in open water. "When did we leave the dock?"

Rose stood several feet behind her answering, "Shortly after you boarded."

Ally collapsed on the deck tormented by what her life had become. Releasing a mixture of screams and sobs into her hands she wished for nothing more than to be back home in Glenbrook. Drunk dad and all. She had been so completely wrong in thinking her life couldn't get any worse than it was.

"Allow me to help you." It was that rich husky voice again.

Even through her unclear vision she could see those unforgettable sapphire eyes from the Halloween party. Forcefully wiping her eyes to help clear them she allowed him to assist her, forgetting what happened the last time she accepted his help. Standing to her feet Ally looked up into the striking face of Edmund Dalton. "It's you," was all she could get out. Even considering him the monster she thought him to be she found herself enamored by his blinding good looks.

Before anything else could be said they were zipping through the sky in what felt like a protective bubble. Sunrises and sunsets flashed before them making Ally nauseous from it all. No longer able to contain her breakfast Ally vomited into the water.

"Are you okay Ally?" asked Rose pulling Ally's hair back from her face.

After emptying her stomach into the waves Ally used the glass of water Seaman Kidd handed her to rinse out her mouth. This kept Ally from getting sick again.

"He was here," Ally exclaimed searching the deck for Mr. Dalton.

"Who was here?" asked both Rose & Seaman Kidd.

"Mr. Dalton."

The two looked at each other doubtfully doing their best to reassure Ally that she had been alone on the deck the entire time.

"He whisked me off into the sky and it made me sick. It kept switching from day to night so quickly I couldn't take it." Ally saw no change in Rose's expression. "You have to believe me," pleaded Ally.

"I believe you think you saw Mr. Dalton," replied Rose.

"Oh Rose please. You're all I have left of my sanity. Please tell me you believe me," Ally implored.

Rose looked Ally straight in the eyes saying, "I believe you Ally." Rose understood that Ally needed her to believe far more than Rose needed to know if Mr. Dalton had truly been there.

Ally mouthed the words, "Thank you," through quivering lips.

Moving to the upper deck Rose found a bench for them to relax on. No one disturbed them out of fear that Ally would breakdown again. Her strong will and determination to find a way out was making her transition much more difficult than most. By this time the newcomer in the locket was normally well on their way to creating the world they had always wished for. Having every wish come true by simply thinking about it was in itself a dream come true for most. What interested Mr. Dalton about Ally in the first place was now proving to be a rather large obstacle in her progress.

Ally finally broke the stillness between them, "He does have the perfect disguise."

"Disguise?" wondered Rose.

"His looks. It's impossible to believe that someone that stunningly attractive is nothing but pure evil."

"Ally I've told you before don't speak about Mr. Dalton like that," reprimanded Rose. "I've never seen anyone love someone the way he loves Helene. He's not evil Ally. He's helplessly in love with his wife. A wife that he lost far too soon."

Rose had never used such a harsh tone with Ally. She made the wise decision to conceal her feelings and remain quiet. After a moment Ally walked to the bow of the ship. Time passed slowly as the ship remained on course. Then something caught Ally's eye.

"That's not the beach house." Ally squinted and shielded her eyes from the sun. "It can't be."

"What is it?" asked Rose almost reluctant to join her at the railing.

"It looks like," Ally paused not believing her own eyes. With an icy shiver running up the full length of her back she announced in disbelief, "It's Dalton Manor".

Book 3

Soon the complexity and wonder of the mystical world around her fills her with exhilaration. Nevertheless, finding a way out of her captivity remains her sole focus. Until, she witnesses Edmund and Helene's young love firsthand.

<u>Surrender</u>

<u>TABLE OF CONTENTS</u>

Chapter One

Rose confirmed Ally's statement and said with a hint of surprise, "It is Dalton Manor."

"How is that possible?" questioned Ally hopeful that she was back at the party and going home very soon. All other options were far too terrifying to explore. Denial was becoming a constant companion for Ally. It was at that precise moment when her appreciation for this was greater than ever before.

The ship slowed drawing closer to the shore. The ocean waves became tranquil and the water's color changed from its dark blue-gray color to powder blue. The water now so clear Ally could see fish swimming about. She could feel the ships railing shrink beneath her hands and watched in disbelief as the entire ship morphed into a much smaller boat. In no time, The Vision had become nothing more than a small yacht.

"What's happening?" Ally asked.

Before Rose could answer her, Seaman Kidd announced, "We will be docking shortly."

"Docking where exactly?" demanded Ally, but Seaman Kidd had already walked away.

Ally turned back to Rose only to find herself standing on the bow of the yacht all alone. The sound of geese honking in the water below distracted her. She watched the graceful birds swim leisurely over the still water with their goslings following close behind. The gaggle of geese welcoming the boat closer and closer to the shore with their calls.

"Are you about ready to disembark?" It was Rose standing several feet behind her dressed in an elaborate golden evening dress. Her hair was pulled into a sophisticated updo and the v-cut neckline of the dress showcased her flawless skin. Her elegant rose necklace made her appear more regal than ever. Ally studied the dress with its loose hanging three quarter length sleeves and intricate lace pattern flowing seamlessly an inch or so above the neckline. Rose clasped her hands in front of her waiting for Ally's response. This made Ally notice Rose was also wearing her matching bracelet.

"Do I have a choice?" were the only words Ally spoke.

Rose moved closer to Ally bringing out the complex details of her beautiful gown. The crushed velvet with its floral pattern shimmered in the sunlight giving Rose's approach a fairy godmother appeal. The applique cutouts on the corset mirrored the ruffled edge that ever so slightly brushed the yacht's deck. Never before had Ally been face to face with such elegant beauty.

"Quite frankly Ally this is your choice. This is taking place for one reason only. It's your continued resistance to your new world that has brought us here. Mr. Dalton is bringing to life your inner most desires and requests."

The boat's engines gave a final roar pulling next to a small floating dock. Crew members quickly secured the boat causing it to shift sideways knocking Ally off balance. Steadying herself by gripping Rose's arm drew her attention to the hunter green velvet sleeves she now wore. Using the window of the bridge as a makeshift mirror she examined her new outfit. A curved neckline balanced perfectly by the long sleeves complimented the satin flounce skirt. When Ally moved, the pale green skirt shifted colors ever so slightly in the sun's rays. There wasn't anything spectacular about her dress, but it's understated classiness matched Ally's personality.

"Your presence is expected," announced Seaman Kidd in a most professional manner. His demeanor was all business and the usual playfulness in his eyes was absent.

Rose assisted by another crewmember was already on the dock leaving Ally without a stall tactic. Before fear could take hold, she was reassured by kindness returning to Seaman Kidd's eyes. "Be careful what you wish for," whispered Ally taking his arm.

At the end of the dock stood an older gentleman fully engaged in conversation with Rose and a few others.

When Ally reached them he happily introduced himself, "Good afternoon Miss Ally my name is Arthur."

Instinctively Ally extended her hand to shake his trying to remember her manners this time, but instead of shaking her hand he lifted it to his face and lightly kissed the back of her trembling hand.

From Arthur's greeting to the attire of those around them Ally was doubtful yet hopeful she was back at the Halloween party. It didn't seem logical she would be back where this all started, but then again nothing here seemed to be based in logic. So why not tell herself that's where she was?

"Where would you like to go first?" inquired Arthur.

"Go?" replied Ally

"Yes Ally, go. Remember this is your doing?" added Rose. Ally now found herself alone with Rose and Arthur.

"What's my doing? What did I do?"

Responding without answering her questions Arthur stated, "Let's start closer to the beginning. That way you can piece them together with the parts you've already seen."

"That's a wonderful idea," agreed Rose with a twinkle in her eye.

"Wait a minute!" protested Ally, "Where am I? I'm not going anywhere until someone tells me what's going on." Ally almost didn't recognize her own voice. It was assertive and confident camouflaging the fear that was tying her stomach in knots. At this point she knew she couldn't flee the situation. Her only choice now was to try and fight. Feeling very much like a cornered animal she glared at Arthur then Rose impatiently waiting for an answer.

"Take a look around Ally. I think you already know where you are," said Rose calmly.

Ally studied her surroundings, the yacht remained docked in what she now recognized as the lake at Dalton Manor. The bench where she had seen Edmund and Helene exchange anniversary gifts was there and sure enough Dalton Manor itself stood proud in its rightful place. The expansive grounds with its lush green grass and impressively large aged trees with their far-reaching branches arched over the same dirt road she had driven on to the party. The location was painfully familiar.

"Okay. I'm at Dalton Manor but which Dalton Manor? The one I drove to or one from decades ago?"

"Very good Ally," cheered Arthur "Whichever one you would like to visit."

"Whichever?" Ally couldn't believe her ears. Was she going home? Had she fought hard enough to earn her freedom? Could it be that easy?

Knowing what was running through Ally's mind Rose destroyed all hope she had of being right, "Ally I'm sorry there's no going home. At least not in the way you want."

Nearly every answer Ally received was cryptic adding to her frustration. "So I can go back to the party at Dalton Manor but not really and I can go home but not the way I want? What's the point?" shouted Ally.

"Magic. All this is magic. Mr. Dalton has created this world to be everything anyone could want it to be. All you have to do is surrender. Once you do you can have anything and everything you've ever dreamed of," soothed Rose.

"Everything but a real life," whimpered Ally.

Before the conversation could spiral out of control Arthur used his gift of diplomacy to pacify Ally's increasing aggravation. "How about a carriage ride around the grounds? That will give you some much needed time to reflect on the day's events. Then you can decide where you would like to go first."

A carriage ride was as logical to Ally as using a toy water gun to put out a forest fire. She whole heartedly disagreed with Rose. This world was not at all what Ally wanted it to be. Magic could not take away her desire to be back home even with all the problems she thought were unbearable. Ally desperately longed for home and convinced herself that she would happily face any problems thrown her way whether from her dad or life itself. She missed home where life was messy and sometimes boring, but at least it was a real life. Ally believed she would trade everything for her old life. The one that was filled with happiness and sadness, genuine memories, family and friends.

The approaching sound of clip-clopping diverted Ally's thoughts. Quickly bringing her back to the many afternoons she'd spent riding with friends. Not having a horse of her own was disappointing or so she thought when she was young. It was common place in Glenbrook for little girls to actually receive a pony for their birthday. By the time Ally reached middle school she discovered the benefits of not having one of her own. Borrowing a horse meant a small amount of work was involved compared to the daily routine of caring for the animal. With so many friends owning horses she was able to pick and choose which type she liked best. Another added benefit of borrowing a horse.

Pulling a polished black carriage towards them was a noble brown and black horse with a high gait. Ally found herself disarmed by the animal's beauty when it halted in front of them. The sound and smell of the horse took her back to happier times. Glenbrook hadn't always been the dilapidated town it now was.

"She's gorgeous," exclaimed Ally sounding almost happy.

"Yes, she is. Misty is quite the eye catcher," agreed Arthur. Taking a small bag from the coachman he asked Ally, "Would you like to feed her some sugar cubes?"

"Oh yes, I would love that."

Arthur and Rose smiled at each other while Ally gleefully fed Misty a small handful of sugar cubes and then another. Several minutes of interacting with Misty gave Ally the mood boost Arthur hoped for. Finally, her relaxing jaw gave way to a smile replacing her scowl and her voice became light and breezy while talking to Misty, "You're such a good girl."

"Are you ready for your ride around the grounds?" asked Arthur handing Ally a kerchief to wipe her hands.

"What do you think Misty? Would you like to give me a tour of Dalton Manor?" teased Ally fondly petting the horses neck. Misty quickly inhaled then puffed the breath out through her nostrils causing a low snort. Ally took it as a clear message of her agreement.

"If Misty thinks it's a good idea then sure. Let's take a tour."

Arthur already had the carriage door open. Ally studied how Rose took his hand, held her dress and gracefully used the tiny step to board the carriage. Rose made it look easy, but when Ally attempted to follow suit things went very differently. Losing her grip on the dress Ally stepped on the fabric ripping one of the multiple layers causing her to plunge head first into the carriage.

"Miss Ally are you hurt?" questioned Arthur.

She didn't answer but remained on her hands and knees. Then out of nowhere Ally burst into laughter, laughing so hard it made Arthur chuckle. With help from Rose she was soon seated on the billowy seat with her. The overstuffed cream colored seats with rows of scarlet buttons struggling against the puffy filling reminded Ally of sitting in her old bean bag chair.

"Are you hurt Miss?" asked Arthur again climbing into the carriage.

"No Arthur I'm fine," replied Ally in between giggles.

With a puzzled expression Rose inquired, "What's so amusing?"

"I was just thinking that I'm a klutz in any decade," responded Ally then it hit her, "Why didn't you know that? You always know what I'm thinking."

"Not always Ally. I'm trying very hard to stay out of your head as much as possible. By this time, I'm usually not needed anymore."

"Needed? Are you leaving me?"

"No Ally. It's simply that no one has wanted me around as a reminder. By this time most of the others have moved on to their own world. I've never been a part of anyone's world except for Mr. and Mrs. Dalton."

"Ally it's our hope to help you move forward in your acceptance," intervened Arthur, "Please allow us to help you."

The coachman's call to Misty suspended Ally's thoughts and feeling the carriage move turned her focus to the view outside the draped window. Soon the carriage passed the yacht still docked in the lake and after what seemed like miles the lake faded into the distance. A mixture of meadows and forest laid out in front of them. Dalton Manor had disappeared from view prior to the lake vanishing. Ally soon noticed they were surrounded by rolling green hills and questioned, "Are we still at the manor?"

"Yes Ally we are still on Dalton Manor grounds. Isn't it lovely here?"

"It is beautiful Rose. My goodness how big is this place?"

"Whoa!" called the coachman bringing Misty to a stop.

"It's time for lunch," announced Arthur opening the door and stepping from the carriage.

"Lunch? How long of a tour is this?" Ally asked searching the landscape for any sign of where lunch may come from.

"We don't have to tour the entire grounds Miss Ally. However, we do need to give Misty a break and we may as well have a meal while we're waiting."

The coachman was already tending to Misty and Rose was sauntering down a dirt path nestled at the base of a small incline. Arthur led Ally along the path walking quickly to catch Rose. Following a bend around the backside of the hill Ally found herself looking up at an extremely large gazebo sitting proudly at the top of an adjacent hill. The smell of freshly baked bread flooded her senses convincing her that lunch was a marvelous idea.

Making her way up to the impressive gazebo Ally noticed the intricately turned posts and spindles. She had spent so many afternoons watching her grandpa in his workshop she could almost smell the cut wood and sawdust. To this day it remained an all-time favorite scent. He would have loved to see the workmanship of this grand pavilion. Picturing her grandpa inspecting the skillful techniques used and enjoying the craftsmanship caused Ally to smile at the thought.

Before long Ally lost count of how many finger sandwiches she had gulfed down. The fresh homemade bread made the little sandwiches irresistible and paired with the chilled apple cider Ally found herself getting into character. The surroundings, her attire, the servants tending to her every need and a harpist playing softly had her playing make-believe. Acting very much the pampered aristocrat she found herself to be having fun. A fond memory of going with her grandma to watch an old classic movie helped Ally get into character.

"I have always loved this place," commented Rose.

"We all have. It's a beautiful reminder of Mr. and Mrs. Dalton's first outing," agreed Arthur.

Curiously Ally inquired, "Edmund took Helene to the manor for their first date?"

"No Ally he simply built a replica of the gazebo from the park as a keepsake," said Rose.

"Built?" Ally's skepticism didn't go unnoticed.

"Built, recreated or......"

"Conjured?" added Ally to Rose's answer.

Arthur stood and spoke in a soothing tone, "Ally you know Mr. Dalton is a warlock. You are free to select whichever word or phrase you prefer to describe his powers. I realize you are struggling with your transition and that is why you've been brought here. I would like very much to show you how beautiful their love for each other is and for you to understand that Mr. Dalton and his magic are not evil."

There was nothing threatening or frightening about Arthur's words yet Ally felt scolded. She would have rather he yelled at her. Then she could have understood why she was feeling what she was feeling.

"As I said earlier let's go back to Mr. and Mrs. Dalton's early days. To the days when they were first courting."

Ally cut in, "To their first date?"

"That's a wonderful idea. Let us visit that late spring day in the park."

"Under this gazebo's twin?" asked Ally wanting confirmation.

"That's correct Ally," smiled Arthur offering his hand to Ally. "Shall we?"

Chapter Two

Giving Arthur her hand she expected to ride the carriage from Dalton Manor to the park Rose mentioned. Instead Arthur took a firm grip of the gazebo railing instructing Ally to do the same with her free hand. After tightening her grip the gazebo shuddered before lurching violently into a sea of colors.

"Hold tight Miss Ally," shouted Arthur over the noisy commotion that surrounded them.

Ally squeezed the railing and Arthur's hand tighter while bending her knees to try and absorb the floors movement. The erratic motion, deafening noise and contorting colors surrounding them stopped as quickly as they started.

"How are you feeling?" Arthur asked before releasing her hand.

Ally took a deep chest lifting breath and exhaled slowly before answering, "I'm a bit queasy, but not as bad as when Edmund flew me off the boat."

"Very nice. Well this is a little different experience. No one holds the power Edmund has."

Nodding in agreement Ally surveyed the area discovering that Rose was no longer with them. "Where's Rose?"

"She remained at the manor. I will be your guide from now on. At least for your time at the manor. You and Rose will return to the beach house when you're ready," Arthur quickly added upon noticing Ally's concern.

The happy sound of children laughing filled the air. Within seconds Ally spotted them skipping towards the gazebo both holding tight to their brimmed hats. Assuming they were brother and sister Ally smiled when the young boy politely stopped so his younger sister could pick the white puff ball from a dandelion. How she laughed after blowing the seeds into the air. By this time their parents had caught up to them and the entire family headed straight towards Arthur and Ally.

"Relax Miss Ally they can't see us," reassured Arthur at which point the children ran right through the two of them.

Fully expecting to feel some kind of sensation Ally braced herself, but there wasn't even the smallest hint of a touch. It was like twisting or bending a piece of your hair. There's no feeling in hair. Something Ally was thankful for when she used a hot flat iron to try and tame her curls.

"This is so weird," squinched Ally when the parents went through them.

Smiling, Arthur agreed and told her she would get accustomed to it. There was a strange familiarity in his smile. One Ally couldn't place. Who was it he reminded her of?

"That bench will do," said Arthur pointing to a shaded park bench a few feet from the gazebo. Leaving the crushed stone and gravel path they cut across the dense green grass. Ally swooshed away a honey bee flying from one of the large bushes covered in purple flowers. A cool afternoon breeze cut through Ally's dress surprisingly giving her a chill.

Rubbing her hands over her arms made her notice the busy floral pattern on her sleeves, "I should have known. Wardrobe change," she stated without emotion. What had once rattled her nerves was now becoming nothing more than another predictable turn of events. The shock factor of this ever-changing world was lessoning.

Arthur stood next to the bench anxiously waiting for Edmund and Helene to make their appearance. Meanwhile, Ally enjoyed watching the little girl repeatedly make herself dizzy. Spinning in circles until her ruffled blue dress twirled eventually made her tumble to the ground. It was adorably cute to observe. Her father always there to slow her decent.

He lovingly kept her from hurting herself. It reminded Ally of the trust she once had for her own father.

"Here they come," Arthur affectionately reported.

Ally stood and looked in the direction Arthur was pointing. The curved path had taken Edmund and Helene behind a cluster of large trees and several minutes passed before they were spotted crossing a newly painted white bridge. Walking a couple feet apart they were closely followed by Helene's parents. More than halfway across the bridge Helene paused for a moment and pointed at something in the water below.

"They're awfully far away," complained Ally stunned by her disappointment with this. She wanted to get a good look at them and hear what they were saying. Instantly, Ally found herself sitting on one of the many huge limbs of an immense oak tree. The Spanish moss growing on and dangling from the branches made the rough bark quite comfortable. Several feet below stood Edmund and Helene looking like one of those breathtaking couples you only see in the movies.

"Is this to your liking?"

"Yes, this is great Arthur."

From her new perch high above the couple she could hear their conversation. Helene had spotted a duckling wedged between some rocks unable to climb out. Mama duck repeatedly jumped on and off the rocks doing her best to coax the duckling out, but the recently hatched duckling had worn itself out and was now barely moving.

"We must help the poor little thing," urged Helene.

Edmund quickly went into action running from the bridge down to the water's edge. Unsure how the duckling managed to get where it was Edmund headed to the rocks something mama duck didn't like. In a fury of quacks and wing flapping she attacked. Edmund returned her aggression with his own sending her into the water followed by her remaining ducklings.

When he turned around there stood Helene, "You keep mama duck busy and I'll rescue the duckling."

Pleased with her assertiveness and willingness to work together he agreed, "Yes, ma'am."

Mr. & Mrs. Beck on the other hand were quite unsure about their daughter's behavior. They quickly voiced their opinion when she tossed off her shoes, hiked up her dress and waded into the water towards the rocks.

"It's okay little one," cooed Helene reaching in and scooping the duckling from its rocky prison. A quick once-over showed the duckling was "no worse for wear" making Helene smile.

By this time the duck family had made their way around to the opposite side of the rocks. Helene was all too happy to place the rescued family member back into the water to join them. "There you go little one. Hurry to your mama," coached Helene.

Helene's father helped her from the water and offered her a handkerchief to dry her legs and feet. The look in his eyes exhibited both pride and fear. Helene knew he was worried about Edmunds reaction.

"Well done Miss Beck. Bravo!" cheered Edmund. "I can't think of another lady who would put the life of one little duckling above their social status. You are remarkably refreshing."

Mr. Beck turned and thanked Edmund, "Thank you Mr. Dalton for appreciating Helene for who she is. I would be hard pressed to find a gentleman who wouldn't shame her for her boldness."

For the first time in her life Ally truly understood how different her world was from Helene's. How anyone could twist her actions into something shameful was mind boggling. What a strange and almost prehistoric way of life thought Ally and she wasn't done being perplexed. The sight of Cora helping Helene dry off and put her shoes back on wasn't terribly strange, but watching Edmund keep his distance with his back turned was. What wasn't he supposed to see? Helene's calves and feet? Ally studied him while he stood there with perfect posture and patience. He didn't make a move until he was given the "all clear" from Mr. Beck.

His entrancing good looks soared to new heights when he tenderly grinned at Helene. A twinkle in his sapphire eyes brought color to Helene's cheeks making Cora smile warmly at her daughter.

"May we continue to the gazebo?"

"Of course," replied Helene her voice now soft and warm.

By the time they all reached the gazebo Ally and Arthur had returned to the shaded bench. Helene's parents stood on the opposite side of the structure while Edmund and Helene leaned against the railing directly in front of Ally. She had a ring side seat for whatever came next.

Helene nervously fidgeted with her fingernails then involuntarily quivered when the chilly breeze became stronger.

"You're cold," declared Edmund.

"I'll be fine," Helene protested readjusting her dress, but her movement revealed what she was trying to hide. Water dripped from the bottom of her dress creating a small puddle below her.

"Mr. Beck sir, may I?" asked Edmund removing his jacket and motioning to place it over Helene's shoulders.

"Yes, you may."

"Thank you Mr. Dalton," blushed Helene pulling the jacket tighter around her. The scent of Edmund's cologne took her back to the Pegasus dream. She recognized his cologne. But how was that possible? This was the closest the two of them had ever been except for her wonderfully magical dreams.

"Feeling warmer?"

"Yes I am," replied Helene who cleverly used the opportunity to pull the coat up around her neck taking another whiff of his enticing cologne. Without realizing it she closed her eyes and focused solely on the magnetic fragrance.

Edmund fought back a smirk when he caught her doing this and said, "I have been looking forward to this day ever since I received the approval letter from your parents."

"That's nice to hear," Helene paused, "I have as well."

Edmund released the breath he was holding and wondered if she was even more nervous than he was. The bold woman who rescued the duckling was now unsure of herself, but why? He had to know, "Helene have I done something to offend you?"

"No. Why would you think that?"

"You suddenly seem very uncomfortable with me," answered Edmund going straight to the point.

Helene found herself fighting against her dream behavior. Wanting nothing more than to dive into his muscular chest and arms to feel his strength and warmth surround her like in her dreams. Her body betrayed her. She involuntarily flinched towards him at the mere thought of being close to him.

If he could be direct so could she. "It's quite the opposite Mr. Dalton. I feel extremely comfortable around you. Perhaps far too comfortable. Especially at this early stage of our courting."

This time Edmund let his smile shine in all its glory. Finding her irresistible he had to find a way to touch her. Leaning over the railing he plucked a daffodil from the flower bed circling the gazebo and handed it to Helene. It was unmistakable that she had the same wish letting his hand leisurely brush hers in the flower exchange. Each of them taking much longer than needed to pass the daffodil from one to the other.

Not a word was spoken between them but their hands whispered volumes.

Ally swore she could see electricity run between the two of them. It was astonishing to observe. Witnessing such a sweetly simple act of affection overflow with so much allure. There wasn't a romantic movie that had been made where such an impassioned and yet demure scene had been captured. Ally found herself flush with expectancy. She never could have imagined the intensity of their connection or how pronounced it would be. It was remarkable how something as routine as giving and receiving a flower turned into such a passionate expression of their feelings for one another.

Helene held the flower in her hands and within seconds let a flurry of words gush from her mouth. She told him about her piano playing, her best friend Rose, what her favorite and least favorite food was and about her first pony. In the excitement of sharing her love of horses she began telling Edmund about her Pegasus dreams. At which point Cora cleared her throat bringing the conversation to a halt. Much to Edmund's dismay.

Mr. Beck stepped forward saying, "It's time we head home Helene."

Unhappy with Mr. Beck for bringing the date to an end Edmund asked, "So soon?"

"Yes. I'm afraid so Mr. Dalton. There is an important business meeting I need to prepare for."

"I understand sir. We will head back to the carriages this very minute," said Edmund before turning his attention back to Helene. "This way my lady."

Ally surprisingly found herself nearly as disappointed about the date ending as Edmund. Countless memories of Ally's grandparents and the blatantly obvious love between them came to mind. They had a special one of a kind relationship. There wasn't anyone else in Ally's life who displayed the love and respect they willing gave each other. Not even her own parents. She had grown to believe she would never see another couple like her grandparents. No matter how hard Rose tried to explain or even show Ally the love they shared, it couldn't break through her strong belief that Edmund was incapable of loving. Then there was the fact that Ally believed only a select few ever truly find love. Yet somehow watching Edmund and Helene interact on their first date and catching their eyes display the same endearing looks her grandparents shared was changing things. Seeing their love begin to blossom in front of her made her consider she was wrong about Edmund. Was he truly falling in love with Helene? No one was caught more off guard by this than Ally.

Chapter Three

Within seconds she and Arthur were traveling through the same surge of colors as before. The turbulent movement and deafening noise made her hang on to Arthur and the railing with all her might. Attempting to keep the queasiness from returning Ally focused on Arthur instead of the surrounding chaos. Arthur stood steady eyes wide open with no visible effects from their travel. Before long Ally thought she spotted people passing by in her peripheral, but maybe it was her eyes playing tricks on her.

"Welcome back," greeted Rose.

"Oh my gosh! Is there an easier way to do this?"

Rose giggled a bit, "You will get used to it Ally."

That wasn't what she wanted to hear although it was the answer to her next question. Candles had been lit on the table for the sun was going down and darkness was on its way.

"We're not going back to the beach house?"

"No Ally you've got so much more to see. Mr. Dalton hopes to ease your mind and send you on your way into your world."

"My world? There's only one world...." Ally argued.

With a fatherly tone Arthur cut in and challenged Ally, "If that were true then explain where you are."

Stumped on how to reply she let the teenager in her answer. She rolled her eyes and vocally exhaled with a loud huff. There wasn't any point trying to argue her case. Standing there in a gazebo somewhere on the grounds of Dalton Manor having just come back from Edmund and Helene's first date, along with everything else she'd experienced was more than enough evidence to prove her wrong. Edmunds magic somehow created multiple worlds. Ally didn't need to understand it or even believe in it for it to be real.

The coachman appeared and summoned them back to the carriage. Dusk was upon them and the chilly air urged them to walk faster. Ally was concerned about where they were headed. However, not knowing the destination was temporarily far less frightening then knowing. This world was highly unpredictable leaving Ally to dream up horrifying possibilities. She decided to leave well enough alone and simply wait to see where they were going. The entire time hoping it wasn't going to be has terrifying as she anticipated. When the carriage started off and continued on the road heading away from the manor she felt relieved. She told herself there wasn't a chance in Hades she'd spend the night at Dalton Manor. But even if that was where they were headed she couldn't battle against it?

Rose was uncharacteristically quiet in the carriage. Had something happened while Ally traveled with Arthur? Was the emotionally driven rollercoaster Ally seemed to never get off of wearing her out? The thought of Rose leaving her alone at Dalton Manor with Arthur scared her to the point of physical pain.

Like a misbehaved child Ally attempted to make amends, "I can see why you and Helene were, I mean are friends." Rose kept her gaze out the window so Ally went on to say, "Listening to her talk about your friendship was a blast. You're right Rose. She would do anything for you and I loved the way she took control and saved the duckling."

Rose flashed her brilliant smile doing little to ease the feeling of uneasiness Ally was dealing with. There was something very different in Rose's eyes. A seriousness and an almost pleading look of warning.

"What did you think when you saw Edmund and Helene together?" her question came out like that of a teacher asking for the one correct answer to a math problem. Was there only one right answer to this? If Ally answered incorrectly what next?

Looking back on the experience Ally answered honestly trusting the old adage "honesty is the best policy" in hopes it would prove true. "They reminded me of my grandparents. The way they interacted and looked at each other made me think they found a real and true love."

"Think or believe?"

"Isn't it the same thing?" replied Ally trying to remember exactly what she said.

"No Ally they are very different," stressed Rose. Concern was written all over her face.

Feeling like a witness testifying in a court case Ally held her words. She was convinced her testimony would either free the defendant or send them away for a long time. The problem was. She was the defendant. There was one thing she could count on in this strange land. The fact that anything at any time could happen. Rose's current behavior made Ally fear things could get so much worse.

Arthur declared they had reached their destination with a simple, "Here we are ladies."

Not far from the road sat a large rectangular log cabin. The covered porch was held up by half a dozen rustic beams complete with bark and nubs of where branches once grew. The rustic appearance and clothes line in the yard led Ally to believe they'd be greeted by a pioneer woman. The smoke from the stone chimney and glow emanating from the windows meant someone was inside.

Exiting the carriage Ally spoke up, "Now, where are we?

"This is one of the many hunting cabins on the property," boasted Arthur.

Inside the home the fire blazed giving Ally the much-needed warmth she'd been craving. Warming her hands by the fire she watched the flames dance and flicker in the mesmerizing way only a fire can. Staring at the fire so intently made her eyes begin to water. Between the heat and rarely blinking, her eyes longed for relief. Ally turned around to investigate her surroundings. Then waited for her eyes to refocus. Once the blurred vision faded away she studied her new environment. The cabin was organized and clean with a large well stocked kitchen. Open shelving revealed containers of various dry goods, canned fruits and vegetables. It took Ally back to her grandma's cellar. Standing in the ample living room she noticed several bookshelves filled to capacity. The lighting reminded her of camping lanterns which explained the scent of kerosene in the room. Close to the front door was a steep stairway leading up to a second floor.

"You two ladies can sleep in the bedrooms upstairs," stated Arthur. "The coachman and I will sleep in the bunkroom out back. If there's anything you need just call for the servant."

"Servant?"

"Yes Miss Ally. I'm at your service," said a young woman entering from the front door. Her round face and remarkably clear complexion reminded Ally of the "after" picture from an old acne commercial. Which Ally believed had been edited to make the person's skin look too perfect to be real. Yet somehow this woman's skin was that flawless.

Excusing himself Arthur left the women alone. It was nowhere close to bedtime. Ally figured something was up and wondered what she would learn next. There didn't seem to be much point in spending the night in the cabin, but then again it didn't really matter where she slept. Whether at the beach house or cabin she was still trapped in the locket.

"I need an answer to my question Ally."
Any hope of Rose forgetting their earlier conversation was destroyed. It was clear this topic wasn't going to go away anytime soon. Stalling for time Ally said, "Which question?"

"Do you think or believe Edmund and Helene love each other?"

"Before I answer..."

"Ally please. It's imperative you give me an answer," beseeched an unsettled Rose.

Ally paid close attention to the distressed expression in Rose's hazel eyes and the fearful tone of her voice. It was reminiscent of the day she gave her life for Helene. Unclear as to why her answer meant so much Ally reflected on what she experienced with Arthur. However difficult it might have been for Ally she was forced to admit something to herself. She continuously refused to even consider Edmund to be anything but a monster. Digging in her heels Ally made the choice to not believe there was an ounce of goodness in the man. That simple admission clued Ally in on exactly what Rose was asking. Ally didn't merely think Edmund was a monster. She believed it with her whole heart.

"Can we sit down?" asked Ally.

"Of course."

When the two were comfortably seated on the sofa Ally took a deep breath attempting to calm her nerves. She had convinced herself that this was to be the most important conversation the two of them shared bar none. Although she still didn't completely understand why.

"I hate to admit it Rose, but I didn't want to believe Edmund was anything more than an evil monster," Ally motioned for Rose to wait when she started to cut in. "Let me finish. I'm furious beyond words that he stole my life from me. I will never forgive him for it, but and this isn't easy for me to say......." Ally fought hard to get the words out, "After all I've been shown I do believe Helene loves Edmund unconditionally. Perhaps for that reason alone he learned to love. Yes, Rose. I believe they do deeply love each other."

Rose exhaled like she had been holding her breath the entire time, "Oh Ally I'm so relieved to hear you say that." Her words were followed by a hug that squeezed the air out of Ally. In the midst of the hug Ally heard the rhythmic and repetitive song of whip-poor-wills from outside. An owl soon joined in and before long there was an orchestra of forest animals livening up the night.

"My goodness what's all the fuss about?" she wondered.

"We are all so thrilled to hear your answer Ally. We want to celebrate."

"We?"

"We, as in all of us you've met or seen so far. We're simply finding a way to express our merriment," said Rose with a mixture of relief and excitement in her eyes.

"So everyone is watching me?"

"No, but they've all been notified of the good news."

"Okay, let's just stop right there. What's the good news and why would anyone care?"

Now it was Rose's turn to pause and contemplate her answer. Her hesitation made Ally nervous and once again Ally was reminded things here change very quickly. Within minutes the musical score from outdoors quieted down leaving the crackling fire on its own to fill the muted room.

"Ally you have been brought here perhaps on my request. We, Mr. Dalton and I spoke some time ago regarding the difficulty you were having. I also took the liberty to share that the love you experienced was in no way real love. During that conversation, I suggested he show you the love he and Helene share. In hopes you would settle in and stop fighting the inevitable."

Ally fought the urge to confront Rose about her conversation with Edmund and said, "We can discuss all you told him later. What I want to know is what good news is being celebrated?"

"I was getting to that Ally," before continuing Rose took a sip of tea which magically appeared in her hand, "You are not the first to resist the locket's entrapment. There have been others before you."

"Oh I can imagine. Actually, I'm not sure why everyone hasn't fought back. I've never been a fighter or brave by any stretch of the imagination. In all honesty, I've spent most of my life being afraid of all kinds of things," she admitted before going on, "So if I can fight so can everyone else," coached Ally. She couldn't help from wondering. If she somehow managed to start an uprising could they all get out?

"My sweet Ally there's no escaping the locket."

"Then what difference could it possibly make whether I fight or not, or whether I believe Edmund loves Helene?" Ally's voice was tense with disappointed anger.

"That's where the 'good news' comes in." Rose put her cup down and turned to face Ally with her entire body before cautiously proceeding, "Ally the good news is you passed the test. Mr. Dalton always tests the resisters."

"Test?"

"Edmund has done his best to create a world that will make its inhabitants happier than they've ever been. Most here accept their fate; create the world they've always dreamed of and never look back. Then there are those who refuse to accept there's no way out. When that happens, Edmund gives them one more chance to prove there's hope for their acceptance," Rose stopped and verified that Ally was still with her.

Ally's response showed she was, "They are tested like I was."

"Yes, but..." Rose left the word hanging in the air giving another clear sign she wanted Ally to fill in the blanks.

"But unlike me some did not pass."

"Precisely"

Hesitantly Ally asked, "Do I want to know what happened to them?"

"Even if you would rather not know I must tell you. You won't be given another chance to prove your willingness to accept life here."

Keenly listening to Rose, Ally learned that those who battled endlessly against Edmund were banished to a wasteland and never seen again. Rose knew nothing more about the wasteland or it's whereabouts only that there was no coming back from it. On a few occasions, she had unfortunately witnessed Edmund banish someone. First by taking their jewelry from them and then ferociously destroying it. Something only he could do. Then with horrified screams they were swallowed into darkness. A darkness Rose described as moving and alive. She went on to explain how the animate darkness appeared hungry for prey. Vigorously devouring its latest victim into the ghastly horror of its shadows. There was only one other time Ally had seen Rose's eyes brimming with an all-consuming fear. It was seeing Maxwell frozen in the hallway at Dalton Manor. His face contorted in raging fury had pushed her over the edge to help save Helene. The evil Rose was explaining terrified her as much if not more than Maxwell.

Upon hearing this Ally confirmed her necklace was still hanging from her neck. "Hence you telling me I'll die without the necklace."

"Yes. It is our jewelry that connects us to the magical garden which connects us to Edmund. Our enchanted jewelry is the only thing keeping us safe. Without it.....well, you now know what happens without it."

Chapter Four

While Helene read next to him on the sofa Edmund leaned over and surprised her with a lavish kiss. "I love you my sweet," he whispered freeing his lips from hers.

"I love you too my darling," giggled Helene, "What brought that on?"

"My heart was bursting with love for you and I wanted you to know," rang Edmunds playful voice, "What's the point of loving someone if you don't tell them how much you truly love them every chance you get?" he added with a frisky wink.

"Oh, well let me know what I did so I can do it again. That was some kiss my love," cooed Helene basking in their passion.

Edmund's laugh resonated through the house, "You were simply being you." It was a true statement. His heart burst with love for Helene on a regular basis, but this time it was bursting for another reason. One Helene didn't need to know anything about.

Leaving his beloved to her reading Edmund took a walk around the grounds ending up at the stables. Storm energized upon hearing Edmund's approach snorted and pawed at the ground. Unable to resist Edmund was soon galloping off at full speed upon the mighty steed. Storm's special love for Helene was unique, but Edmund also had a unique and special bond with him. Their rides were intense fast-paced adventures. The kind men most often enjoy.

Eventually Edmunds ride brought him to the dirt road where Helene lost her life. With precision, he searched the bushes and studied the area for any clue that could help him understand why Helene was taken from him. It turned out like every time before. There wasn't anything new to be found. With his back against a tree he watched Storm standing at a distance clearly uncomfortable with visiting the sight of the accident. Edmund knew Storm remembered something, but there was no way to find out. The only witness to the tragedy was a horse incapable of telling anyone what happened. No matter how magnificent he was.

The entire ride home Edmund verbally spoke about his thoughts and questions. In part to himself, but mainly to Storm hoping he would somehow react to one of countless scenarios Edmund played through. Leaving the stables Edmund checked on the garden before returning to Helene. It's magical beauty glistening in the moonlight.

Having moved from the sofa Helene sat on the floor reading by firelight. Absorbed in the story she failed to notice Edmund studying her. By her tightly scrunched toes peeking out from beneath her dress he knew she was at a riveting part of the story. With an adoring smile he decided to leave her undisturbed.

"I'll be up shortly," she hollered and before he could respond she said, "You smell like a horse. I hope you had a nice ride and said hello to Storm for me." Her eyes never left the book which she enthusiastically dived back into.

Thrashing in her bed for most of the night Ally awoke feeling exhausted. The images in her dreams were blended together into a mess of fearful portrayals giving her the worse night's sleep in a long time.

"Wasteland," she muttered looking at her displeasing reflection in the mirror. With swollen eyes, tangled hair and pillowcase creases on her face it made her want to climb back into bed. So, she did.

No sooner was she getting comfortable did Rose knock on the bedroom door, "Ally time to get up. Arthur has a full day planned."

Ally groaned and reluctantly climbed out of bed not understanding the point of continuing with her visit at Dalton Manor. She'd passed the test and now she just wanted to go....go, where? She no longer had a home or a life. She merely existed somewhere between life and death. For a split second she thought, "this is worse than death," but quickly recanted her thought fearing death would become an instant reality. Were others listening to her thoughts like Rose. Suddenly an even more distressing thought came to mind. Was Edmund listening in?

Arthur greeted Ally with such an enthusiastic smile Ally couldn't resist his charm. His rambling about the plans for the day made her remember the first time her grandpa took her fishing. Due to her tender age and complete lack of fishing experience his long explanation was a bit much for a four-year-old, but grandpa was never one to use baby talk. He loved to debate this with anyone. He argued saying, "It was just as easy for a child to learn the proper word for something as some 'absurd' made up word". Each time she went fishing with grandpa she listened with eagerness. Learning more each time he went through the well-rehearsed fishing lesson. By the time she was seven Ally was amazingly proficient with fishing terminology and reeling them in. Arthur had accomplished what grandpa always had. Making something sound so exciting and fun she couldn't wait to get started.

Their first stop was Helene and Edmund's second date to a traveling fair. Edmund showed off his shooting skills at the shooting gallery before strolling through the aisles of street sellers. Helene was a natural animal lover. She was quickly drawn to the goldfish-hawker with tables of goldfish globes in various sizes. Each filled with a treasure all its own. When Helene's eyes zeroed in on a particular globe Edmund gestured for the glass orb to be brought to her. Wanting to make the sale the hawker held the globe at eye level allowing Helene to get a better look.

Helene gushed, "He's beautiful. He's so bright he looks like one of my garden's tomatoes." It was quite an accurate description of the little fish who outshone the others with its deep rich color. "Why hello there," greeted Helene when the little fish swam towards her. The sound of her musical laugh brought smiles all around.

"What are you going to name him?"

"Name him?" Helene sounded genuinely surprised that she would be taking the fish home. Edmund adored and appreciated her unassuming nature. She was nothing like so many other privileged women he'd known or seen. Their spoiled self-centered and ungrateful attitudes were a pet peeve of his. Helene was solid evidence that not all women were the same and more importantly she also proved all humans weren't the same.

It was endearing to him how seriously Helene contemplated the potential name of the fish. After much thought she proclaimed the fish to be, "Ember". With great dignity Edmund was introduced to the little creature followed by introductions to her parents. Smiling a motherly smile of days gone by Cora relished the pure joy in her daughter's eyes. The child-like innocence of her flamboyant little girl was a sight for sore eyes. Helene was no longer a prisoner of adult heartache. The pain of Luther's deceptive love may have left her scarred, but she was moving on. The most important part was her recognition of true love possibly existing.

By the end of the day and having experienced several outings with Edmund and Helene, Ally realized something intriguing. Edmund hadn't used magic once on their dates. Knowing Rose's story Ally understood Edmund couldn't make Helene love him, but he could use magic to impress and charm her and yet he wasn't. This revelation further chipped away at her belief that Edmund was nothing but evil.

During her travels with Arthur the lodge had become a full-scale hunting lodge. Although Ally wasn't sure why it was referred to as a hunting lodge. There wasn't a deer or moose head mounted above the fireplace, actually there wasn't an animal head mounted anywhere. Ally wanted to talk privately to Rose once she was back at the cabin, but regrettably it was bustling with activity. It was disappointing at first, but in no time Ally found herself enjoying the company of those around her. The magical ambiance of Dalton Manor and its grounds were becoming impossible to resist.

When the delightful evening finally wrapped up Ally wanted nothing more than to get some sleep. This time, her dreams were packed full of sweet visions of Helene with Edmund. Like snapshots in a photo album she thumbed through page after page of the happy couple. Helene was a remarkable woman in any decade. Strangely making Ally wish she could meet her. She was the kind of woman most other women wanted to hate but many found impossible to do. Her physical beauty was undeniable which made many around her feel jealous. However, her beauty didn't stop there. Her heart was equally if not more beautiful. Her kindness, honesty, gentle nature and all around likability helped ease the jealousy of most.

Ally recalled a particular date when the social elite had gathered and Helene's selflessness outshined the sun itself. It was a private concert held at the Bennett's mansion. Ally would soon discover the event was to showcase Margret Bennett's singing voice. Despite Miss Bennett's wishes there wasn't any way not to invite the Beck family. All she could do was hope Helene would decline the invitation. Which didn't happen.

Within minutes of the Beck's arrival Edmund left his assigned seat and walked Helene to hers. Their tables were as far away from each other as possible. Another eligible bachelor begrudgingly traded seats with Edmund. When he sat with the Beck family, Ally caught sight of the livid expression on Margret's face as she peeked out from behind the stage curtain. The Bennett's had spared no expense in creating a full-blown stage for their pampered daughter to perform. When the curtain opened after a lengthy and pretentious introduction Margret took the stage with her head held high.

Her voice was impressive with a wide vocal range. She sang with such gusto all eyes were on her or so she thought. Soaking in the admiration of her guests inflated her ego beyond it's normal exaggerated size. Pridefully her eyes made their way to Edmund who failed to notice her yearning gaze. His eyes never strayed from Helene. Thoroughly infuriating Margret making her voice crack during the final song. At the sound of the embarrassing noise she lost control. She stopped singing and banged her clinched hands on the piano keys thrilling most of her female peers. Very few women were fooled by Margret's false moments of sweetness. The ugliness and selfishness of her heart was constantly on display. Especially when someone was paying attention. The abhorrence she felt for most people was evident in her eyes. Then there was the condescending tone in which she spoke. Unfortunately, most men only noticed her physique or that's all they cared about.

Margret's embarrassment didn't sit well with Helene who rushed to her aid, despite her temper tantrum. "Oh Margret don't stop. You were getting to the best part of the song," shouted Helene rushing the stage. "Perhaps I can help," suggested Helene making herself comfortable at the piano. Without sheet music Helene played from memory. Margret took center stage and completed the song doing her best to block the crowds view of Helene. Even Margret's overstated effort didn't help. She found herself playing second fiddle to Helene's skill of tickling the ivories. At this point the entire audience was doing their best to watch Helene. Adding insult to injury Margret noticed Edmund was beaming with love as he focused solely on Helene.

After the applause died down Margret angrily turned towards the piano determined to tell Helene she'd ruined her day only to find her gone. Margret was so involved in trying to recapture the spotlight she hadn't noticed Helene make a quiet exit offstage.

Helene hurried back to her table. Thanking everyone with a sincere smile for their compliments as she rushed passed them. Samuel and Cora were already standing in anticipation of their daughter's next words, "It's time to go."

Samuel agreed and escorted his family to their carriage and once inside the conversation began, "I'm so proud of you Helene. I know there's no love lost between you and Margret Bennett which makes your kind act even more impressive. You are an exceptional woman."

Agreeing Cora chimed in, "I wouldn't expect anything less from our daughter."

"Thank you," blushed Helene. "Maybe someday Margret will see it that way. I'm sure she'll twist my assistance into something less than helpful. Let's hope my quick exit and leaving her to be the center of attention will subdue her wrath."

Back at the Bennett's house hors d'oeuvres were being served. Margret along with her father were making the rounds. With false humility, she finally made her way to the table where Edmund sat weary of the drama. It wasn't until everyone else paid their compliments did he speak up, "You have a grand voice Miss Bennett. I especially liked the final number. Helene's piano playing complimented your voice remarkably well. It's a shame she didn't stay around to receive her accolades."

Margret was too angry to speak. A common issue her father had grown accustomed to. As was customary he defended his bratty egotistical daughter, "Well I'm sure she understood her place and that's why she left. After all, this day was Margret's day not Helene's. I'm sure Margret would have done just fine on her own."

That brass ungrateful comment reminded Edmund how much he wanted to destroy the Bennett's. Not only had their forefathers killed his parents and tried to end his life they were now trying to separate Helene from him. Margret's blatant attempt to get his attention had succeeded in doing only one thing. Convincing Edmund to make his and Helene's courtship official.

Chapter Five

Ally and Rose finally found themselves alone at the hunting lodge after having spent several more days traveling down memory lane with Arthur. With birds happily chirping outside, the wind rustling the leaves of the forest trees and the newfound peace Ally was experiencing she had to admit something. At least to herself. She felt honestly happy for the first time in a long time.

She was growing surprisingly accustomed to the long frilly, layered and at times constricting dresses. However, she still preferred the more casual days. Those dresses were cooler, lighter and easier to move in, but either way Ally found herself maneuvering about effortlessly. It took some thought to remember the last time she knocked something over or stumbled about.

"Is that a smile?" asked Rose.

Ally had to admit it was, "Yep. I feel great."

"I'm so glad to hear that Ally," Rose was wary about using the word relieved understanding that Ally's attitude could falter in a second. So, she just admitted she was glad about her happier mood.

Being completely immersed in Helene's world not only persuaded Ally into believing Edmund wasn't evil, but it also managed to make her feel sorry for him.

Thinking about their fairytale life being cut short was beginning to anger her. From this different vantage point Ally wondered, "With all the time traveling I've done with Arthur. I don't understand why Edmund doesn't go back before Helene's accident and just prevent the whole thing."

"I have wondered the same thing," Rose commented with an ambivalent expression, "but I'm sure there's a reason. Otherwise Mr. Dalton would have done so."

The ripples caused by one woman's death had and were continuing to disrupt the lives of so many. This fact demonstrated under no uncertain terms how connected we all are. Considering everything she knew brought her back to Rose and Maxwell. Rose had been faced with the fact that someone was going to die on that pivotal day. "I'm sorry Rose," Ally said regretting her question. She knew Rose was thinking about Maxwell and how differently that day could have gone.

Ally's father may have become an angry drunk leaving his family in disarray. Still, his deep-rooted upbringing had so far kept him from becoming physically violent. Thankfully he always passed out shortly after returning home, but not before giving Ally and her mom an uncensored rant about one thing or another. As difficult and painful as that was it wasn't anything close to the hellish life Rose went through.

Days had blended together leaving Ally to wonder how long she'd been at the manor. Everything before it was fading away from the beach house and boat trip to her college classes. Glenbrook seemed to be the one thing that was fading the most. Struggling with this Ally tried to remember the names of kids she'd grown up with. Each time coming up with nothing. How and why was this happening?

Her lifelong friend who betrayed her trust left the largest void in her memory. All she could remember was feeling heartbroken about something someone in her past had done. No matter how hard she tried there wasn't a detail to be found. Diving deeper into her recollection from her previous life Ally discovered there were only faint memories of happy times lingering in her mind. All the hurt and disappointment she once felt about her life dissolved when she focused on it.

"Ally look out the window. It's a doe with her fawn. Oh, my goodness there's two fawns," exclaimed Rose quietly pointing out the front window.

Moving with stealth like steps the two made their way closer to the window. Calmly lying in the green grass at the base of a tree sat a doe. Her two young fawns romping around in the open area between the lodge and their mother who watched them with keen awareness. Their playfulness made both Rose and Ally laugh under their breath. It was a sight neither of them wanted to ruin. When the doe's ears twitched towards them and her eyes met theirs they were fearful they had done exactly that.

Frozen the girls waited and watched relieved when the doe broke her stare. "That was close," whispered Ally.

Rose nodded in agreement. The girls stood motionless and soaked in nature's beauty for as long as they were allowed. The mother deer soon decided to move on with her fawns bounding behind her.

Somberly Ally asked, "Am I going to forget everything about my life?"

"Not at all Ally," comforted Rose.

"Then why is it fading away? My 'real life' doesn't seem real anymore. It's like my family and Glenbrook didn't really exist. I'm starting to feel like those memories are nothing more than a dream," her voice now sad.

"Edmund wants this place to be better than your past life. He created this world to be everything its inhabitants desire. There's not too many limits on what you can create Ally. In order to keep you cheerful Edmund removes pain from your past. He leaves you with only happy memories."

Ally considered this, "Then my life must have been worse than I thought because there's not much left."

"There's more than you think Ally. Mr. Dalton will return your best times once you've settled in," Rose paused and her face looked sullen as she continued, "Sometimes unwanted memories can or will come back. Including some of a person's worst memories." It was clear thoughts of Maxwell still lingered in Rose's mind.

"Edmund is extremely powerful," stated Ally with a thoughtful expression. Her eyes glazed over as she was clearly deep in thought. Soon Rose half expected to see smoke escaping her ears. Several minutes passed before Ally spoke up, "Not only is he back with Helene in their world. He's created this place where each of us can build our own world. Seriously how many worlds exist here and how does he keep it all straight?"

"Yes Ally. Edmund is remarkable," was the only answer Rose offered. She feared if she commented too much Ally would circle around to her body being used to bring Helene back. Those conversations never went well.

"Remarkable? I'm not sure that's the word I would choose." Ally took a deep breath and wanting confirmation said, "The bottom line is either I accept my fate or be banished to the wasteland," Ally paused again and stated, "Pick my poison I suppose."

Rose was thankful Arthur interrupted their conversation announcing the carriage was ready to take them back to the manor. She felt deeply concerned Ally's happiness would be replaced with bitter anger. Rose was convinced Ally was still in a very fragile condition.

Instinctively Ally walked to her room, but once there realized she didn't need to pack anything. There wasn't one thing that belonged to her or that she had brought with her. She knew she'd wake tomorrow morning with new clothes and everything else she needed.

Exiting the room, she jokingly said, "Well, this type of travel makes it easy. No packing or lugging around your stuff."

Misty greeted Ally like a long-lost friend with neighs and snorts. Taking a moment to say hello Ally placed her forehead against Misty's neck, closed her eyes and slowed her breathing trying to counteract the nervous anticipation overtaking her. Butterflies filled her stomach making her wish she hadn't eaten such a big dinner.

Sensing her discomfort Rose placed an encouraging hand on hers, "There's no need to worry Ally," was all she said doing very little to subdue Ally's nerves.

By the time they could see they were closing in on Dalton Manor it was night. The manor was left standing as a huge dark shadow in the night. With only a waning crescent moon left in the sky the grounds were mainly concealed in blackness. Beyond the manor Ally began to see a soft incandescent glow. It's hypnotic beacon calling out to her.

Standing several feet from the gardens gate Ally inhaled the common yet haunting fragrance that no longer left her. Each plant vying for her attention with its own uniquely brilliant glisten made Ally grin. Moving her eyes from one flower to the next made each one's shimmer become conspicuously more vibrant. "It's so beautiful." Ally's voice was hushed fearing the light show would cease.

The evening air blew through the garden causing a lively wave of colors to explode. Ally noticed a long stem rose bush in the center of the grand garden. With its scintillating array of varying reds, she felt a strange connection to the brilliant flowers. It was then she realized where she was, "It's the magical garden!" Ally turned to Rose for confirmation, but she was gone and so was Arthur.

A gripping fear swallowed Ally. Her body shuddered and she heard herself scream when branches of the large oak moved in her direction. Ally was mesmerized as the tree's pigment transformed into a psychedelic show of dazzling colors. She couldn't help but watch. A trail of multicolored sparks ran up the trunk of the tree onto every branch until they burst from its leaves. Alive with energy the mighty oak lit up the night. Illuminating the manor as if the world's largest pyrotechnic show were taking place. Catkins began sprouting from the branches reaching towards Ally with their long apetalous yellow-green clusters. The cylinder-shaped flowers flickered at a manic speed. It was more intense than any strobe light she had ever seen causing Ally to squint and turn her face. Fearful the tree was about to explode.

The oaks rustling leaves seemed to wail her name. Merging all the vibrant color-filled light into the trunk of the tree was remarkable to watch. The oak contained the brilliance making the ground beneath Ally's feet tremble. She swore the roots of the tree were emitting light up through the dirt. The reaching branches had stopped only a few feet from her. Then from behind she heard her name. "Ally," greeted a familiar voice.

Shielding her eyes Ally peered at the human form in front of her unable to make out the glowing transparent figure. A grand finale of light filled the darkness. It was reminiscent of the climactic end of an over the top firework display. Sparks of light darted from the tree and shot into the sky from the garden. Then in a flash it was gone. Leaving a solitary silhouette only a few feet away from her in the dim light.

Backing away Ally struggled to adjust to the darkness only to find herself tangled in the train of her dress. Bracing for the looming impact of the ground Ally was pleasantly surprised to feel herself caught before doing so.

"That was close," spoke the familiar voice.

Peering up at the man who held her she wished for a flashlight or something. Then on cue several lampposts lit up the night.

"Hello there, Ally," said Artie his friendly face a sight for sore eyes.

"Artie?" implored Ally, "Is it really you?"

"Yes, it's me Ally."

"Oh my gosh what happened? I had the most vivid and terrible nightmare....."

Before she could continue Arties face gradually matured into Arthur's. Then regressed back to Artie making Ally wiggle free from him. Landing hard on the ground she scooted away from Artie until her back hit something solid. Aghast with emotion Ally's body went haywire. Leaving her lightheaded making it look as though the garden was spinning around her.

"Ally. Ally come on wake up," pleaded Rose.

With a few moans Ally slowly came to, "What happened?"

"You fainted."

"Huh. I've never done that before."

"Well, you experienced quite a shock," Rose said helping Ally sit up.

Surveying her surroundings Ally asked, "Where are we?"

"We're back on The Vision. Mr. Dalton figured it was best for us to spend the night here."

That simple answer reminded Ally of why she had fainted. The magical garden with its impressive light show and mystical oak tree. Memories of the huge magnificent and terrifying oak tree flooded her mind. Then another memory burst through, "Artie is Arthur?" screeched Ally.

"Yes he is Ally," was all Rose could say. Her tone clearly without surprise.

"You already knew that," replied Ally.

"Yes."

"Are you anyone else?" Ally needed to know although she wasn't sure she wanted to know.

"No Ally, I'm still just me. In the past or future. I'm always the same. I don't transform into anyone else or age for that matter."

Her relief from Rose's answer lasted a mere second, "You don't transform or age meaning others do?"

"Very few, but yes some have been given those abilities," at which point Rose gazed up at Artie standing across the room.

Artie smiled the same congenial smile he had when Ally chimed in on his storytelling so long ago. The Halloween party felt like another lifetime. His friendly, warm and hopeful smile stood the test of time whether

337

young or old he was likeable and easygoing. Now knowing Artie and Arthur were one and the same. Ally could see the resemblance. Especially in his or their smile.

"I didn't mean to startle you Ally," Artie's voice was filled with sincerity.

"I'm not sure how an electrified garden and moving oak tree that bursts with colors like a 4th of July firework show wouldn't startle anyone. To be completely honest I'm surprised I didn't pass out before your appearance," expressed Ally.

Rose chuckled, "You make a valid point."

"Are we going back to the beach house?"

"Not yet Ally," Artie gradually moved in closer, "Mr. Dalton has a proposal for you. That is the sole reason you were shown the garden and the manors ancestral tree."

"Proposal?" questioned Ally dreading the answer.

Noting Ally's understandable concern Rose intervened, "We can stay here on the ship for a few days if need be. We will do our best to wait until you're ready." She knew Ally was far too fragile to be pushed so quickly into what was coming next. The protectiveness Rose felt over Ally was written on her face. It also came across loud and clear in the tone of her voice.

Arties expression was less than thrilled, but he nodded in agreement. "Ally if you don't feel up to it Rose is correct in saying we can give you a couple days. But no longer." This reminded Ally that even though Arthur was personable he was responsible and professional. He worked for Mr. Dalton and when it came to loyalty Ally knew one thing. His duty far outweighed anything else in his life.

"A couple days then," agreed Ally noting Arthur had changed it from a few days to just a couple. She didn't know how to prepare or if she even could, but she would have to accept the fact. She would see Mr. Dalton face to face very soon.

Chapter Six

The gentle sway of the boat peacefully woke Ally from her shockingly restful slumber. Rolling onto her back she studied the room with its rich cherry stained wood and single oval window on each side of the vessel. There was a distinct air of elegance about the stateroom. The odd shape of her quarters made it clear she was in the bow of the ship. Hearing the sound of footsteps above her caused Ally to wonder how long she'd been asleep. Astonished that her mind didn't race all night or cause nightmares Ally felt refreshed and ready for anything.

Finding her way up to the deck she found Rose laughing with a young woman who greeted her warmly and surprisingly very casual, "Hi there Ally it's wonderful to see you again."

Recognizing the round flawless face of the servant from the lodge Ally greeted her, "Hello," her tone revealing the surprise she felt at seeing the servant on the boat.

"We didn't get around to full introductions at the hunting lodge so allow me to introduce Sallie," Rose motioned for Ally to come closer.

Sallie added, "Not only didn't we have time, but I had a different role to fulfill."

"Role?" asked Ally hoping there wasn't going to be another face morphing scene.

"All in good time Ally," replied Sallie.

With an endearing smile Rose inquired, "Sallie do you remember the last time we stood on the bow of The Vision?"

"Do I remember? Of course, I do Rose. I remember it like it was yesterday. You could hardly contain your excitement," her voice lively with remembrance.

Rose and Sallie were so caught up in their banter it was like Ally wasn't even there. She listened for clues as to what was going to happen when she met with Edmund. Unfortunately, there were no details given about their memory, but something very special had been shared between Rose and Sallie. It made Ally feel like a third wheel. The way they understood what the other was thinking or saying without either of them uttering much of anything. What an interesting and bewildering conversation. Ally found it impossible to track. As far as she was concerned they were talking mainly gibberish, but each of them knew what the other was saying or going to say. They completed each other's sentences even after two or three words we spoken. It was remarkable and disturbing at the same time. Where they reading each other's minds, or using telepathy? If so why were they speaking?

341

Rose continued, "The new picture...."

"at the lodge," added Sallie.

"It can't...."

"Yes, it's him," finished Sallie breaking the two of them into belly laughs.

Ally wasn't sure if they were laughing at the crazy way they talked to each other or about whoever was in the picture. Either way their uncontrollable laughter sucked Ally in and she laughed alongside them.

During breakfast Rose and Sallie continued their bizarre conversation sending the three of them time and time again into uninhibited bouts of laughter. Something Ally desperately needed. The seemingly never-ending journey of alternating emotions that took Ally from feeling renewed one moment to frustration about being confined inside the locket had met its match. The abundance of tension and resentment that had continued to build in Ally with each passing hour of captivity was now being pulled from her. Not by magic but through the simple act of laughing.

"Laughter truly is the best medicine," quoted Sallie which wasn't necessarily a funny comment, but her giggling through it made it funny.

"Oh my gosh stop," Ally begged, "my stomach hurts from laughing."

Regaining control Rose said, "Oh my goodness Sallie it's always so wonderful to see you. I've needed a good laugh session although not as much as Ally."

"It's always great to see you too Rose," agreed Sallie her adorably cute round face now pink from so much laughing.

Completely off topic Ally blurted, "Can either of you tell me what to expect when I see Edmund?"

"Ally there's plenty of time to discuss that. How about we hold off for a while and have some more fun?"

"I don't have plenty of time Sallie. I have a couple days and I come face to face with my murderer," Ally's voice wasn't angry so much as it was alarmed.

"Murderer?" that's an awfully powerful word commented Rose.

Ally didn't want to get into another conversation about Edmund being evil so she trended carefully, "Okay maybe that's a poor choice of words, but I'm worn out. One minute I'm feeling happy the next scared beyond my wildest dreams. Then I bounce from one of a dozen other emotions only to repeat the process in a different order. Every day, all day it's the same wild ride. When will it end?"

Rose began to speak, but Sallie's gaze stopped her before the words escaped her lips. "Ally I understand what you're feeling. It's the normal process we've all gone through with the exception of my dear friend Rose."

Lowering her head Rose mouthed the words, "Thank you."

"So Edmund stole your life too?"

"Ally, I prefer to say Mr. Dalton saved me from my previous life."

"I'm confused."

"You know how and why Rose is here. She voluntarily gave her life for Helene as an act of pure love. The life she had before was filled with pain, misery and inevitably a painful death. I also had a life filled with pain and suffering. Although the cause was very different. When I found myself in the locket I was free from all that. For me there was no turning back."

"So like I said Edmund took your life as well," it was no longer a question, but something Ally believed to be factual.

"I suppose you could view it that way," Sallie responded having accentuated the word "could."

"Well you said you found yourself here which means you didn't volunteer to jump in on your own."

Rose interrupted, "No Ally she did not. I'm the only one who knew where I was going. Much like you, Sallie was brought here and as she's admitted it saved her."

"Bottom line Sallie you didn't have a choice. You didn't volunteer," snapped Ally raising her voice.

"I didn't volunteer to come into the locket you're right about that Ally. Nevertheless, I volunteered to stay forever," Sallie's words and her placid voice sent a spine-tingling sensation down Ally's back.

More confused than ever Ally rambled, "Well I haven't volunteered to stay for one minute let alone forever, but I've been told over and over that I can't get out. As a matter of fact, I've recently been told about a 'wasteland' that I could be sent to for flunking a test. A test Edmund gave me that I didn't know I was taking or really understood and......"

"As you wish Mr. Dalton," addressed Rose bringing Ally's rant to a sudden stop.

Terrified to look behind her Ally stood paralyzed in fear. Studying Rose's face, it was indisputable that she was looking at Edmund. Listening hard she couldn't hear anything until Rose spoke again, "Of course sir."

More silence followed and Ally noticed Sallie smile in the same direction as Rose's stare. Closing her eyes in anticipation of Edmund coming out from behind her. Ally held her breath.

"Ally how about a game of croquet?" Rose suggested.

Squinting one eye open Ally looked for Edmund, but she couldn't see him. She verified before opening both her eyes, "Did he leave?" It was only then Ally realized they were no longer on the ship.

"It's just us girls," Sallie declared holding a croquet mallet.

Offering a few mallet choices Rose asked, "Which color do you want Ally?"

Thinking it completely absurd Ally grabbed the mallet with bands of thick black paint near the edges. It reflected the mood she was in dark, miserable, frustrated and afraid.

Arthur returned and announced the croquet court had been set up near the lake. Between Arthur's instructions on how to properly play the game, Rose and Sallie continuing to talk in their peculiar way Ally found it difficult to concentrate on her worries.

By the end of the first game which Rose easily won Ally was enjoying herself. She found the competitive side of Rose quite entertaining. Helping to bring out Ally's athletic skill. She was usually the top athlete in whatever sport she played. This was a complete contradiction to her often clumsy mishaps, but for some reason organized sports brought out a side of her no one knew existed. She decided to try harder during the next game and give Rose a run for her money. Throughout the following game who was in the lead was continuously changing. The banter between the girls took on a mischievous tone, "Awe, that's too bad Rose you were so close," poked Ally with a sideways look.

"Ally's going to catch you," Sallie teased with a snicker.

"We'll see about that," proclaimed Rose anxious for her next turn.

Sallie overshot her ball. It rolled in the direction of the lake teetering on the edge of a gradual downslope only to be accidentally bumped with Sallie's mallet when she approached. That's all it took to send the ball careening towards the water, "Oh no, stop ball stop!" she shouted chasing after it.

Tickled by the hilarious sight Rose and Ally laughed and cheered Sallie on, "Faster Sallie it's getting away!"

Inches from the water's edge the ball was snatched from its unexpected journey. "Why thank you Mr. Dalton sir," curtsied Sallie.

With the sunset solidly behind Edmund it was impossible for Ally to make out his features. Flashing back to the hallway painting she once again yearned to see his face. When his silhouette drew nearer she knew she was about to get what she wished for.

"You will address Mr. Dalton as such," were the only words Rose spoke before bowing her head to him.

Ally followed suit only lifting her eyes when Arthur began introductions, "Ally it's my honor and pleasure to introduce you to Mr. Dalton."

"Hello Mr. Dalton," wanting to take back her casual "hello" and replace it with, with? She didn't know but something better than hello. Although it was better than the "hi" that almost automatically came out.

Unfazed Edmund bowed slightly, "I see you are giving Rose some competition." His intense sapphire eyes and mesmeric features left Ally speechless causing him to turn to Rose, "Are you ready to concede defeat?"

"Never sir," answered Rose respectively with an undertone of humor.

"I'll let you finish your game," Edmund casually stated, "I will wait for you on the porch," he stated with authority and with that he walked away.

Unable to help herself Ally watched him saunter onto the porch and disappear into its shadow. For the second time the hallway painting flashed in Ally's mind. She couldn't help but wonder who he was waiting for. How she hoped it would be either Rose or Sallie, but something deep inside Ally told her it was she he wanted to meet with.

Rose and Sallie did their best to get Ally to refocus on the game, but knowing Edmund was watching distracted her. So much so she swung and missed her ball more than once. It was an easy win for Rose after that. Ally couldn't contain her thoughts any longer and asked, "He's here for me?" whispered Ally hanging her mallet on the croquet rack.

"He is Ally," confirmed Rose then trying to ease Ally's nerves added, "but Sallie will stay with you."

"No offense Sallie. Can Rose stay with me?" Ally's voice now riddled with nerves.

"I apologize Ally and I'm sorry you're so afraid," expressed Rose glancing at Sallie with an imploring look, "You are in good hands." Turning back to Ally she added, "I will see you very soon."

"You promise," begged Ally.

Rose didn't want to lie to her, but she knew there was a remote possibility she would never see her again. That concern kept Rose from immediately answering. "I will not leave the manor," was the only answer she could give Ally.

Hugging Rose tight for what she believed may be the last time Ally cried bittersweet tears. Ally felt Rose release and pull herself free without another word. Then she nudged Ally in Sallie's direction.

"Mr. Dalton is waiting Ally," said Sallie in the same nonchalant way an airport's gate agent will announce passengers say their goodbye's and board the plane.

In an unexpected turn of events Sallie walked away from the manor. It didn't take long for Ally to spy the magical garden directly in front of them. "What happened to my couple of days?" she asked.

"Your curiosity trumped that Ally. Mr. Dalton didn't see any reason to hold off any longer. Especially since answers are what you seek most of all."

Like a teenager cramming the night before a final exam Ally wanted more information, "You said you chose. What did you choose?"

"There'll be time enough for those answers with Mr. Dalton."

"Okay, if you can't tell me that can you tell me what he wants from me?"

"He wants you to accept where you are and be happy here."

In a frantic tone and pace Ally asked, "Then why do I have to see him? Can't I just go back to the beach house and pretend everything is okay?"

"No Ally, there's no pretending," Sallie stopped to look Ally straight in the eyes, "Without complete acceptance there's complicated concerns that Edmund doesn't need or have time for. His number one concern is Helene and their life. Anyone who increases the risk of sabotaging their time together is dealt with in one way or another."

"The wasteland."

"Yes Ally the wasteland is an option."

"Rose said I passed the test," exclaimed Ally afraid somehow things had changed or Sallie didn't know.

"Yes Ally you did," smiled Sallie, "You needn't worry about the wasteland right now."

"Then..."

"As Arthur explained last night. Mr. Dalton has a proposal for you to consider."

"Hello ladies," greeted Arthur, "Mr. Dalton is now waiting for us at the gardens gate."

Chapter Seven

By the time they arrived at the resplendent garden Mr. Dalton was standing in the middle of the vegetation admiring the long stem red rose bush. It's brilliant shimmer brighter than all the surrounding plants had no doubt earned the right to be displayed in the prominent spot. Edmund neither acknowledged their presence nor took his eyes from a single red rose perched high on its stem. The blossom was sizably larger and almost a foot above the other roses covering the bush. The full-bloom with its stunningly deep red hue shifted from one tantalizing shade to the next. Not only a dazzling show for the eye's it also roused something unexpected in Ally.

Even with everything Ally had experienced at the garden the previous night there was an undeniable sense of tranquility and excitement rushing through her. Not at all what she had expected to feel once back at the garden and most definitely not in Edmunds company. With a smirk Edmund turned and strolled down the path taking his time to notice each individual flower or plant bringing them to life. Each with its own special dance of light happily greeted Edmund. Some simply glowed too bright to even look at, others flashed like a strobe light and still others were unexplainable in their effervescent shine.

Following Edmund on the serpentine path through the garden soothed Ally so much she wasn't bothered when he spoke, "Here we are Sallie."

Reaching down Sallie tenderly rubbed her fingertips over the countless petals of a single large peach colored chrysanthemum. The delicate way Sallie caressed the ball of petals reminded Ally of how her mom would brush her hair when she was little. There was an unusual connection between Sallie and this bush. To the point that all the other flowers on the bush leaned towards Sallie's hand. It reminded Ally of the children in line to see Santa when she worked as an elf to earn extra money for Christmas. Sallie gazed at the flowering plant like it was her child. Ally swore her fingers captured the flowers electric charged lightshow. Sallie's hand soon mirrored the flowers glisten merging the two into a blur of light until she slowly withdrew her hand.

"This is my plant Ally. My safe haven," declared a cheerful Sallie making Ally feel like she should introduce herself to the bush. With each new revelation Ally found herself more confused leaving her struggling for what to say or do next.

With glazed over eyes Ally stared straight ahead without focusing on anything. Her chaotic mind had a hard time remembering her own name. She vaguely heard Mr. Dalton and Sallie having a friendly conversation, but found it impossible to remember even the last word spoken between them. None of her senses were working properly, her sight failed to focus, she couldn't feel the breeze blowing or the sun on her skin and the delightful garden scent vanished. She was sure that if she was given something toxic to drink she wouldn't be able to taste the poisonous liquid. Disconnected from all sensory perception left Ally numb to every emotion. In a robot-like state she remained unmoving as if waiting for someone to hit the "on" button.

An undetermined amount of time passed before Sallie patted her on the arm. That simple touch snapped her back from the frozen void she was stuck in. It wasn't until that moment she noticed the sun had moved to the other side of the sky and there was a hint of coolness in the air. Had hours or days passed by? They were all dressed the same as before, but there was no guarantee that the same clothes meant it was the same day. Nothing was real in this place. Everything could be manipulated especially by Edmund.

"So what do you think of my beautiful flowers?" asked Sallie, but before Ally gave her answer Sallie continued, "I know a lot of people don't like the herb smell of the flowers. They think it's too earthy but I enjoy it."

Ally didn't remember ever smelling a chrysanthemum and after Sallie's description she wasn't sure she wanted to. She decided to take the safe route, "They're very pretty. They look like big peach bubbles waiting to float off into the wind."

Sallie giggled at Ally's comment saying, "Yes they do. They're round like me and sometimes I float." Sallie spoke as if there wasn't anything unusual or strange with her comment. Showing Ally "her flowers" in an introduction type way, saying it was "her safe haven" and now stating that "she sometimes floats" was absurd.

Mr. Dalton snickered and proceeded down the winding path alone. His regal and confident walk drew Ally in and no matter how hard she tried to avert her eyes from him she couldn't. There was an undeniable appealing and irresistible force gushing from every inch of him. His features, voice, walk, stance, physique and the list went on kept Ally totally focused on him. Wanting to feel hatred for Edmund now felt inconceivable. There was nothing but calm admiration for the very man who had taken her from her own body. Having brought her to this strange and remarkable world where she could do things she never dreamed of almost gave her comfort. What an idiotic thing to think or feel and yet that's all that consumed Ally.

"Mr. Dalton wants you to be happy during your stay here Ally," it was Rose's voice coming from behind her.

Ally couldn't turn around and hug Rose quick enough, "Oh my gosh you're back."

"I never left the manor Ally because Mr. Dalton thinks having me here will make things easier for you."

Sallie smiled, "I agree. Rose was a huge help when it was my turn to choose."

"Choose?" stressed Ally.

"Yes way back....oh my goodness I can't even recall how long it's been, well it doesn't matter," Sallie said in her casual way. Regardless of how peculiar her words were to Ally. Floating, time travel and whatever else she referenced when talking to Ally didn't matter or at least Sallie didn't feel it did.

Controlling herself was much easier with Edmund nearby, "Would someone please tell me why I'm here?" Ally begged with a crack in her voice.

With an abruptly serious tone Sallie began, "This morning you wondered about my volunteering. You are right Ally I didn't volunteer to come into the locket any more than you volunteered. It was Edmund who decided to use your body for his wife, but there is a choice you must make. The same choice each of us must make at some point once inside the locket. Regardless of why or how we were brought here."

Terror swept over Ally and she regretted asking the question. She tried to recapture the frozen void from earlier by staring blankly at the garden. Doing nothing more than making her eyes water. Out of the corner of her eye Ally watched Edmund continue to stroll through the garden fully expecting him to zoom back to them in a flash. After all, wasn't he the one with the question to ask?

"If you could ask one question before Mr. Dalton asks you his. What would it be?"

Ally searched Rose's eyes in a desperate attempt to be led to the right question. Perhaps Rose would tune into her thoughts and give her some kind of signal when she thought about the right one to ask. Frantically running through a list of questions caused no visible change to her gorgeous hazel eyes. Had Ally failed to come up with the right question or was Rose not listening?

"There isn't one right question," Sallie said.

"Was Sallie listening in?" thought Ally.

"Sallie's correct Ally. In time, you will learn all you need to know, but for the time being what is causing you the most confusion?"

A blur of thoughts raged in Ally's head. How could she possibly narrow it all down to a single question? Unsure if she zeroed in on the inquiry of greatest importance or it was the sight of Sallie tending to her flower something prompted her. She ultimately spoke up, "I want to know about this magical garden. My guess is Edmund sending messages through it is just the tip of the iceberg. Artie or Arthur coming out of the large oak last night proved that," Ally pointed at the oak. Before anyone could answer or comment on her plea she added, "I want to know everything there is to know about it," demanded Ally.

"Smart girl," declared Sallie. "More evidence that you were a great choice."

"Most definitely," agreed Rose with a beaming smile.

Sallie continued gushing over Ally, "Combine that with her kind heart, her friendly demeanor and determination to get what she wants we have a winner. I don't think there's much that can stop her."

"You left out her athletic ability, natural beauty and deep sense of empathy," praised Rose with a prideful smile.

Listening to the two of them compliment her was strange. Ally hadn't really thought much about her strengths and most assuredly not in the way they boasted about them. "I'm still here," she broke in. Unlike most people she was quite uncomfortable being the center of attention whether for good reasons or bad.

Laughingly, both Sallie and Rose said, "Let's not forget her humbleness." That's all it took for them to start another bizarre and difficult to track conversation.

Before the conversation could gain too much traction they instantaneously stopped, turned their focus towards Edmund and appeared to be listening to him. He never turned towards them or opened his mouth. He quietly proceeded around the other end of the garden and went out the gate.

Relief washed over Ally as Edmund disappeared into the manor, "He doesn't want to talk to me?"

"No, he still needs to discuss something with you, but Helene called for him."

For whatever reason, Ally hadn't considered that Helene was inside the manor. Knowing her body was so close sparked something deep within Ally. She was ready for a fight. A fight she hoped would set her free.

Crushing her optimism Rose said, "Ally it's impossible. You will never see Helene in your body. Arthur and I are the only ones permitted to see the true Helene."

"True Helene?" More ambiguous talk thought Ally, "If there's more than one Helene why doesn't he just stay with the first one?"

"All in good time Ally."

Becoming flush with heat as her temper flared Ally tugged on her Victorian dress, "I'm so tired of these constricting clothes. I'm so tired of all of this!" she shouted causing the garden to burst into an explosion of colors. Particles of glimmering light blew towards Ally gathering together until they whirled around her and as quickly as her temper had flared it vanished. Before the specks of light dissipated around her she swore she heard "wasteland" in the hum of their movement.

"Help me!" screeched Ally.

Rose used that same stern tone from the day aboard The Vision, "That's what we're trying to do."

With a forbidding expression and harsh tone Sallie showed a side of her Ally soon wished she didn't know existed. The happy go lucky and bubbly woman had been replaced with a menacing warrior of a woman. Her dark blue skirt and hooded cape was offset by the hazelnut leather corset that covered her cream-colored blouse. The quiver hanging from her back was full of arrows and she wielded an exquisite bow. "Let us get back to your question before it's too late," declared Sallie visibly on alert.

Concerned that anything she said next would make things worse Ally gave a slight nod. Time seemed to move in slow motion as Ally watched Sallie relentlessly scan their surroundings. Fearful of what may come into view Ally diverted her eyes back to the garden specifically to Sallie's chrysanthemum. The bush had bloomed into a countless number of flowers each beaming with its own independent luster.

"Come with me," coaxed Rose.

Without a word Ally followed Rose back to the proud red rose where Edmund stood when she arrived at the garden. The towering stem which held the lone rose swayed in the breeze leaning closer to Rose when she reached for the blossom. Inhaling its captivating perfumed fragrance brought a breathtaking smile to Rose. "This is my flower Ally. It's the gardens original flower. Mr. Dalton planted it with his own hands."

That simple acknowledgement caused the light bulb in Ally's head to flicker. "Okay. Rose was the first one to help Edmund and her flower was the first one in the garden," she thought. Ally knew it was significant, but why did Rose and Sallie need their own flower?

In a gentle whisper Sallie said, "Watch."

Quickly checking to see that Sallie was back to her old self Ally turned her gaze back to the lush garden. In a rhythmic display of light flowers took turns bringing forth men and women just long enough for them to wave hello to Ally. Before Ally could respond they dematerialized back into their respective flowers. Their cordial smiles made her feel like she was home. Ally no longer felt fearful and miraculously all her questions faded away. It was the same feeling she would get when she visited her grandparents as a child. The feeling of complete acceptance and although she hated to admit it, love.

"This garden is our safe haven Ally. Whenever we aren't needed we slip through the garden back to our created world and return only when Mr. Dalton calls upon us." Sallie's voice was filled with warmth and kindness a far cry from the intense defender she was minutes earlier.

Looking around at the countless plants Ally watched more and more people cheerfully welcome her. Many of who she remembered from her time on the ship. "I still don't understand why Edmund I mean Mr. Dalton needs so many people. If all he wants to do is give Helene a body what does he need everyone else for?"

"Each of us have a specific task to perform," replied Sallie.

"What type of tasks could Mr. Dalton need us to do?"

Sallie began to speak and her appearance returned to the warrior, "I am a hunter Ally. My task is very different from Rose's task."

"What do you hunt?" asked Ally crossing her fingers that it was something ordinary. Like something she'd be willing to eat for dinner.

"Several different things but one thing in particular," answered Sallie changing back to her previous self.

Rose winked at Sallie before proclaiming what her task was, "I fulfill Mr. Dalton's main objective. Basically, I'm the closer."

Taking some time to consider what she just learned Ally had an epiphany. Looking straight into Rose's eyes she proclaimed, "You pretended to be my friend so you could give me the locket. You were just doing your job," Ally's voice quivered with this realization. Fighting hard against the tears seeping from her eyes she went on, "I was nothing more than the next task on your "To Do list." Ally's words were filled with more hurt than anger. She needed to know. Were she and Rose truly friends? Rose was the only thing keeping Ally from completely losing her mind.

With sincere eyes Rose pledged, "You're wrong Ally we are friends, but that doesn't change the fact that I have a promise to keep with Mr. Dalton. Not to mention my love and lifelong friendship with Helene."

The look of urgent sincerity in Sallie's eyes helped persuade Ally that Rose was being truthful. Then she went on to remind her of some important facts. "You know why Rose chose to help Edmund and please never forget that. Mr. Dalton saved Rose from Maxwell. There isn't any doubt that he would have eventually killed her. I'm convinced he would have quite literally gotten away with murder. Not once has he been held accountable for his heinous behavior."

Mental pictures of Rose's battered face and the memory of her agreeing to help Helene rushed in. Sallie was right. Rose dying at the hands of her husband was undeniable and they all knew it was only a matter of time. Ashamed of herself Ally apologized to her friend. Coming to the conclusion that Edmund's desire to have Helene back ruled not only his life, but anyone else's he needed to use to make that happen. The extensive garden made it apparent Edmund needed numerous people to help accomplish his goal. Although Ally was unsure why.

"So each plant belongs to a person with a specific job to do for Mr. Dalton?"

"Yes Ally, we all have our own plant or flower," answered Rose thankful to see Ally regaining control.

"But why?"

Edmund's voice reverberated from behind Ally, "I will take it from here ladies."

Chapter Eight

Ally's body tensed overflowing with apprehension. Then ever so slowly and cautiously she turned to face Edmund. A sudden gust of wind enveloped Ally in the gardens perfume causing her nose to tingle. Making eye contact with Mr. Dalton's unforgettable eyes released all her fear. Leaving her in an anesthetized state and without any instincts. Ally was unable to decipher whether he had cast a spell on her or that simply being so close to the most attractive man she'd ever seen dulled her senses. Ally greeted him with a shy smile. His captivating grin sent waves of color to her cheeks making her feel downright embarrassed by her reaction.

"Follow me Ally," he politely instructed.

With Rose and Sallie following a couple feet behind Ally walked alongside Edmund. Ally had to take at least two steps to Edmund's single step just to keep up. It was clearly evident the section of the garden they approached was newer. The few tiny plants that were scattered about in a rather orderly but natural layout were doubly protected. In addition to the garden's surrounding fencing each new plant was sheltered by its own chicken wire cloche.

Ally's necklace ever so gently trembled against her skin when Edmund stopped in front of what appeared to be a recently planted shrub. The petite plant covered in delicate pink daisies with large yellow centers varied ever so slightly in their color. From whitish pink to bold hot pink hues the flowers danced with a glittering shine swaying in Ally's direction. An unexpected wave of sentiment flooded Ally. Within seconds she was kneeling next to the seedling and pushing her fingers through the chicken wire. Tenderly her fingertips grazed the young blooms, but unlike Sallie her hand failed to mirror the daisies light show.

Feeling connected to the plant in the same way she felt connected to her family Ally wondered with anticipation, "Are these my flowers?"

"That is for you to decide Ally." Edmund's stance was serious. Hands behind his back, shoulder's square and an "at attention" posture made him an even more authoritative figure.

Realizing she was about to hear the proposal she'd been waiting on Ally knew she should stand, but her fingertips refused to pull away from the flowers. Touching the fragile blooms was filling her with boundless serenity helping her to understand why Sallie had used the words "safe haven" to describe her flowers. Those words best illustrated the bond she immediately felt towards the daisies. Ally didn't understand this anymore than anything else occurring in this magical world. But for the first time since she entered the locket she felt positively at home. Rose and Sallie each took an arm lifting her to her feet.

The entire magical garden including the massive sentinel oak near the gate began emitting a humming sound. Ally labored to hear the faint and unusual melody the garden was softly playing. The event reminded her of a pivotal movie scene complete with a perfectly matched film score. There wasn't anything sinister about the tune. Ally could think of only one way to describe it "other-worldly" a more than fitting description for where she was.

Lowering their faces Rose and Sallie took a step back changing Edmunds solemn expression into one filled with expectancy. The weight of the moment lifted when Edmund's voice rang of optimism, "I'm hopeful Ally that you will agree to join the garden. You will be of great assistance to me and all the others with keeping Helene safe."

Ally was at a loss and in all honesty said, "I'm not exactly sure what that means Mr. Dalton." Addressing him formally felt completely normal. She no longer felt comfortable calling or even thinking of him as Edmund. Ally continued, "Mr. Dalton would you be willing to explain exactly what you're offering me?"

Somewhere in the deepest recesses of her mind she wondered why she was speaking the way she was. Drowning out this lone thought was the undeniable feeling of being interviewed and the aspiration that she would meet with Mr. Dalton's approval. Contrary to what she expected to feel about the anticipated proposal Ally found herself jittery with excitement.

"The position I would like to offer you is similar to the task Sallie handles for me. I'm sure she can answer all your questions," his tone was pleasant enough, but his face showed signs of concern. A silent exchange between Rose and Mr. Dalton lasted a mere second before he bid farewell to them. Adding he would give Ally until nightfall the following evening for her answer.

Unable to pull her eyes off Edmund she watched him rush up the steps and through the front door of the manor. Ally was unsure if her eyes were playing tricks on her, but she swore she noticed a faint displacement of light when he passed through the doorway. Reminding Ally of the when her Grammy would gingerly reach into her treasured fish tank. With careful and gentle movements, she would rearrange the plants to keep from spooking the fish making only the slightest ripple in the water's surface.

"Oh Edmund," cried Helene falling into his embrace.

Feeling her body quiver against his prompted Edmund to tighten his squeeze. Cuddling her so powerfully close Helene slowed her breathing and released her clenched muscles. Concern oozed from every word he said, "I'm here my dearest. What has happened?"

Helene tried to replay the nightmare that startled her from her nap. A far-off gaze remained in her eyes while she recounted what details she could remember. Frustration built as the remaining foggy memories of the dream faded during the course of her sharing it with Edmund. "Why can't I hold onto the memory?" Helene moaned.

Nightmares were not uncommon after Helene was transported from the locket to her new host body, but this time they seemed to linger. She was experiencing far more difficult days than good days. Helene rarely napped more than a few days after the switch and Edmund wondered "What was making this time so different?" Ally's body was extremely fit and healthy making it so much harder to understand the delay in Helene being back to her old self.

Helene's eyes flashed with remembrance, "Oh. I remember looking in the mirror and not recognizing myself. When I spoke, it was my voice with my mannerisms and the woman in the reflection was wearing my favorite blue dress. She also wore my beautiful anniversary gift around her neck," Helene paused then shot a look at Edmund with distressed eyes. "You wrapped this stranger in your arms proclaiming your unending love for her," she said tearing up.

Edmund's skillful intelligence snapped into overdrive fearing what had caused this all too close to reality dream, "My love," he soothed, "My dear sweet Helene you are the only woman I will ever love. My love for you and you alone will last until the end of time. Without you I would cease to exist." Lifting her tear soaked face to his he continued. His love now more powerful than his fear. Motivated to safeguard the love of his life he reminded her, "Helene you lost a close, trusted and beloved friend in Elizabeth. You are hurting more than you're willing to admit. If you recall our conversation after her passing it's understandable that you would have a frightening dream of us losing each other."

Helene's grief-stricken expression withered away and with a deep cleansing breath she released the dream. Edmunds loving explanation for her nightmare was reasonable enough. Helene was a highly logical woman. She had painfully learned her lesson about letting her emotions run her life. She came so very close to missing out on her life with Edmund. Allowing the fear and heartbreak Luther had left her with to control her. She promised herself she would never again let fear have that much if any power over her.

Helene's adoring eyes locked onto Edmunds and with that simple gesture her sorrow and fear were replaced with comfort and peace. Tilting her head toward his they each closed their eyes. Standing forehead to forehead they let silent minutes' pass between them. Patiently Edmund waited to feel Helene back away from their connection. She was the one in need of comfort and he would remain by her side until she sent him away.

Helene spoke tenderly, "Thank you my love. You are so good to me. I don't know what I did to deserve you."

With a swelling heart Edmund responded, "Deserve me? It's I who never stops wondering what I did to deserve you," his words were sincere and factual. A day rarely passed where he didn't feel humbled by the fact that Helene came into his life and more importantly she truly and deeply loved him.

Choosing to ignore everything other than Helene for the rest of the day Edmund and she enjoyed a walk around the grounds, a visit to the stables and a boisterous piano session where Edmund sang song after song proclaiming his undying love for Helene. Her skillful playing and his noteworthy singing livened the mood throughout the manor. The cooks stirred and chopped to the tempo of the lively songs and the doors to the cellar where left open. This made it possible for the worker's downstairs to faintly hear the impromptu concert.

Life at the manor had returned to an environment of normalcy. At least for the rest of the day. Edmund remained hopeful that Helene had overcome the final hurdle of nightmares and would soon regain all of her strength. He looked forward to years of enjoying time with his beloved wife before having to go through yet another body switch. Refusing to let the future destroy their present happiness Edmund pushed aside all thoughts of another host being needed. Letting his heart rejoice in the pure happiness that his wife had returned soon had him reeling in their extraordinary love.

Helene proved that she was feeling so much better when she seduced Edmund later that evening. They spent the night within the clutches of impassioned carnal affinity. The way only a sincerely loving and committed husband and wife could. Their phenomenal night of love ended with the best night's sleep either of them had had in weeks.

Lazily they rustled in bed as the sunrise skipped across their skin. Helene cuddled against Edmund glowing from the night's activities. Stroking her hair released the soft scent of the rosemary tea Helene used to rinse her hair after a thorough washing. Reminding her that she would soon need more egg yolks to rewash her hair, "Who is it that I should ask to assist me in bathing and dressing?" Helene whispered bringing back a tinge of pain knowing Elizabeth would no longer be helping her. Over the last couple of weeks, a different servant had helped Helene with her daily routine. The rotation of servants made it easy for Helene to convince herself that Elizabeth would be returning from a much-needed vacation. No matter how much she knew that wasn't true. Believing even for a moment that Elizabeth would be back eased Helene's sorrow.

Considering his options Edmund stated, "I believe Dorothy would be a good permanent choice."

"Awe yes, Dorothy," agreed Helene.

Edmund replied in a business-like tone, "I'll summon her and let her know she'll be replacing

Elizabeth as your housemaid," Edmund quickly added, "Not that anyone could come close to replacing Elizabeth. She was truly one of a kind."

Helene forced a smile through her sunken expression. She knew Edmund didn't mean to sound callous about Elizabeth being gone. He had done nothing more than answer her question. Yet it was then that it truly hit her. Sadly, she said, "Thank you darling and yes there's no replacing Elizabeth, but Dorothy is a wonderful choice." Still wrestling with the fact that she would never again dress with Elizabeth's help made Helene miss her friend even more. They had become so much more than employer and employee over the years.

Edmund returned with Dorothy on his heels, "Good morning Mrs. Dalton," she greeted. Her frizzy blonde hair doing its best to break free from the multiple hair pins and white cap she wore.

"Good morning Dorothy."

Dorothy wasted no time getting to business, "It's another beautiful day not too warm or too cold. This should be just fine," she announced pulling a peach and coffee colored dress from Helene's closet.

Helene agreed, "Yes, that is a favorite dress of mine."

Dorothy moved about the room with ease making it look like a well-rehearsed dance routine. Perhaps it was nerves for she buzzed around so quickly from one task to another that Helene was astonished how quickly she was ready for the day.

Joining Edmund in the dining room for breakfast Helene sat near the head of the massive table where Edmund always sat. There wasn't a meal they shared where they couldn't reach across the table and hold hands. The love they shared was evident whether at home or in town, all alone or in a crowd. It didn't matter. They couldn't help it, their love radiated all around them and at times consumed their surroundings.

"You look beautiful my sweet," boasted Edmund with a kiss on her cheek.

"Thank you darling," she blushed. Although it was part of her everyday life with Edmund. He never failed to make her blush with a girlish bashfulness. The adoring and endearing look in his eyes when he complimented her was something she never took for granted. She habitually reminded herself that he was the man of nearly every woman's dream and to her own shock and amazement he had chosen her.

Enjoying a relaxing meal and lighthearted conversation built on the afterglow from the night before. They soon lost themselves in the simple act of relishing their happiness. "Other than an appointment I have later this evening Helene my day is open to spend with you. Is there anything in particular you would like to do?"

It took Helene only half a second to reply, "I would like to go to town. I can't remember the last time I went."

With a playful wink Edmund smiled as he said, "Your wish is my command."

"That would be lovely Edmund. Perhaps we could have a picnic in the park?"

"Today is a great day for a picnic," he agreed. Edmund turned to the butler giving him instructions to alert the kitchen staff and have them ready a meal for their picnic.

"It'll do me some good to get out of the manor for a while. I feel like I've been a hermit lately," Helene stood, kissed Edmund and proceeded to the stairs only to return and ask, "Have you heard from Rose? Maybe we can send word that we will be at the park this afternoon."

Avoiding the question Edmund asked his own question, "Did she say anything to you about traveling the last time she visited?"

"Not that I can remember, but I was still feeling ill at the time. Why do you ask?" Helene inquired after realizing Edmund hadn't answered her question.

Picking his words carefully he said, "She wouldn't contact me directly my love. Any correspondence she would send would be addressed to you and I haven't seen a letter or note from her," his answer was truthful and Helene had no reason to question him further.

"That is true. I suppose I was hoping I had missed something from her. If it had crossed your desk I would have gotten it."

Helene's disappointment was soon replaced with concern for Rose prodding Edmund to nip it in the bud, "Yesterday in town I did overhear that Maxwell was delayed in coming home so there's no need to fret over Rose."

With Helene satisfied with his answer she headed upstairs to prepare for their outing. Meanwhile Edmund sent a message through the garden that he may need Rose that afternoon.

***

"Did you see that?" Ally asked.

"See what?" answered Rose.

"That weird rippling when Mr. Dalton went into the house."

"I wasn't watching," was all Rose said.

Frustrated with her reply Ally pushed the issue, "Okay you may not have seen it this time, but I'm guessing you've seen it before."

Very naturally in a style and tone all her own Sallie switched the topic back to Mr. Dalton's proposal, "We should really stick to the topic at hand Ally. Mr. Dalton's question for you."

"Sallie has a valid point Ally. There's plenty of time for you to learn more about the locket's magical spell. For now, you have a decision to make," agreed Rose adding an important fact, "You need to have your decision by tomorrow night."

The hum of the garden went silent and her little daisy shrub lost some of its luster. Immediately transferring it's sadden look to Ally, "It's okay sweeties," addressed Ally to the flowers perking them up. Their happy reaction to Ally's words also brightened her mood, proving to her that their emotions were entwined.

Enthusiastically Sallie suggested they return to the hunting lodge and begin giving Ally the details she would need to help make her decision. Ally agreed and after bidding farewell to her little bush they were on their way.

Chapter Nine

The hushed carriage ride back to the lodge seemed shorter than normal. Primarily because Ally was altogether preoccupied. She found herself contemplating so much more than Edmund's proposal. Her thoughts were mainly focused on the garden with its spectacular visual effects. Which Ally believed was just the tip of the iceberg. Her matching flower with its own unique sheen, the peculiar way she felt in the garden and lastly the decision she had to make before sundown the following day.

Exiting the carriage Ally stopped dead in her tracks, "Hunting lodge," she deciphered, "You're a hunter and this is your home."

"Yes Ally, when I'm not out hunting this is where I choose to live. The manor and its grounds are far better than anything I had in my life before Mr. Dalton rescued me."

There was that word again, "rescue" a word she would never choose to use about Mr. Dalton. Ally may not have had the perfect life, but who does? Yes, things were bad at home and progressively getting worse. Going away to college put enough distance between Ally and her painful home life, but she knew she would one day return home. Now there wasn't any way to return home. Ally feared she would never see her family again. This thought brought Ally to the brink of tears and her thoughts snowballed into a trail of heartbreaking questions.

Subdued tears vanished in her welling eyes and without hesitation she stated, "I wasn't rescued Sallie. I had my life stolen from me." Ally's tone had a reserved strength to it. With a clear mind and in full control of her emotions she asked, "So tell me Sallie. What exactly do you hunt?"

Proudly Sallie began, "I hunt enemies of Mr. Dalton, his family and of Dalton Manor."

"So you're like his own private security?"

"Not exactly, more of a covert liaison for Mr. Dalton."

"Could I get a straight answer for once?" Ally's voice was agitated. "What in the world makes Mr. Dalton think I would be good at hunting enemies? I've never been in a physical fight and I'd prefer not to start now. Especially in this unpredictable world."

Rose cut in, "Sallie that may be the favorite part of your job, but Ally would have plenty of time to work up to that. Shall we start with what she would be hunting first?"

Knowing Rose was right, Sallie explained, "I hunt down replacement bodies for Mr. Dalton. There are always a couple of backup hosts in case the switch fails. I also take out enemies I come across in my searches,"

Sallies exuberance for this part of her job was highly evident.

"Oh my gosh! He wants me to help him kill other girls to use for Helene's soul?" Ally's voice shrieked with horror.

"Ally let me remind you that you are not dead," said Rose.

"Well I'm not alive either. I'm in this, this...." she struggled for the right phrase, "this fantasy limbo!"

"Ally you must calm down. You don't have time to waste rehashing facts that upset you."

"Oh I'm sorry Rose is my anger at losing my life interfering with your task?" It was the first-time Ally had spoken sarcastically to Rose and she regretted it as soon as the words left her mouth. A strong wind threw open the front door uncloaking a rotting figure before them. In a hoarse voice the grotesquely frightening manifestation groaned, "Wasteland," then vanished as quickly as it appeared. Leaving behind a fetid odor that turned Ally's stomach.

Sallie and Rose appeared mildly shocked by the event, but it left Ally sickened by the stench and grizzly sight. Swaying in the throes of nausea she was assisted to the couch by Rose. Meanwhile Sallie resumed her warrior persona. Once she felt confident that there wasn't an imminent threat she returned to her friendly self.

"What exactly was that?" asked Sallie.

The magical gardens sweet scent funneled through the house overpowering them all. Calm filled them and it was obvious that Rose was listening hard to new instructions.

With a determined expression Rose relayed the message, "Ally, I don't have time to explain all the reasons Mr. Dalton believes that you would be an excellent hunter. For now, you have to trust me when I say he's never been wrong in his selections."

"That doesn't explain...." Ally interrupted.

Grimacing with annoyance Rose interjected, "Would you let me finish?"

"Miss Ally, you need to take this seriously," added Sallie seemingly as interested in hearing what had happened as Ally was. Having added "Miss" in front of her name clued Ally in on the importance of the conversation.

"Mr. Dalton has given you an opportunity to remain here with us for all eternity. To create the world of your choosing or live at the manor like Sallie. However, your continued battling and unending questions have put you at a terrible risk." Rose took a slow deep breath before continuing. With sadness in her eyes she spoke words that were difficult for her to say, "Mr. Dalton is highly concerned that you'll forever be a threat to him and

Helene. If you don't show marked improvement in your willingness to accept your fate," Rose paused then in no uncertain terms stated, "He will send you to the wasteland."

"But I passed the test. I believe he loves Helene and she loves him," reminded Ally.

"That is true Ally and yet you keep ending up at the same place. Back at square one. Refusing to accept you're here permanently." Rose took a deep breath before stressing, "There is no way out," declared Rose enunciating each word with conviction.

Sallie urgently tried to help, "Please stop viewing Mr. Dalton as the enemy. Plain and simple. He loves Helene more than life itself. He would have switched places with her in a second, but it was impossible, even for him. Mr. Dalton couldn't handle an eternal life without her. Think about it Ally. Imagine what it would be like to have someone love you so much he would do anything within his power to keep you alive and with him."

Rose and Sallie continued to plead Edmunds case going on and on about his love for Helene. Repeatedly stating he wasn't evil. By the end of their heartfelt testimony Ally understood one thing. Mr. Dalton was a hero to them both.

"So who was the creepy person at the door?" Ally asked in an effort to change the subject. Besides, she believed Sallie was wondering the same thing.

"I don't know who he was. All I know is Mr. Dalton sent him here with one message," Rose locked eyes with Ally and warned in a strange growling voice, "This is your last warning. Next time you are defiant the wasteland is where you'll find yourself."

"I promise I'll be good. No more angry outbursts. I'll do whatever Mr. Dalton wants me to do. I won't ever say he took my life ever again," surrendered Ally.

With a weak unconvinced smile Rose replied, "I hope you keep that promise Ally. I cannot help you if Mr. Dalton decides to send you away."

"Of course she'll keep her promise," replied Sallie enthusiastically. She firmly squeezed Ally's shoulders. The strength in her hands sent a clear message even though her voice was pleasant and upbeat. Sallie's strength both mental and physical could prove helpful or harmful. Ally wanted to avoid the latter at all cost.

Wanting to prove to Rose that she intended to keep her promise Ally asked, "Okay. What's the first thing I need to learn?"

"Before your training can begin there's a few magical garden details we should cover," suggested Rose with a nod to Sallie.

Sallie took her cue saying, "Let's start with the garden plants. Shall we?"

Ally sat on the edge of her seat completely focused on Sallie and doing her best to be a model student. Holding tight to her necklace's main daisy she concurred, "Yes. I want to know everything there is to know about my pretty little plant."

After taking some time to prepare Sallie started from one of Ally's questions, "You wondered why we each need a plant?"

"Yes I did," cheered Ally sounding like a child listening to Santa give away his trade secrets.

Seeing that Ally was completely tuned into Sallie, Rose stepped back from the couch, closed her eyes and evaporated into nothingness. Ally didn't find it frightening. There was a peaceful expression on Rose's face and the always remarkable scent of the garden engulfed the lodge. Feeling once again like she was home Ally smiled at Sallie anxiously waiting for her to continue.

"Rose has returned to the garden through her rose bush," explained Sallie.

Considering this for a moment Ally giggled, "It's like beam me up Scotty."

Sallie laughed with her whole body, "That's a clever way of putting it."

Surprised by Sallie understanding her comment Ally teased, "I didn't think you'd get my reference."

"Oh Ally. I've traveled to so many different places in time. I'm a wealth of earthly knowledge."

Caught up in their laughter Ally failed to notice Rose had returned. "I'm glad to see you two are having a good time."

"That's kinda cool Rose. What does it feel like?"

"It feels like it looks. All of a sudden you're lighter than air until there's nothing left to feel. The next thing you know Mr. Dalton is summoning you from a blossom and you're standing with him. Usually in the garden."

"That still doesn't explain why we have a plant. Can't he just call us to him?"

A strange sensation pulsated through Ally's veins and in no time, she began to feel weightless. Unlike her travels with Arthur and their sputtering movements with color-rich abstract lights buzzing by, Ally found herself in a sea of tranquility. Muted colors floated by while the aromatic bouquet of countless flowers filled her heart with comfort.

"Ally come forth," commanded Edmund.

Her vision gradually cleared from what could only be described as peering through a delicately thin piece of fabric. Through the haziness she could see the most picturesque sight she'd ever seen. Standing high on the edge of a mountain Ally soaked in the beauty around her as her eyes cleared. For as far as she could see there was mountain range after mountain range. Towering snow covered peaks sat far off in the distance. The clear blue sky was home to large puffy white clouds and the sun blazing from behind the largest cloud made it's silver lining visible. It smelled like Christmas. A strong breeze carried with it an almost overpowering pine scent. Ally couldn't help herself. She breathed deeply with closed eyes and smiled at the remarkable fragrance. Memories of Christmas flooded her mind. Quickly she opened her eyes in an unlikely effort to be back at home.

It was then that she noticed she was standing precariously on the edge of a lofty cliff. Amazingly it had little impact on her comfort level. With bold confidence Ally stretched out her arms, threw her head back and hollered at the top of her lungs, "I will be good!" Her pledge repeatedly echoed through the canyons. When the last echo dwindled away she suddenly found herself back at the hunting lodge.

"Mr. Dalton is big on dramatic messages," Ally stated. She understood what the symbolic visit to the mountain top meant. Even though she was unclear as to how she knew its meaning.

"Where did you go?" quizzed Sallie.

387

Rose gave Ally an encouraging look which was all she needed, "Well it wasn't the garden as I expected. Instead Mr. Dalton wanted to show me how very close I am to the edge."

"What edge?"

"The edge of things ending badly for me. If I continue to be defiant."

"Oh, Mr. Dalton is so gifted," bragged Sallie, "I get it now. Basically, you were teetering on your willingness to help him which means he's teetering on where to send you."

Ally wasn't sure she had the same appreciation for Edmunds flare of theatrics that Sallie had, but she was happy Sallie understood how much danger she was in. Clinging to hope Ally trusted that Sallie and Rose would help her from falling off the cliff into the wasteland. Ally was now more determined than ever to be on her very best behavior. Using such a beautiful sight to send the message of her possible downfall was more terrifying than their earlier visitor. Reminding Ally that sometimes incredibly dangerous things can appear harmless before they strike.

It was well after midnight and the day's events had worn Ally out. Exhaustion was now beginning to win the war on trying to stay awake. The sight of Ally's eyes repeatedly taking extra-long blinks convinced Rose that it would be counterproductive to try and explain anymore about the garden.

"Let's get to bed," urged Rose, "We have all day tomorrow to fill Ally in on the gardens details."

Sallie agreed with a yawn and was the first into her room. Rose gave Ally a friendly hug of encouragement before Ally proceeded upstairs. The longer than normal hug was a clear sign that Rose was hoping beyond hope that Ally would finally and completely surrender to her new life.

Once Sallie and Ally were behind closed doors Rose disappeared at the speed of light, burst from the rose bush and rushed towards the manor.

<u>Chapter Ten</u>

Not long after Ally climbed into bed was she sound asleep. Fuzzy images floated by in a mist. Disappearing before she could make out who or what it was. Finally, one image came into focus. It was the garden or what should have been the garden. The large mature oak stood alone. Not a single plant was to be seen, nor was the fencing there causing Ally to notice something more. The oak itself wasn't quite the magnificent tree as the night before. The bevy of contorted branches held sturdy by the bulky trunk were much smaller in scale. It was clear that the tree was considerably younger. Hovering above the ground Ally swooped in closer only to be stuck in place. She suddenly found herself suspended roughly fifteen feet above Edmund.

With meticulous movements Edmund's hands compressed the soil around the freshly planted rose bush. Then he gave the plant a healthy drink of water and with a wave of his hand the intricate garden fencing appeared. In amazement Ally watched the little rose bush triple in size then shoot one stem high above the others. In seconds a bud appeared and bloomed into an enormous and blindingly intense red rose.

"Come forth Rose," whispered Edmund gently.

A startled Rose materialized before him, "Where am I?"

"You are safe at the manor," assured Edmund.

Examining herself Rose discovered she was healed of all her injuries and felt unbelievably refreshed. The dress she wore was one Helene had given to her as a birthday gift. This immediately reminded her of her last memory, "Helene? Is she alright?"

"Yes Rose. She is doing well with the transition. Of course, she tires easily but that is to be expected."

Rose didn't feel dead. She felt fairly normal except for a strange tingle making its way through her body. Pins and needles swelled through every muscle. The dull sensation reminiscent of her foot falling asleep became more intense worrying Rose. She commented through welling eyes, "I'm starting not to feel very well, Mr. Dalton."

"That's normal Rose please have a seat," motioned Edmund to a bench that instantly appeared.

Rose noticed the rose bush once she was seated and asked, "You're planting a garden?"

"Yes I am. A very special garden Rose and you are the first to see it," Edmunds voice rang with happiness and pride. "You are also the very first to have her own flower."

The puzzlement on Rose's face managed to sum up nearly all of Ally's questions and confusion in one single expression. Ally addressed Rose in the dream unaware that she was speaking out loud in her sleep, "Exactly how I feel Rose."

Edmund was quick to address the questions he knew Rose was struggling with. He explained to her in an encouraging tone how her soul was now locked in the locket and her body now hosted Helene's soul. This wasn't new news to Rose or Ally, but his following words were.

"This rose bush is your lifeline Rose. When your body gives out I will be forced to once again trap Helene's soul in the locket leaving you without a body to return to."

"I'm confused Mr. Dalton I thought I would live for eternity. Isn't that what you offered me? An eternity of safety away from Maxwell and to be forever with Helene and you?" Rose asked terrified she'd been fooled.

Calmly Edmund explained, "That is why I've planted your rose. When the time comes, you will return to the rose and I will use its viability to create your eternal existence."

"You turned me into a plant?" shrieked Rose.

"No, I did not turn you into the rose bush. You will always be you, your soul simply needs a living organism to gain strength from," expressed Edmund with a run-of-the-mill attitude. He then added, "It also allows me to use its existence to give you physical form."

Rose being a highly intelligent woman quickly asked, "What happens if the rose bush dies?"

"Fear not, the garden is magical and protected day and night by the large oak. Besides having its own bodyguard, the iron fencing conceals the very existence of the garden from everyone. I alone am the key in and out of the garden."

Unsure if it was the ceasing of the tingly sensation or Edmunds at-ease behavior Rose felt comfortable and serene with her decision. She anxiously wanted to know what would happen next. Then a thought hit her. "But I feel like myself. I mean I can touch my face and clasp my hands, so I'm guessing this is the physical form you spoke of. Do I look like myself?"

Ally watched Rose continue to speak but no longer heard anything. The damp earthy smell of impending rain engulfed Ally whisking her away from the garden. She found herself high in the rafters of an old church. Her disappointment at being pulled from what she was sure would be an enlightening conversation was quickly forgotten.

Below her was an overfilled church bursting at the seams. Every seat was taken. There were people standing alongside the exterior walls and numerous people outside the rear doors aching to enter. The chapel's chancel was blanketed in elegant floral arrangements and candles. There was very little room left for the minister who stood near the ostentatious casket. Edmund and Helene were seated in the front pew to the left of the alter. Ally focused hard on Helene before looking at the picture on the casket. The crown of the casket was free from flowers. This allowed the framed photograph of Rose to draw the mourners in. Bewildered Ally wondered why Helene seemed so untroubled at the funeral of her dearest friend.

Helene turned and looked up at Ally who was still floating among the rafters. With a friendly wink Helene turned into Rose. Thankfully the magical force that was supporting Ally midair held tight. She didn't fall to the floor even when she tipped backwards. Rose was attending her own funeral disguised as Helene. Ally couldn't imagine how surreal and intensely painful that must have been.

With a loud arrogant and disgustingly unfazed spirit Maxwell greeted all those in attendance. Not surprisingly he turned his eulogy about his deceased wife into a dedication to himself. Ally found herself seeing past the mourner's uniform façade at his speech. Soon she could hear their internal rumbling of disbelief and disapproval. The hatred they were all overwhelmingly feeling for him was second only to the collective fear Maxwell had instilled in the town. Witnessing his menacing behavior had convinced the townspeople to yield to his every wish. Rose's death had only reinforced their fear. Although no one could prove Maxwell had anything to do with her death there wasn't a single person there that believed the story he told.

Edmund stood with Helene or Rose as soon as Maxwell finished his inappropriate speech and headed straight for him. Before they said a word, Maxwell announced loudly, "My wife's horse has been destroyed for his violent act," as if that was what everyone was bothered by.

That statement weakened Rose making her knees buckle and Edmund had to help her regain both her physical and emotional balance saying "Helene we should head outside. It's far too stuffy in here. Let's get some fresh air and let you regain your composure. You are too upset to speak with anyone."

Others standing near them agreed with Edmund reaffirming his advice. Many suggested Helene follow her husband's counsel. What an unusual vantage point Ally had. She could see Rose as clear as day standing with Edmund, but if she shifted her focus Helene came back into view. Slipping through the ceiling of the church like it wasn't there Ally followed the procession out to the graveyard. After the final hymn was sung the crowd dispersed leaving Ally alone to watch the casket be lowered into the ground. She couldn't help but wonder if there was even a body inside the coffin.

Ally blinked normally and was back at the manor watching Edmund lovingly push Helene on a tree swing. No longer could she see Rose posing as Helene. Changing her focus, squinting or even covering one eye at a time had no effect. There was no one there except Helene and Edmund. Making Ally wonder if any part of her dream was real when she awoke.

Throwing on some clothes Ally rushed downstairs. She found Rose and Sallie enjoying breakfast at the kitchens hefty wooden table. Filled with nervous energy Ally wasted no time getting to the point, "Was everything in my dream last night what really happened?"

"Yes Ally. Mr. Dalton often uses our dreams to send messages and answer questions we may have," replied Rose before sipping her tea.

"So my daisy will keep me alive for eternity?"

"If you wish. Mr. Dalton gives you the choice to remain here and assist him..." Sallie stopped mid-sentence when Rose cleared her throat.

Rose tried to prevent Ally from asking the question that was already on her lips saying, "Would you like some breakfast while we discuss the gardens magical power more in-depth?"

"I'm not hungry Rose." Ally braced herself then asked, "What if I don't want to live for an eternity?"

"Then you don't have to Ally. Again, it's your choice," replied Rose preparing her thoughts for Ally's next question.

"Okay. It's my choice. So, what would happen if I chose not to assist Edmund and become another hunter of bodies he needs to hijack. I mean borrow?" Ally corrected herself quickly in hopes of avoiding punishment for her unwise phrasing.

Rose took her time in responding knowing full-well that her answer would hit Ally with a vengeance. "You will remain safely in the world you chose to create inside the locket," Rose paused briefly before stating the cold hard facts, "Until your body expires. Then your soul will be released from the magical spell."

Ally thought she had come to grips with the fact that she would never find a way to break the curse and free herself from the locket. However, hearing Rose confirm her suspicion did exactly what Rose expected. Ally landed hard on one of the wooden chairs sending a shock wave up her spine. Wrestling with her endless captivity took its toll and she wanted nothing more than to retreat back into bed.

In typical Sallie fashion, she tried to help lighten the mood, "Ally did you ever wish you could fly as a little girl or dream of time traveling?" not waiting for Ally to reply she went on, "Your life can become the fairytale you've always wanted it to be or you could be a superhero like in the movies. Mr. Dalton will grant you your heart's desire. He wants to repay you for your help."

Ally's gaze bounced between Sallie and Rose. Focusing on their seemingly unwavering happiness with their choices made her consider making the same choice. After all, what options did she have? Ending up in the wasteland if she decided to continue fighting for her freedom or living out her life in a make-believe world until her body died.

"Hello ladies," greeted Arthur from the doorway.

"Good morning Arthur," responded Sallie almost singing the words.

Rose smiled while clearing the dishes and without a word went about the business of cleaning the kitchen. Sallie and Arthur had moved into the main room leaving Ally and Rose alone. The only sound was that of Rose washing dishes and the distant conversation between Sallie and Arthur.

"Have you ever regretted your decision Rose?"

Placing the final plate back in the cabinet Rose joined Ally at the table, "No Ally I haven't. Not for one second."

"But none of this is real. I mean isn't a difficult 'real' life better than a perfect 'fake' one?" The hurt look on Rose's face reminded Ally how very difficult Rose's life with Maxwell had been, "Well your life was beyond difficult Rose it was a living hell. I understand you not ever regretting your decision, but...."

"Your life wasn't anywhere close to mine," added Rose.

"Exactly."

"I don't know the details of what laid ahead for you Ally. All I do know for certain is that Mr. Dalton only selects those whose lives are either shattered or about to be. He does his very best to rescue people who need to be rescued even if they don't know it yet."

"My family," gasped Ally, "Are they okay?"

Rose shrugged and said, "As far as I know your family is doing well."

"Can he see into the future? What in the world was I rescued from?"

"No. Mr. Dalton cannot see into the future. However, if the hunter does their job correctly they soon discover secret information that could shatter the life of a potential host. As far as what you were rescued from we will probably never know."

There was that utterly inappropriate word again "rescued" sending Ally's mind scrambling. Filled with scenario after scenario Ally searched for the possible tragedy headed her way. Did it have something to do with her father's alcoholism? Did her mom die? What about her grandparents? What in the world was coming that would shatter her world?

Attempting to soothe Ally's mind Rose stated, "There is no use trying to figure out what would have happened. Ally it's pointless to even try."

"Maybe I could have helped prevent it?" cried Ally, "Maybe there was something I could have done?"

"Ally," Edmund whispered in her ear, "there wasn't anything you could do in the mortal world, but perhaps if you prove yourself in this magical world I can give you powers that would help."

The opportunity to possibly help save her family from an unknown tragedy tipped the scales. Ally gave Edmund a resounding "yes" to his proposal, "Mr. Dalton please let me help you so I can help my family." Nothing else mattered in that moment. Ally had made-up her mind long before nightfall and happily gave her answer.

Immediately following Ally's acceptance of Edmunds offer people from her time aboard The Vision streamed into the lodge. Each one welcomed Ally with kind words and friendly faces. Hugs and congratulations ensued from all those at the lodge. There wasn't anyone or anything that didn't seem to be celebrating Ally's answer. With animal calls throughout the forest to the sound of a musical wind there was an uprising of an exuberant and jubilant symphony.

"Welcome to the family," cheered Rose lifting her cup of tea as a toast to the crowd and smiling at Ally in absolute merriment. For the first time in a long time the twinkle in Rose's appealing eyes returned. It was then that Ally realized how very concerned Rose had been for her safety.

Complete happiness and relief washed over Ally. Much to her surprise. The now exquisitely soothing fragrance of the magical garden made her large brown eyes glitter with contentment. Without the slightest hint of doubt Ally confidently asked, "What do I need to learn first?"

Chapter Eleven

Laughter erupted throughout the lodge. Ally gladly took center stage thanking everyone for their support. Feeling more than comfortable being the life of the party. Something she had never done before or even aspired to. She quickly found herself amusing the guests with her quick wit.

Catching her image in a mirror Ally almost didn't recognize herself. Rose joined her during the methodical examination of her newly impressive reflection. With an endearing smile Rose commented, "It's quite something the first time you see yourself after...."

Curiosity got the best of Ally and she interrupted Rose. "What's different? I can't put my finger on it," asked Ally scrutinizing her own image from every angle.

"You're magical now Ally."

"Magical? Like I can do tricks?"

Sallie came up behind Rose and giggled, "Not tricks silly girl. Honest to goodness magic."

"Like," Ally paused, closed her eyes and wished for a strawberry milkshake. Opening her eyes, she found her hands empty, "Well that didn't work."

"You're not a genie Ally," snickered Rose and with one look the lodge cleared out leaving Ally alone with Rose and Sallie.

"I know. I just thought I'd give it a try," shrugged Ally.

"You will slowly learn how to perform necessary magic in tune with your talents." Rose motioned for them to have a seat on the couch.

"Talents? Well unless Mr. Dalton has a need for a mediocre softball player I'm not sure what talents I have," Ally commented doing her best to downplay her athletic abilities.

"Let's begin with the basics first," replied Rose.

Sallie asked frankly, "When you first met me Ally what did you think of me?"

Recalling the first time she met Sallie, Ally remembered a demure round faced servant girl with a flawless complexion. With that recollection Ally was transported back to the moment they first arrived at the lodge. There was however one clear difference. Ally was absent from the memory. In the spot where she had stood was a strange muddled distortion. It was equivalent to blurred out faces on a television show protecting someone's identity.

"What did Mr. Dalton say," asked Sallie.

Heavy with concern Rose responded, "Mr. Dalton isn't sure he wants to bother giving Ally another opportunity to prove herself."

"I think she could be as good if not better than I am. Doesn't he see that?"

"Of course he does, but there's something troubling him and Helene's continuing nightmares are only making it worse," Rose's concern for her best friend was clearly evident.

"Does he know what's causing them?"

"If he does he hasn't shared it with me or even Arthur. At least to the best of my knowledge."

"Very unusual, but I'm not sure how Ally figures into all this," Sallie remarked beginning to pace the floor.

"Neither does Mr. Dalton which is why he's going ahead with his plans on recruiting her. I think he's hoping it's nothing more than a strange coincidence between the transition to Ally's body and Helene's nightmares."

A spilt second later Ally observed Sallie sitting in the farthest corner of the bleachers in a large stadium. She wasn't paying any attention to the exciting football game or the roar of the crowd as the score was tied. The hail Mary pass had worked sending the running back into a celebratory dance. The crowd jumped to their feet cheering their team on and sending popcorn into the air. Ally had almost forgotten how much she enjoyed going to her high school football games. The lights, smells and band music took her back, at least momentarily.

Sallie was still sitting next to a girl wearing a poodle skirt. The girl's hair was pulled into a high ponytail secured by an expertly tied pink ribbon. Even though Ally couldn't hear the conversation between the two the stranger's body language spoke volumes. She was clearly in a world of hurt. Like a quick movie edit Ally witnessed the very same girl wearing the identical blue Victorian dress she wore to the Halloween party. Ally further noticed she was wearing the locket as she made her way up the steps to Dalton Manor.

"Oh!" gasped Ally as the next scene materialized. Sallie dressed in her warrior garb was in fierce combat with some sort of evil looking being. Darting back and forth above the beast's bloody claws Sallie aimed and repeatedly shot her arrows into its scarred flesh. Each arrowhead glowed from within the puncture wound. Within a short time, there was a web of light surging from one arrowhead to the next and so on. Before long the light dominated the creatures dark skin. A blaze of dazzling white consumed the beast leaving nothing behind except for a foul stench.

Wincing from the sight Ally kept her eyes closed wary of what she would view next. Hearing the casual conversation between Rose and Sallie plus the wonderful aroma filling Ally's every breath was proof someone was baking. This persuaded her to open her eyes. They were seated at the kitchen table enjoying tea and freshly baked muffins.

Rushing to them Ally nearly shouted, "Mr. Dalton expects me to fight monsters!" Filled with adrenaline she couldn't sit down. Instead she flounced around the kitchen rambling, "I'm not a fighter. I couldn't destroy that, that, whatever it was. I don't like scary things so what in the world makes him think I could face them? What was it anyways? Oh, don't tell me I don't want to know, I can't do what he wants me....."

"Calm down Ally. Mr. Dalton is perfectly aware you're not prepared for battle. You have plenty of time to train and work your way up to that," commented Rose blocking Ally's path. "Ally you were shown both tasks you will eventually handle. No one expects you to tackle them immediately. Remember, you have an endless amount of time to reach that point. You're here for eternity."

"Eternity," whispered Ally. Saying it out loud was surreal. She would outlive her parents, her schoolmates and everyone she's ever known. However, the sadness she expected to feel was sidetracked into thoughts of her tasks. The job that laid ahead of her abruptly became of utmost importance. "Okay. Why have I been selected to do what Sallie does."

"Good question," applauded Sallie and with that she led Ally outdoors into the bright sunshine. "Let's take a stroll around the grounds."

Walking such a distance that the lodge was no longer visible Ally wondered why Sallie hadn't said anything. The next couple of steps made her feel like she walked through a massive spider web, "Oh yuck, spider web!" yelled Ally brushing it from her face. Suddenly the sticky web clinging to her vanished. No longer were they walking along the dirt path at Dalton Manor, instead Sallie and Allie stood on the sidewalk of a busy street. Clearly they had traveled beyond the manor. Horns honked as automobiles bustled along and the bright theater marquee caught Ally's attention. Reading the title out loud, "The Big Parade," she wondered whether it was a play or a movie.

"Ally. I need you to listen and pay close attention," whispered Sallie pointing to a couple walking their way. The dim street light made it impossible to make out who they were. As the two shadowed figures drew closer Ally began to hear the conversation between them. She recognized the upbeat cadence of the female. Astonishment filled Ally when her eyes confirmed what her ears heard.

It was Sallie's cheerful and friendly voice, "Oh, I believe I understand."

407

"You do? Go ahead and explain it to me then," replied the male's unfamiliar voice.

"No one would ever expect me to be a threat. This allows me to travel behind enemy lines without detection," boasted Sallie.

"Exactly right Sallie, but long before you battle Mr. Dalton's enemies you will search out replacement bodies for him."

"That's easy enough," Sallie replied. Then quickly added, "Once I've mastered that I can move onto fighting the enemy?" Sallies voice was dripping with excitement when she spoke of fighting the enemy. This duty was obviously her favorite part from day one.

"Don't take your first assignment too lightly," warned the bearded man walking with Sallie. Years of sun exposure had left him with tanned leathery skin which Ally believed was why he had such thick facial hair. He was attempting to hide as many of his deep-set wrinkles as he could.

Sallie nodded in humbled agreement. The modest young woman Ally first met was back, "Of course not sir."

"It's time to get your feet wet Sallie. I'll accompany you on several excursions starting with your first. Take my arm and we'll begin lesson one," instructed the bearded man. Then the two began to melt away. Standing next to Sallie while simultaneously watching her in the past was extremely weird, but it soon moved beyond that. Well into the realm of bizarre.

Sallie gabbled, "Let's tag along," while she took Ally's hand and reached for the bearded man before he disappeared.

With burning eyes Ally tried to focus through the smoke-filled room. Horns blasted away and patrons danced along to the lively jazz music. Everyone was either dancing, dining or laughing in exuberant conversation, everyone that is except for one dark-haired beauty standing in the shadows. Her curly and extremely short hairdo was highlighted with a feathery headband. Obviously made to go with the dress. The sleeveless frock with its dropped waist was accentuated with a black belt dripping with black fringe overtop the soft pink dress. Lifting the opera length cigarette holder to her mouth the woman took a long drag. Then gracefully moved her hand away from her face blowing the smoke from her ruby red lips. Ally was more than thankful she couldn't smell the cigarette smoke in the cloudy room. Drawing her attention to the fact that her eyes were no longer burning.

"You will make friends with her Sallie and report back," and with that simple explanation the bearded man vanished. Sallie stood alone in the jazz club looking confident. After a quick glance at her black and silver beaded flapper dress Sallie made her way over to the unaccompanied woman. Rather quickly the two were deep in conversation. Moments later they slipped out of the club and made their way into a small café. Ally listened as the young woman shared her troubled life with Sallie. After a rather lengthy goodbye Sallie was instantaneously returned to the manor's grounds. The bearded man greeted her warmly.

"Well done. She appears to be a perfect candidate. Now all you have to do is organize the events into sequence and then you can hand off the prospect to the closer."

"How exciting Mr. Burns," exclaimed Sallie just before a flash of light.

Quickly dropping backwards Ally plopped rather hard onto the couch at the lodge. Sallie giggled then apologized, "Sorry for the harsh landing it's been awhile since I've traveled with someone."

"No problem."

Readjusting herself comfortably on the couch Sallie looked prepared saying, "Go ahead ask me anything you wish."

"If I'm guessing correctly you basically interviewed the pretty brunette for Helene's body replacement."

"Exactly, go on," encouraged Sallie.

"She was chosen because she's been alone and poor since her husband's death and the only men she's been attracting aren't good for her," summarized Ally remembering the secrets the woman had shared. Yet she couldn't help but add, "Well she shouldn't give up hope. Maybe she'll find happiness and a good man."

"Since that was my very first outing with Mr. Burns I had to accept that others had confirmed she would remain in danger. I trusted she was in need of being rescued. Now I do all my own research before making that decision. We learn in steps Ally."

"Humm."

"Go ahead tell me what's on your mind."

A term the bearded man had used came to mind, "What is a closer?"

"That's my job," answered Rose from behind the couch. "After the arrangements for procuring a replacement for Mr. Dalton have been set in place. I step in and close the deal."

Fitting together the puzzle pieces she'd been given Ally wondered, "Who interviewed me?"

"Does it really matter?"

Ally thought for a second and said, "I suppose it doesn't Rose, but couldn't I learn from it?"

"Sallie will teach you all you need to know about research and setting up a prospect. There's no need for us to go back to your hunter," Rose sternly answered, "Sallie is one of our best and you two share so much."

With a distraught expression Sallie forced a smile at Ally making it clear that Ally's line of questioning had hurt her feelings. Although Ally wasn't exactly sure how she did this.

"I'm sorry Sallie. I didn't mean to be insulting," Ally didn't know what to say next. The hurt in Sallie's eyes intensified after her apology.

"Sallie would you excuse Ally and I?"

"Of course Rose," and with that Sallie retreated to her room.

"Ally you must stop looking back at what 'once was' and focus on the 'here and now'. It's for your own good and everyone else's."

"I didn't mean...."

"You don't have to mean to do something for it to happen. Part of your training will be learning how to be more careful with what you say. Each word you use has the potential to destroy all your hard work. Which increases the risk of ruining Mr. Dalton's hope for having Helene back. Something that is absolutely unacceptable."

"I'm sorry Rose," declared Ally feeling even more guilt.

"Let me explain why Sallie was handpicked to be your trainer," and with that statement Ally was swept up into the air surrounded by a star filled dome.

Sallie's voice came at her from every direction. No matter which way Ally looked there was Sallie. Invisible movie screens each played their own story. There were several showing Sallie with various people revealing her peacemaking skills. Others showed her love of animals and there were dozens of Sallie practicing her archery skills. Selecting to focus on one scene in particular sucked Ally into the motion picture where she studied Sallie. Going from one honorary skit to the next Ally soon noticed one thing standing out. Sallie had a friendly, tender and warm heart very much like Ally. They shared a gentle nature that welcomed people in. It never took very long before a stranger would share closely held secrets and fears to either of them. The more Ally viewed Sallie's life the more it became apparent that they were cut from the same cloth. The mere thought of wanting to talk to Rose brought Ally back to the hunting lodge. Naturally Rose was patiently waiting for her to return.

"People open up to us. That's how we can confirm someone is in need of being rescued," proclaimed Ally with assuredness. It was the first time she happily referred to taking the life of another as rescuing them. Filling both she and Rose with unimaginable excitement. There was a new intense sensation shooting through her veins. Ally not only wanted to achieve her goals but also felt like she needed to accomplish the assignment given to her.

The rest of the night was spent reaffirming Ally's thoughts. Understanding how her natural ease with others would soon be used to acquire new bodies for Mr. Dalton. Somehow it now seemed as normal to Ally as going shopping for a new outfit.

Chapter Twelve

The sunrise greeted Ally while she stood at the window to her room. Falling asleep hadn't been a problem. Staying asleep however, well that was another story. An endless array of questions took charge when Ally simply repositioned herself during the night. The otherwise normal activity of rolling over in bed was all it took for her mind to begin racing. Wide awake in the dark she ricocheted from one inquisitive thought to the next and back again.

The mornings dim light played tricks with her eyesight. Believing the garden was being pulled closer to her Ally remained motionless. Doing her best not to blink fearing any movement on her part would halt the illusion. Her focal point was none other than her flowers. She could see the little plant now blanketed in daisies had not only gained in size but also in splendor. Unable to proceed past the fencing Ally spoke to the dainty flowers, "Good morning sweeties," and in response they all turned to face her. Joyful laughter escaped her lips sending the garden back to whence it came.

Edmunds voice filled the room, "Very impressive Ally. You are ready to shadow Sallie on today's adventures."

"Yes, sir."

In an hour's time the girls were dressed, had eaten breakfast and gone over the rules for shadowing. Ally understood she was to observe without comment and study how Sallie worked. All questions would be addressed when they returned to the lodge. Until then Ally was to act invisible even to Sallie. It sounded simple enough, but Ally worried she'd forget her questions and asked to bring along a small notebook and pencil.

Traveling through time and space took Sallie very little effort. Doing nothing more than declaring, "Bring me to Hattie," the pretty girl from the roaring 20's or "Let me see the summer of 1953" where they found themselves levitating above a crowded beach. Patiently they waited for the opportune time for Sallie to make her presence known. The conversations she had with current prospects were easy enough to grasp. Verify they needed to be rescued from someone or something in their life, get them to confess a deep-rooted desire and finally ease them into chasing that dream.

Ally had trusted her decision to attend college after that fateful morning at the school's career day. She convinced herself it was her own deep-rooted desire. Now she began to wonder if chasing that dream led her to Rose whose job it was to close the deal. Being trapped inside the locket no longer caused Ally pain, but something still bothered her. She couldn't help but ponder whether or not the friendship she and Rose shared was real. Even considering the possibility that it was only a ploy to help Rose do her job deeply upset Ally. Unfortunately, her thoughts distracted her at the wrong time.

If she hadn't been distracted she would have noticed the lurking enemy of Edmund in the distance. It's eyes resembling those of an albino zeroed in on Sallie's every move. The beasts glaring caused it to make a chattering sound like a cat watching a bird from a window sill. Its deformed face made worse by the murky charcoal tint of its skin. Hearing the strange noise caused Ally to turn her focus away from Sallie. When her eyes landed on the creature her heart skipped a beat. Simultaneously her necklace sparked resulting in Sallie's bracelet responding in kind. The flashing jewelry went unnoticed by the perceived threat and it boldly moved towards Sallie.

"Please excuse me Hattie. I completely forgot to run an important errand," Sallie told the young girl. Without waiting for so much as a wave Sallie was around the next corner, transformed into her warrior self and sent arrow after arrow into the menacing essence. She didn't stop her attack until it imploded leaving behind the distinct odor of sulfur.

417

Returning to the lodge Ally couldn't wait to speak, "What in the world are all those creepy things you keep killing?"

"Enemies of Mr. Dalton," replied Sallie adjusting the latest Victorian dress she found herself in.

"That doesn't help," snorted Ally, "Who are his enemies and why are they so gross?"

In a calm slow paced answer Rose explained, "They are guardians of dark magic Ally. They would like to destroy Mr. Dalton and all he's worked so hard to create."

"Dark magic?"

"The evil side of witchcraft Ally. That is why we were all so terribly offended when you continued to refer to Mr. Dalton as evil. He practices only light magic like his parents and their ancestors. For countless generations, light magic has fought against the darkness. They do all they can to overcome dark magic. Including doing good in the world."

Playing the devil's advocate Ally pursued further, "Forgive me, but how is taking the lives of humans for his dead wife's soul good?"

"Mr. Dalton is saving humans from pain and suffering they need not endure. Most importantly he has learned that a human can love a warlock with pure, honest and true love. His family and other witches like him want to prove that light magic and humanity can peacefully coexist. Something dark magic could never do."

Ally meditated on Rose's explanation before saying, "There's still a part of me that believes doing the wrong thing for the right reason is still wrong."

"One could argue that case, but there's more you need to know," replied a tactful Rose managing to somewhat agree with Ally while still making her point.

Curious Ally listened with eagerness. She knew a deep dark secret was about to be revealed. Rose and Sallie were clearly apprehensive. Before Rose spoke a curtain of green draped the lodge removing all sound from the outside. Having the lodge consumed in a noise canceling state Rose divulged, "Mr. Dalton's parents were murdered by an angry mob of humans which is how he was given immortality."

"Oh my goodness," sighed Ally.

"That's only the beginning. Once dark magic heard the news they were determined to turn Mr. Dalton to their side. They hoped to change the course of his family's destiny and gain generations of power. What they couldn't understand was the fact that Mr. Dalton would never disgrace his parents or his family's legacy that way. The only revenge he wished for was to punish the descendants of the families responsible for his parent's death. He wanted them to have agonizing lives filled with unending torment and sorrow like they had given him. As far as other humans Mr. Dalton learned to tolerate them, but unlike his parents he wanted to steer clear of them as much as possible. Until Helene walked into his life," beamed Rose.

Discovering that there was so much more to Dalton Manor and its legend intrigued Ally. She was beginning to think it would take an eternity to learn it all. "Does he still want to punish the mob's descendants?"

"No. Mr. Dalton is entirely focused on his beloved Helene and keeping her safely with him until the end of time."

"Okay, a battle of good vs evil complete with a romantic hero and his damsel in distress," summed up Ally without any hint of sarcasm. She was happy to discover that she was at least on the side of good. She was far less than thrilled, actually she was terrified, about having to someday destroy those from the side of evil. It wasn't that they didn't need to be destroyed. It was more a question as to how she would accomplish it. With a throbbing head brought on by all she'd seen and heard she finally asked, "What's with the strange green drapes?"

"Not everyone here needs to know the specifics. For most of the garden's inhabitants Dalton Manor is the only home they've ever known. Magic is nothing more than fun tricks you see at the circus," Rose replied.

With wide eyes Ally questioned, "So they don't know they're in danger?"

Sallie fielded this question, "Because of their ignorance they're not worth dark magic's time. Harming an unsuspecting human is like a human stepping on an ant. Unless they become a nuisance, they're left alone to go about their tiny meaningless lives."

"Well I think that's enough of a lesson today. I'm going to go to bed and hopefully sleep until early afternoon," jeered Ally and with that the green curtain insulating the lodge withdrew into the night's sky.

Exhaustion prevailed shortly after Ally slid between the sheets. Downstairs Sallie and Rose discussed how Ally's determination would work to her benefit. They were waiting on one thing. For Ally to completely surrender entirely to her new role. Although she had verbalized her surrender and promised to be good. There were still times when Ally's expressions betrayed her lingering bitterness.

"I have no doubt Ally's strong will was one reason Mr. Dalton elected to offer her a place in his garden," suggested Sallie.

"Most certainly," concurred Rose, "I'm thankful he didn't give up on her. I'm going to do all I can to make sure she keeps her promise. It would be wonderful to have another friend around to work with. Very much like having you around Sallie," Rose said fondly.

"I can see it now Rose. Ally will sneak behind enemy lines without any indication of who she really is. Once she's found her target that fierce determination of hers will make her victorious."

The two laughed heartedly at the thought. Abruptly Rose quit laughing and said, "Maybe Ally will be the one to discover what's causing Helene's escalating nightmares?"

"Mr. Dalton must be terribly worried," commented Sallie.

"Worried doesn't cover the half of it. He's beside himself with concern. He's extremely fearful that if we don't figure out what's causing them and put a stop to it. He will lose her."

"I don't recall a switch ever running its course this quickly. It's very peculiar. There's usually decades in between the need for a new host."

"I agree Sallie and I hate to disrupt our conversation, but I suggest you venture off and select a few backups for Mr. Dalton."

Taking her job extremely seriously Sallie smiled with acceptance and darted off to another place and time. Rose sat alone on the couch briefly and wished Mr. Dalton would return her to the garden.

"Perfect timing," celebrated Edmund with a fetching expression.

"I do my best," smiled Rose tucking a loose strand of hair back into the hair comb struggling to hold her lengthy locks at bay.

"Dorothy is helping Helene dress and she's been told you're already here. So, you best be quick."

With very little effort Rose crossed the distance between the garden and the manor. Moving so quickly the only thing visible was a blur of red zooming across the lawn. Her hair having fallen from the hairclip created a streak of crimson resembling a shooting star.

Reaching the steps of the manor Rose whipped her hair back into the updo with ease. While simultaneously making it through the front door, into the parlor and positioning herself comfortably on the sofa before Helene was out of her room.

"I hope you haven't been waiting too long," welcomed Helene with sincerity in her eyes.

"Not long at all," replied Rose rising to her feet and moving at a normal pace. She greeted Helene with a warm hug.

Helene wasted no time in addressing concerns, "Has Maxwell returned?"

"No Helene. He's been gone for an unusually long time. Not that I'm complaining mind you," teased Rose.

"I'm so glad to hear that. However, isn't it a bit strange that he hasn't sent word of when he expects to return?"

It was clear that Helene wasn't about to let this line of questioning go. It was up to Rose to cleverly find a way to change the subject and knowing her friend so well made it easy, "On my way in Edmund was telling me that he plans to stud Storm out this year."

Helene's eyes came alive with excitement, "Oh yes, Edmund was sharing that with me just the other day. I can already imagine the beauty he'll father. I don't care if it's a colt or a filly. I just hope the foal has Storm's coloring."

"He is remarkable in every way and I agree his distinct coloring usually catches your eye first."

Convinced the coast was clear Rose let their conversation flow naturally to the next topic. To her dismay it didn't take long for Helene to come back around to Maxwell's absence. Deciding to change to an offensive position Rose asked, "I get the feeling there is something important you need to discuss with me Helene?"

A higher than normal pitch gave Helene away. Regardless of how hard she tried to deny there was something else on her mind, "What makes you ask that?"

"Helene have you forgotten who you're speaking with? We know each other far too well to be able to keep secrets from each other."

"That is so true," acknowledged Helene. Despite the fact that she was entirely unware that Rose and everyone around her were keeping an unbelievable secret from her. Something they accomplished only through the tremendous power Edmund possessed.

Chapter Thirteen

Reluctantly Helene confessed her battle with her nightly nightmares. After a lengthy pause, she went on to explain how they were now happening any time she slept and were progressively getting worse. Through the course of the conversation it became clear she wasn't being completely honest with Edmund.

Rose posed the question, "Have you explained this to Edmund?"

"He knows I'm having nightmares."

Helene's answer prompted Rose to delve deeper, "Does he know you're having them every night, all night and now during your naps? It also doesn't sound like you've shared they're becoming more vivid."

Defensive that Rose had backed her into a corner Helene rationalized, "Edmund is already far too stressed with everything on his plate. He doesn't need to be bothered by his wife's silly dreams."

"Stop justifying your behavior Helene. Remember who your husband is. There isn't anything he doesn't want to know about you. Unlike Maxwell who couldn't care less about me." Without meaning to Rose had brought the conversation full circle. She quickly did her best to rectify her error, "Perhaps discussing the nightmares in their entirety with Edmund will help. It's possible that together the two of you could figure out the root of your fear and the nightmares will go away."

Helene was quick to answer, "I'll agree to tell Edmund all there is about my nightmares," and her pause made it clear that there was about to be a condition to accepting Rose's suggestion, "if you'll stop avoiding my questions about Maxwell."

"Agreed," replied Rose knowing further debate would get her nowhere.

A victorious smile lit up Helene's face and she immediately went back to her line of questioning, "Have you sent a messenger to look for Maxwell?"

"Oh no Helene. Maxwell wouldn't tolerate me checking up on him."

Nodding in agreement Helene tried another suggestion, "How about a simple letter from his wife stating how much she misses him? You could send it to his last known location. With any luck, it'll find its way to him and he'll respond. Then at least you will know where he is and maybe he'll clue you in on when he plans to return."

"If it makes you feel better I'll send a letter," affirmed Rose then following Helene's example masterfully changed the subject back to her nightmares, "You are unusually interested in Maxwell's whereabouts Helene. Do your nightmares have anything to do with him?"

This question led to answers Rose didn't expect. Helene explained that not only was Maxwell absent from the nightmares, but Rose was as well. The convoluted web of events that changed Helene's dreams from pleasant to frightening always involved Rose being just out of sight or hidden behind a stranger. Whatever entity was haunting her dreams remained hidden from view causing her even more fear. Whether spotting a shadow moving out of the corner of her eye or an unseen creature beneath the lake's surface it didn't matter. In her heart Helene felt something terrible was on the prowl. She fully believed it was after her happiness.

Hearing Edmund enter the manor ceased their conversation. Although Helene was convincing in her portrayal of woman without a care it was the look in Rose's eyes that clued Edmund in on the truth. After the three of them enjoyed a late breakfast Rose excused herself saying she had to tend to business at home. With renewed strength from the wonderful morning Helene asked Edmund to push her on the old swing hanging from the oak.

Closing her eyes and tilting her head back Helene focused on the rhythmic swaying of the swing. Edmunds gentle pushes kept the momentum going as Helene felt the tension from the latest round of nightmares melt away. Dragging her feet against the ground slowed the swing causing Edmund to take hold of the ropes. Immediately stopping its movement.

"I love this oak tree," beamed Helene, "I always feel calmer when I'm near it. Maybe we should add a bench or table with chairs under the cool shade it offers. It seems rather lonely out here all by itself. Besides the swing only allows one of us to have a seat."

"That's a wonderful idea my beloved."

Helene stood up from the swing and circled the oak taking in the surrounding area, "Over here would be the perfect spot," she announced spreading her arms wide and spinning around unaware that she had chosen a spot directly in front of the magical gardens gate.

Edmund watched the fencing surrounding the garden shift out of Helene's way. This caused the plants within to scoot about the ground mirroring the fence's movements. Every dainty step Helene took sent electrified energy bursting from the garden making Edmund smirk. He was unsure which was more radiant. Helene filled with excitement at her idea or the happy and illuminated dance the garden performed around her. His smirk quickly turned to a chuckle.

"Am I amusing you darling?"

"You are too adorable for words my dearest Helene. Name your desire and I will make it so," boasted Edmund lifting her up into his arms. He hugged her tightly and breathed in the sweet scent of her perfume.

Rose managed to get a couple hours of sleep after returning to the lodge noticing that Sallie was still away on her assignment. Ally made good on her comment from the night before and slept until one in the afternoon. When she finally stumbled downstairs in her pj's her eyes were swollen from such a sound night's sleep. Her voice croaked a lazy good morning to Rose.

"Good afternoon," teased Rose, "Would you like breakfast? I mean lunch?"

"Either one," said Ally unable to keep from yawning during her answer.

Hurrying around the kitchen Rose prepared roast beef sandwiches. Which she served with sliced apples and pears one of Ally's new favorite meals. The freshly baked bread that Rose made almost daily was first slathered with butter. Then the succulent lean beef topped with finely chopped celery and a little mustard was added. Ally was bound to once again overstuff herself. She gulped down what was left of her whole milk, which had taken some getting used to, after swallowing the last mouthful. Hunger had kept Ally focused on eating. It wasn't until she cleaned her plate did she notice Sallie wasn't around.

"Where's Sallie?"

"She returned late this morning so I instructed her to go take a nap. She's not much use to you or anyone else if she's beyond exhausted," replied Rose who herself was wishing she could nap.

"Back at the beach house you said you don't need a lot of sleep. Was that true?" Ally asked feeling like that was a lifetime ago.

"It was. I along with Sallie and eventually you only need a couple hours a night."

Rose recognized this line of questioning would be better explained through visuals. Prompting Rose to take Ally's hand who instinctively shut her eyes. Faint at first then more pronounced Ally could see rose bud after rose bud appearing. The buds opened into a full bloom when Rose held one within her hand only to have the petals dry up and blow away. The entire process from beginning to end took less than a minute.

Repeating this course of action over and over Ally noticed a visible difference in Rose. Her hair became shinier, her expression less worn and even her clothes seemed newer. Looking refreshed and more than model perfect Rose said, "All better," then released Ally's hand.

Needing nothing more Ally stated with assurance, "When we need strength we gather it from our flowers."

"You're learning quickly Ally. I'm impressed."

"One question though. How do I call my daisies to me?"

"Use your necklace Ally. Gently press it into your chest while thinking about your flowers. Then call them to you. You must make sure you remain solely focused on them." Rose's final words were clearly a warning.

"I want to try," exclaimed an animated Ally. At last she was given a chance to test out her new magical abilities.

"Go ahead. It's all you Ally."

Adrenaline pulsed through Ally's veins as she prepared to perform her very first magical act. She was on her own. Part of her believed she would accomplish her goal, but a much larger part doubted her abilities. Ally took a deep cleansing breath.

Focused on her flowers and closed her eyes. Pushing harder than she needed on her necklace made the metal tingle against her skin with a new intensity. As the tingle switched to a burning sensation Ally heard Rose's voice. The single word, "gently" was coming from inside Ally's mind. Doing as Rose instructed made the burning stop. Refocusing her attention Ally recalled what her daisies looked like. She soon had a clear picture of them in her mind's eye. Mouthing the words just above a whisper she summoned, "Come to me," hoping it was that simple.

Through the grayish haze Ally could see tiny daisies floating towards her. With both hand's she reached out allowing the delicate blooms to drift into the palms of her hand. When the first flower landed, she felt a slight jolt. Reminding Ally of the static electricity shock she would get after dragging her feet across the carpet and touching her mom. Making both her mom and Ally jump before laughing.

After about a dozen or so flowers Ally broke her train of thought. In the amount of time it took to exhale she found herself back at the lodge. Rose was prepared for Ally to come home. Sitting across from where she would rematerialize with a mirror in hand would allow Ally's reflection to be the first thing she saw upon her return. Her swollen eyes were gone and her ratted hair was clean and styled. She also noticed her muscular arms were much more defined in the cap sleeved dress she now wore. Physically she looked like a million bucks, but the exterior was nothing compared to how incredible she felt inside. "I feel like I could take on the world," Ally said ecstatically.

"Well you're not quite ready for that Ally," replied Sallie who was now seated at the table with them.

"Sallie is correct," agreed Rose whole-heartedly, "Learning to travel on your reconnaissance missions will take more practice and time then you might think. Not to mention the power you will expel. You will have to build up your endurance."

In disbelief Ally argued, "I don't find myself tired when I am out with Arthur or Sallie." She truly believed this to be a valid point.

"Of course not Ally we're using our magic to bring you along. As of yet you haven't received much of what Mr. Dalton will eventually gift you with," proclaimed Sallie in between bites of her lunch.

Disappointed with this new information Ally changed subjects, "If Mr. Dalton created this world to be everything any of us wanted. Why does it sound like I'm going to be busy doing nothing more than working for him?"

"You won't Ally," vowed Rose, "No one needs to spend all their time working for Mr. Dalton. There's plenty of time to live happily in the world each of us creates," hesitating for a moment Rose then continued, "This is the world I simply prefer..."

Sallie interjected, "Me too."

"This world?" Ally questioned.

"This world where Helene is alive and married to the man of her dreams. I'm with my best friend and I don't have to fear Maxwell," said a blissful Rose.

Taking some time to consider her options Ally asked, "So when would I be able to create my own world?" It was difficult to imagine especially for Ally. The inconceivable had taken place. She had ultimately reached the point of accepting her fate or as it had been explained to her surrendering to her fate.

"Once you've completed your basic training and Mr. Dalton trusts you'll be safe."

"Oh I see, after I'm trained and useful he doesn't want to lose an asset," acknowledged Ally with an undercurrent of distaste in her tone.

As expected the profoundly subtle tone in Ally's voice didn't go unnoticed by either Rose or Sallie, but it was Sallie who was quick to mention it, "Don't test Mr. Dalton or me for that matter Ally," she warned in a threatening voice. The flash in her eyes and the body posturing reminded Ally about the warrior just below the surface. Not to mention how proficient she was at her job. Sallie had made a promise to do the task given to her with an unwavering resolve. Even if that meant taking down one of their own.

Understanding she needed to be fearful of turning against Edmund was clear. However, learning that Sallie could also pose a threat to her was unexpected. The fear on Ally's face while she absorbed this fact calmed Sallie. She returned to her friendly-self and reassured Ally by saying, "I'm sorry to be so harsh, but my job is to protect Mr. and Mrs. Dalton against 'all' enemies."

Needing no further explanation Ally understood that if she were perceived to be a continued threat her existence would end. There were plenty of ways and people who could easily terminate her. Quick thinking on Ally's part helped to ease the tension, "Wow. You guys weren't kidding when you said I needed to be careful with what I said. I deliberately threw in the littlest amount of attitude to see if you'd catch it and you did."

Rose remembered warning Ally about saying the wrong thing and without a shred of doubt believed Ally's explanation. Sallie took a little more convincing, but by the time she left to follow-up on a prospect all doubt had been removed.

The remainder of the day was lesson free. Rose and Ally talked and laughed about the silliest of things. Just an old fashion girl-fest discussing a wide range of topics. Mostly things which boys would find mind-numbing. The simple pleasure of casual conversation was something they were both in serious need of. Up until now each day had been filled with learning and visiting different places and times. Both Rose and Sallie were trying to teach Ally as much as possible in the shortest amount of time.

Sallie returned before long and the three of them talked into the wee hours of the morning. Delirious, they giggled until their belly's hurt from the nonsense they jabbered. Before long their minds grew weary. In the distance a soft glow appeared signaling that dawn was approaching. That was all the encouragement they needed. Lazily they made their way to their rooms still laughing at some of the silly comments each of them had made.

Settling into bed Ally understood one thing very clearly. She would have to rethink her strategy. There was only one thing that remained unequivocally true. She had not and would not give up hope.

BOOK 4

Believing there's only two choices Ally decides to choose between the lesser of two evils. Will her choice make things worse endangering everyone around her? Will the old saying "The enemy of my enemy is my friend," prove to be accurate?

TABLE OF CONTENTS

Chapter One

As a reward for training so hard over the last couple of weeks Ally was given the gift of traveling into town with Sallie. Rose believed it would be good for her to spend a day away from the manor. Thanks to the beautiful weather Sallie and Ally were traveling into town with the hood of the cabriolet carriage folded down. The coachman stood on the rear platform watching over the two of them. Misty's gait had an extra bounce in it and Ally was unsure why. Was it the gorgeous day or was Sallie's bubbly personality coursing down the reins filling the mare with a happy feeling? Showing the same expertise Sallie appeared to possess in everything she did she brought the carriage to a smooth halt.

Buried deep within her own thoughts the rambunctious game of "kick the can" went primarily unnoticed by Ally. The boy's shouts were nothing more than background noise. It wasn't until Misty reacted to the can ricocheting off a wheel of the carriage did Ally snap back to the present. Up until that point she hadn't even noticed they had arrived in town.

"Easy girl," quieted Sallie her voice full of bold confidence and reassurance.

The coachman leaped from his perch and snatched the can from the ground. With nothing more than a disapproving glance he scattered the boys off in every direction. Pleased with himself the coachman smirked triumphantly and taking the reins from Sallie said, "Well done miss."

"Thank you sir."

Unsure what she expected Ally was surprised to see so many buildings and people milling about. She had long given up trying to figure out if what she witnessed around her was real. At this point it no longer mattered whether they were really with the townspeople from Helene's life or if they were all imaginary. She had suffered far too many headaches trying to find answers to those lingering questions. Ally was no longer bothered by it. When she stopped caring what decade or year she was in, it gave her the peace she longed for. When all was said-and-done she would have the ability to travel to whichever time she desired within the parameters she would be given.

"A penny for your thoughts," Sallie said quietly.

Shaking her head Ally responded, "Oh it's nothing worth sharing."

Being away from Rose gave Ally the opportunity to think about anything she wanted without concern. If Rose was still listening in on her thoughts she hadn't mentioned it, but Ally couldn't take the chance. With the coachman's help Ally now stood on the cobblestone sidewalk and asked, "Where to first?"

441

"I was thinking Annabel's would be a great starting point."

"Annabel's?"

Sallie headed for the nearest door and almost sang the words, "The best dress shop around."

Not understanding the reason to go dress shopping when all her clothes magically appeared in her closet, Ally still found herself eagerly going through the door Sallie held open. Instead of finding racks of dresses there were several counters lined with employees showing women countless fashion sketches. The walls behind the counters we stacked with fabrics from floor to ceiling. Bustling with activity the store hummed with the sound of women's voices, but it was a young woman with a radiant smile in the back of the store that caught Ally's attention. There was no doubt she was trying on a wedding dress. With her mother's blissful approval, they stared at her reflection and agreed the dress turned out exactly how she wanted. Ally's heart permeated with the pain of missing her mom, but before it overtook her Sallie interrupted her thoughts.

Sallie's voice and mannerisms were laced with animated enthusiasm, "I thought you may want to create your very own dress Ally."

It felt like a waste of time, but Ally couldn't take hurting Sallie's feelings, "My own dress?" Doing everything she could to sound thrilled at the idea and take her focus off the soon to be bride with her mother.

"I'll never forget the day I was able to design my own dress. Before living at the manor all my dresses were hand me downs usually in need of serious mending. Although the dresses at the manor are splendid there isn't anything quite like dreaming up one's own design. It gets even better when it becomes a reality."

"Would you help me?" Ally asked knowing full well what Sallie would say.

Sallie's face lit up and with a pink glow to her cheeks she agreed and quickly got busy scanning the walls of fabrics. Moments like this reminded Ally that deep inside Sallie was a hurt little girl begging for love and acceptance. She believed Sallie would never see herself the way everyone else did; a highly trusted and skilled hunter, a loyal friend and a beautiful intelligent woman. The lies her parents repeatedly told her remained in the deepest corners of her mind. Even here in this magical self-created world Sallie couldn't quite silence their hateful words. No matter how untrue they were.

Relinquishing control Ally sat back and watched the dressmaker bring fabric sample after fabric sample to Sallie. It took some time until she narrowed the options down from several dozens. Not being a big shopper, Ally already felt drained after selecting a dress from the books of sketches. Who knew there would be so many options? At least for the wealthy, something Ally was completely unfamiliar with. Considering the multitude of choices in front of her Ally decided on the pastel pink fabric that was light and airy. The dressmaker rotated the striped fabric in her hands. This made the one shade darker pink stripes stand out against the pale pink stripes. Having them run vertically down the dress seemed like the best choice.

"Yes, vertically would look best," agreed Ally.

"Oh Ally you're going to look amazing," Sallie cheered.

A growling stomach reminded Ally how much time had passed. The dressmaker politely ignored the entertaining sound and processed the order. Sallie on the other hand giggled her joyful laugh stifling it before Ally turned too many shades of red.

Thankfully they were quickly on their way and to Ally's relief she was told reservations had already been made for them at The Copper Tavern. A flash of recognition crossed Ally's face which was more than enough for Sallie to comment on, "Yes, you know the name. It's a favorite place of Mr. & Mrs. Dalton as well as Helene's parents." This reminded Ally that Sallie didn't need to read her mind she was a master at deciphering expressions alone.

It was in part Sallie's highly tuned observation skills that aided her on her missions. Of course, it was useful when locating a new host body, but primarily this talent repeatedly proved to be an indispensable defense against evil. The smallest hesitation, a minor slip of the tongue or even an inconsequential twitch from someone never failed to alert Sallie to impending danger. Always giving her the upper hand enabling her to strike first and defeat anyone or anything that came up against her. Ally could only hope to someday be half as proficient.

It was no surprise Sallie deduced what Ally was thinking. Stating, "Don't fear Ally you will be more than prepared when you're faced with evil for the first time. I will make sure of it."

"I trust you completely. It's trusting myself to do what needs to be done that worries me," replied Ally with a weak smile.

"All in good time. Don't get ahead of yourself," Sallie stopped walking, turned to face Ally and with an intense stare continued, "Help is never far away. If I ever found myself at risk of my own demise help would immediately be sent. Every single one of us from the garden can trust in that." While her words hung in the air Ally watched a glint of color surge in her eyes. The pulsating influx of color became a multicolored parade of blinding light.

The feeling of home embraced Ally relieving her of every single fear, "I believe you."

"Good, now let's get you fed."

The Copper Tavern glowed like a shiny gold coin. Each elaborately arched doorway, mirror and window were framed with intricate carvings. The large windows were draped in heavy scarlet drapes adding another layer of elegance to the restaurant. The maître d' politely seated the ladies directly in front of a large mirror giving the illusion of an unending row of tables. Ally was thankful she didn't have to sit in the straight back chair and took her seat across from Sallie on the booth side of the table. There was so much to look at and it wasn't until Ally studied some of the carvings did she notice several tiny birds in them.

The table setting reminded Ally of the manor's museum so long ago and her comment to Artie about not knowing which fork to use. Fiddling with the white linen table cloth Ally looked at the wide array of utensils in front of her and sighed.

A waiter quickly filled their water glasses and asked, "May I offer you some tea?"

"Yes, please," Sallie answered.

"I'll have the same," added Ally.

In no time the waiter returned with a basket of warm bread and a copper tea kettle. He poured the tea then left the girls alone to review the menu. Ally soon found herself once again distracted by the overdone décor of the restaurant. It was so busy. Not only with patrons trying to get in, but with the sheer detail covering every square inch of the interior. Soon making a game out of trying to locate more bird carvings Ally was enthralled in her search. Quietly and not wanting anyone else to hear Ally leaned forward and whispered, "I think they should have named it The Golden Tavern."

Sallie smiled glancing around the place and agreed, "Yes that name would have worked; however, the family made their fortune mining copper hence the name." Smiling brightly, she winked at Ally then lifted the knife furthest from the plate and buttered a slice of bread.

By the time they finished their meal Ally had managed to use every single piece of silverware for its intended purpose thanks to Sallie's discreet clue's. Just as they were preparing to leave Ally heard a voice she recognized. She turned her gaze to the entrance with a racing heart hoping she was mistaken. For if it truly was who she thought it was; what would happen next?

In a loud condescending tone Maxwell barked, "Three at my favorite table." His order sending the restaurant staff into a frenzied state. With speedy care, they verified his table was in pristine condition even replacing a once used candle with a new one. Out of the corner of his eye he watched the alarmed staff move at a panicked speed and smirked arrogantly.   Similar to watching "The wave" in a packed stadium Ally witnessed tension move across the restaurant.   Women lowered their eyes while each of the men focused on their posture before nodding their heads respectfully to Maxwell. Every person, including Ally, knew it was fear not respect that motivated their behavior.

With reserved composure Sallie reminded Ally that he believed his wife to be dead, to breath normally and follow her lead. Ally couldn't care less that he thought they were so far beneath him to even warrant a glance, or whether it was his desire to impress the couple he was with, but either way they slipped by Maxwell without him acknowledging their presence. Escaping the restaurant undetected was all that mattered, until she heard the young woman with him giggle in a flirtatious manner, sending a chill up Ally's back.

Stepping onto the sidewalk Ally spotted their carriage and released the air in her lungs. The coachman noticed her trembling hand when he assisted her on board and asked her if she felt ill. Her less than enthusiastic nod gave him little comfort. Before Sallie was settled in the carriage the coachman handed Ally a blanket, pulled the hood up to help shield her from the wind and took control of the reins urging Misty on her way.

Never considering the possibility of seeing Maxwell in person Ally struggled to remain calm. A mixture of fear and hatred towards the man who almost cost Rose her life boiled through her veins. Plaguing her thoughts were mental pictures of his contorted face when he stood frozen outside of Helene's room on the day Rose gave her life to help Edmund. The only image proving to be more horrifying, was the one of Rose having been beaten within an inch of her life by that very man. Rage brewed throughout Ally before rising to the surface, "Why doesn't Mr. Dalton kill him?" she snarled.

Sallie lowered her head, "I don't know the answer to that question."

"He's evil Sallie. Look what he did to Rose and she was his wife!"

"I understand Ally and trust me I've despised him for much longer than you," was her only reply.

"Well if Mr. Dalton won't kill him, why don't one of us?" It was the very first time Ally had referred to herself in that way. As one of them, as one of the many who work for Mr. Dalton doing whatever task they've been assigned.

An elated expression replaced Sallies downtrodden one, "I, along with all of us and most of all Mr. Dalton sincerely appreciate your enthusiasm at being part of our family..."

"But?" interrupted Ally her voice still agitated.

"But Maxwell Griggs is off limits and until we're told differently from Mr. Dalton it'll stay that way."

"I don't get it...."

"Ally, Mr. Dalton has his reasons," stated Arthur who had replaced their coachman. Or had it been Arthur the entire time and he merely waited until now to morph back into himself?

Huffing in frustration Ally gave up that line of questioning and moved onto another, "Shouldn't someone let the woman he's with or her chaperone know he's dangerous?" Without being given an answer Ally continued, "We can't sit back and let him wreck another woman's life and what about Rose? Does she know he's back in town?"

"Whether she does or not it's not our place to mention it to her," answered Sallie continuing to ignore Ally's first question.

In a shrewdly authoritative manner Arthur reaffirmed his position as Mr. Dalton's right hand man and declared, "Mr. Dalton and I will inform Miss Rose if need be. You need not worry about Mr. Griggs. He will be handled."

Clearly this topic of conversation was closed and no further discussion from either Ally or Sallie would be tolerated. Mr. Dalton had put into place a very strict chain of command at which he alone was in control. He was the equivalent of the president, the king or the emperor to all of Dalton Manor. The bottom line was Mr. Dalton was in charge.

Bothered that Maxwell had ruined what was otherwise an enjoyable trip into town Sallie did her best to ease Ally's mind. "We will go back into town in a couple months for your fitting. If you aren't already excited about your new dress, you will be."

Concern about running into Maxwell again shadowed Ally's face and it was Arthur who came to her rescue, "Don't fear Miss Ally. Mr. Griggs departure from town prior to your dress fitting will be arranged."

Ally held her tongue something she was struggling with but slowly beginning to master no matter how agonizing it was for her. The questions she longed to ask Arthur bounced around her head making her hesitant to say anything else fearful she'd have a slip of the tongue. With all that was going on inside her mind she used as few words as possible to thank Sallie for a wonderful outing. She said a quick hello to Rose when they arrived at the lodge and excused herself to her room sharing that one of her all too common headaches was coming on.

Chapter Two

When the sky filled with stars and the creatures of the night began to roam in the fields below Ally became aware that she had been seated by the window for hours. It didn't take long for her little white lie about having a headache to become the truth. It was little consolation that Mr. Dalton and the entire garden would keep Rose safe. Ally was sure the mere sight of Maxwell would send Rose swirling into the past, figuratively of course or at least she believed so. Either way she had to protect Rose as much as she could.

"I won't let you cause her any more pain," muttered Ally picturing Maxwell hiding in the shadows. Having no idea how or what she could possibly do she had to trust that Arthur would somehow get Maxwell out of town. Until then, Ally would keep Rose within her sights hoping to minimize the chances of her running into her wicked husband.

Hearing Rose's footsteps outside her bedroom door provided the opportunity she needed. Smearing her makeup and ruffling her hair gave her the look she wanted before opening her door, "Rose?"

"I'm sorry Ally. Did I wake you?"

"No I've been tossing and turning for a while." It wasn't a complete lie she had been quite restless in the chair.

Rose looked Ally over, "Well of course you're not sleeping well. I can't sleep fully dressed and I'm accustomed to the dresses."

Trying hard not to tell anymore half-truths Ally nodded in agreement and took Rose up on the offer to help her unbutton the countless buttons on the back of the dress. With speedy precision Rose had the buttons undone almost in the time it would have taken to unzip a zipper.

"That was fast, thanks," commented Ally.

"Years and years and years of practice," Rose replied with a laugh then asked, "Why didn't you call for help sooner?"

"I guess I dozed off when I sat down for a moment," answered Ally.

If Rose was listening to her thoughts she would have known she was lying and yet Rose didn't say a word. Stepping over to the window Rose watched a family of raccoons scrounge for food. Silent minutes passed before Rose turned to face Ally who had climbed into bed. Clearly there was something on her mind.

Attempting to deflect whatever Rose was about to say Ally spoke first, "Rose I was wondering...." pausing to collect herself she realized what she was about to ask was truly what she wanted. Ally was so distracted by that realization she didn't finish her sentence.

"Wondering?"

Ally shook the thoughts from her mind and asked, "I was wondering if you and I could spend some time together? I've been swamped with training and away with Sallie so much we haven't really talked or anything."

It took longer than Ally wanted before Rose responded, "Ally I would like that very much," her face all aglow.

"You seem surprised," responded Ally with a tilt of her head.

Now it was Rose's turn to reign in her emotions, "Ally you have no idea how special you are to me. You are the first in all these years to want me around after surrendering to Mr. Dalton's wishes."

Puzzled, Ally pointed out that Sallie was her friend and there were dozens of others who she'd seen with Rose. "What about the magical garden? They are your family. Our family," reminded Ally smiling sweetly.

"Let me rephrase that, you are the first who surrendered her body for Helene who has ever wanted me to stick around."

"I don't understand."

"There's far too much involved to go into it tonight. I promise we can talk about it tomorrow," said Rose opening the door to leave adding, "As long as we talk about other things too. I don't want our time together to be nothing more than an extension of your training. Well, at least not most of it."

"Agreed," said Ally wanting desperately to ask Rose if she still listened in on her thoughts, but concerned that asking would give Rose probable cause to start if she wasn't already. Keeping herself from concentrating on the secrets she kept in the back of her mind Ally refocused her attention on making sure Rose remained at the manor. It was Ally's hope to greatly minimize the risk of running into Maxwell. Ally had made up her mind and was determined to protect her friend. She would keep Rose busy day in and day out until Arthur gave her the all clear.

"Sweet dreams Ally."

"Thanks, you too Rose."

Emotional and mental exhaustion seized Ally helping her drift off to sleep quickly. In an uncommonly deep and heavy slumber she snored softly something she usually only did when she had a cold. From the furthest recesses of her mind the questions Ally had tried to bury traveled to the forefront of her subconscious. Scattered visions darted back and forth until they blended into one fluid whirling chaos of images.

"Mmmmm," moaned Ally. While sleeping she fought to see all the sights around her. Her body's natural reflexes jerked her head back and forth. Eventually she drew her hands in front of her face shielding it from the incoming shadow. This was her last movement. A strangely mystical sleep gripped her with all it's might leaving her paralyzed within its grasp.

Unable to move even in her dream Ally stood immobile. Her body felt like lead and other than the ability to breath and blink she remained stuck to the gravely ground beneath her. In no time her bare feet ached from standing on the small rough stones. The murkiness surrounding her soon weakened and Ally noticed a bright light far off in the distance. Slowly it began to flutter like a butterfly. One minute coming closer then heading off in another direction the next. In a flash, it bolted directly towards Ally exploding into daylight and leaving her blinded by its intensity. Once her eyes adjusted she fully reopened them.

She was now standing on the grounds of the manor. With the garden and mighty oak in the background Ally watched people materialize one by one until a large crowd was formed. There wasn't a face in the crowd that she recognized and although their friendly smiles greeted her Ally was leery of them. Convinced something was terribly wrong and something bad was about to happen she fought to run away, but it was useless. Feeling like the weight of the world was literally weighing her down Ally was powerless against it.

Her fears were confirmed when Edmund came through the parting crowd carrying a dying plant. As he approached he left behind him a trail of petals that were falling from the pitiful looking bush. He stopped short of reaching Ally and stated void of all emotion and without a threatening undertone, "Consider your choice carefully Ally and never forget I won't allow you to go back on your promise." Clearly this was a factual statement not a poetic threat. Ally understood he was basically reminding her, when one's heart stops beating life ends. There was no arguing with this certainty. It was simply the cold hard truth.

By this time, the crowd had regrouped behind Edmund and with sorrowful faces they bowed their heads. The same mystical humming sound from before echoed in the night and the crowd again separated this time divulging the secret they shielded behind them. Edmund placed the shriveled plant on the ground and pointed at the young girl lying motionless in the dirt. Mustering all her remaining strength she opened her pleading eyes and mumbled the words, "Keep your promise," to Ally and with that final act she watched the dying plants last few petals tumble to the earth. When the last petal touched the ground the young girl took her final breath.

Reminiscent of Ally's grandpa blowing the sawdust in his workshop into a neat little pile the dead plant blew towards the deceased girl although the air was eerily still. A swirl of dried plant particles encircled her body and in an instant vanished into the ground taking her and the crowd with it. Still incapacitated Ally stood alone and powerless in front of Edmund.

"Ally, please don't make a promise you can't or won't keep," his voice pleading in a way she had never heard before.

Unable to move a muscle Ally remained fixated on Edmund's movements. Walking over to where the young girl had been, he knelt down and brushed his fingers over the dirt before pausing. He looked back at Ally with a grim expression and with nothing more than a slight flick of his hand sent Ally off.

A sudden stop jerked Ally's body with enough force to send her extremities out in front of her. Like a rag doll they hung from her torso inches above a manicured lawn. The black marble headstone in front of her was blank and she wondered whose burial site it was? Tears begun flowing from her eyes while she remained helplessly suspended above the grave. When her vision blurred to the point that she could no longer see clearly, a complete darkness bubbled up around her leaving her in a place void of all light.

Faintly she heard her mother's voice calling her name, "Ally, Ally where are you?"

"I'm here Mom, I'm here," she screamed at the top of her lungs, but the words never left her mouth.

"There you are," cheered her mom, "Daddy will be home soon let's get you washed up." The sound of a little girl giggling while her mom sang a bath time song changed Ally's tears from fearful ones to happy ones. Soon realizing she was the little girl laughing Ally repeatedly opened and closed her eyes hoping to see her mother's face. How she wished the darkness would release it's hold and allow her to witness the memory she had recovered. Unyielding the gloom around her remained, but Ally's other senses heightened. The faint sound of her dad coming into the house echoed and she could soon smell the cologne he wore especially for his wife.

"There's my two favorite girls," exclaimed her dad and with that Ally could physically feel him wrap her up in an oversized towel, lift her into his arms and sweetly kiss her cheek. Her heart burst with love and comfort as she nestled deep into the plush towel and arms of her father.

459

Comforted inside her father's embrace Ally rested peacefully and slept until the first rays of the sunrise peered through the window. Stretching a long satisfying stretch Ally felt happy recalling the dream of her parents only to have it snowball into despair. How she missed her happy family and what they once were. Now she believed an unknown disaster was heading their way. With the speed of light her thoughts went from wondering what that could be to whether her parents knew she was missing and if her father would be sober enough to understand it. Hearing Rose already making her way downstairs brought back the other dreams Ally had experienced. She couldn't even begin to decipher what those meant or whether they were dreams at all. Had she actually been with Edmund last night?

"Enough Ally!" she scolded herself, "It's not always about you. You have to protect Rose."

In an almost frenzied state Ally washed up, dressed and hurried downstairs. To her relief she found Sallie and Rose preparing breakfast and asked, "How can I help?"

Sallie gave Ally a sly smile acknowledging that she was doing the same thing. Keeping Rose busy even though her tactics were a bit different. Instead of a casual day of relaxing and talking Sallie had insisted on a full-blown breakfast. One that would take the majority of the morning to prepare and clean up after.

Rose looked about at the countless items strewn around the kitchen and suggested, "How about dicing up the fruit?"

Ally replied, "Sure, I can do that," and playing coy asked, "Where's all the kitchen staff?"

"Sallie gave them the morning off. Of course, before deciding she wanted a king size meal. If you ask me I think she had the whole thing planned," commented Rose.

Thankfully Ally's face was turned when Rose answered. Then she deliberately looked over the fruit trying to avoid letting Rose see her "the jig is up" expression. Sallie on the other hand never even flinched. Her staunch poker face held true before she said with a smile, "Awe you found me out Rose. I overheard you and Ally last night and wanted to have some time to relax with you both. I figured a big breakfast would do the trick before I'm off for the day."

Ally was thankful for Sallies support in keeping Rose occupied and the morning went off without a hitch. Until they realized they had made far too much food for the three of them to consume. The small icebox couldn't possibly hold all the food needing to be kept cool and not wanting to waste any of it Rose suggested she and Ally ride into town to give it to the orphanage.

Sallie briskly addressed this unexpected and unwanted turn of events, "That's a wonderful idea Rose, but allow me to take the food. I've intruded long enough on your time with Ally."

"Are you sure?"

"Yes Rose I am sure. It won't take me long and besides it'll be my way of thanking you for graciously permitting me to intrude in the first place," winked Sallie cleverly sending Ally a message that the potential problem was handled.

Ally did however disagree with one thing and spoke up, "You didn't intrude Sallie, it was fun. Besides we didn't have set plans. I just wanted a day off from training to spend with my roommate." Ally couldn't remember the last time she had referred to Rose as her roommate. Her more than cheerful countenance acknowledged how very good it felt, "Just like old times, right Rose?"

Her ever brilliant smile flashed looking more dazzling than normal because of the genuine happiness behind it, "Yes. Just like old times," agreed Rose with a twinkle in her eye.

Sallie took the cue and excused herself, "I'll see you both tonight."

Following Sallie outdoors they said their goodbyes and lounged on the front porch taking turns pointing out the various birds in the trees. All at once every bird flew from its perch scattering off in a single direction and filling the air with a flurry of wings.

"Wow! What caused that?" Ally asked.

"I'm not sure," answered Rose searching the horizon, "Oh that's why," she pointed.

Soaring high in the sky was a large brown bird with cream colored highlights near the tip of his expansive wings and along his tail. Gliding effortlessly through the air the sun shone through those pale feathers resembling the soft glow of a night light. At great speed the eagle dive bombed the ground snatching a squirrel from the meadow and then was greeted midflight by a similar but slightly smaller bird.

"Oh no, she's going to try and take his meal," exclaimed Ally fearing a fight was underway.

Chuckling Rose said, "Don't worry Ally that's her mate and no he won't take her meal."

"Her? She's the bigger one?"

"Yes," giggled Rose, "They usually nest nearby."

"I've never seen such a large bird," Ally admitted rising to her feet to get a better look. The male took this as an invitation to land in a large pine tree near the lodge giving Ally a chance to absorb his magnificence and leaving his mate to return to their nest with her catch. His dark brown plumage came to life when the sun hit it just right. Rays of sunlight made the feathers on his head and neck shimmer with golden flecks, giving him the appearance of royalty as he surveyed his kingdom. Turning his head back towards Ally his piercing eyes with their deeply rich caramel color hypnotized her. He returned Ally's gaze pulling her into the cavernous mystery they held.

Joining Ally at the railing Rose agreed, "He is rather spectacular."

Breaking her stare with him Ally answered Rose. This gave him the opportunity to take flight. Silently he faded into the late morning sky leaving Ally hopeful she'd see him again.

"I'm not sure there's much I can do to top that so how about we settle for a cool glass of lemonade."

"That sounds great," said Ally following Rose inside knowing she had numerous hours left to keep Rose busy. After the morning's turn of events with the extra food she knew she'd have to remain on her toes.

Chapter Three

Remembering how easily the two of them could spend hours back in school talking about nothing in particular, Ally decided an honest to goodness old-fashioned conversation would work great. She managed to think of it as two friends just hanging out and not as a ploy to keep Rose out of town. No one was more surprised by this truth than Ally. Even after everything that had taken place they were in fact friends. Imagining they were back in their dorm room Ally brought up ice skating and whether or not the lake at Dalton Manor would be safe to skate on come winter. In no time Ally's wish to have a stress free and fun conversation is exactly what happened. Their conversation flowed naturally and everything that had occurred between the Halloween party and the present continued to fade away.

There wasn't any tension or anger between them. The foundation they built in their budding friendship back at school had not only survived but was deepening. Rose soon shared something that had been on her mind, "I can't quite put my finger on it Ally and I wish I could. Well it doesn't matter, either way Mr. Dalton was absolutely correct in choosing you. There is something extra special about you."

"Special about me?" Ally's surprise evident in her expression and tone.

"Yes, it's like something is waiting to be discovered and only you can uncover it. Something is just out of sight, around a corner or locked away and you alone have the key."

Humbly Ally refuted, "Oh Rose you are giving me far too much credit. That doesn't' sound like me at all. I mean what could I discover that Mr. Dalton doesn't already know?"

"I'm not sure..." Rose trailed off to think or she was listening to something unheard by Ally. She finally continued, "I don't know Ally, but there's something coming. I can feel it."

Unable to control her thoughts Ally wondered if she would be successful in finding a way out of the locket. Could that be the discovery she would make? She hoped so. More than anything else that was her hope and yet that didn't make any sense. Why would Edmund choose someone who could escape his spell? Were Ally's thoughts betraying her?

"Ally, Ally," whispered Rose waving her hand in front of Ally's face.

"I'm sorry," she said shaking her head realizing the perfect opportunity had presented itself, "Aren't my thoughts available to you free of charge?" teased Ally trying to keep the mood light.

"Sticking around in your head after you've surrendered would be a little rude. Don't you think?"

Hiding her relief with Rose's admission Ally nodded in agreement concerned her voice would give her away. With one of her nagging questions answered Ally pushed forward, "Why hasn't any of the other hosts for Helene wanted you around?"

"Each of them had a different reason," Rose held her words then expressed with sorrowful eyes, "Although, I believe they all shared the same root issue," and with misery looming in her eyes she almost whispered, "Each of them found it impossible to forget the betrayal they felt towards me."

The obvious pain this caused Rose was enough to end that topic of conversation. Deciding it didn't really matter in the big scheme of things Ally let it go. She could easily see both sides of the argument, something her Grammy had passed down to her. Whenever tempers began to flare it was Grammy who remained the neutral level-headed one. As the family's peacemaker, it was usually Grammy to the rescue. Her natural ability to put herself in each person's shoes and relate to both sides was a remarkable talent.

Evening fell and the smell of dinner beckoned the girls to the dining table. Once the kitchen staff was out of ear shot Rose took Ally's hand saying, "Thank you for today."

"You're welcome. We needed to catch up and I had a blast, but the night's not over yet."

"Very true, but I'm referring to you being protective over me and wanting to spare me pain."

Not wanting to let the cat out of the bag about Maxwell's return, if it wasn't already, Ally pretended she didn't know what Rose was referring to. Stalling, she tilted her head in puzzlement by Rose's comment and was more than relieved when Sallie entered the lodge. So much so Ally nearly shouted, "Just in time for dinner."

"I'll be right down," Sallie unnecessarily shouted back as she headed upstairs. Which only drew more attention to Ally's awkwardness.

"Ally it's fine. I know Maxwell is back in town, but there's no need to worry about me. He can't cause me anymore harm."

So many questions ran through Ally's mind and she started to ask Rose how and why before stopping mid-sentence when Rose's expression grew sad. Ally's inquisitive mind wanted answers, but none of the answers were more important to her than Rose, so this too was let go. Other than her morbid curiosity there wasn't a justifiable reason to discuss Maxwell any further and the conversation was quickly changed, "Will Mr. Dalton give me my hunting instructions himself or does someone else handle that?"

"They will come from someone else. Mr. Dalton rarely if ever personally deals with his hunters," replied Rose.

"He's a very busy man Ally," added Sallie who had joined them at the table.

Agreeing, Rose said, "To put it simply."

"You won't be given any hunting instructions for a while Ally. Before Mr. Dalton sends you off on a mission we need to make sure you can travel on you own without any problems. I was hoping to have you ready to go in a week or so," announced Sallie.

Butterflies filled Ally's stomach and it took both Rose and Sallie to settle her down. The conversation progressed quickly. Which helped Ally discover the anxious jittery feeling making her body tingle was based in excitement as much as it was in fear. Ally felt like she had become a superhero. Excitement flowed through every inch of her and she could hardly wait to test out her new talents. Naturally she pictured her favorite hero. Images of Peter Parker discovering his 'Spidey sense' made Ally giggle and she understood the need to practice her skills before she actually needed to use them. Unlike in a comic book or movie she knew she could end up in real danger and shuddered to think what would happen if she wasn't ready. Unforeseen and unimaginable threats were in this magical world. Ally wondered if she would ever be fully prepared.

By the following morning Ally was determined to watch Sallie with a renewed intent. Every move, word spoken and glance Sallie made would be given great attention. Sallie had repeatedly proven she excelled beyond measure at her task and Ally was determined to use this to her advantage. Knowing she would soon venture off on her own without Sallie to protect her was a massive reality check. Shadowing Sallie would not last forever. It was up to Ally to take each lesson seriously and thoroughly pay close attention. It was imperative to learn what to do and how to be victorious. Merely watching with casual interest could cost Ally her life. Then an even more troubling thought crossed Ally's mind. Was there something far worse than death when battling evil?

Located high above the bustling street Ally turned her focus on Sallie instead of the people below her. With an almost rhythmic scan of the city Sallie surveyed their surroundings. It wasn't restricted to the people below or to the open windows of the skyscrapers, but from everything on the ground to the sky above them. Even though Ally had already located the target of their visit she soon realized that was the easy part. At last Ally comprehended what she had failed to acknowledge in her previous weeks of training. It was not what was visible that needed her full attention. Quite the opposite. It was all that was hidden from view that needed to be addressed first. Nothing could be accomplished with the target until any and all threats were eliminated.

Hearing herself vocalize her thoughts was surreal, but there was no escaping the truth behind them, "The humans can't really hurt us. But the unseen of the world not only could, it wants to," whispered Ally so softly it was nearly inaudible. How bizarre to call the people humans. Wasn't that what she was? Wasn't that what they all were?

"Yes, it's time to move Ally," blurted Sallie plunging the two of them towards the ground. When they landed, it wasn't on the busy city street below, but on the front deck of the lodge.

Fearful she hadn't noticed something important Ally snapped, "What did I miss?"

"Rely not only on your eyes Ally," and with that Sallie vanished.

Running into the lodge shouting, "Rose! Rose!" Ally ran right into her.

"My goodness Ally what's wrong?"

471

"I'll never be able to do this Rose. Sallie caught sight of something in our travels and I completely missed it. I was doing all I could to see what she was seeing and I still didn't see it," gushed Ally.

"Where is she?"

"She went back to where we were."

"Did she say anything?"

Dread had replaced last night's adrenaline rush about being a superhero and with a shaky voice replied, "She told me not to rely on my eyes."

Doing her best to comfort her friend Rose nudged Ally over to the couch. "That's extremely good advice and you should take it to heart."

By the time Ally had pulled herself together Sallie the warrior had returned. Her face glistening with perspiration, evidence of the battle which took place. "You're safe. Oh, thank goodness," exclaimed Ally rushing to give her a hug.

"Of course I am Ally. Now go sit back down."

Between Sallies commanding presence and take charge way of speaking Ally quietly returned to the couch. Rose gave her hand a squeeze and retreated to the other room without a word.

"Close your eyes Ally."

Ally did so without a second thought. What seemed like minutes passed causing Ally to consider opening her eyes, but she was afraid Sallie wouldn't like that. Deciding to wait awhile longer Ally listened hard. She could hear Rose in the kitchen pouring something, the birds singing happy songs outdoors and the leaves rustling in the wind. That was all fine and good, but what she wanted to know most of all, was whether Sallie was still there. Fine tuning what she was listening to she pushed aside all the other noises until she could hear Sallie breathing. At first her breathing was quick more evidence a battle had ensued, then it began to slow down and become almost too faint to hear. When that happened, Ally struggled for another way to verify Sallie's presence.

Sniffing the air Ally smelled the leather corset she knew was part of Sallie's warrior dress. She also picked up on the slightest hint of sulfur reminding Ally of the charcoal skinned creature Sallie had killed some time ago. Ally was convinced Sallie was still in the room. Zeroing in on the rotting scent Ally turned her face towards where Sallie now stood and keeping her eyes shut gave a sly smile.

"Very nice," approved Sallie, "You can open your eyes."

Opening her eyes to Sallie's expressive grin caused Ally to smile proudly and say, "Rely not only on my eyes."

473

"Now you get it. There's several ways to spot danger. You must learn to use and pay attention to all five of your senses Ally."

"I understand, but...."

"Don't worry Ally I will train you to use all of them. Someday you will notice the slightest shift in the air around you and know danger is close. Your taste buds will become so acute you will be able to detect the slightest drop of an elixir in a sea of water. You've already proven you understand how sound and smells can assist you. There's no doubt you will master them all," Sallie said with unmeasurable confidence.

Rose returned to the living room mere moments before Sallie was off again. "Sounds like you had a successful and eventful morning of training."

"To say the least," Ally replied.

Picking up where Sallie left off Rose told story after story of Sallie's conquests. Pointing out how each of her natural born sensory perceptions were used to her benefit. Accepting that she could use her senses in heightened ways was the easy part. Believing she would reach Sallie's level of excellence was entirely another thing. Ally had never been the best at anything. No matter how good she became at whatever she was learning or playing. There was always someone better.

"It's not a competition between you and Sallie. As a matter of fact, there isn't a hunter that can match her evil fighting skills, but that doesn't mean they aren't valuable and excel in a different area."

Ally couldn't shake the mounting fear taking hold, "How am I ever going to battle the evil that's out there?"

"There's no need to worry yourself about that. You will not be expected to go up against Mr. Dalton's enemies until you are completely prepared."

"I'll never be ready!" hollered Ally, "I don't know how to fight and I'm not sure I want to learn."

Becoming frustrated with Ally's determination to wallow in her self-doubt Rose asserted her position, "Ally that's quite enough. You are your own worst enemy sometimes. You will be kept safe throughout eternity and you will someday realize you're far more capable of accomplishing what you want then you give yourself credit for."

Ally knew better than to argue with Rose giving her an unconvincing and pitiful smile. It's not that she didn't want to believe her, she did, but the odds seemed stacked against her.

"Where did we meet Ally?"

Without understanding her line of questioning Ally answered, "In college."

"Exactly," pointed out Rose with a "told you so" expression.

Unclear of the point Rose was trying to make an exasperated Ally asked, "Exactly?"

Throwing her hands in the air Rose continued, "Who truly believed you would get into college?" Before Ally could reply Rose answered her own question, then persisted with her line of questioning, "Almost no one! Even your adoring grandparents who wanted it almost as much as you thought it may be a little out of reach. Sure Mr. Griffin and your mom cheered you on, but it was your determination that eventually got you there. Who took the tests? Who studied and studied? Who refused to give up?"

"Me," mumbled Ally.

With Rose's hazel eyes literally blazing she asked, "Who?"

Proudly and with confidence Ally stated, "Me. I did what I said I was going to do and left Glenbrook. I went to college!"

Satisfied with that answer Rose pushed harder, "Who was determined to protect me from Maxwell?"

Inundated with fearless courage Ally calmly said, "I was. I am. He will never cause you anymore pain, not as long as I'm around."

"There she is. The determined and strong-willed girl who can reach any goal she sets for herself. No matter the odds, no matter the naysayers, no matter the obstacles. That's the girl who will eventually become the hunter we all know she can be."

Rose was right and Ally knew it. There wasn't anything Ally couldn't accomplish when she set her mind to it and that acknowledgement would keep Ally going. Now more than ever she was determined to reach her goals.

Chapter Four

Brushing her long blonde hair while Dorothy offered her one hair clip after another Helene admired the reflection of the locket hanging from her neck. The delicate chain captured the morning's sun sparkling vibrantly, but it paled in comparison to the brilliance of the locket itself. Helene had quite the collection of fine jewelry and yet this locket alone gave her an unexplainable and illogical feeling. Helene believed in her heart that her and the locket were united in a very special way. She had no idea how true her belief was and Edmund was determined to keep that fact to himself.

Helene's body warmed with the feeling of being completely loved by Edmund. Closing her eyes, she recalled their anniversary and how he had surprised her with the beautiful gift. Refusing to take the locket off it remained a constant companion of Helene. A testimony to the love she and her husband shared. It was Edmund himself who had to convince her to remove it during her bath and even then, it remained safely in its porcelain trinket box. Always within eye sight.

Edmund purchased the dainty cream colored trinket box covered in red roses especially for the locket. No other piece of jewelry ever went into the exquisite oval shaped box. Little did Helene know that the enchanted box wouldn't have allowed another piece of jewelry inside. The mere thought of misplacing or losing the gift shattered her heart. This assured Helene was diligently aware of its whereabouts at all times.

Watching Dorothy twist the front half of her hair into a loose bun Helene was distracted by the almost blinding twinkle of the locket. "Have you ever noticed how bright my locket shines?" she asked Dorothy.

"Yes, my lady," responded Dorothy pausing for a split second then returning to her work on Helene's hair.

How Helene missed Elizabeth's enthusiasm and the bond they shared. Knowing Dorothy was still relatively new at helping her and perhaps concerned how friendly she could be as her lady's maid; Helene did her best to put Dorothy at ease. "I wonder how Edmund accomplished it?"

This had obviously never crossed Dorothy's mind leaving her befuddled and without an answer. Not wanting to be rude Dorothy stopped what she was doing and took a long look at the locket. She watched it as it seemed to dance with life. Waves of light seemed to twirl across the silver locket quickly changing direction and intensity. "I have no explanation for its unique shine. If I didn't know better, I would say there's a flame trapped within it."

"What an accurate description Dorothy. It does remind me of dancing flames. Wouldn't that be a neat trick?" exclaimed Helene with enthusiasm hoping it would energize Dorothy and inspire her to continue the conversation.

Finishing with Helene's hair she answered, "Yes, that would be some trick."

Looking over her finished look she thanked Dorothy before her attention was drawn back to the locket. Grinning with utter sincerity Helene summed it up, "It must be the flame of our love, strong, uncommon and everlasting." Helene refused to give up so easily hoping her truthful admission of love for Edmund would allow Dorothy to let her guard down.

Nodding in agreement Dorothy smiled the first genuinely heartfelt smile Helene had seen. There was something in her eyes that was equally happy and sad. That simple act clued Helene into a possible reason why Dorothy remained so professional yet distant. She had her own story of love and from the looks of it her heart was still broken.

After a quick knock Edmund burst into the bedroom, "Helene my love, are you ready?"

"Yes Edmund what's all the fuss?"

"I have a surprise for you."

"Oh I love surprises," cheered Helene her chestnut eyes beaming with anticipation.

Excitement built between the two of them as they made their way downstairs. One would be hard pressed in deciding whether Edmund was more excited about giving Helene her surprise or if she was more excited about receiving it. Either way, they were both beside themselves with pure joy.

"Close your eyes," instructed Edmund before guiding her outside. Carefully he helped her down the steps, across the lawn and after finding the perfect spot, he positioned her where to stand and slowly backed away.

"Can I open them?"

"Not yet," he answered taking several more steps away from her. Then enthusiastically gave the go ahead, "Now my sweet!"

There in the exact spot she had selected sat a silver painted wrought iron bench. Nestled in the center of the basket weave backrest sat a single heart reminding Helene of her locket. Swirls bordered the backrest and arms, continuing down the legs and across the seat. It was the most intricately stunning bench Helene had ever seen. With a gasp, she enthused, "Oh my darling it's gorgeous." Rushing to the bench Helene quickly noticed the heart was engraved to match her locket, "E & H" sat proudly in the heart's center. Crashing into the arms of her husband she squealed, "Edmund I love it! It's more beautiful than I thought a bench could ever be."

More than pleased with her reaction he kissed her waiting lips. Lost in their embrace the world disappeared. All that remained for either of them was the death defying love they shared.

"I love you," whispered Helene sinking deeper into Edmunds broad chest.

Squeezing her in his muscular arms careful not to use too much strength he returned her words, "I love you my dear sweet Helene."

Together they sat on the bench and watched the clouds leisurely make their way across the sky. Gradually shifting from one shape to another. A double acorn dropped from the oak landing on Helene's lap making the two of them laugh. "Good thing it didn't hit me in the head," taking a closer look at the acorns Helene added, "Look they're a happy couple as well." With a giggle Helene tossed the acorns into the hidden garden.

"Yes, good thing," agreed Edmund. "I imagine breakfast is ready. Shall we go?"

If Helene had not been so hungry she would have stayed on the bench all day with Edmund, but breakfast sounded too good to pass up. Accepting this she agreed, "Yes, we should."

Clearing her plate Helene leaned back and swallowed her last bite before saying, "My goodness, I was hungrier than I thought."

"Yes you were. I was beginning to fear you would help yourself to my plate as well," teased Edmund. "You're feeling much better I see."

It was true. Helene had been feeling so much better over the last couple weeks. The nightmares had become few and far between, her strength was returning and for the first time in a long time she felt like her old self. Edmund had been cautiously hopeful and now it looked like the worst was behind them. At long last his Helene had returned to him, and she was ecstatic that she never had to share with him how bad her nightmares had become.

Life at Dalton Manor was returning to normal. A welcome relief to everyone. Other than the issue of Maxwell being back in town there was happiness all around. Edmund was already dealing with Maxwell's unexpected return. Edmund being the shrewd businessman he was had lined up a deal with a longtime colleague, assuring that a potentially lucrative deal would cross Maxwell's desk. Without a doubt sending him off to make it his own. The only thing that came close to being as large as Maxwell's ego was his hunger for more wealth and unlimited power.

While Helene tended to her garden, something she had been missing, Edmund checked on the status of Maxwell leaving town. From the sounds of it he would be leaving in a day or two. Helene would never know he was back. She was nowhere near ready for a trip into town, but Edmund knew his wife would soon want to venture from the manor, so time was of the essence. Maxwell's hatred towards Edmund meant he would never visit the manor. Fueled by jealousy and his inability to frighten Edmund their paths rarely crossed. Both did their best to avoid the other.

After hours in the sun Helene returned to the manor with dirty hands, a smudged face and feeling happily exhausted from a productive day. Heading straight up to her room she requested a bath and in no time the staff had prepared one for her. Dorothy helped Helene out of her dress and under her careful watch removed the locket and placed it gingerly into the trinket box. Invisible to their eyes the box glowed with bright colors keeping the treasure within safe and protected.

Assisting Helene with washing and rinsing her hair Dorothy went into autopilot mode. She didn't have to think about what to do she just did it. Being a housemaid was the only life Dorothy had ever known. At this point, it was second nature and took no thought at all. Becoming the lady's maid for Helene was a natural step in her profession. Well trained and competent at her job she had Helene dressed for dinner in no time. The quiet between them was nearly deafening.

Accustomed to her friendship with Elizabeth, Helene wanted to help Dorothy feel more comfortable around her. Perhaps for partly selfish reasons, and on the other hand Helene truly believed Dorothy would enjoy a closer relationship, similar to the one she and Elizabeth shared. Helene's desire was to make sure the large staff felt like the manor was home not just their place of employment, especially her personal help. She believed if they felt connected to her and Edmund their work would be done with more care. It had worked so well for her family. The loyalty, love and respect they forever showed the Beck family was an inspiration.

"Dorothy?"

Unware that Helene had asked her a question Dorothy shamefully said, "My apologies my lady. What was it you asked me?"

A forgiving smile put Dorothy at ease and Helene restated her request, "Would you please fetch my locket?"

Taken back and quite astonished that Helene had used the word please Dorothy couldn't move quick enough. Nearly dropping the locket in her rush to unclasp it, Helene surprised her again. She quietly grasped the locket and held it still so the clasp could be undone. Once secure on her neck Dorothy stepped back and waited to be dismissed.

"Thank you Dorothy."

"It's my pleasure," she replied with a curtsy ready to make a quick exit. As far as she was concerned she had not done her job to the best of her ability.

"May I have a moment of your time?" questioned Helene.

"Of course my lady." Dorothy prepared herself for what she believed was coming. She was convinced she would be relieved of her duty and sent back to her previous position.

In a soothing tone Helene spoke, "Dorothy, please be yourself around me. No one could fill Elizabeth's place in my heart, but that doesn't mean we can't have an equally wonderful relationship."

There was that word again "please" and although Dorothy's past experiences were screaming at her not to buy into Helene's kindness she ignored them, "Yes my lady. I will work harder to accomplish that goal."

"I'm glad to hear you say that. My hope is in no time you won't have to work at being yourself. It'll simply be the natural thing to do."

At dinner Helene spoke with Edmund regarding her conversation with Dorothy and how she hoped it would improve things between them. Having a robot, regardless of skill level, tend to her needs wasn't what Helene wanted. Naturally Edmund offered to find someone else to assist her, but Helene being who she was refused to give up on someone without at least trying to make it work.

"That's my sweet Helene. Always making sure everyone around her is happy and well. One of the many things I love about you."

"I like to help."

"Yes you do, from stranded ducklings to your lady's maid," remarked Edmund launching them into a trip down memory lane. That simple comment took them into the wee hours of the morning as they recalled memory after memory. Another sign Helene was regaining her strength. Edmund couldn't remember how long it had been since they sat up talking and laughing all night.

The hours of reminiscing had reconnected them in a way they had both been longing for. Overpowered by the magnitude of their emotions they enjoyed a heartfelt night of fiery lovemaking affirming their bond and love for each other. Far above their physical attraction and compatibility there was a mutual respect, a shared intelligence, a kindred spirit and above all a selfless love and desire to put each other first.

In the following weeks not only did Edmund and Helene enjoy picnics, leisurely horseback rides and boating on the lake, Dorothy was letting her guard down. Helping Helene dress in the morning was quickly becoming one of her favorite tasks. Both being morning people they were inevitably sent into bouts of laughter more than once before Helene was dressed.

Everything appeared right with the world. Maxwell had left town as expected, Helene showed no sign of ill effects, Dorothy was becoming friendly while retaining her professionalism and Edmund at long last felt optimistic about Helene's transition. Believing she would be around for some time before needing another host. He had become so confident in this that he had not checked with Rose in days.

He trusted Rose and Sallie would prepare Ally to do her job and do it with ease. The magical garden was thriving under the watchful eye of the gardener's. Whenever Edmund and Helene went out to her new bench he could see for himself just how robust and hardy the plants looked.

These were the days he dreamed of. Days filled with peace, happiness and his beloved Helene by his side. The only thing bringing him sadness was knowing Helene would not remember all the new memories they were creating. When the time came to replace Ally's dying body Helene would return to the days before their one year wedding anniversary and the healing process would once again begin.

How he wished he could share with his beloved all the memories she had forgotten. So many years of wonderful days and nights locked away in a hidden room within the manors walls. To avoid a slip of the tongue and prevent him from accidentally bringing up something Helene would not remember, Edmund would expel his recollections of their time together while in one host body and capture them in a vial for safe keeping. Allowing him the opportunity to revisit them whenever he liked. Which was a huge help for Edmund in dealing with Helene's absence between transitions.

"Is something troubling you?" asked Helene.

Edmund's mind had wandered to the vials of memories while focusing on the wall they hid behind, but he was quick to reply, "No my beloved, I was thinking about business. Shame on me. What did you say?"

"I was wondering if you were ready for bed?"

"In a little while you go on and head up. I promise I won't be too far behind."

"Alright," Helene replied with a yawn.

While preparing for bed Helene could tell something was on Dorothy's mind. "Are you thinking about business too?" Helene teased.

"No ma'am. I was wondering if I could ask you a question."

"Of course."

"It's rather personal," muttered Dorothy.

"Well the good news about questions is that sometimes a polite refusal to give an answer is an answer in itself," sending a clear message that Helene would only give the answer she was comfortable with.

"I was simply wondering what pictures are inside the locket," Dorothy took a breath, "I've never heard any mention of its contents and I have to say it surprises me. In all our time together you've never once opened it to show me. Is it empty?"

Helene laid her tiny fingers across her necklace and thought for a moment, "I haven't had the heart to tell Edmund is doesn't open. Thankfully he has yet to ask me about it."

"Aren't you curious what's inside?"

"Of course I am; however, not at the expense of making my husband feel bad."

"That's true, but I'm surprised you haven't shared it with him. There's a chance he could fix it or get you another one."

"Oh I would never want to risk damaging it and there is no replacing this one. Even with its identical twin.

This is Edmund's anniversary gift to me in celebration of our first year of marriage. It will be with me forever."

"Well, it's not my place to interfere. It is your choice my lady and your secret is safe with me."

"Thank you Dorothy. I know it'll come up at some point, but until then I know whatever is inside is safely locked away."

Chapter Five

Having spent the last couple of days practicing time travel on her own had done very little to raise Ally's comfort level. She knew Sallie was trying to build her confidence. Nevertheless, the little trips to the past or future safely within the boundaries of the manor weren't helping. It didn't take long for Ally to master the skill of traveling on her own, once she figured out what the trick to her travel was. A deep inhale and quick exhale while zeroing in on her destination was all it took. In a literal flash, she would arrive at her intended stop. The best description she could give was traveling on a lightning bolt. Her travel was so fast and blindingly bright it forced her to shut her eyes tight in anticipation of the dazzling light that followed her exhale.

Lying in bed for hours was doing nothing more than adding to her fears. She knew Rose would be waiting at the lodge for her to return. Meanwhile, Sallie would wait at the appointed destination in order to verify her arrival. It sounded great in theory. Ally trusted she would be protected at either location by one of her friends. Yet there was this nagging concern. What if she didn't actually arrive where she wanted? How would they find her?

It wasn't until she decided she would argue this point in the morning and earn more practice time did she fall sound asleep. Relaxed in the belief that she would be granted more time unfortunately allowed her mind to wander. Going places she never wanted to go.

Everything was black and when the moonlight reappeared Ally found herself standing on a small boulder surrounded by horrifying noises. Lurking in the shadows she heard growls and raspy grunts circling her, but something or someone was keeping them at bay. A sigh of relief escaped her lips when she spotted a figure perched above her yielding a bow and arrow. The woman dressed in a hooded cape and leather corset peered into the shadows. Expecting no one other than her favorite warrior Sallie, Ally was caught off guard by the face under the cloak. It belonged to someone else. Someone Ally had never seen before.

Afraid to move and unable to speak Ally remained where she was, while the animalistic sounds grew in their intensity. She watched her defender take aim and release what she thought was a warning shot into the darkness only to hear something whimper in pain and confirm the arrow had hit its target. In dismayed horror Ally listened to the whimper of pain become screams of intense suffering. She could only imagine what was happening in the murkiness around her. Pressing her hands solidly over her ears trying to block the agonizing sounds Ally cried out, "Help me!"

The ground beneath her shook knocking Ally from her precarious perch onto the ground. Terrified she opened her eyes and discovered a warm glow lighting up her surroundings. She quickly spotted countless creatures with misshaped bodies fleeing on twisted limbs. Ally couldn't pull her eyes away until the very last beast escaped into the shadows. Next to her stood the unknown warrior only now she was at least triple the size as before. The giant woman offered her glowing hand to Ally while simultaneously shrinking to a more normal height. Giving this stranger her hand sent a shock through Ally and she awoke in her bed listening to the words, "You are never alone."

The sun was already rising and Ally decided what little sleep she'd gotten was more than enough. Fearing another nightmare was waiting for her she dressed and headed downstairs. Surprised by her appearance the night watchman who was still on duty offered her some tea.

Graciously Ally accepted and questioned him, "If we're all safe on the grounds of the manor why are you here?"

He simply stated, "Mr. Dalton would never make the mistake of assuming evil would never try and besiege the manor. He is far too wise to make such a potentially dangerous error.”

Appreciating his frank honesty was a bit much in Ally’s current state of mind. How she wished he had humored her and made up some false yet comforting reason for being there. “Oh, that’s what I was afraid of,” she admitted.

Rose made her way into the kitchen just as Ally finished her tea. The watchman and Rose exchanged greetings and he was gone. Rose poured herself a cup of tea and refilled Ally’s cup then piled a plate high with scones and biscuits saying, “Out with it Miss Ally.”

There was no reluctance in her sharing and Ally hoped her nightmare would persuade Rose to believe she wasn’t ready. Making sure not to leave out the tiniest of details Ally recapped the nightmare. She even tried to imitate the gruesome sounds she heard. At least until doing so bothered her too much to continue. Sallie joined them moments before Ally finished explaining all that took place.

“Oh you met Jane,” exclaimed Sallie with amusement.

“Really? That’s all you have to say?” snarled Ally.

Rose shushed them both saying, “Enough. Trust me Ally we all understand how frightening this world can be.

I, for one know it all too well. Remember I was alone here for quite some time."

"I know Rose, but...."

"No, stop right there. Let me remind you that Mr. Dalton hasn't lost a single plant from his garden to evil. We are all so wonderfully connected that if any of us are in dire need the entire garden is alerted and ready to assist. Not to mention Mr. Dalton himself."

Agreeing Sallie put in her two cents, "That's probably why Jane showed up in your nightmare last night. She sensed your fear and came to your rescue."

"So the nightmare was real?" gasped Ally.

Calmly Rose intervened, "No Ally, the nightmare was nothing more than a dream; however, your fear was real and for that reason alone a family member came to your aid."

"Family," whispered Sallie giving Ally a bear hug.

"I'm still afraid," Ally reminded them.

"Of course you are. I would be concerned if you weren't. A little fear isn't necessarily a bad thing. If used in the right way it can heighten your senses," remarked Sallie.

Rose agreed and between the two of them reassuring Ally she soon felt like she was back on solid ground, at which point Ally started to argue her point of needing more practice. Patiently they both listened to her side nodding at the appropriate times and not interrupting her once.

When finished Rose politely said, "It's clear you have thought this through...."

"But?" interrupted Ally.

"No, not a but an and. You have a valid point wondering how we would find you and it's wise to be concerned. So let me reassure you that as long as your necklace is around your neck you can be located. To reiterate what Jane told you last night, 'You are never alone,' Don't ever forget that."

"I know but..." Ally rebutted.

"It's not up for discussion Ally. You have to trust me in saying you are safe and you do not need to know specifics," chastised Rose.

Sallie knew that tone and wasted no time moving onto the task at hand, "Let's go into the living room and do one last practice run."

Reluctantly and with nerves upsetting her stomach Ally followed Sallie. After taking a seat on the couch she prepared for her first trip. Picturing the stables Ally inhaled deeply and automatically exhaled quickly. There wasn't any time to change her mind or even think about what she was doing. It all happened too fast. Ally's countless practice runs were making her travels become second nature and this helped reduce her fear of getting back home in a hurry, if need be.

Misty neighed a friendly hello when Ally appeared sending a clear message that this was common place for the horses. They all remained calm in their stalls completely unaffected by the burst of light preceding Ally's arrival. The sun was just beginning to rise confirming she had gone back to hours earlier.

"See that wasn't so hard," proclaimed Sallie from inside Misty's stall, "Now back to the lodge at the time you left."

Immediately after a final stroke on Misty's forehead Ally returned to the lodge where Rose was still washing the cups and plates from their breakfast. Sallie was only seconds behind and it didn't take long before she told Ally it was time to select a location and time far from the manor.

Rose suggested a revisit to the duckling rescue. It was one of Ally's favorite stories of Edmund and Helene, not to mention evil free. She knew Ally was deliberately stalling so selecting a fun memory was a safe bet.

Thinking for a minute Ally agreed, "Yes, that's a great idea," and with that she and Sallie readied themselves for the trip.

Returning to the exact branch above the bridge where Arthur had taken her, Ally sat waiting for Edmund and Helene to make their appearance. While she waited, she took the time to confirm Sallie was nearby and she was. Sallie was seated on the river bank in the shade of another tree. Motioning for her to come closer Sallie floated over to the branch looking almost angelic with her dress blowing in the wind.

"They will be here any second," guaranteed Sallie.

"I know, but that's not want I was wondering."

A curious Sallie asked, "Then tell me what's on your mind."

"In almost every travel experience with you there has always been evil hiding nearby. When I traveled with Arthur he didn't have to battle evil once. Why is that?"

Sallie laughed so hard she nearly came off the branch, "I can see how that's puzzling. Let me explain," but before she could Edmund and Helene made their appearance.

"It's like watching a rerun of an old show," commented Ally, "I know what's coming next and I can even quote their words."

Nodding in agreement Sallie said, "That's a good analogy."

After rescuing the duckling Edmund and Helene proceeded to the gazebo as expected. Ally on the other hand wanted to stay put on the oak to discover something new. She didn't know what she was looking for but figured this was as good a place as any to try out some of her other senses. Closing her eyes, she could hear the duckling's squeaky peeps in response to mama duck's calls. The gentle flow of the river was faint but noticeable, children played a game of tag in the distance and the smell of a woman's perfume made Ally sneeze. A shift in the wind brought in a cooler breeze marking the approaching dusk. Moments later she heard the Beck family and Edmund leave for their carriages.

"What did you discover?" Sallie questioned.

"More than I expected. I know I'm nowhere near your level of expertise and yet my senses seem sharper than ever before."

"Yes they are and they will gradually become more fine-tuned. Before you know it, you won't have to focus so hard. Your senses will simply be on high alert."

"Will they overwhelm me? I mean I don't always want to hear, smell and sense everything so strongly around me. That sounds exhausting."

Sallie's change in expression gave her away. Danger was near, "Let's go home and I'll answer that question," and with that Sallie disappeared immediately after Ally left.

Back at the lodge they were surprised to discover Rose had gone to visit with Helene and would return shortly. The coachman from their trip into town was taking Rose's place until either she or the two of them returned. Now that they had he made a quick getaway. Grabbing a few pieces of fruit Sallie sat on the floor next to the coffee table and offered some to Ally. Lunch would soon be served, but Ally's stomach was rumbling with hunger so she took a green apple. Time travel was proving to significantly boost Ally's appetite. Her first bite into the tart fruit caused her to make a funny face entertaining Sallie.

Sallie began, "Your senses will always be on high alert which is why they build slowly. If they didn't then yes, you would feel overwhelmed."

"That may help, but to always be listening, smelling and feeling everything so strongly it's gotta be more than you can stand. I don't think I'm going to like that at all," worried Ally.

"It becomes normal. If someone has always had amazing sight they are accustomed to it. It's their normal way of seeing things and they don't give it a second thought."

"Yeah, but my senses have never been close to what they are now and they're going to get stronger." Ally then asked, "I mean I get why we need them. It's for my own safety, but how in the world am I ever to relax?"

"Fear not Ally you will adjust. You'll soon discover relaxation isn't as hard to find as you think it'll be.

501

Besides, you will also notice the time you spend relaxing will be so much more tranquil."

Remembering Sallie's expression before returning to the lodge quickly brought up another topic, "You sensed evil at the park?"

"I'm home," announced Rose.

"Welcome back. Did you have a nice visit?" asked Sallie.

"Yes, I did," replied Rose. Not wanting to risk upsetting Ally by discussing Helene she said no more and asked, "How was your outing?"

"It was good," Ally politely cut in returning her focus to Sallie, "The evil at the park?"

"Yes I detected something, which is why I suggested we return home."

"That's my point! No matter where I go with you there's a battle on the horizon," grumbled Ally, "Why is that?"

Sallie hesitated and blushed, sending a clear message to Rose to step in. Rose calmly answered the question, "Sallie's far too humble to give you the best answer, so let me explain." Rose sat next to Ally on the couch, "Do you remember when Sallie's instructor Mr. Burns reminded her she wouldn't be allowed to hunt evil until she mastered locating a host body?"

"Vaguely," admitted Ally.

"Well for that reason alone Sallie pushed herself to the point of exhaustion trying to excel faster than anyone else in securing a host. Needless to say, she reached that goal and quickly moved on to battle training. Fighting evil has always been Sallie's first passion. The thrill of the hunt, the inevitable battle and the conquest over evil is the driving force behind Sallie. She rarely if ever passes up a chance to eradicate darkness, even if it's not her main objective, she will find a way to squeeze it in."

Sallie chuckled an almost villainous laugh, "Oh how I enjoy obliterating the enemy."

Mulling over what she'd been told Ally finally spoke up, "So you're looking for evil all the time?"

"Basically," answered both Sallie and Rose.

Another pause then she said, "So evil must be everywhere because you always seem to find it."

Rose knowing Ally better than Sallie attempted to defuse what was sure to escalate quickly, "Good and evil are always around us. Each doing their best to conquer the other. It doesn't mean we're always their target. Sallie simply chooses to make evil her target every chance she gets."

This fact obviously didn't help Ally feel any better. She slumped into the couch her mood becoming troubled. The emotional rollercoaster ride she longed to get off of had only managed to find more twists and turns.

Standing with confidence Sallie warned her, "Ally, evil looks for human weakness. It hunts down those who are vulnerable. Remember Ally you are now gifted. Your human frailty is hidden securely behind the protection of magic. And never forget we were selected for our ability to appear friendly and harmless. This allows us to strike from behind enemy lines when necessary," Sallie paused then added with a smirk, "Or desired. I just like defeating evil so much I chose to fight every chance I get."

Knowing this was more than enough for one day Rose requested lunch be served on the porch, where the three of them could relax in the cool air and talk about nothing in particular. As long as they steered clear of today's events.

In total agreement Ally led the way doing her best to push aside all she had just learned. It wasn't going to be easy, but she was running out of choices and yet a small part of her held onto the idea that the more she learned the better off she truly was. "It's always darkest before the dawn," she thought to herself.

Chapter Six

Examining her necklace in the mirror Ally pressed it between the palm of her hand and chest. Instinctively her eyes shut and she could see the enchanted garden. Focusing solely on the center rose she tested her theory and thought, "Rose can you hear me?"

Clear as day she heard Rose's voice inside her head, "I'm here Ally. I will always be here."

At first Ally was surprised. Then she remembered Rose used to listen in on her thoughts, making her think Rose answering her wasn't a big deal. Wanting more proof of the gardens connection she decided on an entirely different target. She wasn't quite sure Arthur's plant was the mighty oak, but that is where he materialized from. Convincing her it was worth a try. "Arthur are you there? Can you hear me?"

She heard nothing and opened her eyes after waiting only a couple seconds and found Arthur standing within the mirror asking, "Yes Miss Ally is everything alright?" with obvious concern.

Her body automatically jumped in response to Arthur's unexpected appearance. "You startled me," exclaimed Ally.

"My apologies Miss, but you summoned me. I thought something may have...."

Rose burst through the bedroom door already apologizing to Arthur for the unwarranted intrusion. A quick explanation of Ally not knowing all the ins and outs of communicating through what had been named the "bloomvine" Arthur returned from whence he came. Arthur's stern expression before he vanished combined with the look of "Are you kidding me?" on Rose's face confirmed Ally's suspicions. She had made a terrible mistake.

"The bloomvine? Isn't that a little cheesy?" Ally teased trying to delay the lecture she knew was coming.

Rose ignored Ally and headed straight for the kill, "Ally I realize we haven't gone over all the do's and don'ts, but you are far too bright not to have figured out that contacting Arthur anytime outside of an emergency would be wrong. I can't imagine what you were thinking. You will never under any circumstance outside of a true emergency call out for Arthur."

Deep down Ally knew before she even tried to contact Arthur that it probably wasn't a good idea. Her apology wasn't received well until she accepted full responsibility for her error in judgment. Vowing to never repeat it, Ally crossed her heart and said, "I promise Rose. I will not summon Arthur unless my very life depends on it."

Rose didn't join Sallie and Ally for breakfast. Figuring it was due to her earlier behavior Ally ate in silence. Even though she wasn't entirely sure why calling Arthur was so wrong. This time however she listened to that inner voice telling her asking about it now, was a bad idea. Instead Ally decided on what she believed to be a safe subject, "So what's on the agenda for today's lesson?"

Sallie's answer clearly showed she knew about Arthur's earlier visit, "Well after this morning's lesson the rest of the day will probably seem a bit dull."

"Oh you heard?"

The only reply Sallie gave was, "Yep."

A forgotten memory came to mind and Ally could hear her grandpa telling her "If you find yourself in a hole the first thing to do is stop digging," so she remained quiet through the rest of breakfast. It wasn't until they cleared the table, washed and dried the plates did Ally test the waters. She couldn't believe her own words, "I'd like to venture off completely on my own and see how I do."

With a hint of surprise in her voice Sallie still agreed, "I think that's a grand idea."

Ally had expected a little resistance and wasn't quite sure what to do next. There wasn't any reason she couldn't go ahead and leave, however this new freedom was terrifying. Thankfully a change of clothes was needed because she had dripped honey on her dress. That would delay her leaving for a short time, but then what? She found herself wandering around aimlessly upstairs until Sallie checked on her, knowing full well what Ally was up to.

With her friendly smile returning Sallie reassured Ally that she would be fine. Reminding her that she had already tested out her necklace that morning adding "You are never alone," repeating the words Jane had said to her in her nightmare.

Before departing Ally asked, "Is there anything I need to know?"

"As long as you stick to the rules you've been given thus far. You will be just fine," Sallie said sounding very motherly. Ally understood she was in control of how well or poorly this trip would go by how well she followed the rules. The undercurrent of Sallie's tone reminded Ally of the first time she borrowed her mom's car. Her mom had basically said the same thing. Only she had spent much more time reviewing the rules before handing Ally the car keys.

Deciding to revisit the day Edmund and Helene met Ally was instantly transported back to that place and time. Choosing a different location to view the party Ally sat upon the porch railing and noticed there wasn't a porch swing. There were several differences about the manor, but what caught her attention was the obvious difference in Edmund. His smile was clearly forced when he greeted his guests until the moment he came face to face with Helene. Ally knew what followed between the two of them having seen it several times before, so there wasn't any need to go with them to the stables. The whole reason she chose this day was to see if she could discover something new. Something she hadn't already seen or heard about.

Moving among the guests she heard conversations ranging from secret business deals to not so secret town gossip. Before long the number one topic of conversation for everyone was Edmund's disappearance with the Becks. Ally couldn't help but giggle at every eligible lady's concern with the matter and some of their spoiled behavior. Some pouted, others cried and a few were angry, especially Margret Bennett. Her anger quickly escalating into full blown fury. Although she hid it amazingly well behind her smiling mask of superiority.

Mr. Bennett tried to soothe his daughter's temper whispering in her ear, "Margret my angel. Please calm down. What can I do to help?"

Behaving in a very un-angel like way Margret snapped at her father. Through a clenched jaw Margret replied while maintaining a sham of a smile, "I will not calm down. How dare you allow Mr. Dalton to be lured by Helene."

"Wow," whispered Ally unsure what shocked her more. Margret's two-faced behavior or her father's inept attempt to calm his pampered daughter. The entire conversation was ridiculous and getting more so the longer it went on. That was Ally's cue. The following second she was back at the lodge still shaking her head in disbelief.

Rose had returned and was sitting quietly reading. Looking up at Ally's expression she had to ask, "What's that face for?"

"Boy Margret Bennett is a piece of work."

Laughing in agreement Rose said, "Oh, you don't know the half of it."

"If she ever needed to find work she'd be a great ventriloquist," stated Ally.

"How so?"

Making herself comfortable on the couch Ally explained, "You should have seen her smiling and waving to other guests at the manor while throwing a personal hissy fit for her father. She was fit to be tied about Edmund and Helene leaving the party together."

With a chuckle Rose said, "Oh yes. I do remember being the only one thrilled that day to see Helene walk off with Edmund. Although I don't really remember Margret's behavior so much. I tried to avoid her as much as possible. I'm sure you understand why," teased Rose.

Ally laughed in agreement adding, "Her father created quite the monster."

"Yes he did and Margret's behavior is rather ironic if you ask me."

"Ironic?"

"Well her spoiled brat behavior isn't. It's the whole I want Mr. Dalton for myself wish."

Not understanding what Rose was trying to say Ally replied, "Well, she's not the only one who felt that way. She was just the one being the most deceitful about it. Her sugary sweet expression and words were completely opposite of how she was feeling."

"Both true statements. Mr. Dalton was or is quite the catch, but I'm referring to her family's relationship to the Dalton's." The look on Ally's face made it clear she had not connected the dots. Rose helped her out by saying, "Margret Bennett? The Bennett's are the family who led the murderous mob to Dalton Manor that horrible night."

Feeling silly Ally gave a nervous laugh, "Oh my gosh! How could I forget that?"

Rose shrugged her shoulders wondering the same thing and this prompted her to give Ally a quick recap of how Edmund was granted immortality from his parents. This caused everything to come flooding back. Edmund had held the party for one reason alone. As a ploy to set up his revenge for the death of his parents. Little did he know he would meet Helene and she would change all that.

Wanting desperately to change subjects Ally asked where Sallie had gone. Rose told her she had some business of her own to tend to. Figuring her training was done for the day Ally relaxed saying, "What should we do for the rest of today?"

"We? Well, I'm going to spend the majority of the day reading and you will spend the rest of the day doing more solo traveling."

"Oh, I just thought...."

"You thought since Sallie was away you could take a day off from training. You can't possibly think you'll master your craft if you don't practice, practice, practice?"

Knowing Rose was right and that she was already on shaky ground, Ally made the wise choice to keep her excuses to herself and not even try to stall. Unsure where to go next it soon came to her. Ally had been wondering about something in particular and cautiously asked Rose, "Does Helene know Edmund is a warlock?"

Closing her book after sliding in a ribbon to mark her page Rose sat up straight and asked, "Do you remember when Edmund gave Helene the brooch in the park?"

"Yes, the one with the couple painted on it?"

"Exactly. Go back in time to that day, only go back late in the evening but to the Beck's home instead of the park," instructed Rose, "There, you will find your answer."

"How late?"

Rose opened her book to where the ribbon was and casually replied, "Almost bedtime. Around 9:00 PM should work."

After repeating the directions Rose had given her Ally nervously left the lodge. Reopening her eyes after the flash of her traveling light disappeared she found herself atop Helene's piano while she played an upbeat song. Ally spotted Edmunds recent gift pinned to her dress confirming Ally's travel was successful. The happy melody was no match for the ear-to-ear smile on Helene's face. When finished, she kissed her parent's goodnight and bounced up the stairs to her room in complete bliss.

Ally waited for something to happen, but all she witnessed was Helene falling fast asleep. Mystified as to why Rose had sent her to this time Ally began to second guess her trip. Believing she had heard Rose incorrectly. After several minutes Ally was ready to give up and return to the lodge. Then something caught her eye. Entering through the open window was a trail of fireflies. They headed for Helene stopping short before abruptly turning away from her and rushing over to Ally. Swirling around her she heard Edmund's voice, "Come with me Ally."

513

That's all it took. Ally was swept into the dancing cloud of floating insect lights. The next thing she knew she was back at the park only this time Helene sat alone on the bench. No chaperones, no Edmund, no one else for that matter. Emerging from thin air Edmund greeted Helene and she rushed into his arms. The kiss they shared immediately clued Ally in. They were in Helene's dream.

"You've been gone so long," whispered Helene holding tight to Edmund.

"I'm here now."

"Where have you been?"

Ally wondered what Helene was referring to. She could see the brooch still pinned to her dress. What did Helene mean when she commented that Edmund had been gone? Struggling to hear what they were saying Ally moved closer to the happy couple, until she was able to hear them clearly. Much had been said in a short time and Ally wondered what she had missed.

"I don't understand what you're saying," mumbled a melancholy Helene, "Sure about what?"

"I wanted, no I needed to make absolutely sure you loved me in the same way I love you," soothed Edmund.

Forlorn eyes showed how much Edmund had hurt Helene's feelings, "You doubted my love?"

Placing a tender kiss upon her forehead Edmund asked her to forgive him, "Forgive my foolishness my beloved. It wasn't doubt that kept me away from your dreams. It was fear."

"Fear? You're afraid of me?"

Ally found herself impatiently waiting for Edmund to answer Helene. She couldn't imagine the turmoil that must have been going on in Helene's heart and mind. Ally no longer felt hatred towards Edmund. Even so, she was still a long way off from liking him a whole bunch and yet his back and forth pacing was driving her crazy. This made her forget her place. For Helene's sake, she cried out in her mind, "Answer her!" hoping Edmund would be able to hear her.

Suddenly Pegasus made a grand appearance landing just feet from where Edmund stood. "Remember our ride?"

"Oh my goodness, yes! It was in one of the very first dreams I had of you."

"Then you remember me asking if you believed in magic."

By this time Helene was standing near Edmund stroking Pegasus, hopeful another ride was about to take place, "Yes I do. I said if magic were real it would be delightful."

"Your exact words were delightfully wonderful," corrected Edmund with a grin.

"All right, if you say so," conceded Helene before remembering Edmund still owed her an answer. "Did you bring Pegasus here to avoid answering my question?"

"Do you think I have the ability to do such a thing?"

"Mr. Dalton," replied Helene in a stern tone, "You are deliberately being evasive. I would like you to answer why you've been afraid to dream the night away with me."

One thing was clear to Ally. Helene believed she was dreaming of Edmund on her own and for no other reason than her intense love for him. In Helene's mind dreaming of the man she loved was as normal as a child dreaming of the Christmas gifts they wished for. Ally wondered if Helene ever discovered the truth.

Chapter Seven

Helene's frustration continued to grow while she waited for Edmund to reply, until he looked at her with a softness in his eyes unlike anything she had ever seen. The piercing unnatural sapphire-blue of his eyes, which reminded her of a masterful painter's work, was now shrouded behind distress. Whatever he was hesitant to say was weighing heavy on his heart. This quickly changed Helene's frustration to concern. Was he about to destroy the unimaginable happiness she felt earlier that day?

Tenderly Helene tried to reaffirm their love by squeezing his hand, "Edmund please, whatever it is you can tell me."

At last he spoke, "I was fearful you would turn me away........because not only do I believe in magic I practice the art."

Helene was speechless, then fighting back the laughter building inside she said, "Oh Edmund you're a magician. Why in the world would I dislike that? I will admit I'm a little surprised a man of your standing would play around with magic, but I guess it could be an entertaining way for you to unwind."

Ally dropped her head into her hands thinking to herself, "She doesn't believe him." She didn't even consider the possibility of Helene misunderstanding Edmund. His next words made Ally look up from behind her hands.

"Let me show you," offered Edmund.

Helene stood back and watched Edmund pick up an ordinary pebble from the ground and turn it into a sparrow. With glee, she shouted, "Oh Edmund that was amazing! Why would you be afraid to tell me you're such a talented magician. I should have known you would excel at magic like you do at everything else you attempt."

"Helene you don't understand."

"Oh wait, I'm dreaming. I wonder if I can do magic too," and with that she quickly picked up a pebble waved her hand saying the magic words "hocus pocus" and poof. Nothing. Disappointed she sighed.

"Helene please listen," begged Edmund.

Hearing the urgency in his voice Helene gave him her undivided attention, "I'm sorry darling. Please continue."

Realizing he needed to be more direct he spoke slowly, "I'm not a magician Helene. I am so much more than that," at which point her expression grew curious and for the second time that evening sent a wave of nerves through Edmund. "There is light magic and dark magic in the world. Do you believe me?"

A bit unsettled by what would happen next Helene gave a simple nod mouthing the word "yes".

"Do you understand the difference between the two?"

This was a question Helene had never thought of and she struggled for an answer, "Well.....I suppose light magic is fun like the bird trick and dark magic is......scary?"

"That is primarily true," confirmed Edmund noticing Helene had gone from curious to concerned. At which point he tried to calm her nerves by saying, "I only practice light magic my sweet."

Helene closed her eyes repeatedly telling herself, "This is just a dream, this is just a dream."

A nudge on her shoulder made her reopen her eyes. Pegasus had moved close to her with Edmund now seated upon the splendid animal. Looking like he was preparing to fly into the sky Edmund delayed Pegasus's departure and gave Helene a sad smile saying, "Yes Helene, this is a dream. Nevertheless, if you truly wish it to be real it can be."

Pegasus bolted away while Helene shouted after Edmund hollering, "How?"

Flying low overhead Edmund dropped a silk bag telling Helene to follow the instructions within. Helene couldn't open the bag quick enough. Inside was a handwritten note on Edmund's personal stationary.

> My dear sweet Helene,
> How I've longed to reveal myself to you.
> If your heart's desire is to know and accept
> my magical world and make it your own,
> hold your brooch in your hand and call to me.
> With my eternal love, Edmund

No sooner had Ally finished reading the note over Helene's shoulder did she find herself back in Helene's room. Helene stirred then shot up in bed. In a panicked haste, she rushed to her dresser picked up the brooch and called to Edmund. Worrying as to why it wasn't working she talked to herself under her breath, "What did the note say? My heart's?" she repeated time and time again. "Oh, come on Helene think. My heart's desire!" she finally squealed. This time she closed her eyes, took a deep slow breath, then affectionately called with her whole heart, "Edmund my darling. I call you to come to me."

A dim glow outside her bedroom window drew her over. When she opened the window, there stood Edmund in midair while the tree branches behind him swayed in the evening breeze. The shock was too much for Helene and she swooned, but before hitting the floor Edmund had her safely in his arms. Tucking her into her bed he was bold enough to kiss her lips fearing it would be the last time. Whether in a dream or reality.

Exiting through the window Edmund left Helene peacefully asleep in her bed, but before he disappeared into the night's sky he turned to where Ally stood and said, "Hurry, go to the manor early tomorrow morning."

Ally did what she was told mainly to see what would happen next. She didn't know what time early was so she tested out a theory and thought of Helene arriving and that's all it took. Riding on what she would soon dub "The Ally Bolt" she showed up just in time to see Helene's arrival. Mr. & Mrs. Beck had sent a servant to chaperone her due to an unexpected visitor at their home. Ally was pretty confident Edmund played a role in that.

Helene was greeted by Arthur who showed her in and then nervously waited for Edmund to join her. While she waited, she studied the collection of fine artwork on the mantle. Carefully she picked up the porcelain figure of a dancing couple making them come to life and dance, by twisting her wrists one way and then the other. She smiled when she caught sight of Edmund's reflection in the large mirror hanging above the mantle. The adoring look in his eyes was something her heart would treasure forever.

"I never realized what splendid dancers they were," he joked.

Blushing, Helene placed the figurine down and said, "Perhaps they were simply showing off on my account."

Edmund didn't know how much of last night's events Helene could recall so he proceeded with caution. "I was a little surprised this morning to be notified you were visiting."

"Do you mind?"

"Of course not Miss Beck. It's always my pleasure to spend time with you."

Helene's restless behavior and repeated glances at her chaperone made it clear she wished Edmund and she could speak in private. Knowing full well that her current chaperone disliked horses due to a severe kick he received as a young boy Edmund suggested they walk down to the stables. Pulling Storm from his stall encouraged the chaperone to stand at a distance where he could see Helene but not hear their conversation.

Speaking softly Edmund questioned, "Is there something in particular on your mind?"

Unknowingly to Helene, Edmund was more nervous than she was about what needed to be discussed, but her apprehension didn't stop her from asking. She needed to know if anything from the night before was real. "I had a dream about you last night Mr. Dalton," she paused before facing her fear head on, "But you already knew that. Didn't you?"

At this precise moment Edmund wasn't sure he appreciated Helene's boldness. Understanding that he needed to be honest with her, especially if they were to marry, was of little consolation. The fear of losing her forever argued against being completely honest causing him to consider hiding the truth from her. In the end, the desire to have Helene love the true him outweighed all the foreboding arguments. There was however, some concessions he was willing to make. Convincing himself that being a warlock was more than enough for Helene to handle. He saw no reason to go into depth about his parents and the spell of immortality they cast upon him.

"Yes Helene, I knew that."

There was something in the way he said her name that rang a bell. It was the same tone he used in her dreams. One of love and familiarity something he had never done in person. It was the tone alone that proved more than his affirmative answer that the events from the night before truly took place. That did it. The flood gates were opened, "You were levitating outside my bedroom window last night?" she inquired causing Edmund's eyes to flash with excitement. She stopped questioning and stated, "I summoned you through the brooch you gave me. I wasn't dreaming. It all happened. Somehow you performed actual magic." There was more she wanted to know, "Did you really fly off on Pegasus? How do you, what are....." rambled Helene.

Edmund froze the people at the manor giving him and Helene the chance to take their time with this delicate conversation. There was no going back now. He figured showing her who he was and what he could do would be easier than trying to explain it. "Would you come sit with me Helene?"

"Where?"

"There's a bench just outside the stables in the shade of a tree," Edmund said slowly. He could tell Helene's mind was racing and although she was doing her best to hide her growing fear. It was beginning to reveal itself.

Walking past her chaperone she noticed he was as still as a statue, "What did you do?" Helene's voice now trembling.

Edmund tried his best to reassure her, "He's unharmed Helene. I merely froze him in time so we can talk without concern of being heard."

Thankfully they had reached the bench for Helene's legs were shaky. Landing hard on the bench she looked at the man she so intensely loved wondering if her first impression of him was right. Was this the terrible secret she had once told herself he must have? Helene struggled with the conflicted thoughts in her head leaving her numb and silent.

Afraid Helene's mounting fear would pull her from his reach he blurted, "Helene I'm a warlock. A warlock of the light, the good and honorable side of magic. There's no need to fear."

"Warlock?" she repeated with glazed over eyes.

"You said it yourself. It would be delightfully wonderful if magic were real. It is real Helene. Let me show you," and with that Pegasus rushed from the stables and rearing in excitement greeted Helene.

Face to face with an imaginary being even one she loved and dreamt about as a child was both thrilling and unbelievable. Helene couldn't resist and cautiously approached Pegasus who sensed her anxiety becoming quiet and still. Slowly she lifted her hand to his cheek and a soft rumbling nicker made it clear he was thrilled to see her too. Touching the powerful animal sent a chill throughout Helene's body. Tears of joy came to her eyes as she lightly grazed his wings with her fingertips. Utter amazement filled Helene, "He's really here!"

"Yes, Helene. He's here just for you," smiled Edmund, his heart leaping for joy at her excitement. Little did he know the relief he was feeling about Helene's acceptance of him being a warlock was minutes away from being crushed.

In disbelief, Helene continuously petted and spoke to the magnificent animal. She came very close to asking Edmund if she could ride him. The sight of the frozen chaperone brought her fear raging back. "A warlock? You can bring Pegasus here; you can levitate and freeze people. What else can you do?" Helene said backing away.

"What do you wish?"

Edmund may have meant his reply as an offer to grant Helene another wish, but she wasn't interested in having another childhood fantasy come to life. She was a woman in love with a man. A man she just discovered was no ordinary man, but a warlock. Something she couldn't even begin to understand. There was one thing she needed to know above all else. "Did you use magic to coerce me into loving you?" her voice rang with terror. No matter how afraid she was of his answer, she needed to hear it.

"No Helene," Edmund pledged, "I would not and more importantly could not do that. Human emotions are untouchable by magic."

"How do I know you're telling me the truth? Based on what I've already seen there doesn't seem to be limits to what you can do."

Edmund stepped closer his eyes pleading for Helene to trust him, "I promise my sweet Helene, the love we have for each other is pure and natural."

"Look what you did to my chaperone! You want me to believe you've never cast a spell on me?" Helene's emotions now ruled her heart and tears streamed down her face crushing Edmund's hope.

Afraid his biggest fear was coming true and he was about to lose the only woman he truly loved Edmund stood helpless and watched Helene's tormented sobs continue. Heartache swallowed them both and he longed to wrap her in his arms and hold her one last time. Realizing he couldn't convince her of the truth gave him an idea, "Helene please take this," he said offering his handkerchief to her. She accepted his offer and wiped her face. Edmund waited for her to catch her breath before speaking, "How do you feel?"

Annoyed at his question Helene snapped, "I feel betrayed, angry, scared and a fool."

"I understand why you would feel that way. Now do me a favor and consider my next question carefully before answering. If it were possible for me to control how you feel wouldn't this very moment be the perfect time for me to do so? Wouldn't it make complete sense for me to cast a spell and make you accept my secret without question?"

527

Much to Helene's dismay her logical brain kicked in and she found it hard to dismiss Edmunds point. Minutes passed while she tried to pick a point to argue and finally she came up with one no matter how weak it was. "Perhaps you're simply choosing not to control my emotions so you can convince me you can't."

Edmunds eyes flashed with pain, "If you think that little of me Miss Beck then I have failed to be the gentleman I hoped I had become. A man of honor, valor and integrity. A man whose word is his bond and most importantly a man in whom a woman like you could love."

At that moment Helene no longer saw a warlock in front of her. The only thing she could see was the man she loved more than life itself. She wasn't completely sure what Edmund being a warlock meant for their life together, but she was determined to find a way to make it work. Rushing into his arms she declared her love, "Oh Edmund forgive me. I love you so much my darling. We will work this out somehow. I trust our love can conquer anything. Even you being a warlock," Helene smiled up at him then looked back at Pegasus, "Who knows, having magic in my life may have some pretty interesting perks."

"Yes my love we have a lifetime to figure all this out. Besides I don't have to perform magic if it makes you uncomfortable. Being a warlock isn't all that I am. It's merely a part of me."

Deep in thought they both considered what effect Edmunds admission would have on their relationship. Neither of them were quite sure what would come next. Even if they weren't ready to admit to each other how nervous it made them, they each promised themselves they wouldn't give up. The one thing they trusted in was the love they shared. A love unlike anything they'd experienced before. A love they would both fight for, no matter the challenges or how difficult the obstacle in front of them may be.

Chapter Eight

Surprised by the tears in her eyes Ally decided to return to the lodge where she found Rose waiting for her with hot tea and her favorite sandwich. Wiping the tears from her face Ally smiled and said, "No matter how much I try. I can't seem to stop rooting for Edmund and Helene. Whenever I'm near them it's as if I can physically feel how much they love each other. They're like that one rare famous couple you really hope make it, even though the odds are stacked against them."

"They are a one-of-a-kind couple," agreed Rose.

Not realizing how hungry she was Ally didn't speak again until she had almost finished her meal. Stopping the shaky and dizzy feeling her hunger had brought on was more important than getting to the questions she wanted answers to. "So Helene just accepted Edmund being a warlock?"

With a rather simplistic answer Rose replied, "Yes she did."

"That's a little anticlimactic don't you think? I mean coming face to face with an actual magic conjuring warlock or witch, during my time would have bothered me. Way back then wasn't it a death sentence? It's hard to believe it didn't cause more problems or questions."

"We could analyze or debate this for eternity Ally, but I'd prefer if you simply take my word for it, but I will share a few more details with you. Then we'll simply agree to accept it the way Helene did," proposed Rose.

Ally read between the lines knowing this would be the first and last time this topic was to be discussed. Faced with this knowledge brought a single question to the forefront. Ally waited to see if it would be answered in Rose's list of details.

"Helene and Edmund came to an agreement. Magic would be used for fun things like Pegasus rides, creating full-blown winter storms allowing them to play in the snow on a hot summer day and traveling to far off lands in an instant. She didn't want to strip away any piece of him. Helene believed magic was an important part of Edmund and helped to make him the man she loved. Edmund fully understood she would have frowned on him using magic for selfish reasons or to gain an advantage in business. Which he himself would never think of doing or..."

Cutting in Ally said, "She doesn't know about his plans to get revenge on the angry mob."

"No Ally she does not. She also doesn't know Edmund's parents were murdered by the angry mob or that they gave him immortality." The expression on Rose's face clearly showed this topic of conversation was done and to drive the message home she stated, "They came to a mutual agreement about magic and neither of them ever looked back."

Agitated that the one question she wanted an answer to couldn't be asked Ally huffed louder than she meant to. The sideway glance from Rose solidified the end of this particular topic. Ally made the wise choice to heed the warning. Noticing the clock on the mantle Ally then decided to venture off for one last practice run.

Clearing the table Ally casually announced, "I'm going to take one last trip today. I shouldn't be long. Thank you for lunch Rose."

"Of course Ally. Good for you," encouraged Rose. Selecting a random day after Edmund and Helene were married to make sure she'd find what she was looking for Ally focused on Storm and Helene. Sure enough, she found Helene preparing for her morning ride. Storm appeared to be captivated with the same adoring love for Helene as Edmund was and even though Ally had seen them both lose control in one form or another Storm not unlike Edmund was gentle, attentively protective and loving when it came to Helene.

Following them around the grounds of the manor proved to Ally more than ever that Helene was an excellent rider. Storm loved to be ridden by Helene magnifying the beautiful dance-like journey they enjoyed in the cool morning breeze. Storm responded to the slightest movement of the reins by Helene and carried himself in a more dignified way. Something he did exclusively when Helene rode him. There was a distinctly uncommon bond between the two. That alone begged the question; How was it possible for Storm to someday cause her death?

Hours passed while Ally observed Helene relishing the simple pleasure of riding. Ally soon found herself laughing along every time Helene burst into her musical laughter. There was a uniqueness about Helene that pulled you in. Ally was saddened when she remembered she would never be able to meet this remarkable woman. Whether Ally liked how Edmund handled her death or what he's done to keep Helene with him was fading into the background. Ally found herself understanding why he did what he did and appreciating his ability to do so.

"They are quite the pair," said Arthur in a hushed voice.

His best effort failed and Ally jumped in fear, "Oh Arthur you startled me."

"My apologies miss," he said before his face transformed into Artie, "Oh yes I remember the stairway conversation. You scare easily," and then Arthur was back.

"You know that still creeps me out," exclaimed Ally leaning away from him. She would have been mad, but Arthur's normally serious expression was now one of playfulness. The years between Artie and Arthur vanished as his friendly smile proved to be ageless. "What are you doing here? Is something wrong?" she asked.

"No Ally, everything is fine. Rose was merely wondering what was taking you so long and I volunteered to come get you. Besides, I wanted to make sure you understood your error in judgement this morning and to let you know I understand and forgive your mistake."

Ally didn't want to offend Arthur by confronting his use of the word "forgive" and her gut feeling convinced her to hold her tongue. To her dismay she had already opened her mouth to speak giving her away.

"Go ahead say what you were going to say," urged Arthur.

He didn't have to ask twice. Ally had been chomping at the bit all day with questions she couldn't ask, "Is it because you're Edmund's right-hand man that I can only call you in an emergency?"

"That is part of it."

After a lengthy pause Ally remarked, "And that's all you're going to tell me."

To her amazement Arthur didn't reply with a yes and although his professional manner had returned with a vengeance he asked, "What is it you would like to know?"

Caught completely off guard by his reply Ally stuttered and said the first thing that came into her head, "The.....the tree is your safe haven?" It was one of the least important questions she had running around in her mind and she was mad at herself for letting it escape her lips.

"It's so much more than my safe haven Ally," he said offering her his hand. The same shuddering movement and kaleidoscope of colors danced around them while they traveled to another place and time. Ally found it remarkable how each person's travel was unlike another. Rose was right again, she had grown accustomed to time travel. When they arrived, Ally felt no queasiness or ill effects.

Under the shade of the mighty oak Ally scanned her surroundings something that was becoming second nature. They were at the manor and by the size of the tree Ally surmised they had returned to the present. A quick look into the garden confirmed her suspicions. Her plant had more than tripled in size and was completely covered in petite little flowers.

"This ancestral tree has been protecting and watching over the Dalton family for centuries. I am the latest to have been given the honor of being a guardian over a family member," replied Arthur with an absolute sense of reverence for his position.

"Guardian? I thought you were human like me and Edmund selected you after...."

"Allow me," Arthur said once again extending his hand.

Ally took his hand and watched him place his other hand on the massive tree trunk. Before she could pull her hand away or say a word she felt energy pulsing through her, making her feel extremely powerful and quite invincible. Feeling like she could take on the world and win she boldly asked, "What is in that tree?"

Breaking the connection with the tree Arthur put both his hands behind his back. "The sentinel tree holds all the magic of the Dalton family. From the first generation through today."

"So without this tree Mr. Dalton would be powerless?"

"No, Mr. Dalton's power is within him. When a Dalton dies, their magic joins the tree for safe keeping. It helps to protect the next generation from dark magic."

"But Mr. Dalton can't die," Ally blurted repeating her earlier question, "Are you human?"

"Yes Ally I was born human and I became part of the Dalton family when I was a little older than you are now."

Figuring she had solved at least part of the mystery Ally stated rather arrogantly, "So, after Mr. Dalton gave you a new life you worked your way up to his guardian."

"It was not Mr. Dalton who gave me my new life it was his wonderful parents who offered this opportunity to me," clarified Arthur. His voice quivering at the mention of them. "Mr. Dalton's parents granted me the position of guardian in part for the years I spent with their family. My loyalty was sealed when I faced down the angry mob that horrible night. They knew they would never find another so dedicated to their son's safety."

Speechless Ally stood in front of Arthur and the magical tree. It was becoming abundantly clear that the Legend of Dalton Manor was so much more involved then she could have dreamed of. Ally remembered Edmund being concerned about telling Arthur what he truly was and now come to find out Arthur had known the entire time. "There's so many secrets here. Secrets upon secrets," was all she could say.

It was clear to Arthur that Ally was overwhelmed and needed some time to reflect on the day's events. Especially in regards to his latest disclosure. "Ally you should head back to the lodge and get some rest. You've had an insightful day," said Arthur.

Nodding in agreement Ally closed her eyes, breathed in a deep chest lifting breath and before

537

completely exhaling she was back at the lodge. Rose and Sallie were already having dinner and were surprised when Ally opted for bed instead of a meal.

"Looks like Ally's rough day got rougher," commented Sallie.

Pausing briefly before answering, Rose agreed and reminded Sallie how finding out the truth about Arthur took everyone by surprise. Including Edmund. Up until bedtime they relived and shared memories of their first year with Mr. Dalton and how it was quite an adjustment. So much time had passed since then that their memories felt more like dreams and who they once were scarcely existed.

At last the lodge was silent. Sleep had welcomed each of them that evening and in its midst they found the rest they longed for.

Arthur knew Edmund was waiting for him in his office and proceeded on his way shortly after Ally had left for the lodge. The door was ajar, but Arthur still asked to come in. "Good evening sir. May I enter?"

"Hello my good man. You may enter," Edmund responded then added, "Please, close the door."

"Has the mistress retired for the night? I didn't see her in the parlor."

With a chuckle Edmund answered, "Not quite yet. Dorothy is helping her wash her beautiful long hair."

"They seem to be getting on much better these days."

"Indeed they are. I know Helene was missing Elizabeth terribly and I'm hopeful Dorothy will ease some of Helene's pain."

Arthur took a seat and waited patiently for Edmund to finish what he'd been working on when he came in. A few corrections on a letter he drafted and a couple signatures on some other paperwork finished his business for the day. Before leaning back in his chair Edmund put everything inside folders then added them to the proper pile making sure they were nice and neat. "How did it go with Ally?"

"She was overwhelmed by the news of course, but most new family members are."

"Point taken," Edmund remarked, but it was clear more was on his mind.

"Is there something troubling you sir?"

"You have always been up front with me Arthur, well after you shared you're my guardian that is," said Edmund with a smirk, even though the lingering pain of his parent's death and how Arthur became his guardian was still evident. Edmund knew Arthur had no control over what happened that night and he was thankful his parents made sure he wouldn't be alone, but not knowing for so many years who Arthur truly was had left a scar.

Recognizing that Edmund's pain was rooted in the loss of his parents more than anything else Arthur was patient and understanding. "Yes sir I have been."

"My apologies Arthur. You were simply following orders."

"Of course sir no need to apologize."

Pushing aside painful memories Edmund returned to what he wanted to ask, "Arthur I would like your honest opinion about Ally's participation in helping me."

"Could you be more specific sir?"

"I don't believe it's a coincidence that Helene's nightmares have lessened at the same time Ally seems to have accepted her fate. Her resistance to surrender almost ended this transition. I selected Ally because she has a talent that could be invaluable to us all, yet at the same time she almost single handedly sent Helene prematurely into the locket."

Taking a moment to consider his answer Arthur finally voiced the requested opinion, "I agree Ally has a unique gift. She can and does see things in a way most can't or don't. That could prove to be helpful in many ways. Add the various similarities she shares with Sallie and we have a wonderful asset. Your concern over her stubbornness to surrender is valid; However, I do believe she's come to terms with her situation."

"You don't think I have to worry about her?"

"No sir. Why do you ask?"

"The other night I had a nightmare. Helene's host body gave out and it caused me to regret not sending Ally to the wasteland. After that night, I've struggled with not listening to my instincts causing me to second guess my decision."

"That's a horrible dream sir. I'm sorry you experienced that," replied Arthur with sincerity in his eyes. Arthur gave Edmund a moment before continuing, "Mr. Dalton if there were any concern over Ally's, so be it late and reluctant surrender, I would be the first to inform you. Today I witnessed her watching Helene riding Storm and laughing along with her. I also heard from Rose that when Ally returned from exploring a particular place and time this morning she had tears in her eyes. She witnessed the moment you shared your magical identity with Helene. It moved her to tears sir."

"Interesting," said a relieved Edmund. "I hope they were happy tears."

"Yes sir. Both Rose and I believe they were. Furthermore, I also believe Ally has grown to appreciate the woman Helene is. Like all of us she's been captivated by your wife and wants nothing but the best for her."

Feeling like a huge weight had been lifted from his shoulders Edmund thanked Arthur for his input and excused him for the night. That evening a restful night's sleep was had by all at the manor.

Chapter Nine

The day had arrived for Ally's dress fitting and just as Sallie had told her she found herself excited at seeing her creation. Casual conversation helped the time pass quickly and before long they arrived at the dress shop. Sallie couldn't help but smile when Ally presented her receipt and happily asked to try on her dress.

To add to the anticipation the clerk didn't bring the dress out for Ally to examine. Instead she invited Ally into the dressing area saying she would bring the dress to her there. Time slowed while Ally waited and she began fidgeting on the floral-patterned stool in her dressing room. Gently spinning back and forth in expectancy she heard Margret Bennett's growly voice from one of the other tiny rooms. Expecting to hear Margret fuss about a dress or something along those lines meant Ally was even more surprised by the conversation she overheard.

"They're already married," faintly said another female's voice.

Margret was doing her best to speak softly but her obvious anger overrode her attempts and Ally could hear her plain as day, "Grant it that does complicate things, but I will get what I want. I always do," proclaimed Margret her voice dripping of venom.

Whomever Margret was speaking to, gave one last plea, "I'm concerned about you Margret. I've never seen you so enraged. I'm afraid of what you may do. Please don't do anything you may live to regret."

"Don't waste your concern or fear on me. I'm not the one you should be fearful for," Margret stated in such a haughty tone it sent chills down Ally's spine.

Just then the clerk knocked on Ally's dressing room door startling her. The clerk had returned with Ally's dress naturally ending Margret's conversation and while Ally tried on her dress she heard Margret leave. When Ally exited into the main dressing area and stood in front of the angled mirrors she was astonished by how perfectly the dress fit. The off-the-shoulder neckline with its swag of pink lace hung across the front, draped across both arms and ended in a bow between her shoulder blades showcasing Ally's muscled arms and shoulders. The vertically striped pattern along with the A-line cut made Ally appear taller than she was. Sallie had been right. Creating her own dress did fill her with a renewed energy. Perhaps it was the feeling of having control over something or simply that the dress was exactly what she hoped it would be. Either way Ally felt at home and happier than she'd been in a very long time.

The clerk broke Ally's train of thought when she asked, "Would you like any alterations miss?"

Turning this way and that the only adjustment she could think of was to add some lace around the waist to mirror the neckline and to accentuate her curves. Pleased with her appearance Ally sashayed out into the main store to show off her design to Sallie. The expression she gave Ally solidified how wonderful she looked in her new gown. After spending several minutes approving time and time again how incredible Ally looked it was time to change and head back to the manor. The simple alteration would take about a week making Ally very happy and with that they returned home.

It wasn't until after she shared her shopping experience with Rose while having lunch in Helene's gazebo did Ally remember Margret Bennett's conversation. Instead of going back to the manor with Rose, Ally decided to follow up on the morning's events. Daily travels to and from different places in time were now a normal activity for her. She didn't have to give a reason or destination any more. Ally was trusted to continue mastering her talents on her own. Part of her knew this would eventually lead to her first assignment from Mr. Dalton, but for now it was just fun learning as much as she could. Ally now felt exhilarated when she discovered something new. She especially liked when she uncovered something no one else had caught.

Hovering near a wall of fabrics Ally waited for Margret to make her appearance. It didn't take long before the pretentious Miss Bennett swaggered in tossing her coat and hat on her young servant. While she struggled to unbury herself from the coat and hold onto the hat without either of them touching the floor Margret scolded, "Do be careful you klutz."

The more Ally saw of Margret Bennett the more she wished she could tell Sallie, her warrior friend, "Sic 'em!" She may not have been an actual element of evil, but she sure acted like one. There was such a strong darkness about Margret that it was an embarrassment to say she was human. As Margret approached the counter Ally witnessed the clerks do their best to scatter and find something else to do trying not to appear like they were fleeing from her very presence. This made Ally giggle and shake her head when Margret interpreted their actions the way she wanted. Clearly she felt those scurrying about were inadequate in helping her, when the truth was not one of them wanted to help her.

After the unlucky clerk was pounced upon Margret began her list of demands and showed herself into the dressing area. Ally wasn't sure if she should wait where she was for Margret's friend to arrive or follow Margret into the other room. She chose the latter.

It didn't take long for the few women who were in other dressing rooms to exit after hearing Margret's voice. Clearing a room seemed to be a natural and expected result when Margret made an appearance. The strange fact was everyone understood why people scattered. Everyone that is, except for Margret who chalked it up to others feeling inferior to her and finding it impossible to compete with her. In Margret's twisted mind she believed they left for no other reason than their overpowering wonderment of her beauty, wealth and charm, which was non-existent.

Time passed and no one came into the dressing area including the clerk. Ally made a quick trip into the main store to find the clerk running around the store like a crazy person trying to fulfill Margret's demands. It took Ally less than a minute to do this and when she returned she could hear Margret speaking with someone. This didn't make any sense no one had gone through the dressing area entrance. Ally searched for another door, but there wasn't one to be found. There was but one way in and out of the dressing area. Who could Margret be talking to?

Curiosity lured Ally into Margret's dressing room where she soon couldn't believe her eyes. Unlike the dressing room Ally had used this one held a free standing full-length mirror. The large mahogany mirror had a

Heater Shield shape except the very top was a gentle arch that curved down and across to meet the sides rather than the top's typical sharp point. It was unlike any mirror Ally had ever seen. With it's simple yet elegant style it was certainly the most unique mirror in existence. Ally would soon discover why she felt that way. The inlaid mirror was glistening like the sunrise on a calm ocean.

"Mother please I didn't come here to be lectured," remarked Margret.

Caught off-guard that Margret had used the word please was nothing compared to what happened next. Ally watched the mirror's shimmer start to fog over and through the misty white cloud that maneuvered about on the glass a figure appeared. An elegantly beautiful woman with dirty blonde hair and a long slender neck boasting a pearl choker filled the mirror. She was stunning. Her red lips contrasted her pale complexion and the sweetheart neckline of her dress showcased even more of her flawless skin. Her hair was pulled into a tall updo adding several inches to the woman's height with only a few loose curled strands framing her model worthy face. The look was completed with a feathered hairpiece which matched the red of her lips and gown.

The woman who didn't look old enough to be Margret's mother spoke clearly, "Look at me Margret," the woman's light brown eyes pleading for Margret to listen.

In typical spoiled behavior Margret tilted her face toward the mirror with a bothered expression and said, "What is it Mother?"

"I know it's been hard for you my dear losing me at such an early age. However, that's not an excuse or reason for you to be reckless with your life."

"I'm not being reckless," argued Margret.

"They're already married," replied her mother bringing Ally back to the moment she first heard Margret's conversation. Ally had been so involved in trying to understand who and how a woman was in a mirror she hadn't noticed herself come into the dressing room or had she? The next thing she knew she was back at the lodge feeling like she had been thrown there.

"Whoa!" Ally blurted trying to remain on her feet.

Rose looked up at her with a knowing smile and said, "Ran into your present self, did you?"

Steadying herself by placing a hand on the wall Ally asked, "Is that what happened?"

Half giggling her answer Rose explained, "It's far too early for you to visit so close to the current date and time."

"A little warning on that would have been nice."

Sallie was coming down the stairs in time to hear their conversation. Adding her two cents on the topic,

"Now what fun would that be Ally? We all experienced it and laugh about it now."

Rose added, "It is sort of a rite of passage or as some would say an initiation. There's no risk of harm and it has been quite amusing to see the wide range of expressions and reactions over the years."

Ally was less than amused and had more important things to discuss so she quickly changed the subject. Without so much as a segue from one conversation to the next Ally dived right in, "Is Margret's mother alive?"

"Margret Bennett?" asked Rose.

"Yes, do you know another?" snipped Ally.

Rose's disapproving glance reminded Ally to mind her manners and Rose returned with her own attitude, "Actually I do Ally. There are numerous Margret's in my life."

Sallie played peacemaker, "Ally you have to remember Rose has been around for centuries and knows thousands of people. You would be hard pressed to give her a person's name she hasn't come across."

Solidly put back in her place Ally apologized then rephrased her question, "Is Miss Bennett's mother alive?"

After sipping her tea Rose answered, "No. Mrs. Bennett died when Margret was a very young girl. I'm not sure how much if anything she would remember about her. Why do you ask?"

By this time Sallie had taken a seat next to Rose and appeared just as interested in knowing why Ally was asking such an unusual question. Ally walked over to the adjacent chair and sat down. She began to explain how she overheard Margret earlier that morning speaking with someone in another dressing room. Neither Rose or Sallie seemed surprised or concerned when Ally mentioned Margret was being rude. Furthermore, they were puzzled why Ally felt the need to go back and listen to Margret throw yet another tantrum.

"Margret was simply being Margret," commented Sallie.

Ally didn't want to waste time going into the details of what Margret had said, at least not yet, her main objective was to find out more about this magical mirror. Was it possible for Margret's mom to materialize in it? Picking up from the moment she heard Margret talking in her dressing room Ally explained, "I didn't understand how anyone could have gotten passed me and yet someone must have because Margret was already involved in conversation.....That's when I joined her in her dressing room................" Ally's pause this time was too long.

Rose coaxed her on, "And?"

"And there was this mirror in the dressing room,"

Sallie interrupted, "How strange. They don't usually have mirrors in the private changing rooms."

"Oh having a mirror in the room is just the beginning," Ally replied. "The mirror is no ordinary mirror. It's magical."

Simultaneously Rose and Sallie asked, "Magical?"

"Yes. The mirror first shimmered like the sun on the ocean. Then it fogged over and ever so slowly a woman appeared in it," said Ally.

Rose and Sallie looked at each other clearly having a silent conversation before Rose suggested Ally go slower in her description. It was imperative that Ally explain in great detail what happened next, including what was said. Her first request though was for Ally to give them as many details about the woman's appearance as possible.

Stopping Ally when she finished her account of the woman Rose agreed, "That sounds like Mrs. Bennett."

"So it was Margret's mother?" Ally asked.

"It appears so. My guess is Margret referred to her as such? affirmed Rose.

"Yes, but she wasn't very nice to her mom."

Sallie shook her head in disgust, "From what I've been told about Mrs. Bennett she was a wonderfully kind woman. I would have given anything to have a loving and kindhearted mom."

Rose stopped Sallie from traveling any further down memory lane, "That's correct. Mrs. Bennett was the black sheep of the family. Of course, she wasn't born a Bennet. She married into their bloodline so that explains why she never truly fit in."

"How did she die?" wondered Ally.

Rose gave a short and direct answer, "She died of tuberculosis," then pressed Ally for more details.

When Ally finished sharing all she remembered she questioned Rose, "If Margret's mother is dead. How was she in the mirror talking to Margret like she was alive and well?"

"She's a ghost Ally," stated Rose undoubtedly too busy with her own thoughts to break it gently to Ally.

"Ghosts," moaned Ally, "Of course there's ghosts here. Why wouldn't there be?"

Allowing Rose to concentrate on what she needed to consider Sallie did her best to make sure Ally didn't grow concerned, "Ghosts can't hurt you Ally."

"I wasn't worried about that. Ghosts seem like child's play considering the creatures of the dark I've seen. I'm more curious as to why the ghost of Margret's mother would use a mirror to contact her. Why not just show up?"

"I like this new confident Ally," cheered Sallie.

"Thanks. So why the mirror?"

Sallie explained as simply as she could, "They need a portal to contact humans. It crosses the divide between the supernatural world into the human world."

"So Margret isn't magical?"

"Oh my goodness no," shuddered Sallie.

Ally's question brought Rose back into the conversation, "Could you imagine the destruction Margret would cause if she had powers? There's no doubt she would fight for the dark side of magic."

Jumping from the couch while instantaneously turning into her warrior persona. Sallie took aim with her bow and arrow. Her eyes were deadly focused and vied for the opportunity, "I would gladly remove Margret from this world if it were within my rights." The thrill of the hunt coruscating in her Pu-erh tea colored eyes.

Rose and Ally giggled at the sight, but Sallie remained staunchly focused on her day dream. Pretending to send the arrow off complete with a whooshing sound added the perfect effect before announcing, "And poof she's gone!" That sent Rose and Ally into such a laughing spell that soon both their stomachs hurt. Sallie broke her focus on the imaginary Margret and soon joined in the laugh fest.

Chapter Ten

With only a few hours' sleep Ally headed downstairs to find Sallie almost finished with her breakfast. Rose was nowhere to be found and the full kitchen staff had returned. They were quick to prepare a plate full of eggs, ham, bacon, toast and fresh fruit for Ally. It was quite the feast and she graciously thanked them, in part because she knew the busy day she had planned would expel tons of energy, and partly because she didn't have to help Rose and Sallie prepare or clean up another meal.

"It's busy around here," Ally said while spreading preserves on her toast.

Sallie agreed, "Yes, it is."

Low on patience from her lack of sleep Ally laid out her lists of questions, "Where's Rose this morning and why is the full staff back? Should I be worried about something? Have I made another error in my travels? Is....."

"Whoa, hold on there. One question at a time," said Sallie cutting in. "Rose had business to attend to. The staff is back to take care of things around here so we can get back to doing our jobs more fully. No, there's nothing to worry about and no you haven't done anything wrong."

"Am I done with my training?"

Sallie made a bit of a scoffing sound before answering, "Oh no Ally there's so much more for you to learn."

"Then how can I do my job if I haven't completed my training?"

"It has more to do with Rose and I doing our job. In the meantime, you have some extra time to continue mastering your time travel."

Ally's first instinct was to dig deeper into Sallie's explanation, but something inside made her pause. Giving her time to think about it and realize this could work to her advantage. Trying to be as nonchalant as possible Ally replied, "I have taken up most of your and Rose's time. I suppose more practice would be helpful." Giving in so easily wasn't something Ally did often and she hoped it wouldn't cause Sallie to be suspicious. Whether it did or not wasn't clear from Sallie's expression, but either way it didn't matter. All Ally knew is that she was being left alone for the entire day and that's what she surprisingly hoped for.

Her first stop was the dress shop's changing rooms where Ally hoped to get a better look at the mirror. To her dismay the mirror wasn't there. After confirming it hadn't been moved into another dressing room Ally decided there was only one place or person to follow. Knowing it wouldn't be easy and more than likely it would be infuriating. Ally did what she felt had to be done. She was right, hovering over Margret Bennett all day was exasperating and that was putting it mildly. The woman was so high-maintenance she made the diva starlets from Ally's time seem more like humble and kind maidens. Ally recalled a narcissistic family member and how they managed to turn every situation around, resulting in the issue being all about them. Whether a world event or a family matter.   Inevitably they never failed to ruin everyone's day from birthdays to holidays, but that now seemed like a walk in the park. Margret was absolutely void of empathy and there was no reasoning with her about anything. She proved to be the most exhausting person Ally had ever seen bar none.

For the next few days all three of the girls were so busy with their own projects they had very little time to talk.   They were thankful the staff was cleaning and cooking for them. Allowing them to get earlier and earlier starts on their days and returning later and later each evening. By the fifth day Ally had almost given up hope on relocating the mirror. That's when a new tactic came to mind. Instead of traveling to the days after she first saw the mirror she decided to follow Margret on the weeks leading up to it.

Her idea worked and somehow Ally managed to select the exact day to find what she was hunting for. It was well within the hour of Ally's arrival when Margret started sketching the mirror in a small silver notepad she pulled from inside her boot. A small pencil was held secure in the attached pencil holder on the side of the notepad. The front and back covers were identical with a not quite perfect circle in the center and swirling vines that wound their way from it to the edges. It reminded Ally of the pumpkin in her Cinderella storybook before it became the magic coach.

When Margret completed her sketch she carefully held the rag paper in one hand while she slipped the notepad back into her black boot. From the stretched-out section of her boot, it was evident Margret had been in possession of this notepad for some time. Once the notepad was safely in its hidden location Margret took the piece of paper, held it over her heart with both hands and whispered something unrecognizable before throwing her arms open wide. Releasing the paper into the wind.

The smell of sulfur filled the air and Ally watched as the paper transformed into the very mirror she had been searching for. Ally's heightened senses caught a glimpse of black smoke emanating from the center of the mirror for no more than the blink of an eye. She was sure Margret couldn't see it or any non-magical being for that matter. This mirror was most definitely an element of dark magic. Ally wondered how and why it was in Margret's possession?

Hearing Mrs. Bennett greet her daughter halted Ally's thoughts and immediately brought her focus to their conversation. Unlike the conversation in the dress shop this one went much smoother. The stories Sallie had heard about Mrs. Bennett were correct. She was a very kind and loving mom. This time Margret almost seemed tolerable when she spoke with her mother. A side Ally truly thought didn't exist. Perhaps Margret's more acceptable behavior was in part to her mother's kind compliments about her. That idea was quickly confirmed when Margret's mother stopped complimenting her daughter and told her she had considered Margret's question and her answer was "no."

In a rage Margret picked up the nearest rock from the forest floor and hurled it at the mirror. Splintering glass flew in every direction, but before any of it could fall to the ground the mirror was sucked into a black void roughly three feet in the air. Margret's temper boiled over. Between the screaming, stomping and kicking this so-called adult woman was doing, Ally couldn't help but think any two-year-old would be proud of the tantrum. It didn't take long for Ally to spot a black aura begin to surround Margret followed by shadowy tentacles reaching for her from every crevice. As one after another

559

reached Margret they continued beneath her skin sending up a line of smoke as if a candle had been blown out. The smell of hot tar filled the air and Margret's all-consuming temper grew in intensity. Ally made the mistake of moving closer to get a better look causing a shadowy tentacle to falter before touching Margret. Thankfully Ally was becoming extremely perceptive and her reflexes uncannily sharp. She returned to the lodge before the shadow detected her.

"Are you all right?" asked Rose.

Doing her best to pretend her heart wasn't beating at the speed of light Ally answered Rose, "Sure, I'm fine."

"I think our jewelry would argue that point," disputed Sallie who was dressed for battle.

The puzzled look on Ally's face caused Rose to lift her necklace from her chest and point to Ally's necklace stating, "They're lit up like blazing fires."

Looking down Rose was accurate in her description. Ally's center daisy was shooting waves of light up the chain to the smaller daisies making them come to life. Both Rose and Sallie's necklaces were glowing bright. Caught red handed Ally tried to pacify them without explaining what she was up to, "Wow, we sure are connected aren't we? I just managed to scare myself. You know letting my imagination get away from me. In the back of my mind I still worry about the very real danger lurking about." It wasn't a lie Ally did have that fear and although she wasn't sure the shadow detected her it did scare her. It could have been her imagination making more out of the shadows slight hesitation than was necessary, but it wasn't worth taking a chance.

Her explanation was accepted and within a minute the necklaces were normal and Sallie was out of her battle gear. Being together at home for the first time in nearly a week they decided to spend the remainder of the day together. After eating a delicious dinner, they sat outside on the porch looking up at the stars and listening to the concert of frog's croaking in the nearby stream.

Other than a few minor details here and there not one of them said what they had been up to. Figuring this was the normal process of no more work talk before bed Ally didn't put much thought into the reason for it. Besides, she didn't want to share what she was doing until she thought she had something truly worth sharing. As far as the mirror was concerned Rose and Sallie had already been told about it and Ally really hadn't learned a great deal more.

Cautiously Ally did pursue one line of questioning, "So was everyone's jewelry from the garden electrified like ours was earlier?"

Sallie answered, "No just the three of us."

"You are Sallie's student and I am your closer meaning our connections are the strongest. If you had been in such a dangerous spot that the three of us couldn't handle it, the entire garden would have been electrified, generating enough power to defeat whatever enemy we faced," elaborated Rose.

Spending a moment considering the answer before replying Ally queried, "Basically you're my personal body guards and the garden is the Calvary?"

"That's an accurate and creative way of putting it," chuckled Rose.

A shooting star caught their attention and each of them made a private wish. Unclear when or how the whole "wish upon a shooting star" came to be Ally found it entertaining that they all not only knew about it but made a wish. It was rather ironic with the powers each of them possessed. They didn't have a need for wishes they could make most of their wishes come true themselves.

Ally decided to take advantage of this safe topic and questioned, "Why do we wish upon a shooting star?"

Sallie looked at Rose giving her the floor, "I'll let Rose explain. She's better at history than I am," Sallie went on to tease Rose, "In part because she's lived through so much of it," she said with a wink.

Ally found Sallie's joke funny, something she wouldn't have just months earlier. The locket world felt like home at this point and Ally trusted both Rose and Sallie more than any friend in the real world. Was it possible for Edmund to be controlling her emotions? Sure Ally was born human, but now she had magical powers and Ally wondered if that changed the rules. Was it now possible for him to control how she felt?

"Ally are you listening?"

"Oh, forgive me Rose I was just trying to imagine the answer for myself. Go ahead I'd rather hear the truth."

"Wishing upon a star is a legend dating further back then Dalton's Legend. It dates back to the Greek astronomer Ptolemy sometime between 127-151 AD. He wrote that when the Greek gods were bored or curious they'd peek down on earth sometimes causing a star to shoot across the sky."

"Interesting," Sallie remarked.

"So the Greek gods became shooting stars?" Ally wondered.

Rose explained further, "No, the Greeks believed when the gods peered through the spheres between earth and their world the stars sometimes slipped from the gap, creating a shooting star. Because of their origin it was believed that wishes would come true."

"Huh, I didn't know that. It's kinda a cool story," commented Ally before adding, "Wait, you said it was a legend. The Legend of Dalton Manor is real that means the shooting star legend could be real..........Pegasus is from Greek mythology, right?”

“Yes.”

“Okay, Helene and Edmund ride Pegasus so mythology is real?”

Rose didn't have time to answer Ally's question before she rambled off several more. Patiently waiting for Ally to finish with her “thinking out-loud” chatter Rose and Sallie shared their own internal conversation.

Ally's mind had gone from asking if the Greek gods existed to whether she would run into the tooth fairy in the locket world. For Ally, there wasn't much she couldn't consider real. To her it made sense that every fantasy or magical being was real. Her jibber jabber was progressing into a rant and Rose figured now was the time to stop her.

“Ally, get a hold of yourself,” pleaded Rose. “How do you expect me to answer you when you keep spouting question after question without a breath?”

Clearly Ally also found it a daunting task to remember every question she had asked. A headache brought on by her endless thoughts made her dizzy when she stood up. Sallie who had taken a seat on the porch railing steadied her, “Easy there.”

“It's been a busy few days for all of us let's call it an early night,” suggested Rose.

A wave of nausea swept over Ally as the pounding in her head reached an all-time high. Even the slow almost non-existent nod she gave Rose made her teeter off balance. With Sallie and Rose supporting her from each side they managed to get Ally upstairs and into bed. Giving Rose and Sallie a weak smile before crumbling into bed Ally hoped a good night's sleep would help. At last pure exhaustion overpowered the throbbing ache in her head and a deep sleep pushed the pain aside.

Downstairs Sallie and Rose continued the conversation they had shared secretly on the front porch. Sallie wasted no time picking up where she had left off, "What did Mr. Dalton say?"

"He found the entire mirror revelation intriguing to say the least."

"Has he given you instructions on what to do?"

"He hadn't for days. He wanted to handle it himself. Now he's asked me to keep a lookout for the mirror."

"That's odd. Just a lookout? Why not hunt it down?" Sallie replied.

"I'm not sure. I would have thought he would have eliminated it immediately or had one of us do so."

"He must have a good reason for delaying its destruction," remarked Sallie, "Have you seen the mirror?"

"No, I did take a quick look at the dress shop and the Bennett's mansion but it wasn't at either place," Rose wondered, "Have you noticed anything different or increased activity in the dark magic world?"

"No, it's as bad as it normally is but not worse," Sallie answered, "Maybe we should move Ally's training to a different space in time?"

"I've discussed that with Mr. Dalton; however, the sole reason he selected to bring Ally here before Helene's tragic death was to try and help the host body survive. This has proven to be one of the most difficult transitions."

"I don't understand?"

"Mr. Dalton believed that having Ally's soul closer to her actual body may strengthen it and solidify the switch. Of course, it all depended on Ally's surrender, but he was willing to take the chance."

Sallie contemplated this new information, "A rather risky move I must say."

"Agreed, but he was convinced the switch would fail if he didn't do something drastic and it appears he was correct. Helene is doing well and Ally seems to be at peace with her decision."

"Good point."

Rose went on to say, "Not only did Mr. Dalton's plan for a successful transition work out as he hoped, Ally has uncovered a concern none of us knew existed. A mortal who not only knows about magic, but is using magic. It is a problem for our entire world not to mention putting the lives of each of us in jeopardy. I'm sure the magical mirror came from the dark side."

Sallie concurred, "Another good point. It's unsafe for any human to know about our existence. It puts every one of us in danger. I can't imagine what someone like Margret Bennett could or will do with the knowledge of magic."

Chapter Eleven

Helene knew something had been on Edmund's mind for the last few days. The dark circles forming under his eyes were a dead giveaway. Her concern for him was growing even though he was doing his best to mask his preoccupation with whatever was troubling him. She tried to stay up the previous night in an attempt to catch him wide awake and question him on the reason for his fretting. Unfortunately, she slept soundly and when she awoke Edmund was already up or never actually came to bed.

Joining Edmund at the table for breakfast he greeted her with a kiss laced with concern and that was the final straw. Helene wanted her husband to confide in her. She also wanted or more so needed to try and help him. They were a team, a united front against anything or anyone that came against them. Tenderly she said, "Edmund my darling, would you please share with me what's troubling you?"

He may not have liked that he was unable to keep his concern from Helene and yet it came as no surprise that she knew something was wrong. Their connection had strengthened far beyond words. It was becoming increasingly difficult to surprise each other on special occasions. Causing them to mutually agree not to press each other with questions when they knew the other was up to something. They trusted they would only keep surprises for celebratory times hidden, not secrets.

Edmund found relief in being able to share his distressing concern with Helene, helping his words pour out easily, "I've been notified that there's an element of dark magic nearby. I have spent the last few evenings patrolling and investigating various leads in an effort to locate the evil. It's crucial that I determine whether it has an assignment or is simply loitering about looking for one."

Helene interrupted, "Assignment? Dark magic has assignments? That's more than a little spooky. It's downright unnerving."

Edmund chose his words carefully not wanting to alarm his beloved any more than she already was, "Perhaps assignment was a poor choice of words. Evil has an agenda to search and destroy, meaning dark magic is always looking for someone to use for their purpose. Basically, an effort to spread depravity in the world."

It took a few moments for Helene to respond, "To use someone? Does dark magic cast spells on people?"

Shaking his head Edmund answered, "Not spells necessarily, dark magic doesn't want to be discovered any more than light magic does. Casting a spell on a human could reveal the existence of magic. History has shown even suspecting someone is capable of performing magic has led to countless deaths."

"Very true my darling. Even if a single person believes another to be a warlock or a witch it could cost that person their life. Even without any definitive proof." Helene summed up, then she was hit with a harrowing thought, "Oh my gosh Edmund it could cost you your life!"

The dreadful concern on his wife's face crushed his heart and he wrapped her securely within his arms, "No Helene I'm not in any danger. Fear not my sweet. I am perfectly safe."

Panicked for her husband's safety she babbled endlessly, "I've never told anyone you're a warlock or that you can perform magic. My parents don't know or even Rose and I tell her everything. Maybe someone witnessed us fly away on Pegasus! Oh my gosh, my silly selfish wish put you in harm's way....."

"Shhhh, my sweet," soothed Edmund squeezing Helene tightly against him and placing a lovingly protective kiss on her forehead. "You've done no such thing. Look at me Helene," he lifted her chin until their eyes locked, "Our magical adventures have always started within the safe borders of the manor. No one has seen us. I have taken every precaution to keep us from being discovered. Trust in me my beloved."

"I do Edmund," whimpered Helene.

"That's my girl," Edmund cheered.

Feeling comforted by Edmund's words Helene returned to her first line of questions, "If you don't have anything to fear why go looking for dark magic and its possible assignment? Wouldn't it be safer for you to steer clear of it and not risk making your presence known?"

Navigating this line of questioning put Edmunds truthfulness to the test, "I don't have anything to fear, however dark magic could stir up trouble for the humans in town."

"Like my parents or Rose?"

"It could, but dark magic couldn't touch them directly."

"What does that mean?" squealed Helene.

Methodically he continued, "Dark magic can only coerce a weakened human into doing an evil act. It's highly improbable that one of our loved ones could be used. They are strong goodhearted people, but they could be caught up in the despicable behavior of someone else."

Understanding that family and friends may be in danger Helene asked, "What can I do to help?"

"You're too wonderful for words my sweet," beamed Edmund, "There's nothing I would like more than to work side by side with you on this, but there's nothing you can do to help."

"There must be something," Helene insisted.

"No Helene. I'm sorry there's not," repeated Edmund and yet Helene's saddened face made him think of something, "Perhaps you could have your family and Rose over for dinner and suggest they assist you in planning a party. That would keep them close."

Thrilled with the idea Helene agreed, "That's a terrific idea my darling. I'm sure they would be safer here at the manor than anywhere else...." Helene paused.

"But?"

"Well my father will still have to work and he would naturally leave all party planning to Rose, my mom and I."

"Good point, I will watch over your father."

Satisfied with their arrangement Helene had one remaining question, "What constitutes a weakened human?"

"There's more than a few scenarios, but the most common are humans who naturally tend to be negative, hateful and mean from birth. Then there are the humans who've lost their love and passion for life or have been hurt so terribly that they longer have hope. Any of those can cause their humanity to wane or be completely stripped away. That alone leaves them vulnerable to wickedness."

"That's rather terrifying," Helene said, "Well now that I know what you're up to why don't you head out and see if you can locate the threat?"

A bit taken back by Helene's support Edmund questioned, "Are you sure my beloved?"

"Yes, I'm sure," she answered patting him on the back as if to say "now get" before saying, "I want my husband home in bed with me tonight."

Edmund left shortly after sharing an impassioned kiss with his wife and thanking her for being so very wonderful. Meeting up with Arthur, Edmund informed him on Helene's knowledge of the situation and asked for an update. Although it had only been a few hours after they parted Arthur surprisingly had a juicy tidbit of new information.

"It appears that Margret is not the first Bennett family member to use dark magic," Arthur reported.

"Do tell," prompted Edmund.

Arthur divulged what he had recently discovered, "A distant ancestor of Margret who appears to have been born wicked and appropriately named Jezebel originally came into possession of the magic mirror centuries ago."

"Have you discovered how she came to possess it?"

"No, sir. Dark magic is doing its best to shield as many details of the mirror as it can from the light side."

573

Grumbling at this complication Edmund paced back and forth meditating on this new information. Knowing he had to proceed cautiously in his research and avoid drawing attention to Arthur and himself he made the wise decision to back off for a few days. Going off half-cocked could put all of them in danger. Something he would not risk. There was enough for him to be concerned about. Keeping Helene alive was at the top of his list and adding the dark side's interest in his family would only complicate matters.

Finally, he gave new orders, "Arthur I want you and Rose to keep an eye out for the mirror. If you happen upon it wonderful, but no more active searching for it or its origin."

"Of course sir. I will let Rose know straight away."

There was only one place Edmund felt like going and it wasn't back to Helene at least not yet. There were too many emotions and ideas running through him to be good company for his wife. Besides, his anxious heart wouldn't go unnoticed by her and the last thing he wanted to do was give her more cause for concern.

Storm neighed and pawed at the ground when Edmund appeared. "Hello boy," greeted Edmund. It didn't take long for the two to be galloping off toward the furthest corners of the manor's grounds. Storm kept up the pace while Edmund urged him on and as the trees went by in a blur Edmund's mind slowly cleared. Upon reaching a small glade near a stream the two slowed to a stop. Dismounting the spectacular animal Edmund dropped the reins letting Storm know he was free to drink or graze.

"It sounds like the Bennett family have always been a bloodline of villainous humans," Edmund said to the thirsty horse.

Storm lifted his head from the refreshing water as if to acknowledge Edmund's comment before he went back to sucking down more of the cool liquid. After getting his fill he wandered about grazing on newly sprouted tender plants. His ears turned this way and that while Edmund continued to speak.

"We need to protect Helene from every possible threat Storm. No matter how much I want to know how or why Margret has the magical mirror the most important thing to me is Helene. She is and will forever be my number one priority. That's why I can't risk hunting it down. If dark magic ever found out about Helene and I it could be the end for us," Edmund proclaimed to Storm although he knew he was actually reminding himself not to do something foolish.

An internal battle roared inside his heart. He would never endanger Helene and yet there was a very strong urge to know about Jezebel and how she acquired the mirror. Was it possible that somewhere in her story Edmund would find the cause of his parent's death? Were the Bennett's who were clearly monstrous in their own right made worse by the heinous and diabolical side of dark magic? These were questions he physically ached to have answers to, but never at the risk of his sweet beloved Helene. He always put Helene before himself and even though this particular situation tested his resolve, he would never under any circumstances waver from that decision.

It wasn't until Edmund felt worn from overthinking and analyzing Arthur's update did his heart begin to calm. Now he could return home and spend the evening in the arms of his true love. Storm trotted leisurely back to the stalls where he was given a bucket full of celery, turnips, alfalfa sprouts and beets before being brushed down by a groomer. Edmund said his farewells and sauntered back to the manor.

Smiling at her husband when he walked through the door Helene asked, "Did you take a horse with you on your journey?"

"No," laughed Edmund knowing that was his cue to bathe before dinner. "Storm and I took a ride when I returned. I've neglected him the last few weeks so I thought I better make it up to him."

"Well, I'm sure he appreciated it," Helene said remembering her ride from the previous day.

Edmund proceeded upstairs, but not before blowing Helene a kiss. Catching it in the air with her hand she placed it on her heart and blew him a kiss of her own. She laughed when his typical response of catching it on his cheek made him aware of just how dirty his face had gotten during his ride.

After dinner Edmund and Helene typically relaxed in the parlor where he would sing along while Helene played the piano. On other nights, they'd head out to the porch swing to share hopes and dreams of their future. However tonight would be different. Helene knew her husband was exhausted and it was her turn to dote on him like he had when she wasn't feeling well. Edmund climbed into bed with open arms waiting to snuggle with his wife and let her fall asleep listening to his heartbeat. Instead Helene asked him to remove his shirt and roll over onto his stomach. Edmund was not only too tired to argue with her he was also eager to find out what his loving wife was up to.

Lavender filled the room with its sweetly relaxing scent and the next moment Edmund felt the sensation of warm liquid being dripped on his back. Before it could run down his sides onto the sheets Helene used her hands to massage the oil into Edmund's muscular back. The powerfully solid physique of her husband never went unnoticed by Helene or failed to take her breath away. While Edmund savored the feel of her hands manipulating his sore muscles she soaked in the enticing sight of her man. Edmunds worries and cares faded away. Helene's hands wandered from his broad shoulders over one massive bicep and sinewed forearm until she caressed his hand with firm squeezes. Before moving to his other arm, she pulled the tension from his fingers. By the time she completed the rubdown of his other arm Edmund had regained his strength and to her satisfaction proceeded to return the favor.

The touch of Edmund's hands against her bare skin sent shivers throughout her body. Goose bumps ran the length of her arms and legs giving her away. With a mischievous grin, he bestowed soft amorous kisses along her spine continuing to her neck where he lingered. Helene could no longer lay still. She swiftly rolled to face him and their mouths met sending them into another heated night of passion. When the morning sun rose, they remained tangled among the sheets, both fulfilled and drained.

Content in the afterglow of their evening they slept through breakfast and woke in the late morning. The staff new all too well of the passionate love Edmund and Helene shared, so they left them undisturbed until they were summoned. When hunger drove the blissful couple from their bed the staff was quick to prepare another meal and tend to their every need.

Arthur couldn't help but have an extra twinkle in his eye when he greeted Edmund. "You look remarkably better than yesterday, sir."

"I feel remarkably better than yesterday," remarked Edmund with a whimsical smile.

"What's on today's agenda?"

Edmund considered a few options but surprisingly decided not to set an agenda for the day, "Let's just see how things go today Arthur. I've been so swamped with work not to mention other important details of life that today belongs to chance. Whatever Helene wishes to do I will grant."

Helene entered the room in time to hear Edmund's answer and gave him a hug saying, "How wonderful darling! A day for us to do whatever comes to mind. It's been far too long since we've shared one of these days. Let me think. What sounds like fun?"

Edmund could only imagine what was going through Helene's head. She was creative, smart and adventurous. There was no telling what she would come up with. "Any ideas?" he asked.

"I'm still thinking," answered Helene looking like a child who had just been given three wishes from a genie.

Her expression made Edmund and Arthur chuckle alike.
She was undoubtedly up to something.

Chapter Twelve

On and off throughout the night Ally dreamt of the magical world she now dwelled in. As each dream changed from one warped reality to another she stirred restlessly. The wonderfully tantalizing aroma of bacon cooking dragged her from the current disarray of images before her. Rubbing her tired eyes and trying to remove the fog leftover from her deep sleep Ally squinted in the bright morning sun.

Stumbling downstairs in the all too frilly robe for her liking she found Rose and Sallie eagerly awaiting breakfast. Fully dressed and wide awake they smiled at Ally's appearance and motioned for her to join them. Rose asked, "How's your headache?"

Ally had forgotten about her headache. All she could remember was a night full of puzzling dreams, "It's gone," she said with surprise in her voice.

Sallie teased, "Are you sure? That didn't sound convincing."

"No, it's gone. My head doesn't hurt at all."

"I'm happy to hear that. You do look tired though," commented Rose.

Agreeing with Rose she went on to explain how she had slept sound all night causing her to dream countless dreams. Proceeding to explain one of the dreams Ally soon realized she couldn't, because it neither had a beginning or an end. The dreams all merged from one into another with no rhyme or reason blending locations, people and ideas into a mish mosh of incomprehensible visions. Attempting to give an example of the jumbled mess Ally remembered one vivid yet disorderly sequence, "I was standing inside my home in Glenbrook, but it wasn't my house and yet I knew it was my home. When I stepped outside to leave for school I was suddenly in the magical garden, but the plants were gone. When I looked down I was standing in a muddy puddle which suddenly became a massive swimming pool. I quickly sank to the bottom of the pool and was unable to move. I held my breath as long as I could then began inhaling water before someone pulled me out. When I gasped for air I was standing in my high school math class being mocked by my classmates and friends for being soaking wet."

Shaking her head Sallie replied, "Rose I'll let you sort through all that. I've got to get busy with my day," then turning towards Ally with a smile said, "That headache of yours sure messed with your mind."

"That's probably all it was Ally. I wouldn't put too much emphasis into trying to figure it out," surmised Rose.

Ally felt she was right, but more importantly she wanted to just forget her dreams and get back to her research. She was feeling a renewed energy after breakfast and wasted no time before heading off for the day. It only took a couple hours of monitoring Margret before Ally blamed her for the headache and ensuing dreams she'd experienced. This woman was certifiable as far as Ally was concerned and other than annoying the heck out of Ally nothing had been accomplished.

Turning her focus to the silver notepad within Margret's boot Ally hoped to locate something of consequential value and that's when it happened. Day became night. The clear blue sky was now a dark abyss covered in heavy clouds that permitted only segments of the full moon to shine through. Finding a gap in the clouds the moonlight illuminated the ancient cemetery below Ally. The tall weedy grass and mushroom clusters proved the deceased buried beneath no longer had visitors. Countless tombstones leaned off balance, some had even toppled onto the one next to it. Others were covered in moss and most were chipped or cracked to the point of having various size pieces fall to the ground below what remained of the headstone.

Unsure where she was or how she ended up there, Ally inhaled deeply in preparation to leave. Before she exhaled she noticed an unusual tombstone standing all alone at the far end of the cemetery. The black obelisk headstone was in surprisingly great shape and the area around it seemed to have been tended to. Odd images and carvings covered the four sides of the five-foot pillar. They reminded Ally of the Egyptian hieroglyphics she'd seen in the mummy movies she loved to watch. Before Ally got around to reading the name of the deceased Margret burst onto the scene.

Gaging from Margret's reaction she was just as surprised to be there as Ally was. The old saying "curiosity killed the cat" ran through Ally's mind and she hoped this would be the breakthrough she'd been searching for. In no time her suspicion rang true. Margret pulled the silver notepad from her boot and leaned it against the tombstone. In mere seconds the notepad flew open and the pages flipped one after another followed by the back cover slamming it shut against the tombstone. The sound of the little notepad crashing into the black marble echoed so loudly both Margret and Ally covered their ears.

"What the heck!" thought Ally as she waited for the deafening sound to cease.

When it stopped, there was an extraordinarily beautiful woman standing where the tombstone had been. Ally didn't recognize the woman and yet something about her was vaguely familiar. Margret hit the ground trembling in fear and screaming, "Who are you?"

Ally surprisingly felt fearless, she'd seen enough magic over the last few months that a glamorous woman replacing a tombstone didn't make much of an impact. She actually found herself enjoying the sight of Margret being humbled to tears.

"Rise Margret," ordered the woman with a breathy and rather smoky voice.

For the very first time that Ally could remember Margret did as she was told without a snide comment. Standing with a slight slouch and refusing to make eye contact with the woman didn't help matters. The woman's now raspy voice demanded, "Stand tall Margret and look at me."

"Yes, ma'am."

With a sinister smile the woman commented, "Ah, I see my eyes have been carried through the generations."

Margret examined the woman's eyes closer noticing that they did indeed resemble hers. She was also close to Margret's height and weight. This realization helped to relieve some of Margret's fear and she spoke, "It's wonderful to finally meet you Jezebel."

"The pleasure is ours," she said in a menacing tone. Then without warning Jezebel's gorgeous face became disfigured and deformed as it twisted into a multitude of unnatural contortions. Agonizing minutes passed for Margret as she fought to stay standing and motionless before the parade of horrific faces in front of her. With a nefarious laugh the horde of evil beings melted away leaving Jezebel standing alone with Margret.

Ally had to give Margret credit for remaining still during the spectacle. The events had made Ally nervous, causing her to move further away and ready herself to bolt at any moment. Not knowing who Jezebel was Ally did come to the conclusion that she was an ancestor of Margret's. She deduced that simply by the exchange they shared. How exactly they were related was of little consequence at the moment. Ally was far more interested in why Margret was contacting an obviously possessed and dead family member.

"Very good Margret," complimented Jezebel seemingly impressed that Margret was still standing, "There may be a way for us both to get what we want."

"Oh please help me," urged Margret.

Voices like that of a crowd asked from Jezebel's mouth, "What is in it for us?"

"I'm not sure what I have to offer, but just name it," begged Margret.

In utter amazement Ally felt compassion for Margret. Part of her wanted to shout at her to get away from her ancestor. Struggling with the desire to discover what was happening against rescuing this unsuspecting woman from the evil she was about to bargain with. Ally was shocked to find herself conflicted. Margret was considerably far from being nice, but the creature in front of her was nothing but pure evil. Before Ally could decide what if anything she should do, darkness instructed, "If we remove Helene from Edmund's life our wish is your command," stipulated the throng of evil beings residing in Jezebel.

Having the possibility of Edmund as her own was more than Margret could stand. Jittery with anticipation she agreed, but not before clarifying her own stipulations, "Helene must be removed and I must become his wife."

"As you wish Miss Bennett," agreed the assemblage of darkness living inside Jezebel.

Margret was beside herself with excitement. Completely forgetting she had yet to hear what price she would pay for her desire to be granted. Before discussing the cost of her agreement Margret was given details to follow. In unison, the army of wicked creatures laid out their plan, "When you cry over losing Edmund to Helene capture tears of your broken heart into this vial. Let the ingredients fuse and strengthen for no more than a fortnight in the darkness of the earth. It must be buried into the frost line of the ground."

"I have to wait two weeks? That'll come far too close to their first wedding anniversary. I barely survived their sickening sweet and loving wedding. It made me nauseous. I want her removed before their anniversary," grumbled Margret.

Jezebel's eyes flashed angrily and in her own voice asked, "Do you dare argue with the supreme witches of darkness?"

The rebuke worked and Margret was quick to apologize, "Forgive my behavior. Two weeks is more than acceptable."

Margret's weak and less than heartfelt apology was quickly accepted and Ally was about to discover why. The witches may have been granting Margret her wish by eliminating Helene and allowing her to step in as Edmund's wife, but the exorbitant price she would pay was what the perceived bevy of witches were after.

In its typical fashion evil tempted Margret with the life she would share with Edmund. Going as far as to create visions for Margret to view of their happy life together. From unending wealth and power to a house full of children Margret was beaming with expectancy. The children even ran from the visions into Margret's arms where they laughed and hugged. By the time the children ran off shouting their love back at their mother Margret was ripe for the picking.

In one voice the rabble of witches laid out the cost of their help, "Once married you will give us access into Mr.

Edmund Dalton and at long last the Dalton family will join our side."

"How exactly will I do that?"

"Does it matter?"

Afraid of risking her dreamlife with Edmund it took a mere breath for Margret to reply, "No, of course not. I will pay any price for the life you've shown me."

"We have an accord," announced Jezebel handing the vial to Margret.

The rather plain and simple vial was indistinguishable from any other Margret had seen. The only differing element other than the unusual colored liquid inside, was the silver capped cork which Margret was told could be removed twice. Once when she placed her captured tears into it and finally when the spell would be cast. This information brought to mind a question Margret had failed to ask.

"May I ask how Helene will be eliminated?"

After a considerable time of internal debate Jezebel answered sounding at long last like herself, "Helene typically enjoys a morning ride on her favorite horse. During one of these rides and with the guidance of the supreme dark witches you will be led to a location where she will pass. As she approaches you will throw the vial to the ground shattering the glass and releasing the spell." Jezebel's beautiful smile contrasted with her voice, which was sultry and euphoric at the same time making the evil within her more unnerving.

Margret couldn't help but interject her own wishes, "Helene will disappear into thin air."

That same nefarious laugh burst from Jezebel and her face appeared to be several beings at once, "You have much to learn our pet. Helene will suffer at the mercy of Storm once the spell is released. The dark mist will enter through his nostril's and he will rage over Helene until she meets her disastrous end. Once she has been slayed the power of the spell will be gone and Storm will be released from its grip."

The fearful and appalled expression on Margret's face was not at all what anyone expected to see. Ally herself was unclear what Margret thought would happen to Helene when she agreed to let the dark side remove her from Edmund's life. For a split-second Ally hoped Margret would rethink her agreement, even though Ally knew the witch's description was exactly what would occur days before Edmund and Helene's wedding anniversary.

Jezebel's absolutely breathtaking face returned and in a soft almost pleading tone questioned Margret, "Does that bother you my pet?"

Ally knew Margret's uneasiness had very little to do with Helene's fate and everything to do with risking her future life with Edmund. Her answer would once and for all show just how absolutely selfish she could be. In a robotic and monotone voice Margret replied, "It's fine. I had never really given much thought as to how my wish would be granted, but I want it granted regardless of the cost. It took me by surprise that's all."

"I understand this is all new to you. Trust me Margret once you've tasted just how intoxicating evil can be there will be no turning back," boasted a more than pleased Jezebel.

Margret nodded in agreement and put the vial safely inside her other boot. Jezebel took that as sign to send Margret back and handed her the silver notepad, refusing to release it until Margret looked her in the face. Ally wasn't sure what was going on as the two of them peered into each other's eyes for several minutes without blinking. She did however know it couldn't be good.

Before relinquishing the notepad, Jezebel said, "You have no idea how wonderful it is to finally have someone in the family to pick up where I left off."

"Where you left off?"

"That's a story for another day my pet."

"So I will see you again?"

Jezebel laughed a normal fun laugh at Margret before she confirmed, "Of course you will see me again. We are fettered together from this day on Margret."

"We, as in you and I?"

"Yes, and so much more," leered Jezebel sending an unmistakable message that there was no going back for Margret. She had basically sold her very soul to the side of darkness.

Suddenly Margret and Jezebel simultaneously vanished and Ally wasted no time heading to the lodge, where her first order of business was to take a bath. Her brain told her she couldn't and didn't need to wash evil off of her skin, but feeling like this was something she needed to do overpowered all reasoning. Scrubbing herself until her flesh turned pink Ally clutched her necklace to her. Pulling energy and light magic from the garden until she felt comforted.

When the water cooled to the point of being uncomfortable Ally dressed and went downstairs in hopes Rose or Sallie had returned. The staff was busy doing their jobs, but it was Rose and Sallie that would help Ally the most. Their friendship was like a warm blanket on a cold night. Something Ally could physically feel when they talked and laughed. The bond they shared not only made her feel safe and protected it warmed her heart. Something Ally needed more than anything at the moment. Having discovered something of tremendous importance was what she was hoping for. She was ecstatic about it, although she wasn't exactly sure what do to first with the new information.

There was time enough for that. Right now, her main concern was refueling with friends. Ally remembered seeing her grandparents make wise decisions through patience and careful consideration. Not only had some of her own decisions backfired, she also witnessed her father's rash spur-of-the-moment decisions ruin their lives. She needed time to consider her options and get back on solid ground before deciding how, when and to whom she would disclose the events she witnessed. Holding onto one undeniable fact Ally was sure of one thing. She, and she alone had discovered the answer to one if not the most important question Edmund had. The unbelievable cause behind Helene's death.

<u>Chapter Thirteen</u>

Sleep evaded Ally for most of the night. Fearful over having another bizarre and puzzling night's sleep meant she didn't really mind lying awake in bed. It gave her time to thoroughly evaluate her options. She knew she wouldn't be given a second chance if her attempts to earn back her freedom failed. There wasn't a single doubt in her mind as to where she'd immediately be sent. Ally was confident she'd end up in the dreaded wasteland. She was painfully aware that any plan she came up with must be infallible. Even if the tiniest piece of her scheme went wrong her fate would be sealed.

Ally became discouraged as she ran through scenario after scenario. Would Edmund believe her if she shared the story of Jezebel and Margret? Would he ask for proof? If so, then what? Ally didn't know how she ended up in the cemetery. She couldn't tell Edmund how to get there or where it was simply because she didn't know. Ally believed dark magic was masking Helene's death and keeping Edmund from returning to the moment it happened. It's the only reason Ally could come up with as to why Edmund was incapable of preventing his wife's death or as Ally now understood it. Her premediated murder.

"You're awfully quiet this morning," stated Rose.

"Oh, I'm sorry Rose. I've just got a lot on my mind," responded Ally through a croaking voice.

"I'm all ears."

Ally had backed herself into a corner, but quick thinking gave her a way out, "Oh it's just me being silly. I'm trying to figure out what those weird dreams meant."

Rose smiled and said, "I wouldn't waste any more time on that. If you're bored or need some assistance with your travel practice, I'd be more than happy to give you a few suggestions."

Putting into practice some of the lessons Sallie had taught her Ally paused to think before answering. Making sure not to give herself away, "That's not necessary Rose. I'm having fun exploring on my own and its helping me become more confident and independent in my skills." Ally never considered that learning to hide the truth from a potential host body for Helene would turn out to be helpful against Rose.

"Good enough. Have a successful day," replied Rose heading for the door before adding, "I will see you tomorrow."

Curious Ally asked, "Tomorrow?"

"Yes, I have to take care of something that'll go well into tomorrow, but Sallie should return late tonight."

Ally eased Rose's obvious concern by saying, "It's okay, the staff is here and I can always contact you if I need to," holding her necklace in her fingers signaling how assured she was that help was always nearby.

Smiling with pride Rose expressed her feelings, "You have no idea how happy your decision to join the garden makes me Ally. It's wonderful to have you as part of my family."

In full agreement Ally nodded and hugged her friend before she disappeared from sight. Their friendship was strong and getting stronger, something Ally had hoped for when they first met back in college. Naturally she figured their friendship would blossom as college roommates and not in the unknown realm she now resided. Prompting a new question to cross her mind, "What would become of their friendship if and when Ally was released from the locket?"

She couldn't worry about that now. Ally had more important things to consider. Things like how to use the information she was collecting to her advantage. Feeling like an attorney preparing for the biggest case of their career Ally sought evidence, witnesses and cold hard facts.

Edmund had repeatedly returned to the sight of Helene's death each time coming up empty handed. Ally had at least one advantage over Edmund. She knew who and how Storm was used to end Helene's life. Figuring if dark magic could prevent a warlock with unmatched powers from returning to the actual scene Ally had zero chance of returning there. Ally knew she'd have to try another route. She believed coming at the problem with a different perspective would help. Ally hoped to find a way around the mask dark magic had placed over the tragic event.

Ally returned to the moments prior to Helene's death when Edmund held her in his arms and safely captured her soul within the locket. Unlike the times before Ally wasn't focused on the agonizing sight of Helene's passing. Instead she searched the vicinity for Margret. Was it possible that she had stuck around to witness Helene's demise? Margret was nowhere to be found and Ally voiced her disgust, "You coward Margret."

By this time Edmund had transported Helene's body to the manor and returned to search for the cause of her death. Edmund's rainstorm raged, quickly flooding the area causing streams of rising water to rush along the roads edge and into the forest. Ally zeroed in on one possibility. The silver capped cork from the potion vial. Sensing its location nearly half a mile away from Edmund, Ally caught sight of the cork bobbing in one of the growing torrents. With the silver side beneath the waters muddy surface the brown cork was scarcely noticeable in the surging water. Ally had never been so thankful for her growing talents. All her practice on pinpoint concentration techniques had enabled her to locate an invaluable piece of evidence or leverage. Scooping the cork from the mucky flow Ally looked over the tiny plug and confirmed it was the same cork she'd seen on the vial.

Another piece of the puzzle had been secured. Ally felt a tremendous jolt of satisfaction which passed all too soon. She could tell Edmund all she had discovered and he would be immensely grateful, but Ally was sure it wouldn't be enough to persuade him to release her. She would have to gather far more evidence and monumental intelligence to secure her freedom. As it stood, Edmund would thank her and probably grant her almost anything she asked for barring her freedom. Knowing who caused Helene's death wouldn't change the fact that she still needed a host body and Ally was sure it would only cause Edmund to move forward in his revenge plot against the Bennett's. His hatred for them would no doubt increase to the point of eradicating them from the planet.

Returning to the lodge and securely hiding her treasure in her room Ally enjoyed a solitary lunch on the front porch. It gave her time to plan her next move knowing an error in judgement would ruin her plans if not end what was left of her. It truly was a matter of life and death. The world inside the locket wasn't real, and Ally truly believed surrendering her body, mind and soul entirely would completely wipe out her existence. As far as she were concerned it would be as if she were never born. At the very least, she feared she'd no longer have the ability to differentiate between real life and the lockets magical one.   Walking the tightrope between unconditional surrender and hanging on to the tiniest bit of hope in returning home was tiring, but it was necessary if she ever wanted to escape the locket.

The afternoons silence was broken by the high pitched and rarely heard call of the nearby nesting eagles. Ally searched the sky and right away spotted the pair soaring above the lodge. With their massive wingspan and wingtip feathers spread wide they glided effortlessly on an updraft climbing higher and higher. Entranced by the refined beauty of their rhythmic flight Ally found a similarity between the breathtaking eagles and Edmund and Helene. Each couple unselfishly showcased the other and profoundly exhibited the bond they shared through their actions. It was like a masterfully choreographed dance with each of them doing their part and creating a sight to behold.

Out of nowhere the female soared directly in front of Ally. The magnificent bird was so close Ally felt the cool breeze from her flapping wings hit her face. The male who had visited before was now bolder than ever landing on the porch railing only feet from Ally.   Afraid any movement on her part would send him away Ally froze in place. He surveyed her briefly and at the mere sight of his mate heading back to their nest he took flight. She didn't have to call him to join her, he simply followed her out of devotion. They belonged to each other for as long as they lived, another similarity to Edmund and Helene, with one major difference. The eagles didn't possess magic.

Refreshed with new ideas Ally headed off on another exploration trip hoping it would be as successful as her earlier outing. Time and time again Ally found herself in burial grounds with a black obelisk headstone all of which didn't belong to Jezebel. She had no idea this type of tombstone was so popular and her patience wore thin as she continued to end up at the wrong cemetery. Frustrated that she couldn't locate Jezebel's final resting place Ally reluctantly followed Margret for hours, discovering that her pompous attitude was increasing with the mere anticipation of becoming Mrs. Edmund Dalton. Mr. Bennett noticed the same thing and in his typical spineless way tried to reprimand his daughter, failing miserably as usual.

Margret dismissed her father's comments with a perturbed huff. Then marched herself up to her room stomping out her anger on every step causing pictures to rattle on the walls. Once inside her extravagant room Margret dramatically threw herself onto her frilly bed only to be crying out in pain the next second. Briskly removing her boot, she discovered her notepad was glowing red and scorching hot causing her to drop it to the floor. Examining the outside of her calf she witnessed blisters beginning to form. The notepad slammed open and all by itself sketched Jezebel's headstone bringing her forth.

Snarling in a gurgling voice Jezebel ordered, "Margret Bennett you will behave yourself. We will not allow you to draw attention to our connection."

"I didn't do anything," argued Margret. More evidence that her egotistical attitude was out of control.

Without warning Jezebel transformed into a beast like Ally had never seen. Angrily its putrid appendages reached for Margret who blacked-out from fear. When she came too Jezebel was standing over her and stroking her hair appearing suspiciously concerned, "There, there Margret," she kept repeating.

"Where did it go?" shrieked Margret remembering the repulsive creature. Pulling away from Jezebel she quivered at the far end of her bed.

"My pet, are you trying to anger me again?"

Gripped with fear Margret remained transfixed on Jezebel and said with a cracking voice, "No my liege."

Jezebel took a seat next to Margret saying, "We can do this the hard way or the easy way. It's entirely up to you Margret. Whatever we do will be in response to your choices. Consider them carefully. You don't want to make us do something we'll regret."

Ally couldn't believe her ears. The forces of darkness were blaming Margret for their behavior, coming short of saying "Look what you made us do." It was similar to an abuser convincing their victim they caused their own assault. There was no two ways about it. Margret was going to do exactly as she was told or suffer the consequences. Either way she was doomed.

Margret nodded in agreement and tried her best to appear at ease. Smiling with quivering lips she encouraged Jezebel to explain her error to her. With fear intensifying in Margret's eyes she sat motionless and waited for Jezebel to speak.

Jezebel simply glossed over Margret's question and much to Ally's satisfaction proceeded to divulge more secrets, "Perhaps I was mistaken about you Margret. I was convinced you would be a perfect fit as a new mistress of the dark."

"Mistress of the dark?" whispered Margret clearly still on edge.

"It's the position I proudly hold for the supreme witches. Because of my willingness to allow them access through my body they spread chaos, mayhem and evil into the world," boasted Jezebel.

"Why would they need me if they already have you?"

"You will soon have access to Edmund Dalton in a way no one from the dark side ever has," sneered Jezebel, "This plan surpasses all the previous plans. Even the original plan to annihilate the Daltons."

"Previous plans?" questioned Margret before growing concerned, "Annihilate the Daltons? I don't want Edmund harmed. I want him for myself."

In a repugnant manner Jezebel explained, "Edmund will be yours Margret. The only difference is his power will belong to us. Having his power far outweighs the original plan of ending the Dalton bloodline."

Margret wanted answers, "How could you end his bloodline?"

Jezebel gave Margret a condensed version of the angry mobs attempt to kill the Dalton family, going as far as to summarize how they tried to persuade Edmund to join the dark side after his parent's death. Jezebel didn't quite admit she was the cause of any of it, but Ally believed she was involved somehow.

"Well, that presents a problem I didn't know about," remarked Margret.

"Problem?" asked an annoyed Jezebel.

Margret was now pacing the floor, "So I'll die someday and leave Edmund to marry again. That's not at all what I want."

The band of witches inside Jezebel erupted in dreadful laughter and Jezebel fought for her own voice to rise above it, "I will explain." The laughter ceased and Jezebel began, "You can earn immortality and live forever with Edmund." Jezebel purposely paused and examined a lose thread on her dress which she immediately fixed. She was deliberately causing Margret agony for no other reason than for the fun of it. With an evil smile, she finally continued, "If you help us achieve our long-awaited endeavor of turning him evil."

That was all Margret needed to hear. Living an immortal life with Edmund far surpassed a normal human life with him. She could hardly wait for her new life as Mrs. Margret Dalton to begin. Her exuberant response did little to hide this fact, "I will do whatever you want."

A grisly smirk crossed Jezebel's face and she praised Margret's willingness to be used by evil, "Now that's doing things the easy way my pet. See how much smoother things can go when you don't cause waves?"

Ally had seen enough. Being in the company of such evil sucked the life out of her and she bolted for home before Jezebel melted away. With all she had learned she feared for Helene and Edmund's safety. It was painfully obvious that evil wasn't going to give up on turning Edmund away from light magic. She was also sure that the spell Edmund used to save Helene had put a major wrench into their plans. There was no telling who or what they would use next to achieve their diabolical plan. It didn't take long for Ally to realize that not only were Helene and Edmund at risk but the entire locket world and garden. If Edmund was somehow overtaken by evil, it only stood to reason that everything and everyone under his power would also become evil.

Saving herself from the locket had just hours earlier been her only objective. Now she was faced with the heavy weight of knowing there was so much more at stake. Cupping her face in her hands Ally rubbed her forehead forcefully and tried to find a solution. Sallie came back to the lodge and seeing Ally's anguish asked if she was alright.

Needing to stall for time Ally replied, "Yes, it's just been a crazy busy day and I'm afraid I over did it."

"Are you getting another headache?"

"No, I was doing some preventive maintenance by rubbing my head," blushed Ally from the sound of her own explanation. It sounded too dumb to be real.

Sallie's day must have been equally draining and she didn't press Ally any further. During dinner, they shared a casual conversation discussing weather, favorite foods, books, hobbies and pet peeves. They each needed to give their brains some time off. It wasn't until dessert was served, freshly baked lemon tarts, did the girls come back to life. Perhaps it was a sugar-rush from the four tarts Ally scarfed down, but whatever the reason Ally's mind reeled with questions.

"Sallie, how far back does the magic in the Dalton family line go?"

If Sallie was surprised by Ally's question she didn't show it, "I'm not entirely sure, but my guess is they've always possessed it."

"So you don't know how they became magical?"

"No, it's never even crossed my mind," admitted Sallie.

Ally wondered, "Who decides whether to be on the side of good or evil? Has the Dalton family always been on the side of good?"

"Yes, every one of them has practiced light magic."

Ally thought out loud, "So they've always been a thorn in the side of evil. I imagine dark magic would like nothing better than to crush such a long family line of light magic." Suddenly Ally had an idea pop into her head, "Do evil warlocks and witches marry humans?"

That caught Sallie's attention, "Oh no, evil rarely associates with humans, unless of course they locate one they can use," Sallie was growing curious with Ally's line of questioning and asked, "Why do you ask? Did you come across a poor helpless human that's being used by dark magic?"

Ally was less than honest saying, "No, I'm just being nosy and trying to get a feel for the dark side of magic. Someday I'll have to face it and the more I know the more prepared I'll be." It was in part the truth. Margret was no longer a poor helpless human which brought up another question, "So evil can take over a human without their permission?"

"Thankfully no, but the dark side is a masterful deceiver and humans rarely recognize that the desire they want more than anything is evil in disguise," answered Sallie before reiterating, "Ally you have a long while before you'll be asked to battle the enemy. You haven't finished your training or located your first host. Please don't get ahead of yourself."

"I know," agreed Ally before asking one last question for the night, "Is the reason I still need to rest so much more than you or Rose, because I haven't finished my training?"

Sallie replied, "That's a small part of it. Mainly it's because your powers aren't mature yet. Edmund's masterpiece of a garden limits the energy we can pull from our plant keeping us from draining the very life from it. You have to remember your plant is still very young and fragile."

The explanation Sallie gave her sounded rationale and on that note Ally excused herself for the night. Hoping to have a peaceful and dreamless night's sleep. Ally trusted her mentally frazzled mind would beat out her subconscious allowing her to feel well-rested come morning.

Chapter Fourteen

Ally had lost track of time and forgot she was scheduled to pick up her dress from the boutique until the coachman asked if she was ready to leave. It would be her first trip into town without Sallie and it proved to her that she had earned Sallies trust. The coachman wouldn't leave her side helping settle Ally's nerves. She figured she was going into town for one reason and only one reason, to bring home her custom-designed dress. What could go wrong?

The answer to that question made itself known shortly after Ally changed into her dress. The seamstress wanted to see how the additional lace looked before Ally took it home, prompting her to go into a dressing room and try the dress on. When Ally turned to open the changing room door she discovered the door was gone. In its place was Margret's magical mirror. Startled by the unnerving sight of it, Ally flew backwards solidly hitting her back and head against the opposing wall making her head ring. Trapped in tight quarters with an evil-possessed mirror was something she was less than prepared for. Her mind buzzed with thoughts as she fought to think, and think clearly.

The dressing room no longer had a way out. Ally was for all intents and purposes, trapped. Fleeing seemed the only logical choice and she inhaled deeply giving away her means of escape. Trying to exhale proved to be futile something or someone was preventing the air from leaving her lungs. Horrified, Ally reopened her eyes to see Jezebel standing in front of her. After a succession of coughs and gags in which she regained the ability to breathe normally. Ally stood paralyzed in fear.

Jezebel spoke in a whisper accentuating her breathy voice, "Quiet Ally just listen."

All consuming fear like nothing Ally had known before brought her necklace to life, shining so bright it made Jezebel shield her eyes. Ally swore she could hear distant cries of pain emanating from within Jezebel. Ally wasn't bothered by the light, but was stunned when there wasn't any change to Jezebel's features. Even as the shrieks of intensifying agony coming from within her became deafening. Jezebel remained beautiful.

In a guttural tone Jezebel spoke quickly, "We can help you get even with Edmund. With your help Ally we can sever your bond with his spell and set you free..." before Jezebel could finish her sentence the increasing light from Ally's necklace chased her back into the mirror. In the blink of an eye the mirror vanished.

The next thing Ally knew she was standing in the garden with the mighty oak electrified so intensely it gave off heat like a bonfire. The garden itself was shimmering like thousands of tiny jewels under a spotlight, casting infinite sparks of light to dance on every object it found including the night sky. The illumination from the garden reached as far as Ally could see and she soon found herself at ease. Any remaining doubt she had for her safety was eliminated. She smiled fondly as Edmund approached her.

"Good evening Ally. You've been a busy girl," he said confidently.

In a reflexive manner Ally curtsied saying, "Good evening Mr. Dalton."

"I'm happy you are safely home." His tone was genuine and yet there was something in his eyes that made Ally curious. It wasn't anger or anything along those lines. It was more the look of trepidation.

"Thank you sir. I'm happy to be home."

Edmund's heart melting smile made Ally blush. The man was the epitome of handsome regardless of your "type." His features, physique, mannerisms and voice were nothing short of perfection. Accustomed to this type of reaction Edmund did his best to refocus Ally's attention to the matter at hand. "Where would you like to begin Ally?"

Part of her brain wanted to shout out what had just happened. Then another part of her brain told her to keep quiet. The latter reminded her there wasn't much

Edmund didn't already know about his garden family and he probably already knew what took place at the dress shop. Trusting Edmund didn't know anything about Margret, Ally hesitated before answering and that's when Sallie's training really kicked in, "Perhaps you share with me what you already know Mr. Dalton. Then I won't have to bore you with details of things you're already familiar with."

An amused laugh filled the air followed by a pleased reply, "Excellent Ally. I see Sallie's training has been most effective and you have learned well."

"Yes sir."

"I believe you've located Jezebel and the mirror that allows her to cross between her dammed existence and the world."

Ally wasn't sure what shocked her more. The fact that Edmund was already aware of Jezebel and the mirror or the fact that Ally was surprised by his knowledge. Was it possible he also knew about Margret? He couldn't have. If he did, he would know why Storm pummeled Helene to death and Ally was positive that news would travel through the gardens bloomvine at the speed of light. Keeping her answer tightly linked to his comment Ally said, "Yes sir, although I have to say it kinda found me today. I wasn't looking for it. I was just picking up my dress." At which point Ally noticed she was still wearing her creation.

Edmund took the time to compliment Ally's dress and how wonderful she looked in it. If he was deliberately trying to keep Ally off balance by making her blush like an infatuated school girl, it was working. While Ally struggled to regain her focus, Edmund commented on Ally's statement, "That's what I assessed when the garden notified me of your SOS."

"My SOS?" wondered Ally.

"Yes Ally, your necklace alerted the garden of your perilous situation as soon as your fear became immeasurable. Your garden family knows you are far from being prepared to face evil one on one. They may not have known the exact cause, but they knew I needed to be alerted immediately. Hence the SOS."

"I don't understand. How did the garden know evil was with me?"

"It was the only explanation for your fear level. Your necklace sent an urgent message expressing the absolute horror you were experiencing. I promptly investigated and discovered Jezebel. You, as well as most of the garden is ill-prepared for something as phenomenally evil as Jezebel and the powers that have possessed her."

Ally was extremely grateful that Edmund himself had come to her rescue and shuddered to think what could have happened if he hadn't. He had pulled rank and overshot Sallie, Rose and Arthur in coming to her aid. It was at that precise moment when Ally made the decision to follow his lead and deal directly with him. She would share what she had learned about Helene's passing with no one other than Edmund. Before she could respond to his explanation about rescuing her he elaborated.

This is when the trepidation in his eyes returned, "I'm concerned that dark magic is strategizing to hurt you and the rest of my garden and most importantly Helene." When those final words left his mouth the concern and dread he felt for Helene devoured his love for life. He paced for several minutes before stating, "I can't lose her to evil. I won't lose her to evil!"

Making the wise decision to hold onto the secrets of Helene's death a while longer Ally stood silent. Edmund's fearful state was not the time to divulge such heinous news and she waited for him to regain his composure before saying anything. "I wish there was something I could do to help, but I'm out of my league with Jezebel," admitted Ally something she hoped he would remember.

Edmunds beautiful eyes flashed with excitement and what followed revealed why, "I agree Ally. You are out of your league. At least on your own," this wasn't sounding good and to Ally's dismay he headed in the direction she feared most, "I need you to play along with Jezebel.

Pretend you've considered her evil plot and want to help her get even with me. Once she reveals the details of her plan we can sabotage it and I will conquer Jezebel removing her as an instrument for the powers of darkness."

"They'll destroy me," squealed Ally wanting nothing more than to forget coming face to face with Jezebel.

"I won't permit it Ally. I will watch over you through the garden and prevent any harm darkness tries to inflict. Evil will never suspect I would allow you to contact them and will assume you're acting on your own."

Her fear over Jezebel far outweighed her fear of Edmund and she found herself boldly arguing with him, "I don't ever want to see her again. I can't pretend to be on her side her side terrifies me. Now that you know she's up to something, can't you just deal with her yourself?"

Patiently Edmund explained that he could very easily destroy Jezebel and the mirror, but it would leave one very important detail unknown. The motive behind evil's attack on him and his family. Good versus evil was as old as time itself, but Edmund understood that for him to be a direct target of dark magic, there had to be a specific reason behind their tactics. Something much more than just being on the side of good. The elements of darkness wouldn't be working this hard to find a way to get to him if they didn't have a bigger objective.

615

Eradicating Jezebel would take away Edmund's direct link into their scheme. Which would result in him having to either spend all his time searching for the new mistress of darkness or hope to once again stumble across it.

By the time Edmund had completed his articulate and eloquent speech Ally had been persuaded to do all she could to help. "I'll do whatever I can Mr. Dalton and I trust you will keep me safe," was all Ally said. Without question or doubt on her part, she was at last, fully surrendering all she was or ever hoped to be.

"Wonderful Ally," he applauded, "I'm sure Jezebel will waste no time getting in touch with you. Not after her bold appearance in the dressing room."

After a few more instructions Ally was sent on her way resulting in confusion about what day it was. She had arrived at the boutique in the morning, was transported to the manor in the evening and returned to the lodge during sunset. Making her wonder if time existed in the locket or whether it was just another element of the spell trying to make it appear normal to its inhabitants. It didn't matter either way. Ally was thankful she had until morning before she'd have to leave the manor's grounds in hopes of running into Jezebel. Edmund had explained that dark magic had never tried to invade the manor. Largely in part to it being protected against evil through the use of light magic. Ally figured it was guarded in a similar way to Helene's accident being shielded from Edmund and light magic's discovery of what took place.

Another poor night's sleep added to Ally's nerves as she prepared to leave. She did her best to make it seem like it was just a run-of-the-mill travel day. Whether Rose or Sallie had any suspicions of what she was up to wasn't clear and soon enough Ally was on her way. Figuring the dress shop was as good a place as any to start Ally pretended to be on the hunt for another new dress. Only this time she wanted to try on a few of the dresses that had not been picked up for one reason or another. As expected she was ushered into the changing area where she found Jezebel waiting for her.

Jezebel wasted no time in fear of light magic detecting her presence, "I'm so glad to see you Ally, but I can't stay long. I need you to travel to the future and visit Margret Bennett's grave. There you will find what you are looking for," and with that Jezebel vaporized.

"Margret Bennett's grave?" she mumbled to herself. Perplexed by Jezebel's instructions Ally excused herself telling the clerk she suddenly felt ill and once safe from view bolted to the lodge. Much to her relief she found Rose enjoying the cool morning air on the porch. Greeting her friend with a warm hug they spent only a few minutes catching up before Ally asked, "What time are we in?"

Rose appeared unfazed, "Do you want the year?"

"No, that doesn't matter. I just want to know if right now the time we're in is when Edmund and Helene are alive. I mean I've seen Maxwell, Margret and the old town so I know it's in the past."

"You're right it's in the past," replied Rose, without commenting on Ally's sighting of Maxwell.

Wanting more clarification Ally confirmed, "Okay, the past, but the past before or after Helene's death?"

Now Rose was thrown, "Ally you know it's after Helene's death. You have traveled back to reach that day. What's going on Ally?"

"I'm just trying to keep my bearings and in all honesty from what I've gathered most souls are kept as far away as possible from their own body. It makes me wonder why I'm so close to Helene and her soul residing in my body."

Rose didn't blink an eye, "Mr. Dalton was concerned for Helene and hoped having your body and soul coexist in the same time period would help the transition be successful."

"Did it?"

"Yes, it appears to have been successful."

Afraid of the answer Ally couldn't help but ask, "What would have happened if the transition failed before I surrendered and became part of the garden?"

This was not something Rose wanted to share with Ally and had secretly wished it would never come up. Speaking in a soft library voice Rose broke the news as gently as possible, "Helene's soul would have returned to the locket and waited for another host body and..." Rose paused.

"And my soul?"

"Your soul would have returned to your deceased body," said Rose with a sorrowful look.

Ally leaned back in her chair and bowed her head saying, "That's what I thought."

"What exactly brought this on?" asked a concerned Rose.

Not knowing if Rose was aware of her arrangement with Edmund, Ally put on her best poker face and said, "I ran across Margret the other day and I was wondering what ever became of her. It's more a morbid curiosity than anything else. I guess I was hoping her spoiled behavior finally caught up with her and it made me wonder what could have happened to me if I hadn't surrendered."

Rose wasn't sure how Ally went from Margret's spoiled attitude to herself and she briefly tried to connect the dots before answering, "She died a lonely bitter old woman which ate away at the only thing pretty about her,

her looks. By the time she passed she was nearly unrecognizable even to her family."

When Ally seemed only mildly interested in her answer it made Rose's bewilderment grow and it quickly changed into concern. Rose's expression reminded Ally that she needed to keep up appearances, "I'm sorry Rose, I guess I just needed to confirm that I'm safe. Surrendering to Mr. Dalton means I've been given an eternity here in the locket, right?"

"Yes Ally. Would you like to share what's spooked you?"

Knowing she needed to omit most of what spooked her Ally downplayed her fears and summed it up in as few words as possible, "Nothing in particular. I think it's a combination of bizarre dreams and spending too much time on my own and inside my own head."

Agreeing Rose remarked, "You have been working extremely hard and with Sallie and I gone from morning till night I understand your mental exhaustion. I think we all experienced some kind of turmoil during our training, but the good news is this too will pass."

"Good point, but my confidence level has grown by leaps and bounds so I can't really complain. My grandpa always used to quote Thomas Edison, "Ally, 'There's no substitute for hard work' he would remind me whenever I grumbled about working hard," said Ally doing her best grandpa imitation.

"He sounds like a smart man."

"He was and he was a great grandpa. I loved, oh I mean love my grandparents," Ally corrected herself. Reflecting on her grandparents made her tear up. Choosing not to cry Ally took those downcast emotions and used them to strengthen her desire to reach her goal.

Before leaving, Rose suggested Ally spend the rest of the day relaxing and doing a whole lot of nothing. It did sound like the right thing to do, but between agreeing to help Edmund and Ally's own intentions she couldn't waste the rest of the day. Every moment she delayed getting things done only meant she was delaying her plans coming to fruition.

Chapter Fifteen

Standing in front of Margret Bennett's headstone was surreal. Ally looked over the towering piece of black marble noticing it was void of any carvings or elaborate details. Other than Margret's name and date of birth the stone was primarily untouched by human hands. The only flaws on the perfectly polished slab of stone were mysterious and surprisingly deep scratch marks. They were located exactly where the date of Margret's death should have been. Upon closer observation Ally realized the scratch marks appeared to have been made by claws. Something extremely powerful had clawed away whatever had been written.

Unable to resist, Ally lightly brushed her fingertips along the ragged grooves of numerous lacerations, and felt heat radiating from them. She watched in disbelief as a faint apparition gradually appeared in the stone. The aged and haggard face was unknown to Ally, except for the eyes. Those beautiful yet wicked eyes were know filled with sorrow making Ally assume the elderly woman was Margret. Rose had been correct in saying she was almost unrecognizable in her older years. Standing in silence Ally waited for her to speak. Guessing by Margret's gestures she was unable to say a single word and after persistently motioning for Ally to retouch the scratches she obliged.

Suddenly above the scarred area of the increasingly hot marble Ally watched the smooth surface of Margret's tombstone became a movie screen. As long as one of Ally's fingers remained on the headstone, no matter how lightly, the images continued. Rotating her fingers helped them from being burned too severely. Soon they transitioned from silent films into high definition videos. The first clip was the angry mob marching towards Dalton Manor with Jezebel and her legion of dark witches urging them on. Before the crowd reached the manor's gate the channel was changed. Ally watched as Jezebel pleaded with the supreme witches to spare her the fate Margret would eventually suffer. Jezebel had failed at accomplishing evil's goal of destroying the Dalton's and yet they believed she was still of some use to them.

Ally learned through the progression of dark magic's atrocious home videos how Margret suffered the wrath of the supreme witches, decades after failing to become Edmund's wife, and giving them the conduit they needed to overtake him. Casting the spell to save Helene and keep her with him for all eternity had been an unknown possibility. Regardless of the fact that Margret played no role in Edmund's spell, darkness was insistent on having someone pay for yet another failure. Margret was taught how dangerous becoming a mistress of darkness was and had faced severe consequences over the years for not meeting their expectations. The stereotypical bad guy in gangster movies was reinforced in Ally's mind. Sure, those all too common characters would play nice as long as they were getting what they wanted from someone, but the second that person's usefulness wore out so did their false niceties.

The expression on Ally's face proved she appreciated the informative history lesson, but she remained baffled as to what dark magic wanted from her. She already knew she wouldn't agree to become an instrument of evil, but Ally had to play along. She reminded herself that if for one millisecond she felt seduced by the empty promises or lies of darkness she would use her necklace to be rescued. Ally was there for one reason, to help Edmund understand why his family was targeted and basically get a sneak peek into evil's play book. That way Edmund could protect the magical garden, the manor and most of all, his life with Helene. Ally couldn't have imagined the twists and turns that had taken place from her desire to discover hidden secrets. She had succeeded in getting the bargaining chip she needed for her own benefit, unfortunately Ally had never given a single thought to what else she would uncover.

The preview of what evil wanted from Ally proved without a shadow of a doubt that evil would never give up on ending the Dalton's family line and their power for good. Including the destruction of all Edmund loved. Through Ally and her traveling ability darkness intended to invade the hidden garden, turn its inhabitants to their side and like a cancer overtake Edmund's power. At long last evil would end the Dalton legacy of light magic and rebuild it into an immense legacy of unspeakable wickedness. The only thing Ally needed to do was agree to allow darkness into her heart, something Margret implored her to do.

Withdrawing her slightly singed fingertips from the tombstone broke the connection and Margret was gone. Ally blew on her fingers trying to remove the sensation of heat the stone had left on them. In the blink of an eye a terrified Ally returned to Jezebel's grave site where her fear mounted because she had no control over ending up there. Wasting no time and obviously afraid light magic would come to Ally's aid Jezebel spoke quickly, "Margret is offering you a way out of Edmund's spell. All you have to do is help us capture Dalton Manor and we'll return you to your little life in Glenbrook."

Disturbed by Jezebel's knowledge of where she grew up and referring to her life as "little" Ally wrestled over concerns for her family, the magical garden, the friends she'd made at the manor and even Helene and Edmund. With a despondent groan, she at last thought of her own safety and how to get back to the lodge in one piece. Without meaning to her words dripped of malice, "Trust Margret to set me free? Didn't Margret already have her chance and fail?"

Jezebel smiled an evil smile and said, "She did, however her ingenious plot to use you to get to Edmund has persuaded the supreme witches to give her another chance. You are already connected with Mr. Dalton and with your help we get what we want. Margret regains her youth and we may even allow her to claim her position as Edmund's wife."

There it was, the sickening truth. After all this time Margret was still only interested in herself and what she wanted. She didn't care about helping Ally. True to form Margret was just using Ally to achieve the goal she failed to reach so many years ago. The fact that Ally would never consider being used by dark magic was beside the point. How dare Margret use her as a pawn for her own selfish desires. Infuriated to the point of seeing red Ally boldly announced, "You will have your answer by nightfall tomorrow," bolting back to the manor before Jezebel could utter a sound.

As expected Ally found herself standing with Edmund in the garden and forgetting her place blurted, "Did you see that?"

Edmund's livid expression answered Ally's question and she remained silent while his mood transitioned from unadulterated rage to agonizing fear. She wasn't sure if it was for her benefit or not, but Edmund seemed to be keeping his intense emotions under control. Unlike the storm he created when Helene passed there was a petrifying calm surrounding them, and although Edmund appeared to be in a great deal of pain he maintained his composure. While she quietly waited, she felt a cooling sensation on her fingertips and when she looked down at them she noticed they were healed. Finally, Edmund spoke asking in a slow and direct tone, "Ally, explain to me why dark magic would want Margret to be my wife."

Unsure where or how to begin Ally chose to go way back to the day he met Helene. While explaining how angry Margret Bennett was Edmund interrupted her and strongly suggested she tell him something he wasn't already aware of. A quick summary of Margret's carefully orchestrated, but failed attempts to break Edmund and Helene apart brought Ally to the dressing room scene, where she first overheard Margret arguing with her mother.

"I'm aware of the possessed mirror and the dark magic behind it," interjected Edmund, "Go on."

"Not only does Margret use the mirror to contact her mother she contacts or actually Jezebel seems to contact Margret through it. I'm not sure which happened first."

"Inconsequential," interrupted Edmund.

His assertiveness and mannerisms reminded Ally who and what Edmund was and she tried not to continue rambling, "Yes sir," she uttered. This was not at all how she expected to tell Edmund what caused Helene's death, but there was no way around it. Ally feared this new information on top of what he had just learned would push him over the edge. It was quite possible that he would no longer be able to control his anger.

Aware of Ally's growing fear Edmund tried to put her mind at ease, "Miss Ally, please forgive my abrupt behavior. I permitted myself to be consumed by my emotions and forgot that you put yourself in harm's way to assist me. The information you've already provided will be of great use for me and light magic," and although he never said the word, Ally heard the "but..."

Ally raised her eyes to Edmund where he could see the devastation behind them. Her cracking voice magnified the significance of what she needed to share, "You need to know everything I've discovered."

"Yes Ally I do. If I'm to keep you and everyone at Dalton Manor safe I need to know everything."

For the first time since she discovered the cause of Helene's death Ally found herself looking at the information as so much more than leverage. She found herself choking on the words. How could she possibly tell this man how and why his beloved wife died? She closed her eyes trying to fight back the tears but they flowed through.

"Ally, what's wrong?" it was Rose's voice.

Instantly Ally felt calmer and she leaned into Rose's embrace. Edmund gave them the time they needed before asking them to have a seat on one of the garden benches. The trepidation on Edmund's face had returned while he waited for Ally to tell him what had thus far been too difficult to say. Rose did what only she could do, which is what Edmund had hoped for when he summoned her to the garden. Ally had regained her composure and with a little encouragement from Rose was ready to speak.

"Mr. Dalton sir," began Ally with a shaky voice. "You have spent decades wondering what caused Helene's death," pausing Ally took a deep breath.

"Go on," prodded Rose with a friendly smile contrasting her serious and interested eyes.

Gathering her thoughts Ally laid it all out on the table in one continuous blurb, "Storm was possessed the day of Helene's death. Margret basically sold her soul to the devil and used a potion from Jezebel to turn Storm into an enraged beast. When the spell completed its mission, it came out of him or lost its power. I don't quite remember the exact way Jezebel described it, but either way Margret got her wish. Helene was removed and out of her way. Dark magic promised her she'd become your wife..."

The wind picked up and storm clouds rolled in faster than Ally thought was possible. Thunder roared in the darkened sky and countless lightning strikes raced to the earth. The curtain of electrified bolts created an ominous blue and purplish glow. Rose cautiously approached Edmund saying, "Please sir control yourself," and the look he gave her should have sent her back to the bench, but she refused to yield offering a justifiable reason, "Evil will see your display of power and become curious as to its reason."

Giving evil any clue into his plans of having Ally gather inside information was the last thing Edmund wanted to do. In an instant the storm subsided. Ally was instructed as to what her answer should be if Jezebel questioned her about the volatile yet brief storm at the manor. Edmund knew Rose was right in making sure he maintained control over his tremendous power. He then asked point blank if there was anything else Ally had discovered.

Having regained his composure Edmund began to speak then changed what he was beginning to say, "W....Ally, I want to thank you for discovering the truth behind my beloved Helene's death. I never understood how Storm could have done what he did. It was beyond reason. His love for her would never allow him to cause her the tiniest of injuries. Anything less than a potion from the dark side made such an accident impossible. As does the fact that I couldn't return to the accident and find any evidence of what occurred. Dark magic has kept me from discovering the truth all these years."

Rose appeared nearly as astonished as Edmund and she asked her own question, "How did you discover all this?"

"There's time enough for that Rose I would like more details," Edmund returned his attention to Ally, "I understand Margret's desire to be my wife that's old news. What I want to know is what evil hoped to gain from her becoming my wife."

"After Margret became your wife dark magic was somehow going to use her relationship with you for their benefit. Jezebel never really said how this would work, just that you would be turned evil and join the dark side.

They made it sound like you and Margret would become one of the most evil and powerful couples to ever exist."

Edmund interrupted, "My spell to save Helene thwarted their plans."

"That explains what happened to Margret over the years," added Rose.

To her surprise Ally felt better having gotten such an important and decades old secret off her chest. This caused a few of her own questions to come to mind and without thinking Ally blurted, "So if I'm understanding all of this correctly, Jezebel was used long ago by evil when they attempted to kill your family?"

A mixture of torment and anger flooded Edmund's eyes, "Yes, dark magic was behind that horrible night, although they aren't fully to blame. If the Bennett family wasn't predisposed to evil they could have never been provoked into doing their bidding."

Edmund and Rose spoke in their strange language while Ally sat quietly on the bench, feeling like a traveler in a strange land, which was exactly what she was. She was a little offended that they were speaking in a language she didn't understand. Especially after agreeing to help Edmund by putting herself in danger, not to mention discovering the hidden truth of Helene's untimely death. After all, she was the one who had uncovered the answer to the decades old question of how Helene died. Ally's frustration turned to anger.

An outraged Ally cried out, "Hey, why can't I know what you're talking about? I'm the one who figured out Helene was intentionally murdered." It wasn't until the words left her mouth did Ally hear how bad it sounded. It wasn't like she had found out who teepeed the manor. She had taken Helene's accidental death, something everyone was having a hard-enough time dealing with, and revealed it was cold blooded murder. This revelation was sure to bring on a multitude of different emotions. Some Ally was sure would probably never go away, especially for Edmund.

Ashamed of herself Ally apologized for her outburst, "I'm sorry. I'm so terribly sorry," was all she said. If she had tried to add anything to her apology it would have sounded like nothing more than excuses for her behavior.

"Apology accepted," Edmund replied clearly at odds with how to proceed.

Rose took Ally's hand saying, "Come Ally there's nothing more we can do at the moment. Mr. Dalton needs time to evaluate and contemplate his next move. It's best we let him be."

A gracious nod was all he gave them before he sent them away. Once back at the lodge Rose was quick to remind Ally not to speak to anyone else about what she had learned or her arrangement with Mr. Dalton. It was not her place to divulge the truth about Helene's passing. If and when Edmund chose to share it and with whom was all up to him. Failure to respect Mr. and Mrs. Dalton's privacy, not to mention risking dark magic uncovering her ploy, would make Ally a target of both good and evil magic. No matter how grateful Edmund may be for her discovering all she had, he wouldn't allow her to step out of line and put his family in even more danger. There also wasn't a chance in Hades that dark magic would allow her to get away with what she had done. Pandemonium broke out in Ally's mind as she wrestled with the fact that her nosing around had led to so much more than she thought it would. Had she dug herself into an even deeper hole?

That reminded Ally, "Oh my gosh Rose, I only have until nightfall tomorrow night!" shrieked Ally.

"Before?"

There wasn't time to explain it to Rose and Ally knew Edmund was the only one who could help. "I forgot to tell Mr. Dalton something, something really, really important," exclaimed Ally in a high pitched nervous tone.

Calmly Rose gave Ally instructions on how to ask permission to speak to or meet with Edmund, but not before reminding her that her reason for doing so must literally be a matter of life and death. Ally reassured Rose that it was and then raced up to her room to do as Rose had instructed.

With her necklace held securely in her clenched hand Ally closed her eyes repeating over and over her request to speak with Edmund. Back at the manor he heard her cries and by sheer force pulled himself out of the flood of emotions that were causing him to drown. Edmund had been shaken to his core. Feeling like he had when he first lost Helene and thankfully Ally's worried cries arrived before he was entirely immersed in his sorrow. Grateful for the distraction he greeted Ally and she wasted no time getting to the point.

Nearing hysteria, she rapidly spouted her fears, "I only have until nightfall tomorrow to give Jezebel my answer. I was so mad at Margret and afraid for my life that I said the first thing that came to my mind. All I wanted was to be back home, so I told her what I thought she wanted to hear. What am I going to do?"

Chapter Sixteen

Speaking in a serene tone Edmund stated what was obvious to him, "I will destroy Jezebel before you're to meet with her." Expecting Ally to be thrilled with his answer and feel relieved about eliminating Jezebel, he looked at her less than enthusiastic expression and asked, "Why hasn't that put you at ease?"

Although Edmund's answer would alleviate the current situation, it failed to stop any further attacks on his family. This concerned Ally more than she knew how to express. Presuming she were to spend eternity in the garden, there would forever be the much bigger and constant threat of evil. Contrary to what any of them thought, Ally believed the occasional battles against a creature of darkness was far from the main objective. If history was any indication of how much dark magic abhorred the Dalton family and their practice of light magic, it stood-to-reason that evil would continue lurking in the shadows just waiting for the opportunity to pounce. Ally knew if she expected Edmund to fully put his trust in her. She first had to be completely honest with him. She needed to share her secret plans, but before she could say a word they were interrupted.

Helene burst through the front door of the manor screaming Edmund's name and running directly towards the garden. Ally was stunned since she believed Helene to have no knowledge of the magical garden. Stopping short of the garden's gate Helene's screams became dreadful cries for her husband, "Edmund my love where are you?" She turned one way then the other frantically spinning in circles looking for him. "Edmund please come to me. I can feel you're in danger. Please Edmund please," Helene sobbed plummeting to the ground.

Stepping through the garden gate he materialized before her, then raised her crumpled body into his arms and held Helene tight until her breathing returned to normal. Comforting his troubled wife Edmund whispered, "Shhhhhh, my sweet Helene I'm right here."

Clinging to her husband lessened Helene's fear at least momentarily. Then the reason for her dismay came flooding back. Repeating her earlier statement, "I feel danger Edmund. It's all around us. It's weighing on my heart so heavily I can hardly breath. I can't shake it and it's becoming more powerful."

"There, there my beloved. I will protect you."

"That's just it Edmund. It's not after me. It's after you!" declared Helene.

Ally watched Edmund fail miserably in his attempt to reassure Helene that everything was fine. Clearly the garden remained invisible to Helene and yet her eyes returned to the exact spot where Ally stood motionless.

637

Somehow, someway, Helene was feeling something even Edmund didn't quite understand. Getting nowhere, Edmund changed his tactics from trying to convey all was well to the reason Helene believed danger was close, "Perhaps you should tell me exactly what brought this on. Then we can go from there."

The look in Helene's eyes vaguely reminded Ally of the time her high school invited a hypnotist to perform at an assembly. Her eyes first became teary, but differently from the tearful expression she had when she couldn't find Edmund. Then the same strange glazed-over look her classmates had when the hypnotist made them act like monkeys changed Helene's warm chestnut eyes to empty and cold. Speaking in an unusual cadence Helene explained, "I was reading in the parlor when I felt a blanket of warmth cover me. At first it was comforting and kind. Then it turned into an ugly heavy and menacing sensation. My heart felt broken, aching like never before and just when I felt like the pain would cause me to faint it vanished." Helene's loving eyes returned and without hesitation she said, "As it left me I heard a woman's voice Edmund. It was lovely and lyrical. I've never heard such a beguiling sound," smiled Helene with a twinkle in her eye.

"And what did this voice say?"

That's when terror returned to Helene's face. She stared blankly at her husband and whispered, "Help save my son Helene. He's in terrible danger."

While Helene's words still hung in the air, the leaves of the sentinel oak moved like a mighty gust of wind had blown through, even though it was an uncanny night of calm and stillness. Both Edmund and Ally witnessed the phenomenon which remained concealed from Helene and for the first-time Ally saw legitimate fear in his eyes. Was it possible Edmund's mother had contacted Helene? Why after all this time would she chose to do so and furthermore, if she had the power to contact anyone why wouldn't she contact her son? An onslaught of emotions overtook Edmund and he did something he swore to himself he would never do. He froze Helene and the entire manor except for the garden.

Arthur emanated from the oak and rushed to Edmund's side, "I'm here sir."

"Is this possible? Did my mother contact Helene?"

"It does appear so."

"Has anything like this ever happened before?"

Arthur searched his memory and stated, "No sir, not that I'm aware of. The ancestral tree does hold your family's power and it watches over each generation of Dalton's, but to actually make contact is unheard of."

"Then why now?"

Ally ran to the garden gate yelling at Edmund, "Evil won't stop Mr. Dalton! It will never stop looking for a way to get to you, not until it finds a way in and accomplishes its goal. If not through me, through some other evil plot," Ally abruptly stopped speaking and looked up at the tree standing guard over them. Her gaze made the tree light up as if to acknowledge her stare. With a solemn tone Ally said, "I think it knows you won't win this battle."

Like any typical alpha male Edmund scoffed at that idea, "Preposterous, I've become more powerful than any Dalton in history. Dare I say the most powerful warlock of light magic to ever exist. Let evil give it their best shot. I'm immortal."

Having lived for countless decades Edmund had become more powerful than anyone before him, and thus far he had yet to master any level of humility in the area of magic. Arthur in his own unique way reminded Edmund of this, "Mr. Dalton, I agree you have become a supreme warlock. You possess powers far beyond anyone's expectations. All the same, it is my duty as your guardian to remind you that standing alone against an army of darkness puts you at a massive disadvantage. With all due respect sir, you could lose not only Helene but everything you hold dear."

"The manor is protected and I'll reinforce its shield of light. If need be I'll request assistance from my family," argued Edmund now puffing his chest out in defiance.

Arthur nodded in agreement although he remained unconvinced that Edmund was making the right decision. Ally on the other hand was far from agreeing with Edmunds irrational peacocking and strongly voiced her opinion, "Well, if Helene could be taken from you so could I and I'm not going to allow myself to be sacrificed because you want to prove how big and bad you are!" In that moment, Ally discovered there was a much greater fear than being trapped in the locket forever or even being banished to the wasteland. The fear of being conquered or captured by evil far outweighed any previous fears. This alone prompted Ally to speak to Edmund in a way that only his parents had.

Puffing out his chest even more and with a clenched jaw Edmund snarled at Ally, "How dare you speak to me that way. Away w...." But before he could finish his sentence Arthur came to Ally's rescue.

A coolheaded Arthur reminded Edmund of all she had done, "Please Mr. Dalton sir, don't forget Ally is the reason we know about the extreme danger you're in. Without her agreeing to help you, we could have been blindsided by an unprecedented attack."

"Or is she the cause of evil's plan? If she hadn't persisted in her refusal to surrender, dark magic wouldn't have picked up on her opposition to being here," suggested Edmund.

Ally cut in, "It's true," Ally sighed and bowed her head, "If it wasn't for me fighting you for so long Margret probably wouldn't have thought to use me against you."

Arthur placed his hand on hers, "No Miss Ally. You're not the one to blame for this."

Intrigued she lifted her face and questioned, "I'm not?"

"Do tell Arthur," prompted Edmund.

Taking an assertive stance Arthur listed his reasons, "Evil is to blame. Their eternal battle against the Dalton family has reached its pinnacle of tolerance. Furthermore, if what's currently happening outside of the manor is any indication, darkness is rallying the troops. You should be thankful Ally's delay in surrendering uncovered their plans. Not only did she give you the answers to so many of your heart wrenching and unanswered questions. Ally succeeded in discovering the most wicked plot to date. Something you desperately needed to know. What evil has done and continues to try to do to your family must be stopped once and for all."

The contempt left Edmund's face and he apologized, "Forgive my outburst Miss Ally. My good and trusted friend has reminded me of all you've done to help not only me, but our entire family."

"Apology accepted sir."

Giving her the best smile he could muster Edmund turned back to his wife and said, "Oh Helene, my sweet beloved wife. I promise to keep you safe and find a way out of this."

Looking at Helene for the first-time face to face Ally was awestruck by the sheer splendor of her beauty. Although she wasn't royalty she was exactly what anyone would expect a true princess to look like. Forgetting Helene was using her body Ally wanted nothing more than to talk to her, to be seen by her and to apologize for putting her in even more danger. Helene was not to blame for her murder, any more than Ally was to blame for being in the locket. Her animosity towards Helene and Edmund vanished and at that very moment Ally decided she needed to let Edmund know what she had been up to, "Mr. Dalton I need to tell you something."

"Yes Ally, go ahead."

"I don't think it was a coincidence that I discovered the magic mirror and everything else."

"What do you think it was?"

A quick glance at Arthur sent him the message that she needed him to have her back and his affirmative nod confirmed he did. Speaking barely above a whisper Ally shed the light on her motive for seeking out hidden truths. "I scoured the time before Helene's death purposely looking for something I could use. Knowing I needed to uncover something no one else had...."

"Because?"

Ashamed she admitted the truth, "I wanted to find something I could bargain with."

"Bargain for your freedom," deduced Edmund.

"Yes, sir. I figured if I had something you wanted as much as I wanted my freedom we could come to an agreement."

"Oh, Miss Ally," remarked Arthur.

It was Ally's turn to apologize, "I know, I'm sorry...."

Interrupting her Edmund clarified, "Wanted, you wanted your freedom and now you don't?"

"I'm not going to lie. I would like very much to go home," pausing Ally looked back at the garden, "but not at the expense of harming everyone else. I couldn't live with myself if I thought I was the reason for destroying your garden or turning it evil."

"Thank you for your honesty Ally. You may have started off with selfish desires, but along the way you've become a true family member."

Now that the tension between Edmund and Ally was gone Arthur swiftly returned to the topic of protecting the manor. Candidly he said, "That brings us back to the fight ahead of us."

"Yes it does. Allow me to get Helene up to bed and then we can discuss our options," Edmund said.

Ally posed a question, "Shouldn't she be included?"

"Ally does have a point Mr. Dalton. Your mother would not have contacted Helene if she didn't feel she would be of help," mentioned Arthur.

No one understood more than Edmund how big of a deal it was for his mother to contact Helene. Through all the agonizing years and failed attempts to connect with his parents not once had he received even a hint of a message. This fact alone proved beyond a shadow of a doubt he was in far more danger than ever before. Reluctantly Edmund agreed, "You're right, she should be included. I will explain things to her in the morning."

Ally was quick to point out, "Isn't she going to wonder how she went from standing under the oak tree this evening to tomorrow morning?"

A proud smile crossed Arthur's face, "She has a valid point sir. I told you Ally views things through fresh eyes and I have no doubt being a woman is helping with a different and much needed perspective."

"Thank you Arthur," curtsied Ally.

Edmund couldn't argue against Ally's logic and he stalled for time. After pacing for longer than he realized he eventually shared his concerns over bringing Helene deeper into the threat of evil. Besides her safety he was consumed with how much he should share. How specific would he have to be? Would his omissions about his parent's murder or his immortality cause Helene to stop loving him? How would he keep from telling her about her own death and all that took place since? Once he unlocked decades old secrets there was a chance he could lose Helene forever. Something he knew would kill him if not for his parent's spell.

Arthur tried his best to diminish Edmund's fears, "Sir, I have never seen love like that of you and Helene. She will need time to adjust to everything, but I wholeheartedly trust your extraordinary love will not only overcome the truth. It will bring you closer."

Unconvinced, Edmund asked Arthur to leave, unfroze Helene as if no time had passed and said, "Oh my love there's nothing to fear."

"You're wrong Edmund I feel it. Not only from what happened moments ago but from you. For days, I've been feeling your torment and don't forget you told me dark magic was nearby."

He knew better than to argue with her. This was not the first time their remarkable bond had alerted Helene to Edmund's unspoken distress, and his mother's warning was clearly an indication that he needed her help. "That's right I did tell you I was looking into an evil presence."

"Yes, you did and I'm guessing you've located it?"

The cold night air made Helene shiver motivating Edmund to take her indoors. Ally stood alone in the garden weary of the day's events and before she even noticed what was happening, Edmund returned her to the lodge in the same manner he had brought her to him. Falling into bed was all it took for sleep to strip away her consciousness. During the night Ally and all those within the manors boundaries fell into the trance of a powerfully deep sleep. One they couldn't wake from.

Secure in knowing the entire manor was under his spell Edmund felt relaxed in continuing his conversation with Helene. He wanted to give his beloved wife all the time she needed to process not only his admissions but the impending danger. He was sure her offer to help him battle evil was heartfelt, but neither of them, especially Edmund expected her to actually help. She didn't have powers and although Edmund could return her soul to the locket if things went awry, he preferred to eliminate the current threat without bringing the switch into Ally's body to an abrupt end.

Once inside the privacy of their bedroom Helene asked, "Your mother spoke to me?"

"It appears she did," replied Edmund in a hushed voice.

"Has she ever spoken to you?"

Sadly, Edmund answered, "No," as his sapphire eyes were overshadowed with woe.

This surprised Helene and increased her level of concern, "Then you must truly be in serious danger. Do you have any idea what dark magic is trying to achieve?"

"I don't have all the details, but yes my beloved I do know what it's after."

Unsure as to whether the unknown or known evil terrified her more Helene posed a question with an escape route, "Do I want to know?"

There it was. A valid reason for not giving Helene full disclosure. Her humanity didn't want to know everything, "That's entirely up to you my sweet," answered a relieved Edmund.

Thinking long and hard she finally spoke, "You tell me how I can help and ease into the spooky details. Then I can stop you when I don't want to hear anymore. Maybe that way I can keep my nightmares from returning."

There wasn't much that shook Helene's confidence and this side of her was rarely seen. Reminding Edmund that ultimately Helene was a fragile human, who without Edmund's confession of being a warlock, would still be

ignorant of magic's existence. He could never forget that
or how dark magic had already ended her life once.

649

Chapter Seventeen

Explaining to Helene how she could help wasn't something Edmund could do. He was baffled by his mother's message nearly as much as he was about her connecting with Helene. Magic had never relied on mortals for anything. Especially its preservation. Answering from his heart he said, "I don't know how you can help, my sweet."

"Neither do I, but your mother's message clearly told me to help save you."

"Are you absolutely sure you heard her correctly?

Helene's confidence returned and she replied with an air of frustration, "Yes Edmund."

Aware he'd insulted his wife Edmund apologized, "Forgive me Helene I don't mean to doubt you...."

Inundated with fear for her husband she cut in, "I know darling, you're under a tremendous amount of stress and you're right in saying it doesn't make sense. Let's put that aside for now and discuss what you do know. Have you discovered what danger your mother could be referring to?"

Edmund proceeded with caution and stopped short of giving any specific details away, "Dark magic has targeted the Dalton family."

"The Dalton family or Edmund Dalton?" stressed Helene.

In an effort to downplay the evil plot against him he said, "Dark magic has always targeted light magic and at the moment they seem fixated on me. I'm sure it's nothing I can't handle."

Helene's heart sank and every cell in her being tingled in disagreement, "No my love you're wrong. Everything in me disagrees and our bond has never once steered me wrong."

Prior to responding Edmund caught a flicker of light coming from the dresser behind Helene. He watched in disbelief as the photograph of his parents began to smolder then shoot electrified sparks throughout the room. Helene turned around to see what was bewitching her husband and instinctively reached for the picture. Once in her hands the sparkler display ceased and a new wonder took its place. Helene's eyes widen while the photograph rebuilt itself and in a matter of seconds the picture was restored to its original splendor. Fearful of what was happening Edmund attempted unsuccessfully to grab the picture from Helene. His hand bounced off an invisible force field and he ended up standing beside her with the same astonished expression.

Tears welled in both their eyes. For Edmund, they were tears of remembrance. Helene's joyous tears reminded him that this was the first and only picture Helene had ever seen of him as a young man. She was aware that his parents died in a tragic house fire and other than the remnants of this photograph nothing survived. What she didn't know was the cause of the fire, which was something Edmund still didn't wish to share.

"Oh my gosh!" celebrated Helene, "Look at you, you were adorable."

Modestly Edmund responded, "That's only because you love me so much," trying once again to take the picture from her, "May I see it?"

While Helene was not preventing him from taking the picture it remained locked in her hands. "How very strange," she nervously commented. "Move your hand away from it Edmund I want to try something." No sooner did he lower his hand was Helene able to release her hands at least one at a time. "Now what is your mother trying to tell me?" and that's when an unexpected answer revealed itself. Magically the photograph turned itself around in the picture frame displaying an exquisitely hand written message. The calligraphy's graceful swirls were recognized by Edmund as none other than his mother's. Her expertly and stylish composition was short, "Trust in love."

Reaching exasperation Edmund shouted, "Trust in love! After all these years, all my mother can send is an obscure message?"

Helene did what only she could do. Go toe to toe with her irritated husband and succeed in talking him off the ledge, "Edmund my darling she's right. Don't you see? Love is light and goodness. Even the tiniest candle flame can push back the darkness. It has no choice but to yield its power to light. We can defeat evil though love."

"You are sweet Helene and I appreciate your confidence, but if I'm correct we're up against an assault of monumental proportions. Light from one small candle doesn't stand a chance."

"Then let's create more light."

This brought Edmund full circle to asking the Dalton family for help, "That's what I was thinking. I will contact family members all over the world and they could be here before tomorrow night."

"Tomorrow night?" shrieked Helene, "When were you planning on telling me evil is attacking so soon?"

Abruptly, the sunrise was overshadowed by a thick layer of gloom and the grounds of Dalton Manor quaked in response to the perpetual thrashing against its light shield. Edmund could feel the walloping hits weaken the shield causing him to become alarmed. He immediately took hold of Helene's hand and ordered her to come with

653

him. Racing down the stairs and through the entrance hall they erupted through the front door. Making a beeline towards the oak tree. Pulling Helene through the gardens gate brought its splendor into view. Amazed by the surprising and dazzling sight before her, Helene soaked in its beauty while Edmund busily summoned home all the garden members.

"What happened to tomorrow night?" screamed Helene.

Edmund was far too involved in what he was doing to explore any reason evil had upped its onslaught. Nor did it matter. Now was not the time to explore why. It was time to defend all he loved. The garden radiated more light with every returning family member, strengthening the layer of protection over the manor. The oak tree erupted into an unparalleled spectacle of light causing the darkness to pull back, giving them a minute to catch their breath. This fleeting victory was quickly forgotten when the vile powers of dark magic lashed out against Edmund with a renewed hatred.

Not understanding why no one was coming to Edmunds aid Helene shouted over the rumbling attack, "Where is everyone? Why isn't anyone helping you?"

"They are helping," answered Edmund pulling more power from the deepest recesses of his strength as well as from the garden.

Not fully understanding what he meant Helene witnessed the first casualty of the siege. A young seedling withering away fading into nothingness leaving its mark on Edmund. Wincing in pain he proved how accurate his mother's words were. He was in terrible danger and Helene found herself petrified at the thought of losing her husband. Fear for herself never crossed her mind. All she could see was the love of her life doing all he could to protect her. Even if it meant sacrificing himself. "Edmund they're going to kill you!" she shouted at the top of her lungs.

Time stood still as the sentinel oak reached its mighty branches over the garden covering it completely within an expansive network of limbs. When the creaking sound of moving branches ceased, silence filled the protective dome and Edmund's voice echoed the unbelievable words, "They can't kill me Helene. I'm immortal."

Helene remained speechless while she fought to understand what she had just heard. Discombobulated by Edmund's words she swayed on her feet. Feeling his arms pull her in close steadied her body and cleared her mind, "Immortal?"

"Yes Helene, it was a gift from my parents. It's how I survived the fire that killed them," explained Edmund feeling tremendously relieved at being able to tell Helene the truth about his immortality.

"Then how could you be in danger?"

"The only way evil can cause me harm is to take you away from me," Edmund admitted.

Helene considered this and asked for clarification, "You believe if I die you would be left alone for all eternity?"

"Yes my beloved. Evil knows it would devastate me until the end of time, without killing me. Leaving me a shell of who I am," his saddened voice broke Helene's heart.

Fear relentlessly overtook Helene triggering her to express any thought crossing her mind, "Maybe that's what your mother meant Edmund. Perhaps the love we've shared would be enough to help you survive eternity without me. Once evil witnesses our memory standing strong against them, evil would leave you alone."

"You're wrong Helene."

"You don't know that Edmund," she disagreed and offered him the ultimate gift of love saying, "If I can save you by giving up my life. I will gladly do so," cried Helene.

Rising to his feet and releasing her Edmund snapped, "No!! You're wrong. You couldn't be more wrong. Evil will never stop pursuing victory over me."

His sharp words slashed at her frightened heart, "How do you know that? I'm offering my life to save you and your snapping at me!"

The next thing Edmund knew his own words were betraying him, "Because evil has already ended your life."

"I'm dead?" shrieked Helene rubbing her hands over her body trying to find a wound, "I didn't feel a thing." She was completely unaware that Edmund was referring to her accident with Storm. "Is the battle over?" questioned Helene wondering if the oak had protected her from moving on.

Hanging his head low and fighting back tears he said, "Yes my dear sweet Helene you've passed, but the battle is not over."

Sobs escaped her lips and she whimpered a painful admission, "Then I was wrong. Darkness took my life and they're still after you. Forgive me my love. I couldn't save you." Helene fell to the ground weeping uncontrollably.

Kneeling beside her and gently wiping the tears from her cheeks Edmund tried to calm his grieving wife. At last she caught her breath and he took her locket into his hands explaining how he could use magic to protect her soul and ultimately bring her back leaving out the spells dirty little details.

"I would be a ghost?"

"No Helene you would have a body," he admitted.

Suffering from an aggressive headache brought on by the loud roar of the incessant battle and the mind-blowing fact of her death Helene managed to ask, "How is that possible?"

From somewhere above Helene heard the all too familiar voice of her friend, "I would sacrifice my body for you Helene," announced Rose.

Pulling away from Edmund she looked up at her lifelong friend and said, "Rose, what are you doing here? How could you offer your body?' Then a frightful idea came to mind, "Maxwell! He's hurt you again."

"He can't hurt me anymore."

Reaching the end of her rope Helene spouted, "Does that mean he killed you? I've had quite enough!!!" Moving several feet away from both Edmund and Rose, Helene demanded the truth.

As gently as he could Edmund explained how Rose wanted and needed out of her marriage with Maxwell. Even if that meant sacrificing her life to do so. Comparing Rose's unselfish act of kindness to Helene's willingness to offer her life to save her husband did manage to help Helene maintain control. The oak shuddered under the stress of defending the garden, reminding them all that time was of the essence. There was no way to answer the countless questions tearing through Helene's head so she picked one.

"Will Rose's body live for eternity?"

"I wish it could, but the spell doesn't work that way. I would have to find another replacement body."

"I only have one friend that would willingly give up her life. How would you get another body?" Both Edmund and Rose's eyes said all they couldn't say. Helene was against taking the body of another, "No Edmund that's wrong. I can't let you take the life of another and I'm sure it's not the life you want for us."

"Helene I cannot survive without you."

To ease the fear growing in Rose as she trembled from the non-stop bombardment of evil, Edmund allowed her to listen in on his thoughts. She listened carefully to his plot. If evil destroyed Ally's body, it was only then that Helene's strong-will would be weakened enough for Edmund's spell to be successful in recapturing her soul, and placing it safely back into the locket. For as long as Helene was resistant to surrendering her soul into the locket Edmund's spell was powerless. The sound of cracking branches made them all contemplate the possibility of dark magic being destined to win this battle. Rose wondered if Edmund somehow managed to save Helene's soul in the midst of this clash between good and evil. Would he also be able to save the garden?

Darkness continued to try and breach the web of dense branches with sharp blows creating thuds that vibrated the earth beneath its shelter. Afraid a chink in its coverage was imminent the leaves of the oak danced in a rhythmic display until their shushing sound spoke loud and clear, "Your love," it sang over and over, "Your love, your love...."

Whether it came to Helene on her own or whether it was magically given to her she came up with a plan. She rushed back into Edmund's arms and kissed him like it was for the last time. Releasing his mouth from hers she witnessed the despair she was feeling manifest itself in his weepy eyes. "Edmund my love please I beg of you. Release me. Let my soul go."

Through a wretched voice he spoke, "I can't live without you Helene. You are the love of my life. You are the reason for my very existence."

"Then don't," she suggested.

"There's no way out my beloved. The spell is unbreakable. Take it from me. In my darkest hours, I tried numerous times to break free. Nothing managed to end my life."

Pieces of bark started falling from the mighty oak and the garden responded by sending what little power it had left into the remarkable tree. Meanwhile, Edmund and Helene's eyes remained locked on each other. As the shower of bark increased and began including twigs and leaves it created a strangely beautiful sight around them.

"Come with me," pleaded Helene, "To a place where we never have to part."

"It's impossible,"

"Nothing is impossible with love."

Confirming Helene's words the tree sent one final message to Edmund and he heard his mother's melodious and loving voice say, "You must hold your pain inside."

The look on Helene's face showed she had also heard the message and even though she was horrified beyond measure she implored, "My darling Edmund, let this be your ultimate gift of love for me. Free my soul and trust that somehow we will end up together."

A loud bang echoed in the oaks deteriorating cavern splitting open a fissure and permitting evil to enter. Helene couldn't help but breathe in the shadowy mist that headed straight for her. The garden gave a collective groan when she failed to exhale the murky gas. Dropping to his knees Edmund held Helene's lifeless body in his arms while tortured misery gripped him. As he had done so many times before he prepared to use the locket. Before he could initiate the spell, he heard the faint whisper of his beloved Helene echoing around him, "My darling, allow it to devour you."

Desolation engulfed him with a vengeance. It commanded to be let out of its confinement within his body making the surface of his skin ripple and bulge. Yet

Edmund's unwavering decision to listen to his wife's final words forced his emotions to yield. Pain like he had never experienced consumed his mind, body and soul. Grimacing from the excruciating torment of losing his wife forever, Edmund wrapped his arms tighter around his beloved wife and together they toppled to the ground. Watching the branches above splinter and crack Edmund embraced Helene with all he had left. At long last, the complete and selfless love that had empowered Edmund's parents, so very long ago, to cast the immortality spell met its match. Edmund's exemplary pure love for Helene broke the unbreakable spell. Freeing him from his eternal life. He could feel their powerful spell release its hold on him. When the tingling sensation ceased, Edmund took a deep chest-lifting breath. He closed his eyes before slowly exhaling through relaxed lips, and with that.........he was gone. Gone to be with his dear sweet Helene.

The mighty oak lifted its electrified branches high into the air chasing away the darkness. The flowers of the garden liberated its family releasing them into the now picturesque blue sky and Ally watched as one by one they soared into the clouds. Hovering over her plant Ally wondered why she was still there and that's when she noticed Rose smiling at her from across the garden. Mouthing the words "Thank you," Rose swirled with outstretched arms high into the sunlight.

Ally felt herself evaporating and waited to be lifted into the air, but the next thing she knew she awoke at the base of the magnificent oak. Slowly rising to her feet, she watched a glowing red spark carve the initials "E & H" into the trunk of the tree adding a perfectly shaped heart around them. With a bittersweet smile Ally placed her hand over the luminescent engraving and felt the trees wondrous energy for one last time.

<u>Epilogue</u>

Standing in the shade of her favorite tree on the campus, Ally enjoyed watching dozens of students greet their family members arriving for graduation day. She could hardly believe it was only days before the commencement ceremony. So much had taken place since surviving the lightning strike years before. The strangely beautiful Lichtenberg scar originating in her palm had shot through to the back of her hand, curved its way up her arm, over her shoulder and stopped just below her collar bone. The main vine of the scar branched out into little leafy fronds resembling a fern. Ally continued to struggle with memory loss and Susan did all she could to help fill in the blanks, but there was still so many unanswered questions.

The first clear memory anywhere close to that fateful night was of waking in the hospital surrounded by her parents and grandparents. They had been anxiously waiting for her to regain consciousness. Ally's doctors were amazed at how well she remembered who her family was and that the typically severe headaches resulting from being struck by lightning never transpired. As a matter-of-fact, the headaches Ally had suffered from early childhood and continuing through college rarely if ever occurred. For the most part she was unscathed by the entire experience. Other than the loss of several months leading up to leaving home and being at college Ally could recall most memories. With extraordinary detail.

Frustrated by this unusual reaction to such a harrowing experience her well-meaning doctors continued running tests on her nearly a year later, until her parents finally said, "Enough!" They didn't care that the doctors were stumped or about their unwillingness to admit they didn't have an explanation for Ally's lack of health issues. Other than one particular doctor who was willing to simply say Ally was a walking miracle, the egotistical behavior of the other doctors made Ally's family mad. They seemed less concerned about Ally's health and more concerned with being the one who solved the mystery. Her parents had grown particularly tired of the doctor's competitive behavior and canceled all of Ally's follow up appointments.

Ally's father who sobered up immediately upon hearing about his daughters near death experience was well on his way to becoming the father she remembered. He had found a job, was providing for his family and doing his best to make up for lost time with his daughter and wife. Following doctor's orders Ally returned home where she stayed until the spring semester began at school. Even though her parents were reluctant to let her go back to college. There was no stopping her. One effect

665

in the aftermath of her accident wasn't a health concern but a personality change. Ally had become confident, outspoken and bold. With a new plucky and self-assured attitude, which helped ease her family's mind, she headed off to school. Not being able to remember much of anything from her time in college before the Halloween party, didn't matter to Ally. There wasn't a shred of doubt in her mind regarding her future success.

Returning to her dorm room after enjoying some alone time she found Susan leaving for dinner with her parents, "I'll be back later tonight Ally. Your family arrives the day before graduation, right?"

"Yes they'll be here in a couple days."

Before closing the door, Susan asked one more time, "Are you sure you won't join us Ally?"

"I'm sure Susan, but thanks for asking.....again," smiled Ally.

After waving farewell to Susan as she left for dinner with her parents, Ally looked around the room she'd soon be permanently leaving. Then she giggled from hearing the all too familiar hum of Susan's non-stop talking fade as they made their way to the elevator.

Ally turned on the light above her bed and pulled Rose's old faded note from the hidden zippered pocket in the stuffed bear on her bed. Ally sank into her pillows and breathed a sad sigh. She had read and re-read the note countless times giving the paper a cloth-like feel. Only fragmented memories of Rose remained. Ally could remember her eyes and smile, but if she were asked to describe Rose she couldn't. There wasn't anything more she remembered and everyone deliberately avoided speaking of Rose for fear of upsetting Ally. Once again Ally read the note out loud hoping to trigger a memory.

> My dearest Ally,
> My family has decided I need to leave
> school and go with them. I'm not sure
> where we'll end up or when I'll be able to
> get in touch with you. I miss you already.
> Farewell my good friend,
> Rose

Ally's heart sank when she finished reading the short and fact-less message. How she wished she could remember their friendship or anything about her old roommate. Over the years nothing more had come back to Ally and she wondered if her memory loss was the reason for Rose never reconnecting with her. Had Rose heard of her accident and decided to keep her distance? Was she under the impression that it would somehow be harmful for Ally to have someone she couldn't remember back in her life? If they truly were as close as Ally believed them to be, she couldn't help but wonder. How and why was it possible for Rose to simply vanish from her life? There was no logical answer to that question as far as Ally was concerned.

Stuffing the note back into its secret hiding place Ally turned off the light, rolled over in bed and fell asleep fully dressed. Susan quietly returned to her room, threw a blanket over Ally and also went to sleep. The next couple days were busy with graduation rehearsal and wrapping up loose ends. When Ally's family arrived, she was able to spend only a couple hours with them. The next time she would see them they would be somewhere in the crowd of spectators during the graduation ceremony.

After the benediction and recessional Ally was swooped into her father's arms sending her cap flying into the air. Her mother quickly snatched it in midair saying, "I knew you should have used more bobby pins," impatiently waiting for her turn to hug her daughter. Tears streamed down her mother's face during their embrace and not a word needed to be spoken. Not only had Ally come so far over the last few years she had her entire family there, intact. Understanding how very close Ally had been to dying from the lightning strike still gave her mother nightmares, and yet due to that tragic event her marriage had been restored. It wasn't something she would ever wish on anyone. Most certainly her own daughter, but she had to admit some rather miraculous results came from it. In some weird twist of fate, she not only had a college graduate to brag about she had her husband back.

Her grandpa sat in his wheelchair with his loving wife beside him at the far end of the stadium waiting for Ally. She rushed into her grandma's arms then gently snuggled onto her grandpa's lap. With a proud smile and a kiss on her cheek Grandpa said, "I'm so proud of you Ally. We knew you could do it."

"Yes we did," agreed Grandma.

The thrilled and proud family spent the day touring the campus where Ally showed them her favorite shady spot under the large tree near the cafeteria, her dorm room and introduced them to her favorite professor. By dinnertime they were all famished and happily headed to the restaurant where reservations had been made. Naturally, several trips down memory lane filled the dinner conversation and for the most part Ally remembered them all. Soon enough the conversation moved onto Ally's plan for the future. She had applied to several local elementary schools, a couple where she had completed numerous weeks of internship, but she was still waiting to hear back from any of them. Especially her first choice.

That reminded Ally's mother, "Oh I almost forgot, Mr. Griffin gave me this card to give you. He is so sorry he couldn't make your graduation."

"Oh my gosh. Mom please tell him I understand and that I'm so sorry his wife is ill."

"I will sweetheart."

"Thanks. Is she doing any better?"

"Well, she's not getting worse and that's good, but Mr. Griffin is beside himself with worry."

"I can only imagine. Well I'll send him a card ASAP."

Smiling proudly Ally's mom gushed, "I know you will."

By the time dinner was completed Ally's grandparents were worn out and they said their goodnights. Giving hugs all around, Ally said goodbye to her family and watched them drive off knowing there was a chance she'd see them soon. Largely in part to a teaching position not coming through. Back in her room Ally helped Susan pack what she didn't need for the next few days in preparation to leave the dorm. Ally on the other hand was waiting up until the last moment to move. In hopes she wouldn't have to go back home before accepting a teaching position. She had already made arrangements to rent a room with several of her peers in a house nearby, but without a teaching job, she knew staying there for long was out of the question.

When Susan left for her new home Ally cried happy and sad tears. The half empty room shifted Ally thoughts. She was soon filled with anticipation for the next adventure in her life. Wandering aimlessly around the college campus Ally soon found herself seated under her favorite tree. The early afternoon breeze caused the leaves to break out into its imitation of a rain storm. While listening to the soothing sound Ally was startled by a large eagle landing directly above her. The enormous golden-brown bird briefly surveyed Ally and then took to the air where it circled above. Mesmerized by the bird's flight Ally felt the faint glimmer of a memory fighting to return. Completely focused on the majestic creature and the way the sunlight caused the golden highlights to shimmer on its head and expansive wings, Ally failed to notice another bird perched in a nearby tree. Without a sound the second bird swooped down before Ally and dropped what appeared to be a small branch from its beak.

Walking over to the dropped stick and even with great care Ally still managed to prick her finger on one of its thorns. What she thought to be twig had turned out to be the stem of a dazzling bright rosebud. Never before had Ally seen such a deep red rose, at least not that she could remember. Inhaling the sweet fragrance of the unopened flower sent a shiver throughout Ally's body. For a second time a memory struggled to make itself known. The harder Ally concentrated on recovering the memory the further away it moved. Frustrated to the point of tears Ally decided to return to the scene of the dreadful accident.

Unsure she would be able to find Dalton Manor, which is where she was told the lightning had struck her, she got in her car and headed in the direction she believed it to be. Ally was pretty confident she knew the main road Dalton Manor was located off of. She remembered far too many whispered conversations of fellow students discussing the incident. The manor had been closed within the year of Ally's accident due to a lack of funding. She knew if by chance she managed to find the manor she still may not be able to gain access.

The landscape surrounding Ally convinced her she must be close. There were acres of wide open space, trees, fields and green rolling hills which now lined the street on both sides. All alone on the road and unsure where she was going Ally lowered her speed and carefully searched for any sign of the dirt road that would lead to the manor. There was no sign of a dirt road anywhere. Ally was about to give up when a second look caught her attention. After making a U-turn she slowly drove back to what she thought she saw and to her relief she was right. Overgrown bushes and grasses had been either flattened or snapped by car tires. Someone had recently driven over the brush and peering beyond the evidence, Ally discovered a long dirt road framed with century old trees.

"Maybe someone can let me in," thought Ally out loud.

Throwing caution to the wind Ally drove down the dirt road and found the iron gate wide open. Pulling in front of the manor and taking a quick look around Ally exited her car and hollered, "Is anyone here?" No answer. Nothing but the echo of her own voice reverberating in the quiet. Concentrating hard she studied the weathered manor and tried to imagine what it looked like all decorated for the Halloween party, which had turned out to be the final party held at the manor. Forgetting so many months of her life bothered her more than she admitted to anyone. Even to herself. How she wished she could remember the memories of that night and her long forgotten roommate. Susan's love of talking had failed time and time again to help Ally remember. No matter how long or how many details Susan shared the party and the months leading up to it were permanently gone. At least that's what Ally feared.

The front door of the manor was locked and Ally didn't want to be arrested for trespassing. She worried if someone did show up, primarily the police, she wouldn't be able to explain the reason for her visit. Hopefully the open gate meant it was okay for her to enter the grounds, even though she knew better. Out of nowhere the same pair of eagles from the school appeared in the sky, both landing in the massive oak tree to the right of the manor. High stepping over and through the weeds Ally approached the tree with caution. Noticing the birds seemed far from interested in her approaching them, Ally looked up at the enormous tree and admired its aged beauty. This was the type of tree you couldn't plant yourself and live long enough to see its full magnificence. This was the type of tree you had to be fortunate enough to find on an existing property.

Out of curiosity Ally tried to wrap her arms around the trunk of the tree. She laughed at herself when her arms didn't even reach halfway around the giant trunk. Next she began counting the steps it took to walk around the tree. On her way around the trunk she noticed a carving in the bark. "E & H" she whispered before tracing the heart around the letters with her fingers. As quickly as it came the flashback of a memory vanished, and yet something inside her told her this was precisely where she was found after being struck by lightning. She had unwittingly ended up exactly where she wanted to be. The very spot where a bolt of lightning had almost taken her life.

Deep in thought and doing all she could to force that spark of a memory to return, Ally failed to notice she was no longer alone. Not until a deep masculine voice asked, "Hello miss, may I help you?"

"Oh," blurted Ally startled by the tall gentleman walking towards her. With the sun shining directly behind him Ally couldn't see his face. Until he stepped into the shade of the oak tree. Her relief over it not being a police officer was quickly replaced with self-consciousness. Here she was having spent the morning helping Susan move her stuff out of the dorm and wearing an old faded T-shirt, torn jeans, raggedy tennis shoes and very little makeup. Fidgeting with her messy bun did little to make her feel better. Just when she thought she couldn't feel any worse this handsome stranger smiled with delight at her embarrassment. Her appearance was in complete contrast to this well-dressed man with his extraordinarily handsome features. Suddenly there was something unexpected in his azure eyes. A softness Ally didn't expect. He wasn't making fun of her with his smile, instead he seemed genuinely charmed by her appearance.

From behind they heard a woman's voice calling out, "Mr. Dalton I apologize for being late."

Turning to greet the woman who was having a tough time navigating the overgrown yard in such high heels, he reached out and steadied her as her ankle twisted upon reaching him, "Easy there," he said.

"Thank you," was all she could say. She was thoroughly horrified at her entrance, which was evident to both the gentleman who was still holding the woman's hand and to Ally. That's when she noticed Ally standing there. How quickly she turned the focus away from herself and onto Ally. "Excuse me miss what are you doing on private property?" her voice was annoyed. Then it was like a switch had been hit. She turned her focus back to the gentleman and with an all too sugary sweet tone said, "I apologize Mr. Dalton."

"Mr. Dalton? So, you own this place?" asked Ally.

Interrupting the woman scolded Ally, "This is none of your concern. You need to leave and leave now. Mr. Dalton doesn't have to answer or explain anything to you."

Lifting his hand, he shushed the woman who by this time Ally figured was an attorney based on the scale of justice engraved in the briefcase she held. "Yes miss I am the owner or shall I say the inheritor of the manor," he said extending his hand and introducing himself, "I'm Benjamin Dalton, but please call me Ben."

Shaking his hand Ally introduced herself, "I'm Ally Fischer," she said with a blush.

"Happy to make your acquaintance. Is that with or without a 'c' miss?"

"With a 'c' Mr., I mean Ben. Very good," remarked Ally impressed by his knowledge of the various spellings of her last name.

"Ally Fischer with a 'c' then," he smiled a breathtaking smile.

Without realizing it Ally still had a firm grip on his hand and it wasn't until he pulled his pale blue eyes away from hers and looked at their hands did she become aware of it. "Oh, I'm sorry," Ally replied pulling her hand away and fidgeting nervously before excusing herself, "I better leave you two alone and I apologize for the intrusion."

The attorney sneered at Ally as she headed to her car. Before Ally was out of ear shot she began speaking in lawyer jargon only to be interrupted by Mr. Dalton. "Miss Fischer please don't leave on our account. Mrs. Jones and I can finish up the details later this afternoon at her office. Where I'm sure she'll be far more comfortable."

Less than pleased with this Mrs. Jones grumbled under her breath. With a simple annoyed look from Benjamin she was reminded she worked for him and left without another word. It didn't make sense nor was it particularly smart to agree to stay with this stranger at the manor and yet Ally found herself agreeing to do so. After watching Mrs. Jones disappear down the road Ben turned towards Ally and asked, "So what exactly brings you to the manor this fine day?"

"I'm not really sure. I just had an overwhelming urge to return."

"Return? You've been here before?"

"Yes I was struck by lightning a few years back somewhere near that amazing tree. I don't remember it and I haven't been here since that night but something, actually those two eagles perched in the tree...."

"The eagles?" questioned Ben during Ally's lengthy pause.

Laughing at herself she said, "Oh its nothing," afraid the story of the dropped rosebud would make her sound crazy. At that the eagles flew off over the manor disappearing from sight. Then Ally asked a question of her own, "You inherited the manor?"

"Yes its belonged to the Dalton family for centuries and apparently, I am the next in line to take ownership of it"

Ally looked around and said, "Looks like you have your work cut out for you."

"Oh you don't know the half of it," replied Ben and there was something familiar about his remark.

Agreeing with him she said, "I bet I don't."

Ben politely asked, "Shall we have a seat Ally? I would like to hear more about you surviving a lightning strike. I'm sure that's a remarkable story," he continued leading Ally to the bench under the oak.

Noticing the same heart and initials on the bench that were on the tree Ally commented, "Do you know who E & H were?" Completely distracted by the matching carvings on the bench and tree, Ally failed to notice a tree root sticking up from the ground and tripped. Falling into Ben's arms she felt a small electric shock. Equivalent to the shock one gets from dragging their feet across carpet and touching another person. "Excuse my clumsiness," replied Ally pulling out of his strong arms, "My goodness I seem to attract electricity when I'm here. Maybe we shouldn't stay under this tree. It's been bad luck for me before."

"Attract electricity?"

"Didn't you feel that shock?"

"I did Ally, but how could you attract electricity?" inquired Ben with a sneaky look in his eyes.

Self-conscious for the second-time Ally answered, "Okay maybe I can't attract electricity, but there's something strange about this place. Maybe a magnetic field or, or....I don't know. Can we please just go sit somewhere else?" Ally walked ahead of him and turned around to see where he went, after noticing he wasn't with her. With long strides, he caught up to her and pulling his hand from behind his back offered her a bouquet of little pink daises, "Of course we can Ally."

With a bashful smile Ally took the flowers from Ben and the picture of an intensely colorful and splendid garden flashed before her eyes. Only to be followed by the irresistible scent of extraordinarily sweet flowers. Ben's eyes glistened with acknowledgement and although Ally was unsure what it all meant. Her very core told her she was home.

<u>Author's Note</u>

Life has returned to normal for Ally. She accomplished her goal of graduating college and is looking forward to the future. Her family is back on track and all is right with the world. Is there a chance that magic isn't done with her? Will she recover the lost memories of the garden and all that took place? Is Benjamin Dalton a friend or foe?

I know life is crazy busy, but if you don't mind please leave a review before moving on. Positive reviews and word of mouth, in whichever way you share my books, are some of the best ways to help my books reach more readers. As an indie author, I want to thank you so very much. I truly appreciate your support and feedback.

Remember to follow me on Amazon, Goodreads and/or Pinterest. You can also be added to my email list for updates, book releases and promotions by emailing me at email@tl-stevens.com *and happy reading.*

www.tl-stevens.com

www.ingramcontent.com/pod-product-compliance
Lightning Source LLC
Chambersburg PA
CBHW030325010826
48973CB00004B/863